SOLD FOR THE GREEK'S HEIR

BY

LYNNE GRAHAM

First Published in Great Britain 2017
By Mills & Boon, an imprint of HarperCollins*Publishers*
1 London Bridge Street, London, SE1 9GF

ISBN: 978-0-263-92523-4

Our policy is to use papers that are natural, renewable and recyclable products and made from wood grown in sustainable forests. The logging and manufacturing processes conform to the legal environmental regulations of the country of origin.

Printed and bound in Spain
by CPI, Barcelona

Lynne Graham was born in Northern Ireland and has been a keen romance reader since her teens. She is very happily married to an understanding husband who has learned to cook since she started to write! Her five children keep her on her toes. She has a very large dog who knocks everything over, a very small terrier who barks a lot, and two cats. When time allows, Lynne is a keen gardener.

Books by Lynne Graham

Mills & Boon Modern Romance

Bought for the Greek's Revenge
The Sicilian's Stolen Son
Leonetti's Housekeeper Bride
The Secret His Mistress Carried
The Dimitrakos Proposition

Brides for the Taking

The Desert King's Blackmailed Bride
The Italian's One-Night Baby

Christmas with a Tycoon

The Italian's Christmas Child
The Greek's Christmas Bride

The Notorious Greeks

The Greek Demands His Heir
The Greek Commands His Mistress

Bound by Gold

The Billionaire's Bridal Bargain
The Sheikh's Secret Babies

The Legacies of Powerful Men

Ravelli's Defiant Bride
Christakis's Rebellious Wife
Zarif's Convenient Queen

Visit the Author Profile page at millsandboon.co.uk for more titles.

For Rachel and Michael,
for their unswerving support and their ability to
consider my characters as seriously as I do.

CHAPTER ONE

In the pit, Jax Antonakos climbed out of the low-slung car, adrenalin still pumping fiercely from the excitement of the race. Only a show race for charity, though, he reminded himself wryly, bracing himself as he was engulfed by a large, noisy crowd of people.

He yanked off his helmet, revealing tousled black hair and eyes as strikingly green as emeralds, and the usual collective female gasp of appreciation sounded. While he stripped off his track regalia, photographers flashed cameras, journalists demanded quotes and shot questions at him and beautiful women tried to sidle closer to him, but then all of that was the norm in Jax's goldfish bowl of a world.

Jax, however, ignored all of them to stride over and congratulate the winner of the race and the reigning world champion.

'You gave me a good run for a man who hasn't been behind a wheel in years!' Dirk conceded cheerfully. 'Maybe you shouldn't be pushing numbers behind a desk, maybe you should still be racing.'

'No, Jax is a business genius,' a female voice crowed from Jax's other side, and before he could react the bubbly brunette wrapped her arms round him with enthusiasm. 'Thank you so much for stepping in last minute to do this when Stefan had to let me down. You know how grateful I am.'

'Kat,' Jax acknowledged, frowning as the photographers predictably went for a shot of them as a couple. But he and Kat Valtinos weren't a couple, no matter how much the media and their families wanted them to be, both of them being conveniently young, single and very rich.

Jax stepped back from Kat with a guarded smile. He liked Kat, he had *always* liked her but his father was in for a disappointment if he was still hoping for a dynastic marriage that would unite their parents' massive business empires. Unfortunately the photos would only encourage him in that delusion.

'Let's get you a drink,' Kat urged, closing a possessive arm round his spine. 'I really appreciate you flying out here and doing this for me today at such short notice—'

'It was for a good cause,' Jax pointed out. 'And you're a friend—'

'A friend who could be *so* much more,' Kat whispered with laden intent in his ear.

'I enjoyed the race,' Jax admitted, choosing to be tactful and sidestep her leading comment. After all, there was no kind way of telling her *why* she was wasting her time chasing him and, with his reputation for womanising, it would be sheer hypocrisy for him to do so. Even now he retained fond memories of Kat's raunchy wildness when they were teenagers and he had been on the outskirts of the same social set but he still wasn't willing to marry a woman who had slept with every one of his friends. If that was a double standard, so be it, he acknowledged grimly.

In any case, he didn't want a wife, *any* kind of wife. Nor was he prepared to deliver the grandchildren his father, Heracles Antonakos, was so eager to have. Parenting was a minefield: Jax knew that better than anyone because he had stumbled through his own very unhappy childhood, filled as it had been with constant change and even more constant emotional drama.

His parents had gone through a bitter divorce when he was only a toddler and for the following twenty-five years his father had pretty much ignored his younger son's existence. Heracles's elder son, Argo, had been born from his first marriage. Widowed, Heracles had plunged into his second marriage far too quickly and he had never forgiven his second wife, Jax's mother, for her subsequent infidelity. Jax had paid the price for his mother's extra-marital affair in more ways than one. He had had no safe harbour from which to escape the fallout of his mother's broken relationships, nor any paternal support. He had struggled alone through Mariana's divorces, suicide attempts and regular stays in rehabilitation facilities.

And one of his earliest memories was of hiding in terror in a cupboard from one of his mother's druggie meltdowns. He must have been about three years old, he mused, old enough and wise enough to know that he would be kicked and punched if she found him before the rage wore off. His mother, a gorgeous, much-adored film star on the public stage and a drug-addled monster behind closed doors. That was the woman whose tender mercies his father had left him to rely on as a defenceless child.

And then, when he was twenty-six years old, everything had suddenly and quite miraculously changed. His half-brother, Argo, had died in a bungled mugging in a city street and without the smallest warning Heracles Antonakos had moved on surprisingly fast from his grief and had begun to take a passionate interest in the younger son he had snubbed for years. Of course, Jax's mother had been gone by then, Jax reminded himself ruefully, but he still could not adequately explain or understand the very abruptness of his father's change in attitude. Even so, the paternal recognition and support he had craved from his earliest years had unexpectedly and finally become his. Naturally he still wondered if his father's change of heart would last and life being what it was, of course, he had discovered a whole new set of challenges because life as the Antonakos heir was not all peaches and cream.

As the only son of one of the richest men in the world Jax had more money than he knew what to do with. Everywhere he went in Europe he was photographed and treated like a celebrity. Bands of adoring, manipulative and rapacious women tracked and hunted him much as if he were big game. But in the business field, he reminded himself with determined positivity, he had countless stimulating projects to command his interest and engage his brilliant mind.

One of Jax's bodyguards brought a phone to him, his expression dour and apologetic. Jax compressed his lips and accepted the predictable call from his father. Heracles ranted and raved in a rage about the risk Jax had taken by going on the race track and driving at breakneck speeds. Jax said nothing because over the past two years he had learned that arguing or trying to soothe only extended such frenzied sermons. Since Argo's shocking death, Heracles had developed a morbid and excessive fear of Jax participating in any activity that could possibly harm him and if he could have got away with wrapping his only surviving son in cotton wool and packing him away safely in a box he would have done so. While Jax valued his father's new apparent attachment to him even if he didn't quite trust it, he loathed the restrictive and interfering trappings of expectation that came with it.

Only for the sake of peace had Jax accepted the five heavily armed bodyguards he didn't need and who accompanied him everywhere he went. But he remained every bit as stubborn and fiercely independent as he had always been and when he felt the need to relieve stress he still went deep-sea diving, mountain climbing and flying. He still slept with unsuitable women as well…the sort of women even his father couldn't expect him to marry.

And why not? He loved being single and free as the air because he hated anyone trying to tell him what to do. On the only occasions he had strayed from that practical stance he had ended up in disastrous relationships, so now he didn't *ever* do relationships, he only did sex and uncomplicated sex at that. Once he had run off with another man's fiancée and barely lived to tell the tale, he recalled darkly.

Franca had crept into his bed one night when he was drunk and the deed of betrayal had been done before he'd even recognised *who* he was doing it with. Franca, of course, had simply used him to escape a life that had no longer suited her but he hadn't grasped that little fact. He had fallen hook, line and sinker for her 'damsel in distress' vibe long before he'd appreciated that he was dealing with a highly manipulative and destructive alcoholic. He had betrayed his friendship with his former business partner, Rio, but in the end he had more than paid his dues sorting Franca out. But had he learned? Had he hell. After Franca had come his second biggest mistake…

Yet another female-shaped mistake. So, he didn't want a wife and he didn't want children either and *nothing*, certainly not any dormant desire to please his long-absent father, was going to change that, he reflected cynically as Kat Valtinos approached him bearing drinks and a winning smile…

'I hate you doing work like this,' Kreon Thiarkis hissed under his breath as his daughter brought him a drink. 'It's demeaning—'

'Hard work is never demeaning, Dad,' Lucy declared, her dimples flashing as she smiled down soothingly at him. 'Don't be a snob. I'm not half as posh as you are and I never will be.'

Kreon bit back tart words of disagreement because he didn't want to hurt his daughter's feelings, most particularly because she had only been in his life for the last six months and he was afraid of driving her away by acting like a heavy-handed parent. After all, Lucy had never had a proper parent to look out for her, he acknowledged guiltily. But fiercely independent and proud as she was at twenty-one years old, she had been very much down on her luck when she'd finally approached Kreon, toting his baby granddaughter in her arms, both of them shabbily dressed and half starved. The older man's heart softened at the thought of little Bella, who was the most adorable toddler and the light of his life and his wife, Iola's, for he and Iola had met and married too late in life to have a family. He loved having the two of them in his home but he was firmly convinced that his daughter and her child still very much needed a husband to look after them when he himself was no longer around.

And that would have been *so* easy to achieve if only Lucy weren't so defensive and insecure, Kreon reflected in frustration, because his daughter was an extraordinarily beautiful girl. In the bar where she worked men stopped in their tracks simply to stare at her. With a mane of strawberry-blonde curls reaching halfway down her back, creamy skin and big blue eyes, she was a classic beauty and dainty as a doll. She made more on tips than any other waitress in the hotel and was, he had been reliably assured by the owner, who was a friend, a terrific asset to business.

Lucy went about her work, ruefully aware that the job she had insisted on taking only annoyed her father. Unfortunately, being a single parent was an expensive challenge even with the wonderful support her father and stepmother had given her in recent months. She was very grateful that she had come to Greece to finally meet her long-lost father for he and his wife had freely given both her and her daughter love, kindness and acceptance. Her father was the son of a Greek who had married an Englishwoman and he had grown up in London. Kreon was a wonderfully supportive parent and grandparent. Without a word of protest or reproach he had taken in Lucy and her child even though she hadn't warned him about Bella when he'd first invited her out to Greece.

But while Lucy was willing to accept free accommodation as well as her stepmother Iola's help as a sitter with Bella, she was determined not to become a permanent burden or to take too much advantage of the older couple's generosity. She was willing to admit that she had desperately needed help when she'd first arrived in Athens but she was trying very hard now to stand on her own two feet. Her earnings might be small but that salary meant she could pay for the necessities like clothing for herself and her child and for the moment that was enough to ease her pride.

As she stepped away from a customer, her boss and the hotel owner, Andreus, signalled to her. 'We're hosting an important business meeting here in the rear conference room tomorrow morning at eleven,' he informed her. 'I'd like you to serve the drinks and snacks. I only need you for a couple of hours but I'll pay you for a full shift.'

'I'll check with Iola but that should be fine because she doesn't usually go out in the morning,' Lucy said, before taking off to serve a customer waving his hand in the air to get her attention.

The customer tried to chat her up and get her phone number but Lucy simply smiled politely and ignored his efforts because she wasn't even slightly interested in dating, or indeed in anything more physical, being well aware that the very fact she already had a child encouraged most men to assume that she would be a good bet for a casual encounter. She had been there, done that, lost the tee shirt and got a baby for her pains. Unhappily, as a green-as-grass nineteen-year-old virgin she hadn't grasped that she was involved in a casual fling until it was far too late to protect herself and she had been ditched. In fact, having been treated with such devastating contempt and dismissal by Bella's father, that final humiliation was still etched into her soul like a burn of shame that refused to heal whenever she thought about it…which was why she didn't allow herself to think about it *or* him very often.

In any case, what was the point in agonising over past mistakes and misjudgements, not to mention the most painful and cruel rejections she had suffered? Agonising never did change anything. Lucy had learned that the hard way time and time again when she was a vulnerable child growing up in care, subject to the whims of others and unable to control where she lived or even *who* she lived with. Now it meant that she found it hard to trust people and if she didn't have a certain amount of independence and choice she tended to feel horribly trapped and powerless.

But life, she reminded herself with dogged positivity, *was* getting better because for the first time in years she was daring to start putting down roots. She was happier than she had been in years and hoping to come up with a plan to improve her career prospects for Bella's sake. Very probably she would accept her father's offer to pay for some sort of job training or further education that would enable her to move out of low-paid employment. Perhaps it was finally time to start making some long-term decisions and think like a responsible adult, she told herself firmly.

'You're worth so much more than this kind of grunt work…' Bella's father had told Lucy two years earlier in Spain.

Well, look just how badly daring to have dreams and believe in them had turned out for her then, Lucy reflected, rigid with regret and pain as she stood at the bar to collect an order. Her friend at the time, another waitress called Tara, had been far more realistic about that relationship.

'He'll sleep with you and dump you and move on the minute he gets bored,' Tara had forecast, although the words she had used had been much earthier. 'Guys like that don't stick with girls like us. We're only good enough to party with for a few nights.'

Perspiration broke on Lucy's short upper lip and she wanted to punch herself hard for letting herself drift even momentarily down that bad memory lane, because hindsight only made her more ashamed of how stupid and naïve she had been. It was not as if she hadn't known what men were like, not as if she had grown up in some little princess castle, always protected and loved. She should have known better and she had yet to forgive herself for her rashness.

But at the end of her shift, when she got home to her father's very comfortable small town house and crept into the bedroom she shared with her daughter, she realised that nothing was quite that cut and dried. Bella slept nestled in her cot, curly black hair dark against the bedding, her olive skin flushed by sleep, long lashes screening her bright green eyes. Bella was gorgeous, like a little angel, Lucy thought with her eyes stinging and, although she could be sorry for everything else, she could not find it in her heart to regret Bella's existence in *any* way.

'Come with us to this dinner on Saturday night,' Iola urged over breakfast the next morning. She was a curvy brunette in her late forties with smiling dark eyes. 'It would please your father so much.'

Lucy went pink as she washed her daughter's face clean of breakfast debris. She knew that her dining out with them would please Kreon, but she also knew it would entail fending off the advances of at least two handpicked young men because her father's current main aim in life seemed to centre on finding her an eligible boyfriend. In that line Kreon was old-fashioned because he refused to credit that Lucy choosing to remain a single parent could be a viable plan for the future.

'Mum… Mum,' Bella carolled cheerfully as she was released from the high chair and set down to toddle somewhat clumsily round the room.

Lucy steadied her daughter as she almost fell over the toy box and ruffled her untidy curls. Curls, aside of the colour, just like her own, frizzy and ungovernable in humid weather, explosive when washed. Lucy looked back at her stepmother uncomfortably. She felt like an ungrateful brat for her reluctance to do what her father wanted her to do. 'I'm just not interested in meeting anyone at present…maybe in a few months I'll feel differently,' she added without much conviction.

'You had a bad breakup and you went through a lot alone afterwards,' Iola acknowledged gently. 'But your father's a man and he doesn't get it. I did try to explain to him that this is more of a healing time for you—'

'Yes, that's it, that's *exactly* it!' Lucy exclaimed, giving the older woman a sudden impulsive and appreciative hug. 'I'm not ready right now, not sure if I'll ever be though…'

'Not all men are like Bella's father. There *are* decent caring men out there,' Iola reminded her quietly.

'Nobody knows that better than me. I kissed a lot of frogs before I met Kreon.'

Lucy grinned and then laughed because her stepmother really did understand her viewpoint. A few minutes later, she left the town house and set out to walk to the small select Hotel Palati where she worked. Sited in an exclusive district in Athens, the hotel catered mainly to a business clientele.

Her father had met Iola when he'd engaged her as a PA in a property rental business that had eventually gone bust. But then Kreon had led a chequered 'boom to bust and back again' life and had been divorced once for infidelity. Lucy had respected his honesty with her. Even on the subject of her late mother, Kreon had proved to be painfully frank. Kreon hadn't once whitewashed his own failings or hidden the fact that he had gained a criminal record over some pyramid selling scheme he had got involved with as a younger man. Yet in spite of that honesty, Lucy still wasn't quite sure what actually funded her father's comfortable lifestyle.

She knew that Kreon gambled and took bets on a near professional basis and that he was always enthusiastically involved in some hopefully lucrative business scheme of one kind or another. Whatever he did, he seemed to be successful at it. Even so, she would not have been entirely surprised to learn that some of his ventures skated a little too close to the edge of breaking the law. But basically because he and Iola had given Lucy and her daughter both the home and the love Lucy had never known before, she closed her eyes to that suspicion and minded her own business the best she could.

After all, there truly *were* shades of grey between the black and white of absolute right and absolute wrong, she ruminated ruefully. Nothing and nobody was perfect. Even at the height of her passionate infatuation with Jax, she had recognised that he was flawed and all too human. He had been moody, controlling, domineering and arrogant and they had fought like cat and dog on a regular basis because, while Lucy might be only five feet tall and undersized, she was no pushover. At heart, she was stubborn and gutsy and quick-tempered. Even if Jax hadn't let her down so horribly, it would never have worked between them, she reasoned, feeling pleasantly philosophical on that score and firmly stifling the painful little push of heartache that still hollowed out her tummy. So, she'd had her heart broken just as Iola and thousands of other women *and* men had. It had only made her more resilient and less foolish and naïve, she told herself squarely.

The hotel manager showed her into the lofty-ceilinged back room, which had been comprehensively redecorated only weeks earlier with an opulence that was calculated to appeal to the more discerning customers.

Sometimes when Lucy daydreamed she wondered, if she had come from a more fortunate background, would she have become one of the elegant well-educated young businesswomen she saw round the hotel. Unfortunately she had been handicapped at the outset of life by her birth. Her parents' marriage had broken down after her mother had had an affair.

'Annabel always thought some better man was waiting for her round the next corner,' Kreon had said wryly of Lucy's mother. 'I wasn't rich and I lived by my wits and she had big ideas. We were living in London then where she was struggling to get the finance to set up her nursery business. But my father had returned to Greece after my mother died and he fell ill out here. I *had* to go to him. When I left London I had no idea Annabel was pregnant and when I contacted her to tell her that I was coming back she told me we were finished because she had met someone else. Now from what you're telling me, it seems she may have learned that she had this dreadful disease and she didn't want me around even though she had my child. I can't understand that, I will *never* understand that…'

And Lucy couldn't understand it either because, just listening to Kreon talking, she had recognised that he *had* loved her mother and had planned to return to London to be with her. But the more Kreon had spoken of her mother's beauty and her feverish love and need for fresh male attention, the more Lucy had suspected that there definitely *had* been another man and Annabel had burnt her boats for ever with Kreon shortly before illness had cruelly claimed her future.

Lucy had been two years old when Annabel was hospitalised and her daughter put into care. Her only memory of her mother was of a beautiful redhead lying in bed and shouting at her, so she wasn't sure that the mother who had surrendered her to the authorities had been that much of a loss in the parent stakes. Kreon had described a flighty, selfish personality, ill-suited to the kind of personal sacrifices a mother was often forced to make. And when, to Lucy's very great astonishment, Kreon had revealed that Annabel had actually had two other daughters being raised by her own mother somewhere in northern England, Lucy had been silenced by that shattering news.

Apparently she had two half-sisters somewhere, born from her mother's previous liaisons. Some day Lucy planned to look into that startling discovery but she didn't even know where you started in such a search because, not only had she no money to pursue enquiries, but also no names even to begin with. Naturally all these years on Kreon didn't recall such details about Annabel's background and history. After all, he had never met Annabel's mother and had been stonewalled by Annabel when he'd asked to do so. All he had remembered was that Annabel never went to visit the two little girls she had left behind her and he had said that even then he had recognised that as a warning sign that Annabel's attachments were of the shallow sort.

Lucy had counted herself lucky that she was not equally superficial because she adored Bella and would have laid down her life for her child, counting Bella as one of the few good developments in a life that had been far from easy or happy. On the other hand, had she cared less about Jax she would have been less devastated when he disappeared. My goodness, she had fallen apart at the seams and done stupid stuff, she recalled ruefully. She had been thrown off his father's yacht and warned never to show her face at the marina again while being marched off by security guards. She had been shouted at, called nasty names and utterly humiliated in her fruitless pursuit of Jax. All because she was fundamentally stupid, she conceded with regret.

After all, it had been crazy of her to believe that she meant anything more to Jax than an easily forgettable sexual fling, and when he was done with a woman, he was definitely *done*. The crewman on the yacht had called her a cheap whore as he'd bodily manhandled her off the polished deck and forced her down the gangway. She had fallen, been hurt and bruised by that brutality and she had been pregnant at the time. That was one reason she had never told her father the whole truth about Bella's parentage, preferring him to assume that Bella was the result of some one-night stand with a man in Spain. She knew Kreon would seek revenge and restitution if she ever told him the whole story.

So, in a way, staying silent was protecting her father from doing anything rash, she reasoned uneasily. Kreon was extremely protective. He would hit the roof if he realised that Lucy had been homeless even though Bella's father was a rich man, who could so easily have helped her and their child. A rich man, who was also Greek. That information wouldn't help either when Kreon was so immensely proud of his heritage.

But then Lucy had long since decided that rich people were pretty much untouchable, unlike the rest of humanity. The very rich had the power and the money to hold the rest of the world at bay and she saw the evidence of that galling fact every time she saw Jax in the media. Jax surrounded by bodyguards and beautiful women, never alone, never approachable, as protected and distanced from ordinary people as an exhibit in a locked museum case. Jax Antonakos, renowned entrepreneur and billionaire in his own right with a daddy who had billions also.

Her hands trembled as she set out china on the trolley awaiting her. She hated Jax now with the same passion she had once put into loving him. He had strung her along, faked so many things and she could never,

ever forgive the fact that he had quite deliberately left her stranded in Spain without a home or a job or any means of support. That she had been pregnant into the bargain was just her bad luck, but then Lucy had little experience of good luck.

A cluster of chattering businessmen entered and she served the coffee, standing back by the wall to dutifully await any further requests. Beyond the ajar door there was a burst of comment and then a sudden hush and the sound of many footsteps crossing the tiled hallway outside. The door whipped back noisily on its hinges and two men strode in, talking into ear pieces while checking the exit doors and all the windows, and that level of security warned Lucy that someone tremendously important was evidently about to arrive. The security men backed against the wall in silence and two more arrived to take up stances on the other side of the room. The almost militaristic security detail seemed so over the top for a small business meeting that Lucy almost laughed out loud.

And then Jax walked in and she stopped breathing and any desire to laugh died in her suddenly constricted lungs…

CHAPTER TWO

THE INSTANT LUCY saw that untidy black hair and the gorgeous green eyes so arrestingly bright against his bronzed skin, she wanted to run and keep on running and only innate discipline kept her where she was while she questioned her reaction. Why should *she* want to run? What had she done to be ashamed of? She was not a coward, she had never been a coward, she reminded herself doggedly, unnerved by that craven desire to flee. Indeed if anyone should be embarrassed it should be Jax for the cruel way he had treated her.

Couples broke up all the time but the process didn't have to be downright nasty. She hadn't been a stalker. There had been no excuse for threats and no need whatsoever to run her out of the neighbourhood.

Recollecting that vicious goodbye, Lucy lifted her chin high. Seated centre stage at the circular table, the cynosure of all attention and conversation, Jax mercifully wasn't looking round the room enough to notice her. Lucy might have overcome the urge to run but it did annoy her to find herself in a subservient role in Jax's radius again. In a mad moment she had once fantasised about swanning through some swanky club some day looking like a million dollars and seeing Jax and totally ignoring him to demonstrate her disdain and overall superiority as a decent human being. But now that she was actually on the spot she discovered that she was indefensibly and horribly curious and could only stare at him.

He had kept his black hair short. Once he had worn it long but he had had it cropped not long after she'd first met him, hitting the more conventional note she had suspected his father preferred. In retrospect she found it hard to credit that they had once bonded over their absent fathers. Jax had admitted how recently his father had come back into his life and had shared his grief over the death of the half-brother he had loved, not to mention his mother's abuse and infidelities. None of those deep conversations had fitted into what she assumed could be described as a typical short-term fling. But then that was Jax, a tough individualist, unpredictable, fiery and mysterious…the archetypal brooding hero beloved of teenaged girls with an overly romantic disposition, she concluded sourly.

That he *was* startlingly handsome had undoubtedly influenced the fantasies she had woven, she acknowledged, chewing at her lower lip, fingernails biting painfully into her palms. High cheekbones, strong clean jaw line, stunning eyes set beneath well-shaped ebony brows. Of course his mother had been a very famous and stunningly beautiful Spanish movie star and he had inherited her looks. In a big magazine article she had once read about him, which had been accompanied by a close-up photo, the journalist had raved about those dazzling wild green eyes and the spiky length of his sooty lashes.

Bella had *his* eyes. Lucy swallowed hard, recalling her feelings as her daughter's blue eyes at birth had slowly transformed to an eerily familiar emerald in her innocent little face. Innocent, something Jax was not and had never been. And reading about his sexual exploits over the past two years had helped Lucy to understand that he had always been a selfish, ruthless womaniser but she had been too trusting and inexperienced to recognise his true nature. Her heart was fluttering a beat so fast behind her breastbone that she wanted to press a hand against it to slow it down.

And then the truth of her response hit her and she was aghast that in spite of everything her body could still react to the presence of his. He glanced up from the file he had been perusing and for a split second, a literal *single* heartbeat, she clashed in dismay with his fierce gaze. It was like an electric shock pulsing low in her pelvis, tightening bone and sinew, awakening sensations she had almost forgotten and had never felt since. Every pulse she possessed went crazy, her breath catching in her throat, her very skin as achingly sensitive as if he had actually *touched* her. And then that tiny moment was over and past as Jax blanked her and passed the file back to someone at the table while making some comment about profit margins.

Her Greek vocabulary was slowly growing but in unfamiliar scenarios she still got as lost as any non-Greek-speaking foreigner. And *of course* Jax was going to blank her, she told herself shakily. Had she really thought he would greet a worker bee as low on the proverbial food chain as a waitress? Her mouth compressed as she wondered anxiously how he would react to the news that he was a father were she to tell him. With furious hostility and denial, she reckoned, her skin turning clammy at the prospect. Jax had once been very upfront about the fact that he didn't ever want children. Bearing that in mind, Lucy ruminated grimly, he should have been more careful to ensure that he didn't get her pregnant.

Jax's lean, chiselled features were rigid. He refused to look back in Lucy's direction. He didn't need to. That momentary image was stamped into his brain like a punch. What the hell was she doing in Athens? And her sudden appearance in his presence? Some sort of a set-up? And if so, why? Jax never took anything at face value any more. After all, he had once accepted Lucy for what she appeared to be and learned his very great error.

Bile tinged his mouth as he briefly recalled what he had read in that investigation file on her background: a string of drug offences stretching back years and convictions for soliciting sex. He had felt like a complete idiot. He had rushed off to see her, *confront* her even though it was late at night and then he had seen who she really was for himself...down an alley with a man enthusiastically giving up what she had made him wait weeks to enjoy.

Disgust and distaste flooded Jax, bringing back even less welcome memories of his mother's rampant promiscuity and empty promises of fidelity. He had seen her cheating break more than one man who had adored her. His father didn't know it because he had never dared to ask what his son's life had been like with his mother but Heracles had not been the only man to be chewed up and spat out in pieces by Mariana, who had wilfully followed every stray sexual impulse. As for Lucy, she was a liar and a cheat and he did not forgive betrayal. The entire episode had been sordid in the extreme. So why was he remembering that she had given him the wildest, hottest sex he had ever had?

A stubborn push of raunchily sexual images infiltrated Jax's hind brain even while he fought to hold them at bay and kept on talking about the project on the table. Hard as a rock behind his zip, Jax went rigid with angry aggression. How dared Lucy even walk into a room that contained him? He had always told himself that he had not inherited his father's notorious temper and equally notorious ability to hold a grudge but just then he recognised that he had lied to himself. Had it been possible to bodily throw Lucy out, he would have done so!

One of the bodyguards nudged Lucy's elbow and she glanced up, dragged from her own bemused thoughts with a vengeance. The older man indicated the coffee on the trolley and angled his head in his employer's direction, clearly urging her to get on with her job.

Reddening all the way up to her hairline, Lucy unfroze in an effort to behave normally. Even so she had to fight a huge inner battle to force her legs over to the trolley and pour Jax a coffee when all she really wanted to do was empty the entire contents of the pot over his hateful, arrogant head. Without him looking once at her or indeed acknowledging her in any way, she settled the coffee at his elbow with a hand that trembled slightly. Next she laid out the snacks and topped up the cups, signalling the bar waiter at the door when one of the men requested a shot of ouzo to wash down his coffee.

From below screening lashes and the almost infinitesimal movements of his proud dark head, Jax tracked Lucy's every move like a predator planning an attack. A blinding flash of memory assailed him: skin as translucent as fine porcelain in the dawn light, his fingers knotted into tumbling golden ringlets spread across a pillow, glorious bright blue eyes holding his, a tiny slender body with surprisingly sexy little curves reaching up to his. A little curvier than she used to be, he estimated abstractedly, remembering for a few seconds and then suddenly emerging again from that uncharacteristic reverie to answer a question, angrier and hotter than he had been in years.

The louse could at least have thanked her for the coffee, Lucy reflected with growing annoyance. Even a nod would have been acceptable but then Jax had always been a law unto himself, ferociously uncompromising and challenging, driven to succeed, survive and flourish as if it was in his genes. And perhaps it was. Only in a fantasy could there ever have been a scenario in which she believed that Jax Antonakos would settle down with a humble waitress… Bitterness gripped her and resentment shot through her like a sheet of lightning flashing off all her exposed nerve endings with painful effect.

Who the hell did Jax Antonakos think he was to treat her with such derisive dismissal?

Jax summoned Zenas, his head security guard, with an almost imperceptible flicker of his gaze and passed him a note. Zenas stood back to read it and confusion gripped his features for an instant before discipline kicked in and he left the room to do his employer's bidding. Lucy paid little heed to the byplay and only tensed when her own boss appeared in the doorway and silently summoned her out into the hallway.

A frown line bisected the older man's brow as he studied her. 'Mr Antonakos wants to speak to you in private when he's finished. I'm not sure how your father would feel about that request—'

Comprehension gripped Lucy fast. Andreus had no idea that she already knew Jax. He simply thought that Jax was trying to get off with her.

'Please don't mention this to Dad,' she muttered unevenly, for that was not a connection she wanted made. Once a link of any kind was established, secrets could spill out.

Andreus cast open the door of a smaller room across the corridor. 'Wait in there…but only if you *want* to,' he added with deliberate meaning. 'This is nothing to do with your employment here or with me. I have only passed on his request because I am very reluctant to offend so powerful a man.'

Lucy turned a slow, painful red, rage mushrooming inside her again as she imagined what her employer must be thinking. Jax wouldn't care about appearances. Jax had never *had* to care about appearances. For an instant she almost walked away from the opportunity to tell Jax what she thought of him. But she was too nervous, too aware of what had happened the last time her very existence nearby had become objectionable to Jax Antonakos. He had paid her then boss in Spain to sack her and she had lost her job and the accommodation that went with it. That was the kind of power the super wealthy had. Her boss in those days had been outrageously frank with her, admitting that he couldn't afford to keep her on when so much money to do otherwise was on offer and that he had had a poor summer season.

She paced the floor in the small room that was normally used as an office by the hotel housekeeper, thinking herself lucky that Jax hadn't had a room in the hotel and called her there, which would have looked even worse. Why on earth after ignoring her would he have demanded a meeting? From his point of view that made no sense, she reasoned with a frown. After all, he had ditched her two years earlier without an explanation or even a text. He hadn't turned up for their last date, hadn't phoned, hadn't done anything and when she had tried to contact him he had blocked her calls. Either he had simply tired of her or she had done or said something that had offended.

It hurt to look back and recall how many weeks she had tormented herself by pathetically wondering what she had done to annoy Jax. But nothing could have justified his subsequent behaviour in having her sacked and forced to leave the area like some vagrant whose very presence was offensive. That more than anything was what she could not forgive.

'You literally have three minutes or you'll miss your flight,' Zenas warned Jax outside the door.

Jax strode into the room, absently wondering if there was actual truth in the idea that human beings needed closure following certain experiences because he could not imagine any other reason why he should still feel driven to confront Lucy. Two years ago, he had never wanted to see or speak to her again. But possibly curiosity provided more motivation than he was willing to admit, he reasoned impatiently, angry tension tightening his lean, darkly handsome features.

'What the hell are you doing in Athens?' Jax demanded.

Lucy spun round from the window to face him, inwardly reeling from the shock of Jax in the flesh standing close enough to touch. He was so tall and he radiated restive energy and dominant vibes in waves. Tensing, she lifted her head up but she still had to tip it back to actually see any part of him above chest level. Not for the first time her diminutive height struck her as an embarrassing flaw. Being almost child-sized often meant that people didn't take her seriously or treat her like an adult. 'What's that got to do with you?' she slung back sharply, her tone similar to his own.

Jax drew himself up to his full six-foot-three-inch height and glowered down at her, green eyes luminescent with rage because it had been two years since anyone but his father had challenged him. 'Answer me,' he ground out impatiently.

'I don't owe you any answers…I don't owe you the time of day,' Lucy traded with the kind of provocation that struck a deep and unwelcome note of familiarity with Jax.

'You *will* answer me,' Jax raked back at her in a raw undertone, watching as she angled her head back and struck an attitude, hand on hip. Strawberry golden curls slid round her shoulders, her hair falling round her heart-shaped face, accentuating the defiant blue of her eyes and the lush fullness of her rosy lips.

And that fast, that urgently, Jax wanted to throw her down on the desk and control her the only way he had ever really controlled her, with the seething passion that was the mainstay of his character. For the briefest of moments he allowed himself to imagine the hot, wet tightness of her and the pulse at his groin reacted with unbridled enthusiasm. He reminded himself that it had been a toxic relationship and that she had played him like a con artist with her stories, her fake innocence and her lies. A dizzy surge of rage ignited inside him like a threatening fireball.

'If you don't answer me you will live to regret it,' Jax threatened in a wrathful undertone, every drop of his merciless Antonakos blood burning through him and hungry for a fight.

An angry spurt of fear made Lucy's stomach turn over sickly. He was too influential to challenge as even her boss had reminded her. She knew Jax could cause trouble for her, maybe even for her father as well if she wasn't careful. She might hate Jax but it would be insane to risk such penalties. 'What am I doing in Athens?' she repeated flatly. 'I finally looked up my birth father and he lives here—'

'But that was all lies,' Jax breathed in momentary bewilderment. 'You don't *have* a Greek father.'

Her smooth brow furrowed with genuine confusion. 'Lies? I don't know what you're talking about. I believe my birth certificate is as accurate as anyone else's. At the moment I'm living with my father and his wife.'

'That's not possible,' Jax told her, stiffening as a light knock on the door warned him that their time was up if he planned to make it to the airport. His long, lean frame swivelled as he half turned towards the door to leave, common sense and practicality powering him.

'I just want you to know that I hate you and I'll never forgive you for what you did to me,' Lucy confided in a belated rush of angry frustration that she could not tell him what she really thought of him any more bluntly than that. In truth she wanted to scream at him, she wanted to throw herself at him and hammer him with angry fists for hurting her.

'I didn't *do* anything to you,' Jax parried with complete cool.

'It was vicious...what you did, unnecessary!' Lucy condemned chokily, bitterness almost overpowering her along with a very human need to hit back. 'Having me sacked? Leaving me penniless and homeless and forced to go back to the UK when I had nothing there!'

An ebony brow elevated at that improbable accusation of bullying behaviour on his part, Jax swung back to her just as another knock sounded on the door. Whatever else he might be, Jax prided himself on never having treated a woman badly. 'I don't have time for this and I shouldn't make time for it either,' he acknowledged grimly. 'You're a liar and a cheat—'

'Of course you're going to say stuff like that, rewrite history, because you're so up yourself now,' Lucy shot back at him in disgust as she thought about her innocent, trusting little daughter. 'But I never lied to you or cheated on you and you never once thought about consequences, did you?'

He wanted her phone number but he wouldn't ask for it, wouldn't allow himself to ask for it. He knew what she was. He didn't want anything to do with her. So, having reached that decision and feeling invigorated by it, he could not explain why he then turned back like a man with a split personality and told her to meet him for a drink the following evening at a little bar he patronised on the marina, a haunt of his for quiet moments, which the paparazzi had yet to discover. Even as he walked back out again, he was questioning the decision and regretting it, lean brown hands clenching into impatient fists. What the hell had he done that for?

But what had she meant by 'consequences'? And how come she *did* have a Greek father when according to that file she did not?

He was simply curious, nothing wrong or surprising about that. His libido was not in the driver's seat, he assured himself with solid conviction. Stray memories had briefly aroused him when he saw her again, nothing more meaningful. All men remembered incredibly good sex. Furthermore, he had a little black book of phonebook proportions to turn to when he felt like sex, hot and cold running women on tap wherever he travelled. *That* was the world he lived in. There was no way he could ever be tempted to revisit a manipulative little cheat like Lucy Dixon, he reflected with satisfaction.

Naturally, becoming the Antonakos heir had ensured that Jax became significantly more cynical about women. He didn't listen to sob stories any more, he didn't let his inherently dangerous streak of chivalry rule him. Indeed the sight of a woman in need of rescue was more like aversion therapy to him now. He knew from experience that that kind of woman was likely to be far more trouble than she was worth.

After all, how many times had he felt he had no choice but to race to his mother's rescue? When the men she betrayed became violent as her lies were exposed? When she needed another spell in some discreet rehabilitation facility before she could be seen in public again? When he was forced to lie to protect *her*?

And yet at heart he had always known that his

mother was a deeply disturbed and egocentric human being, undeserving of his care and respect. That was why his little sister, Tina, had died, he reminded himself bitterly. Mariana's self-centred neglect of her younger child had directly led to the incident in which the toddler had drowned. But he had only been fourteen, so what could he possibly have done when so many adults had witnessed the insanity of his mother's lifestyle and yet failed to act to protect either of her children?

Lucy walked home in a pensive mood. Of course she wouldn't meet him, she told herself firmly. What would be the point? *Bella!* Jax was a father whether he liked it or not but she knew he wouldn't like that news any more than he liked her. And why was her being in Greece such a big deal? What was it to him? It was not as though they were likely to bump into each other again in normal life. Jax lived against a backdrop of massive yachts, private jets and private islands. He didn't rub shoulders with ordinary working people.

Yet a giant ball of despair was threatening to swallow Lucy up and she didn't know why. Seeing Jax again, she recognised, had *hurt* and hurt much more than she had expected. It had brought back memories she didn't want. She had loved him and had given her trust to a man for the first time ever. His sudden volte-face had almost destroyed her because she had given him so much she had felt bare to the world without him.

And yet he *still* wasn't married. She had thought for sure that he would marry the wealthy heiress his father kept pushing in his direction, the very lovely but very bitchy Kat Valtinos. But then Jax was bone-deep stubborn. You could take a horse to water but you couldn't make it drink and getting Jax to do anything he didn't want to do was like trying to push a boulder up a steep hill.

Kat Valtinos had organised the party the night Lucy had met Jax on his father's enormous yacht. Lucy's memory wafted her back two years into the past. Back then, Jax had been in Spain setting up a new resort on the coast. When the caterers had mucked up with a double booking, Kat had personally trawled through the local bars seeking waitresses for the event.

'You two will do,' she had said to Lucy and Tara, looking them up and down as though they were auditioning as strippers. 'You're young and pretty and sexy. Just what men like. You put your make-up on with a trowel,' she had told Tara critically and to Lucy she had said, 'You need to show more leg and cleavage.'

If the money hadn't been so good, Lucy wouldn't have done it but back then she had lived on a budget where no tips meant stale bread and going hungry. Their boss didn't feed them for free and they had no cooking facilities in their mean little attic room, which had been hot as hell up under the eaves above the restaurant kitchen. Any extra cash was deeply welcome in those days.

The party had been full of blowhard bellicose men talking themselves up in Antonakos's company and drinking too much. One of them had cornered Lucy when she was sent to a lower deck to restock the bar from the supplies stored there. She had been trying to fight him off when Jax had intervened. Jax, blue-black glossy hair brushing his shoulders, green eyes glittering like shards of glass, who had dragged the guy off her with punishing hands and hit him hard without hesitation.

'Are you OK?' the most gorgeous guy she had ever seen had asked, pulling her off the wall she had slumped against, smoothing down the skirt the creep had been trying to wrench up. '*Diavolos*, you're so tiny. Did he hurt you?'

'Only a little,' she had said shakily, trembling like a leaf and in absolutely no doubt that Jax had saved her from a serious assault because, with the noisy party taking place on the deck above, the lower deck had been deserted and nobody would have heard her crying out.

'Take a moment to recover,' Jax had urged, guiding her into an opulent saloon to push her down into a seat where her cotton-wool legs had collapsed under her as if he had flipped a switch. 'What were you doing down here on this deck?'

He had issued instructions on the phone to a crew member to have the bar supplies refreshed. And the whole time she had just been staring at him like a brainless idiot, utterly intimidated by everything about him from the expensive quality of his lightweight grey suit and hand-stitched shoes to the sheer beauty of his perfect features from his edgy cheekbones to his sculpted mouth. It was the eyes that had got to her the most, the tender concern she'd seen there and then the budding all-male appreciation. He had the most stunning eyes and his rare smile had been like the sun coming out on a dark day.

'Are you OK?' he repeated.

Well, no, in fact from that moment she had never

been OK again. Something she'd needed to survive had lurched into strange territory and softened to let him in, no matter that it had gone against sense and practicality and her life experience. She had truly never been the same since.

CHAPTER THREE

LUCY WAS RIVEN with extreme guilt by the time she finally climbed on the bus that would take her down to the marina.

She had had to lie to Iola simply to get out. She had pretended that she was joining a couple of the other waitresses for a few drinks. To weigh down her conscience even more, Iola had been delighted to believe that her stepdaughter was finally going out and about. Her stepmother had hovered helpfully, urging her to put on make-up and wear the pretty white sundress that Iola had bought for her a few weeks earlier. But how *could* Lucy have admitted that she was heading out to meet Bella's father? After all, she had already lied on that subject by declaring that she had no way of getting in touch with the man who had fathered her daughter. Kreon and Iola had averted their eyes in dismay and embarrassment at that claim, clearly assuming that she did not know the man's name.

Indeed, one lie only led to more lies, Lucy conceded shamefacedly, annoyed that she had found it impossible to be more honest. But Kreon would raise the roof if he discovered that Jax was Bella's father and she didn't want to put Kreon in the potential firing line of Antonakos displeasure.

And why was she off to meet Jax when she had sworn she would not do so?

Obviously she was thinking about her daughter's needs, wondering if there was any chance that Jax could have changed his outlook on children and could possibly be willing to embrace the news that he was a parent. It was definitely her duty to check out that possibility and finally tell him that he had a child, she told herself staunchly even while her heart hammered and her breath caught in her throat at the prospect of seeing Jax again.

You're pathetic, she scolded herself angrily as she marched past crowded bars, ignoring the men who called out to her. He's a very good-looking guy and of course you still notice that but that's all, leave it there. You are *not* a silly impulsive teenager any more, she coached herself, you know what he is and what he's like and *you know better*.

Jax lounged outside the bar with Zenas close by, the rest of his security detail settled within hailing distance. He didn't know why he had come until he saw Lucy, her dress flowing and dancing round her slender knees, the pristine white lighting up below the street lights, her strawberry-blonde ringlets a vivid fall round her narrow shoulders. And then he knew why he had come and he hated that surge of absolute primal lust, raw distaste flaming through him even as his jeans became uncomfortably tight. A wave of male heads slowly turned to check her out as she passed by. Jax gritted his even white teeth at that familiar display.

'The waitress...*really*?' Zenas teased from the shadows.

'I need to have this conversation in private,' Jax warned his old school friend quietly, relieved that Zenas had only joined the team the year before and had no idea of his prior acquaintance with Lucy.

Zenas strolled obediently across the street and plonked himself down on a bench. Jax lifted his newspaper, refusing to continue watching Lucy walk towards him, perturbed by the level of his own interest. He would get answers from her, satisfy his curiosity and leave. There would be nothing more personal and absolutely *no* sex.

Lucy saw Jax outside the bar, arrogant dark head bent, the bold cut of his chiselled profile golden beneath the lights, his black hair still long enough to tousle in the light breeze. And her heart bounced inside her like a rubber ball because she was helplessly reliving the excitement he had always induced in her. There were flutters in her tummy, crazy tingles pinching the tips of her breasts taut and a dangerous hot, liquid awareness pulsing into being between her legs. Just as quickly her entire body felt overheated and she was seriously embarrassed for herself.

As she took a seat Jax glanced up at her from below his ridiculously long lashes, crescents of uncompromising green running assessingly across her flushed face. 'At least you're on time for once...I assume you hurried.'

Lucy blinked and bit down on her tongue hard. Her poor timekeeping had always infuriated Jax because he hated being kept waiting and never, ever understood how time could sometimes run away from her.

He had always contended that being late was rude and indefensible. But then Jax, who was relentlessly practical and full of ferocious initiative in tough scenarios, had probably never had a weakness for daydreaming.

Daydreaming, however, had always been Lucy's escape from challenging experiences. When she didn't fit in at the many different schools she had attended she had floated away on a fluffy cloud inside her own mind. When life was especially difficult, fantasies had become her consolation and she would dream of a world in which she had love and security and happiness.

In the smouldering silence that had now fallen, Lucy forced herself out of her abstraction and registered that Jax was watching her with impatient green eyes as if he had guessed that she had momentarily drifted away with the fairies. In receipt of that aggravated look, she felt her mouth run dry as a bone. In desperation she spun his newspaper round, her attention falling on a recent custody case that had attracted a lot of media coverage. 'Oh, my goodness...' she muttered as she slowly traced the headline with a fingertip while she carefully translated it. 'The *father* got the kid? How could they take a child away from his mother?'

Jax shrugged an uninterested shoulder as he signalled the waiter. 'Why not? Life has moved on. Fathers are now equal to mothers—'

'Yes, but—'

'Read it and you'll see why the family court reached that decision,' Jax said drily.

'I can't read Greek well enough yet,' she admitted grudgingly.

'The father is willing to work at home to be with the child while the mother would be leaving him in a nursery all day. Why are we talking about this anyway?' Jax demanded impatiently.

'It's an interesting case,' Lucy proffered stiffly. 'The mother's a paramedic who doesn't have the option of working at home.'

'While the father wants his child and what's best for his child, which is as it should be,' Jax interposed as a bottle of wine and glasses arrived at the table.

A cold skitter of fear pierced Lucy's tense body as a glass of wine appeared in front of her. 'Is that how you would feel?'

'We're not talking about me. I won't be fathering any children,' Jax declared with a cynical twist of his expressive mouth. 'Don't need the hassle or the responsibility. But if I *did* have a child I certainly wouldn't sit back and allow a woman to take my child away from me…in fact that is the very last thing I would do.'

A quiver of sheer fright rippled down Lucy's taut spine as she reached for her wine. That risk, that particular fear of losing her child, had never once crossed her mind as a possibility. And why hadn't it? Jax might not want children but he *was* a very possessive guy. What was his was very much his, not to be shared or touched or even looked at by anyone else. Once he had treated Lucy like that, enraging her with his determination to own her body and soul and control her every move. Suppose she told him about Bella and he felt the same way about his daughter?

Sobered by that fear, Lucy decided there and then to continue keeping Bella a secret until she had, at least, taken legal advice. In fact maybe the legal route would be the best way to go when it came to breaking that news, she thought cravenly. It would be more impersonal and less likely to lead to confrontation and bad feeling. Just at that moment Lucy could not face telling Jax that he was the father of her child and that because of his behaviour after their breakup she had had no way of telling him that she was pregnant. That was not her fault, she reminded herself. That was unquestionably *his* fault.

'When did you move to Athens?' Jax prompted.

'Six months ago…I was struggling to make ends meet in London,' she confided, almost rolling her eyes at that severe understatement before taking several fortifying swallows of wine.

'When we talked in Spain, you had no plans to track your father down,' he reminded her with a frown. 'You thought he had deserted your mother and you *said*—'

'I was wrong. When I needed help, my father came through for me,' Lucy admitted. 'Why did you ask me to meet you?'

Jax watched her sip at the wine, one little finger rubbing back and forth over the stem of the glass, her lush mouth rosy and moist. Like a sex-starved adolescent, he remembered the feel of her mouth, the flick of her teasing little tongue and he went rigid.

'Jax?' she pressed, setting down the glass.

Lean, dark features taut, Jax topped up the wine. He had tried to teach her about wine once: how to select it, savour it, how to truly *taste* it, and she was still knocking it back as if it were cheap plonk. That had been another lesson that had inexplicably ended up between the sheets. But then nothing had ever gone to plan with Lucy. His self-discipline had vanished.

When he had taken her shopping he had taken her in the changing cubicle up against the wall, stifling her frantic cries with his hand. Yes, she had definitely *earned* that red dress he had later seen her wearing while she gave her body to another man.

'Why?' Lucy prompted in growing frustration at his brooding silence.

Jax inclined his head to Zenas and spoke to him soft and low when he approached. 'We'll go somewhere more private—'

Lucy collided with smouldering green eyes like highly polished emeralds and stiffened in instant rejection of that idea. 'No.'

'I don't know what I was thinking of. This is not the place to talk.' Or fight, Jax reflected, in no doubt that angry words were likely to be exchanged when he challenged her.

Lucy gulped down more wine in an effort to steady herself and think carefully before she spoke. 'I don't want to go anywhere else with you,' she argued.

'Don't lie,' Jax advised in the driest of tones. 'I could have you on your back in five minutes if that's what I wanted...but it's *not*.'

A tide of outraged colour slowly dappled Lucy's creamy skin as she gazed back at him, aghast at his crudity. 'I can't believe you said that.'

Jax shrugged again, a knowing look in his stunning eyes. 'It's only what we're both thinking about.'

Lucy bristled like a cat stroked the wrong way and threw her shoulders back. 'No, it's not. Speak for yourself.'

'I fell for the virgin ploy once. Don't push your luck, *koukla mou*,' Jax advised as he thrust back his chair and began to rise. 'Born-again virgins push the wrong buttons with me.'

'Don't call me that...I'm *not* anyone's doll!' Lucy protested, aware of the meaning of those words because her father used them around Bella.

'Don't push your luck, Tinker Bell,' Jax stabbed instead.

And the sound of that once familiar pet name hurt like the unexpected swipe of a knife across tender skin. It turned her pale because it took her back to a place she didn't want to go, to a period when she had fondly believed herself to be loved and safe and cherished. But it had all been a lie and a seriously cruel lie at that. It hurt even more that she had adored that lie and longed for it to last for ever and ever, just like in the fairy tales.

'You still haven't told me what this is about,' Lucy argued as she drank down her wine with desperate little swallows that pained her throat. 'I'm staying here.'

A long silver limousine purred along the kerb. They were in a pedestrian zone and the car shouldn't have been there but the two police officers lounging across the street did nothing to interfere with its progress.

'Get in the car or I'll throw you in it!' Jax bit out in a driven undertone, what little patience he had taxed by her obstinacy.

He had made a mistake, he thought furiously, turning his head and unexpectedly encountering Zenas's shocked appraisal, registering that the other man had heard that threat.

Incredulous, Lucy giggled. 'You wouldn't dare,' she told him.

And he *did*. He picked her up off the chair and

shoved her into the back seat of the limo as if she were a lost parcel he was retrieving, aware throughout that his bodyguards were watching him as if he had gone insane. But it was entirely Lucy's fault. She would never ever do as she was told. She would never ever accept that he knew best. And the whole situation was going to hell in a hand basket fast and he could blame himself for that because he should never have arranged to meet her in the first place. Why the hell did what had happened two years ago even *matter* to him?

So, she had lied to engage his sympathy and ensnare him, pretending to be younger and more innocent than she actually was. He already knew why she had done it. She had lied to impress him because he was rich and there was nothing more complex behind her behaviour back then than greed and a desire to rise in the world. He had been cunningly targeted and chased by hundreds of other women for the same reasons. Why was *her* deception still raw?

As he swung into the car, radiating blazing tension, his dazzling eyes splintered like green lightning with anger and Lucy stared at him.

'You still have a terrible temper,' she complained. 'And you just kidnapped me and the police did nothing—'

'Maybe you should've tried a little screaming and struggling to demonstrate fear,' Jax mocked, convinced that she was secretly delighted to be in his limo again and probably already planning a lucrative rehash of their Spanish fling.

No way, he swore to himself, black lashes almost hitting his cheekbones as he glanced studiously away from her, sitting there as she was watching him like a little spider planning an intricate web in which to capture him. On the other hand, *he* could play her the way she had once played him, he conceded grimly. And while he was doing that he could do whatever he wanted to do with her. That thought, that very idea took him aback because he didn't usually play games with women. But there was no denying that the concept of playing games with Lucy hugely turned him on.

Lucy breathed in slow and deep to calm herself. She focussed on the strong male thigh next to her own, the fine fabric of his trousers pulled taut across his powerful muscles and across his crotch. Her attention lingered there a split second longer and then hurriedly shifted because it was obvious that he was aroused. Why? Did he *ever* think of anything but sex? Colour warmed her cheeks because once they had had a very physical relationship. It had lasted six weeks, with them only becoming intimate in the last two, but during it she had realised that sex was unbelievably important to Jax and an unapologetic drive he made no attempt to restrain. Bella, after all, had been conceived in a brazen episode in a changing-room cubicle, she recalled in serious mortification. She had *tried* to say no but she had never been very good at denying Jax when her own body burned for his like a fire that couldn't be doused.

'I hate you,' she told him truthfully, still thinking about that changing-room cubicle in which the use of precautions hadn't figured.

'Because I found you out?' Jax drawled in a tone of boredom. 'Or because I dumped you?'

Lucy's nails bit crescents into the soft skin of her

palms. She had told him the truth: she *did* hate him. In fact the idea of wreaking revenge on Jax energised her. He was so unbearably confident, sure of his every move in a way she had never been. He was clever, successful and rich. He was also worshipped like the Greek god he resembled by women more akin to groupies than anything else.

'Where are you taking me?' she demanded curtly. 'Why do you even want to talk to me? It's a bit late in the day, isn't it?'

'Is it?' Jax traded unfathomably, leaning forward to press a button that opened a gleaming bar.

'I don't understand you!' Lucy bit out in frustration.

'Why would you?'

Jax thrust a foaming glass of champagne into her hand, thoroughly disconcerting her. Big blue eyes skimmed up to his in confusion and she looked so lost and bewildered that a momentary pang of conscience pierced his tough hide. Of course it wasn't real, he recognised angrily.

Fool me once, shame on you, fool me twice, shame on me.

He knew he could trust Lucy to put in an award-winning performance. He would get what he wanted. He would get answers and doubtless tears, self-justification and grovelling into the bargain. He positively warmed to an image of Lucy grovelling and a smile flashed across his forbidding mouth. Lucy on her knees poised to please...just what the doctor would order for a bored billionaire.

That was what lay at the root of his bizarre behaviour, he reasoned broodingly. He was bored. Bored with the flattery of too many far too eager to please women. Well, Lucy had never been into the art of hanging off his every word and complimenting him on his brilliance. Lucy had fought him and criticised him and driven him crazy on many occasions. Yet he had only been with her six short weeks interspersed with the business trips that had parted them. Six weeks. That was a sobering acknowledgement. Why did he remember so much about her when generally he was challenged to recall the name of a woman he had shared a bed with only a week ago?

She had hurt his pride. That was why. That was the only reason he still remembered her, Jax decided. Well, that and the supercharged, highly satisfying sex…

Lucy sipped the champagne, bubbles bursting under her nose and tickling, tiny beads of moisture cooling her too hot face. She felt out of control and she didn't like it. She was in Jax's car and she didn't know where he was taking her or why he would want to talk to her after so long. She crossed her legs, then re-crossed them, looking everywhere but at him.

'I want to go home,' she said abruptly.

'No, you don't.'

'I don't trust you. I don't want to be anywhere alone with you,' she told him sharply.

'My housekeeper lives in,' Jax murmured flatly.

'Like that's going to change my mind!' Lucy scoffed. 'Nobody you employ will go up against you. Do you think I'm stupid?'

'A little hysterical,' Jax confided. 'And it's undeserved. I've never harmed you in any way.'

'But your employees will if you tell them to. I was dragged off of *Sea Queen* two years ago and I got hurt,' Lucy told him reluctantly.

Jax turned his head to frown at her as the limousine coasted to a halt. 'What on earth are you talking about?' he demanded.

The door beside him clicked open and then the one beside her. She climbed out onto a well-lit driveway fronting an ultra-modern villa of quite astonishing size. The cool night air hit her hard and she felt slightly dizzy. A large glass of wine topped up by champagne had been too much for her system, she acknowledged heavily. Alcohol always hit her hard.

'We'll discuss this indoors,' Jax ground out impatiently. 'Come on…'

How had she got herself into this situation? Lucy asked herself with angry self-loathing. She didn't know where she was and had no idea how to get home again. She *should* have kicked up a major fuss when Jax had lifted her out of her chair at the bar but she had let him get away with it sooner than cause a public scene. In certain moods, Jax was as unstoppable as a juggernaut. He didn't care what anybody thought. The only opinion he cared for was his own.

'I want a taxi home,' she informed him. 'Right now…'

'I thought you were dying to tell me about the assault on the yacht,' Jax murmured, shooting her a politely enquiring appraisal that she immediately distrusted.

Lucy hovered uncertainly, noting the security team standing around and the older woman waiting to greet them at the front door. Compressing her lips, she forced herself to follow Jax, carefully picking her path up the steps into the contemporary hall. The preponderance of mirrors and multiple reflections confused her and she didn't object when Jax rested a light hand on her back to guide her into a huge reception room furnished with sofas and monochromatic modern art works.

'Assault…yacht,' Jax prodded expectantly. 'When did this happen?'

'About two weeks after I last saw you in Spain—'

'I had already left the country by then. Tell me what happened.'

'I went looking for you and I was told you weren't on board the *Sea Queen*—'

'Which was true.'

'The crew member that dealt with me was horrible. He called me names and manhandled me—'

Jax had fallen very still. 'In what way were you "manhandled"?'

'I said that I wasn't willing to leave until I was given a phone number or an address where I could contact you. Maybe that was foolish,' Lucy muttered ruefully. 'Anyway, this big bald guy got really aggressive and called me a whore and just dragged me across the deck and pushed me down the gangway. I fell at the foot, bloodied my knees and my elbows and nobody helped me. And someone had called the marina security to escort me away and they accused me of trespassing in a restricted area. It was hideous.'

A frown line had drawn his fine ebony brows together. 'I refuse to credit that any member of the crew would be so rough with a woman—'

Lucy bridled. 'Well, believe it…it happened!'

'Nor can I accept that there was verbal abuse. But I can confirm that you would not have been given my phone number or address because I left that instruction,' he admitted grimly.

'Why was that necessary? What did you think I was going to do?' Lucy framed in an angry rush. 'Spring a terrorist attack on you? Turn into a stalker?'

'I didn't want you making a nuisance of yourself,' Jax advanced flatly, turning away from her for an instant, memories interfering with his thoughts.

What she had made him feel had been too intense. In the aftermath of his discovery of her true nature, he had overreacted, he acknowledged with hindsight, stepping back and instinctively protecting himself from further exposure to her. It had seemed imperative that he neither speak to her nor see her again.

'I can't understand why you went to the yacht or why you tried to contact me again,' he said drily, swinging back to her with his brain fixed firmly in the present.

Bitter recriminations bubbled on Lucy's lips and she swallowed them back because she didn't want to make an announcement about Bella in the midst of a heated dispute. And Jax might be poised in front of her as ice cool and expressionless as a glacier but the atmosphere felt combustible and the tension was horrendous.

'Obviously I tried to contact you…but you simply vanished. I didn't hear from you again. Most people would seek an explanation—'

'There was a *very* obvious explanation. I'd grown bored,' Jax murmured with derision.

'Sometimes you are a very nasty piece of work,' Lucy mumbled shakily, appalled that he could throw that humiliating statement in her face.

'Put your cards on the table, *koukla mou*. And maybe I will too.'

'I don't know what you're getting at—'

'Stop acting like a poor little victim—stop faking it,' Jax urged with stark impatience. 'You told me a lot of lies back then—'

'No, I didn't!' Lucy broke in furiously.

Exasperation gripped Jax. She was moving agitatedly round the room, luminous blue eyes fixed intently to him. The floor lamp behind her turned that pale dress almost transparent, clearly delineating the rounded swell of her small, succulent breasts and the shadowy outline of her pink areolae. He went hard, his reaction instantaneous.

'*What* lies?' Lucy demanded hotly, watching the fluid movement of his long, lithe body as he paced the tiled floor in front of her.

He was so beautiful he still took her breath away. It wasn't merely his lean, strong face and stunning green eyes. Jax simply radiated masculine power from the aggressive angle of his arrogant head to the square swing of his wide shoulders and the decisive gait of his long, muscular legs. She was so busy staring, so busy drinking him in with greedy eyes that she couldn't concentrate. A prickling sensation assailed her nipples and tightened them into hard little nubs while a sliding, pulsing warmth began low in her pelvis.

'What lies?' she mumbled afresh, her brain in a fog.

Throbbing with arousal, Jax compressed his sculpted lips. He was done with conversation. Lucy would verbally twist and turn and prevaricate and embellish and evade until he was ready to strangle her. And why was he even bothering? He didn't ever travel an emotional road with women these days. He wasn't interested in their motivations and their deepest secrets. He kept it simple, straight. So, why wasn't he being straight with himself? He hadn't brought Lucy home to *talk* to her, had he? His mouth quirked into a flashing sardonic smile as he studied her.

It was the bad-boy smile Lucy had seen Jax wear a dozen times in glossy photos. It wasn't the smile that had once made her heart jump and fill to overflowing with love. It was a dark edgy smile with a sensual hint of threat in it.

A forbidden tingle of anticipation infiltrated what remained of her defences. She took a sudden step back, struggling to keep her distance and stay in control. But Jax reached out a hand and closed it round hers in a sudden movement, pulling her to him before she could back off. He wrapped both arms round her, lifting her easily off her feet to hoist her high against him.

It was a decisive moment and she knew it, knew she should push her hands down on his shoulders to force him to put her down and release her. But nothing was ever that simple for Lucy when it came to Jax. As he brought her down he nuzzled against her neck, dark stubble scratching her tender skin, and a shudder of awareness powerful enough to leave her dizzy enveloped her. The scent of his cologne laced with clean, husky male flared her nostrils; he smelled so unbelievably good she wanted to bury her nose in his hair. Her hands went round his neck and for a split second as he worked his erotic path towards her parted lips she clung like a limpet.

Just one kiss, she bargained with herself, just *one*, but the man who had once seduced her with kisses had no intention of breaking his perfect track record. He always knew what she wanted and he gave it to her, all the seething passion he had taught her to crave. He kissed her and she went up in flames. Her body flared into shocking awareness and suddenly burned back to almost painful life with every plunging thrust of his tongue. She gasped and quivered, filled with all the hunger she had suppressed.

He brought her down on a firm but yielding surface and her head fell back as he wrenched down her dress to squeeze a straining pink nipple between his fingertips, swiftly following it up as she arched up to him in response with the warm sucking pull of his mouth. It was as if a river of liquid fire ran down through her to engulf her feminine core. A strangled moan of excitement was torn from her as his mouth traced a fiery path down over her twisting body, long, lean fingers clenching on a slender thigh.

And just then she wondered how he had contrived that skin-to-skin contact and the answer shook her so much that she yanked herself violently free and rolled off the sofa, hitting her hip painfully hard in the fall. Her dress fell round her knees. Tears of pain and mortification in her eyes, she got onto her knees and, with great difficulty, clumsily and awkwardly hauled her dress back up over her exposed body, shame roaring through her in long agonising waves.

'Thee mou...' Jax began rawly.

'I want a taxi home. This is not going any further,' Lucy swore breathlessly, unable to even make herself look at him.

Jax wanted to break something. Instead he breathed in very deep. Lucy hadn't changed. She had to have all the ducks in line before she would fire. Two years ago, that simple process of withholding sex had worked on him but he was no longer that suggestible, Jax told himself with fierce conviction. Yet when he touched her, she *owned* him, he recognised, unnerved by that realisation.

As she struggled with a singular lack of dignity or cool to refasten the difficult ties on her slender shoulders, Lucy's hatred of Jax rose like a tide of poison inside her. Ten seconds and he had had her half naked, nothing but a pair of knickers standing between her and total nudity. She had been a pushover. Maybe she was so starved of sex she *did* need a man in her life, she decided, her eyes stinging with hot, angry tears. But that man would not be Jax Antonakos.

'The limo will take you back home,' Jax told her flatly. 'That is if you *really* want to leave.'

'It's my turn to do the walking away,' Lucy framed gruffly, loathing coursing through her slight body in such powerful waves that she trembled with it. 'I wish I'd done it two years ago. What were you planning on happening? Another session of unprotected sex? Haven't you ever had consequences from that?'

'What the hell are you trying to imply?' Jax demanded in a raw undertone.

Lucy flung her head back, all fired up on adrenalin and resentment and bitterness. 'When you got bored and dumped me,' she told him shakily, 'you left me pregnant—'

CHAPTER FOUR

JAX HAD FALLEN very still. 'That's not possible—'

'Why? Are you infertile?' Lucy shot back at him, unimpressed. 'I don't think so because we have a *child*, Jax. A little girl, who's fifteen months old.'

Jax stared back at her in rampant disbelief, hard lines settling between his nose and mouth, his handsome bone structure drawn stark and taut. 'Impossible,' he said again, green eyes brilliant with outraged denial.

'That last week we were together you had sex with me in a changing-room cubicle and you didn't take precautions,' Lucy reminded him angrily. 'Why do you think I tried so hard to get in touch with you that I got thrown off the yacht? I needed help.'

Shock ensured that Jax's brain continued to rebel and tell him that what she was saying was totally and absolutely impossible but his memory was infinitely more accurate. He knew he had taken that risk and had thought nothing of it at the time, indeed revelling in the reality that not even the thin layer of a condom separated him from her. He also realised in that moment that if she was telling him the truth, he had very probably made the biggest, messiest mistake of his life.

Panic hurtled through Lucy when she saw the shrewd dawning of genuine concern in his glittering green eyes. What had she done? Throwing it at him like that? Oh, my goodness, what had she done? Dully she recognised that she had been hitting back at him the only way she knew how. Needing to shock and hurt him as he had once shocked and hurt her with his rejection. But she knew instantly that she should not have used Bella like a weapon against him.

'This has to be discussed,' Jax intoned in a driven undertone.

'Not tonight. I want to go home,' Lucy breathed tightly. 'Right now.'

'You can't tell me I could be a father and then—'

'Yes, I can,' Lucy incised fiercely. 'I can do whatever I like just as you do whatever you like. And it's not a question of "*could* be a father". Bella is yours because I've never been with anyone else!'

Jax knew that was a lie for he had seen her cheat on him with his own eyes but DNA testing would provide proof neither of them could refute. He was appalled by the idea that he could have unwittingly had a child with a woman who not only lied and cheated but also had a criminal record. Even his parents' numerous unsuccessful marriages and affairs paled beside such a development. And the existence of an illegitimate Antonakos heir would send his father through the roof.

'I want to see the child,' Jax told her doggedly.

Lucy lost all her hectic colour. 'No.'

'If that child is half mine, you don't get to say no. I'll call in the family legal team,' Jax warned her without skipping a beat. 'Who looks after her when you're at work?'

That reference to lawyers and the reality that she was a working mum made a cold, hollow sensation of fear spread inside Lucy's tummy. 'My stepmother,' she told him, struggling to suppress the defiance rising inside her because a mood of conciliation struck her as being far more sensible in the circumstances.

'I'll call in with you tomorrow and we'll take care of the necessities,' Jax breathed coldly as he strode out to the hall. 'I need your address—'

'No.' The sense of being trapped built up inside Lucy until she felt almost suffocated by it. She had told him about Bella. She had done it in a recklessly provocative way too, absolutely the worst way to give Jax bad news. As volatile as he was, he didn't need the encouragement. And she had no doubt at all that learning that he was a father was very bad news on his terms because from the instant the concept had set in, Jax had turned icy-cold and businesslike. Now, however, Lucy recognised that she had to deal with the fallout from her impulsive decision and that would entail finally telling Kreon and Iola the truth.

'If you come in the morning I'll be there,' Lucy conceded abruptly. 'I usually only work evenings. My father and stepmother have a funeral to attend, so they won't be at home.'

Jax demanded the address and then stood poised in the doorway of his home watching her clamber into the limousine outside. Lucy tore her gaze from his forbidding stance and told herself that she had only done what had had to be done. He had the right to know about Bella. It was his own fault that he hadn't found out about his daughter sooner. Maybe he wouldn't want anything to do with their child, Lucy reasoned with sudden hope that that might be the case. And then she felt horribly guilty because she knew how much it hurt not to have a father and she didn't want her daughter to suffer the same way.

Yet when she looked back to her affair with Jax she could never have believed that they would have ended up so bitterly opposed. That night after the yacht party, Jax had sought her out and insisted on seeing her back to her room at the bar.

'You *are* over twenty-one?' he had checked. 'I don't get involved with anyone younger than that.'

'I'm twenty-three,' Lucy had lied instantly, adding on four years to her age, determined to make that all important grade for him.

He had told her he would pick her up for dinner the following evening. She had told him she was working.

'Take a night off,' Jax had urged.

'I can't afford to,' she had argued.

'I'll cover the cost of it,' Jax had declared.

'But then you'd be paying for my time and I couldn't agree to that—'

'You're very difficult,' Jax had condemned.

'And you don't understand how to take no for an answer.'

'I want to see you again,' Jax had proclaimed impatiently.

'I'm free Thursday night.'

'I don't want to wait that long.'

'All right. You can see me at midnight tomorrow when I finish my shift…unless that's too late for you?'

'No, that will do.'

'But know upfront I'm not spending the night with

you, so if that's what you're expecting, just forget about me,' she had warned him staunchly.

Lucy had learned to be blunt with men. She thought of it as managing their expectations. She had gone out with so many men who had simply assumed that she would sleep with them at the end of the night and who had reacted badly to a refusal. But her body was the one element in her world that Lucy had always felt was truly hers and until she finally met someone who could make her want him enough to move beyond that she had no intention of sharing her body with anyone. She genuinely hadn't expected Jax to be any different and she had slowly learned her mistake until saying no to Jax had become painful because she hadn't been able to control her own hunger.

'You're too defensive. Not every guy is out to nail you—'

'You mean you're *not*?' Lucy had exclaimed in surprise.

'I can see that trying to be smooth and seductive with you will be a huge challenge,' Jax had laughed, flashing her a highly amused smile.

And she had started falling for him that very night because that glorious charismatic smile of his had stopped her in her tracks and left her short of breath. She had met him the following night, sharing tapas and a couple of drinks with him in an upmarket bar. But sadly, she had dropped off to sleep in the middle of the conversation, bone tired from being on her feet serving all day. He had shaken her awake and taken her home without even attempting to kiss her, confiding that yawns weren't sexy. He had put his phone number in her phone while she slept and the next day he began texting her, first letting her know that he would be out of the country for a couple of days, then arranging to see her on her next free night.

A day later Kat Valtinos had shown up at the bar and cornered her. 'Jax is the ultimate playboy and you're the British equivalent of trailer trash—'

'Probably,' Lucy had conceded, looking back on her troubled poverty-stricken past.

'Obviously Jax will get bored fast and you look like the clingy sort.'

'I haven't had a chance to cling yet but I'm a quick learner. Does he like clingy women?' Lucy had asked, wide-eyed. 'Is he your boyfriend?'

'No, a very good friend,' Kat had declared. 'But you're wasting your time. I intend to marry him.'

'Tell that to him, not to me,' Lucy had advised and got back to work, ignoring the bitchy brunette until she'd finally stalked out in a snit at not being taken seriously.

The following morning, Lucy rose early after a sleepless night of wandering painfully through her mortifyingly fresh memories of being with Jax two years earlier. She watched her father and stepmother leave to attend the funeral. Over breakfast they had been too preoccupied with a sad and affectionate exchange of stories about their now deceased friend to notice how heavy-eyed and silent Lucy was.

But Lucy was also restless with anxiety and operating on pure adrenalin. Now that Jax knew about Bella she had to worry about how he would act on that information. She winced at the knowledge that Jax had power over her again. Certainly he had rights as a father that she could not deny. But would he choose to exercise those rights and seek an active parenting role?

Barely an hour later, Lucy received her first taste of Jax choosing to exercise his rights. A smartly dressed, fast-speaking lawyer arrived and asked her to agree to DNA testing and no sooner had she given consent, her face burning at the humiliating suspicion that Jax could doubt that he had fathered her child, than a lab technician arrived and took samples. That matter dealt with, the lawyer then settled a confidentiality agreement down in front of her. It seemed to be what Lucy had seen referred to as a 'gagging order' in the media and she refused to sign it, sticking to her guns when the older man persisted in his persuasions.

'Mr Antonakos does not like what I shall describe as private matters broadcast in the public domain. If you sign this document, it will form a secure basis for good relations between you in the future.'

'I can assure you that I have no intention of speaking to the press but I'm not prepared to sign anything that says I cannot talk about my own daughter,' she told him quietly.

By the time the older man departed, Lucy fully understood that he had been engaged in a potential damage-limitation plan. And Lucy was utterly unnerved by Jax acting to protect himself and the reputation of the Antonakos family even before he had definitive proof that her child was his. She was appalled that he could distrust her so much that he suspected that she might sell nasty stories about him to the newspapers.

In truth she did have a very low opinion of Jax but she had every intention of keeping that low opinion to herself for her daughter's sake. Whatever else Jax was, he was and always would be her daughter's father and she didn't want to do anything to damage that relationship. That meant, she registered with a sinking heart, that she would have to keep her personal feelings very much to herself. Airing her anger, resentment and bitterness would be destructive and the situation they were in where they shared a child but nothing else would be difficult enough to deal with.

An hour after the lawyer departed, Jax arrived and, for once, not in a limousine. He roared up outside on a motorbike and it was only as he doffed his helmet on the way to the front door that she realised it was him and not someone making a delivery. He was trying to be discreet, endeavouring to ensure that he wasn't recognised, she realised. When she had first met Jax in Spain he had only recently stepped into his late brother's role and as he had been relatively unknown there had been no paparazzi following him around then. Now that a kind of celebrity madness erupted around Jax's every public appearance she was grateful that he was being careful because she did not want to see her face or her daughter's appearing in articles full of embarrassing speculations.

Lucy opened the front door and stepped back. Jax strode in, bringing with him the scent of fresh air, leather and masculinity. In the narrow hall, he towered over her and she thrust the door quickly shut to walk into the spacious front room, which was sprinkled with colourful toys and baby equipment.

Jax slung his motorbike helmet down on a chair and raked impatient fingers through his black hair. 'Where is she?' he demanded.

'Bella's having a nap. I'll get her up in ten minutes. She wakes very early in the morning and then she gets tired again…' Realising that she was gabbling, Lucy flushed, insanely conscious of Jax's stare.

Lucy sported cropped jeans, a pink tee shirt and bare feet. She looked very young and cute and definitely hadn't dressed up for his benefit. Jax was irritated that she had not made the effort. He hadn't slept much the night before. The cold shower hadn't worked any miracle and that sexual tension piled on top of the shocking announcement Lucy had made had done nothing to help. When he had a problem Jax liked a plan to work towards, a plan with firm boundaries. Unhappily there was no convenient plan available to tell him how a man behaved when he discovered he was a father even though he had never wanted that particular joy. But he *had* been reckless with Lucy in the birth-control department and in retrospect he could not forgive or excuse himself for that lack of responsibility. Of course, he reminded himself wryly, the kid might not be his, in which case he was dealing with nothing more than a storm in a teacup.

'Stop staring at me,' Lucy told him, cheeks burning from the intensity of his scrutiny.

'Of course I'm staring. You dropped a bomb on me last night. I'm still reeling,' Jax breathed in a raw undertone, green eyes glittering warily below curling ebony lashes.

'Well, I've been mentally reeling from the minute I discovered I was pregnant,' Lucy confided truthfully. 'With time you get used to the idea. I couldn't bear to imagine life without Bella now.'

Jax scanned the youthful glow of her unblemished

skin and the luxuriant tumble of strawberry-blonde ringlets that merely highlighted her bright blue eyes. He acknowledged her beauty for there was no denying what was right in front of him. As his body began to react he clenched his teeth together hard and wandered back towards the front door, determined not to let his libido take over when there would soon be a child in the room.

'Coffee?' Lucy pressed as the awkward silence stretched when he reappeared in the doorway.

'This is not a social visit,' Jax answered.

A cry sounded out somewhere above them and Lucy scurried upstairs, her face flushed by his deflating statement.

Jax plonked himself down on a sofa and struggled to relax but it had been more years than he cared to recall since he had been around a baby. He was godfather to several but his role had never been hands-on, nor would it ever have been more because nobody expected a single man, who was also erroneously known as his actress mother's only child, to be comfortable dealing with young children. Ironically Jax had learned the daily routine of how to look after a baby when he was only twelve years old. It had been the end of the summer before his mother had finally engaged a nanny because Jax was returning to boarding school.

He heard the creak of the stairs and vaulted upright. As he straightened his shoulders Lucy walked into the lounge and he immediately saw the child in her arms. He froze into a statue in the same moment that he saw the little girl's black curly hair and the green eyes. That fast, that dramatically, Jax knew he didn't need a DNA test to prove to anyone that the little girl was his. Lucy's child was the living image of his kid sister, Tina, and that uncanny resemblance hit him like an avalanche. His mother had had very strong genes, he reckoned ruefully, for both he and the little sister who had died as a toddler had looked far more like Mariana than the men who had fathered her two children. He knew too that his striking likeness to his mother had only been another nail in his coffin as far as his oversensitive father was concerned.

'This is Bella…' Lucy framed, kneeling down to settle the little girl gently on the floor.

A thumb planted in her rosebud mouth, Bella studied Jax fixedly, her green eyes full of curiosity.

Jax bent down and lifted a toy that broke straight into a catchy tune as soon as he pressed the right button. Bella grinned and came closer, steadying herself on one powerful thigh with a clutching little hand.

'She's not scared,' Jax remarked, marvelling that he could still speak normally after being plunged without warning into some of his darkest memories. The remnants of that guilt, anger and pain still resonated powerfully with him.

'No, she's quite confident and she likes men. My father makes a fuss of her and spoils her. I suppose we all spoil her a bit,' Lucy conceded, staring at the little tableau of Jax and his daughter as they each assessed the other. 'She looks very like you—'

Jax skated a teasing forefinger off Bella's determined little chin and swallowed thickly, struggling to master his almost overwhelming emotions. He should not cloud his first meeting with his daughter with such tragic memories, he censured himself fiercely. The past was the past and it would be wiser to leave the sad little ghost of Tina safely buried there.

'What is it?' Lucy prompted, troubled by the feverish glitter of Jax's stunning eyes, their brilliance enhanced by the surround of spiky black lashes. 'What's wrong?'

'Nothing,' Jax insisted, his wide sensual mouth slashing into a sudden forced smile, for he had shared far too much private stuff with Lucy in the past and he had no plans to make himself vulnerable in that way again 'But when she was born you should have moved heaven and earth to ensure that I knew I was a father.'

Unprepared for that criticism when she had tried every way she knew how to contact him, Lucy stiffened. 'That's not fair—'

'What isn't fair,' Jax fielded as he accepted the little plastic doll that Bella brought him, 'is that this little girl and I weren't able to be in each other's lives from the start.'

Lucy's bright blue eyes hardened. 'As you said though, when you dumped me, you didn't want me making a *nuisance* of myself,' she reminded him thinly. 'If you didn't want to hear from me ever again, how was I supposed to tell you?'

Not trusting himself to speak in the mood he was in, Jax shrugged a muscular shoulder in brooding silence.

'Didn't think you'd have an answer for that,' Lucy sniped, leaning down to clasp Bella's hand and guide her into the kitchen where she set about filling a toddler cup with milk.

Bella pushed against the back door, keen to get out onto the patio and play. Lucy opened it and watched her daughter toddle out into the sunlight to retrieve the little plastic pram she loved.

His child, *his* daughter, a new generation in the Antonakos family, Jax acknowledged, watching Bella swig her milk and then set down the cup with exaggerated care before pushing the little pram out onto the small lawn. Somehow, he didn't know how, he didn't care, Lucy *should* have contacted him, he thought angrily.

'I have missed out on over a year of my daughter's life,' Jax intoned grimly. 'That is not acceptable—'

Under sudden attack, Lucy spun. 'No, what was unacceptable back then was the way you treated me!' she condemned with spirit.

Jax thought about the contents of the investigative file he had been given. He saw no point in throwing the contents of that file in Lucy's face now. Likewise her little session in that alleyway. His reaction had been all too human. He had let his anger and aggression take over and dictate his moves. 'I'm afraid it never occurred to me that you could be pregnant,' he admitted in a harsh undertone. 'I should've acknowledged that possibility and made provision for it but I didn't. That was a serious oversight on my part.'

A little of the tension in Lucy's slender shoulders eased. 'Yes, it was.'

'Then let us not waste time stating the obvious and rehashing a past we both prefer to forget,' Jax countered impatiently.

'We can't forget it when Bella was born from it,' Lucy argued helplessly. 'We may not like each other but we'll just have to live with that. I'll make coffee, and not because this is a social occasion but because we need to learn how to act civilised.'

As Lucy left the doorway to switch on the kettle Jax strode out onto the patio, unable to let his newly discovered daughter out of his sight and reach. It crossed his mind that he had no intention of living with his distaste of Lucy and forging a civilised alliance with her as a co-parent. With what he knew about her past, he didn't, *couldn't* possibly trust her to be a caring decent mother. Bella's well-being came first and nobody would ever persuade him that his child could be safe with a mother who had once dealt in drugs and sold her body. It didn't matter that to all intents and purposes Lucy appeared to have turned over a new leaf.

Jax, after all, was the son of a drug addict. He had heard too many promises, seen all too many fresh starts *and* witnessed the subsequent falls from grace. Bella would always be at risk of harm if she remained with her mother, he decided cynically. He would have to fight Lucy through the courts for custody of their daughter. He was sure that she loved Bella to the best of her ability but with her fatal weakness for substance abuse he couldn't trust her to always put their daughter's needs first.

'Are we capable of behaving like friends?' Lucy asked Jax hopefully as she hovered in the doorway.

Jax glanced at her in astonishment, questioning how she contrived to still look so young and innocent in spite of her misspent past. Friends? Never, he conceded wryly. And once Lucy received the first official communication from the Antonakos legal team and realised what he planned to do friendship would be the last thing on her mind. But what other choice did he have?

'You have to stop blaming me for everything that's gone wrong,' Lucy told him squarely. 'In any relationship it takes two people to screw up. Remember that...'

As she spoke Bella fell flat on her face on the lawn and let out a yell, followed by frantic sobbing. Jax strode across a flower bed and snatched the little girl up into his arms, speaking softly to her, smoothing a lean brown hand gently over her shaking back to soothe her before getting down on his knees to show her something on the ground in the clear hope of distracting her from the fright she had sustained. Lucy stared at that seemingly effortless display of child management in sheer amazement, involuntarily impressed.

'Jax...' she muttered in a daze.

Once Bella was restored to calm again, Jax set her down. His lean, strong face taut, he glanced at Lucy, noting how the sunshine lit up the shades of red in her hair and illuminated her perfect skin. Lucy bent to pick up the pram and the shapely curve of her heart-shaped derriere pulled tight below the cropped jeans she wore. Jax remembered ripping her jeans off her, desperate to sink into the damp, welcoming heat of her, and fierce tension gripped him as he suppressed the hunger flaring through him like a dangerous burning brand. 'In a couple of days I'd like to take Bella out. I'll bring a nanny with me if that keeps you happy.'

'I assumed you would be waiting for the DNA results before you did anything official,' Lucy parried, thoroughly disconcerted by his request as she walked back to him.

'The DNA tests will only confirm what I already know,' Jax murmured. 'Are you going to make me fight for access to her?'

Lucy winced and set her teeth together. If in doubt, weigh in with the threats. That was Jax. He could afford the very best lawyers. Ultimately he would be entitled to time with his daughter whatever she did or said and trying to ignore that reality would be foolish. In any case, didn't she want Bella to have a father? Yes, she did, but she hadn't expected to have to share her time with her daughter quite so immediately.

'No, but I wouldn't want her away from me for more than a couple of hours at a time,' she admitted. 'She's still very young.'

'I can agree to that,' Jax traded. 'Give me your phone number and I'll be in touch.'

Bella cuddled to her, Lucy watched Jax swing back onto the motorbike, the lithe powerful lines of his big muscular body moulded by his designer jeans and leather jacket. Across the road a car started up and pulled out to follow him, his security team, she assumed.

When her father and stepmother returned from the funeral, Lucy sat them down and finally told them the truth.

Straight away her father erupted like a raging volcano. '*Jax Antonakos?* Are you serious?'

'Please don't get mad,' Lucy pleaded. 'It will only make this situation worse.'

'You were only nineteen, Lucy,' her father protested with pained condemnation. 'He must be nearly ten years older than you!'

'Well, he can't be blamed for that. When he said I had

to be over twenty-one to spend time with him I lied,' she admitted ruefully. 'I said I was twenty-three—'

'You *lied* to him?' Kreon repeated censoriously.

'Calm down, Kreon,' Iola interposed gently. 'She was a typical teenager and when a handsome young man approached her, she pretended to be older and more sophisticated than she was. A lot of girls that age would have done the same thing.'

'Yes,' Lucy admitted, her cheeks burning.

Iola dragged the rest of the story of those six weeks in Spain from Lucy while Kreon sat fuming, his anger unhidden. 'I knew his father, you know,' he told them abruptly. 'And he was a selfish, arrogant thug of a man too.'

'Jax's father? You *knew* him? *How?*' Lucy asked, astonished by that admission.

'My parents worked for the family of Heracles Antonakos's first wife, Sofia, in London. Sofia and I grew up together and we never lost that friendship even though she lived in a very different world. She was only thirty when she died,' Kreon revealed gruffly.

'I'm really sorry I didn't tell you the truth from the start,' Lucy confessed. 'I didn't want to upset you—'

'Never you mind about me being upset,' Kreon told her through compressed lips. 'Be grateful I'm here to support you. Antonakos sending in the lawyers straight off is your first warning of his plans—'

'What do you mean?' Iola interjected worriedly.

'Well, was what happened this morning a nice or considerate thing to do to the mother of your child? Demanding DNA testing? Trying to browbeat Lucy into signing a confidentiality agreement? As a first warning shot, it tells us all we need to know…'

'Jax is trying to protect himself. I can't blame him for that,' Lucy muttered ruefully, troubled by her father's angry gravity and all too conscious that she was the cause of the lines of stress that had appeared on his weathered face.

'He can protect himself all he likes but not at your expense or Bella's,' Kreon replied.

Lucy was anxious and preoccupied when she went into work that evening and she struggled to remember the drinks orders and deliver them back to the correct tables. Her father's genuine fear of what Jax might be planning had seriously scared her. Not for the first time she wished she had the ability to get inside Jax's head.

Earlier that day he had been strangely distant with her but very different in his wholehearted response to Bella. In retrospect it was hard to credit that he had been kissing her, *touching* her only the night before. Of course, that made sense, she told herself squarely. Everything had changed the minute she'd told Jax about their daughter. She recalled his glacier cool when she had first told him at his house and barely restrained a shiver of apprehension. Her father's concern had set off all her internal alarms and had left her on the edge of panic and thinking thoughts she had believed she would never think again…

What if she simply upped sticks and vanished? She had done it before and she could do it again. But it would be wrong, her inner voice warned her sternly. It would be wrong not to give Jax the opportunity to form a relationship with his daughter. It would be equally wrong for Lucy to run away from the life her father and stepmother had generously offered her. Running away from her problems would be the childish thing to do and she wasn't a child any more…

CHAPTER FIVE

'So, YOU ARE Lucy's father,' Jax commented, lounging back against his office desk with lethal cool, not a shade of what he was thinking revealed by his lean, darkly handsome features. 'Where were you all the years Lucy was growing up in the care system?'

Kreon straightened his shoulders. 'That's my business and Lucy's. She's welcome to tell you if she wants. But I'm here now to protect the welfare of my daughter and my granddaughter.'

'I don't understand how you plan to do that,' Jax remarked.

'Oh, that's very simple,' Kreon told him almost cheerfully. 'I have access to secrets that your father would kill to keep out of the newspapers—'

Taken aback, Jax laughed. 'My father fears nothing. Is this some sort of clumsy blackmail attempt? I advise you to back off now before I call the police.'

'That will be your decision but it won't stop me sharing your family secrets with the press. In fact having me arrested will only add legitimacy to my claims,' Kreon pointed out calmly. 'Your father hates me. I will tell you that for free. But why do you think he leaves me alone? He is afraid of what I might know.'

'You're talking a lot of nonsense and I don't intend to listen to it,' Jax told him, crossing the room to open the door and hasten the older man's departure.

'Your brother, Argo, wasn't your brother because he wasn't your father's child,' Kreon delivered very softly. 'I think Heracles only found that out *after* your brother died and, believe me, he does not want that humiliating truth spread across the newspapers.'

Jax froze, shock washing over him in an almost physical attack that pulled his every muscle taut to breaking point. In a driven movement he thrust the door shut again and swung violently round.

'What do you want?' he demanded of the smaller man, refusing to think of what he had just been told, refusing to join the dots and acknowledge how well that revelation would dovetail with his own quite recent miraculous change of status within the Antonakos family.

'In return for my continuing silence, I want you to marry Lucy.'

Jax stared back at him in savage disbelief. '*Marry…* her?'

'She was a teenager when you wrecked her life. You owe her the security of a wedding ring. It doesn't have to be a life sentence for either of you. But it would give her and Bella the safe harbour and the recognition they need to have a better life—'

'She *wasn't* a teenager!' Jax raked back at him in furious rebuttal.

'Lucy was twenty-one last month. We celebrated with dinner at that hotel where she works.' Kreon shot him a sourly amused appraisal. 'My wife tells me that teenaged girls do lie about their age occasionally.'

'Twenty-one,' Jax repeated thickly, fighting to master the violent anger lashing through him and a powerful urge to strangle Lucy for having dared to lie to him. 'I would require proof of those allegations about my brother, Argo.'

And from an inside pocket Kreon produced a handwritten letter which he handed to Jax. It had been written and sent to Kreon when his father's first wife, Sofia, was terminally ill. Unable to face death with such a weight on her conscience, Sofia had admitted the affair that had led to Argo's conception, although she had not named her lover.

'Why didn't you come forward with this at the time of her death?' Jax demanded harshly a few minutes later. 'With this letter, you were in possession of facts that were unknown to everyone else involved.'

'Sofia couldn't have thought through what she was doing. Your father had just lost his wife and Argo had lost his mother and her letter would have destroyed them both. Back then Heracles had no idea that Argo wasn't his son. What do you think he would have done?' Kreon grimaced. 'He would've disinherited the boy and cast him off.'

Jax stared at the wall, knowing that there was a fair chance his father would have reacted like that in the first heat of his fury. Once Sofia had let that genie out of the bottle there would have been no putting it back.

'I didn't want that responsibility. I'm not a cruel man. It was a secret that shouldn't have been told. I never liked your father and he was a lousy absentee husband but, fond as I was of Sofia, once she was gone I preferred to mind my own business…that is, until an Antonakos threatened the security of my own flesh and blood.'

Long after Kreon had gone, Jax studied the copy of the letter the older man had allowed him to keep. He was still shaken even though the woman had died long before he was born. The contents of that letter would distress his father, although, like Kreon, Jax was inclined to believe that somewhere around the time of Argo's death his father had found out that his eldest son was not actually his son. That would better explain why Heracles had found it possible to move on so fast from that loss and adjust his attitude to Jax almost overnight.

That new knowledge and understanding just about ripped Jax apart, not to mention his view of his family. He had looked up to the big brother he had never really got to know very well and he loved his father. And why *did* he love Heracles, who had proved to be a useless parent when Jax was young and in need of a father? Ultimately, he had recognised that the older man deeply regretted allowing his dented ego and workaholic ways to triumph over the ties of blood. Heracles was hopeless when it came to expressing emotion though and Jax had realised that he suffered from the same flaw. His father had stumbled on blindly after Mariana's infidelity had made him a laughing stock in the media, protecting himself as best he could by avoiding his ex-wife…and unhappily that avoidance had included Jax.

Jax hadn't really thought about how he actually felt about Heracles until that moment, but when he thought of his father being forced to see the tragedy of his first marriage spread across the newspapers he knew he couldn't allow that to happen. Sofia had died after a long drawn-out fight against breast cancer. Heracles was domineering and manipulative and interfering but he had once adored his first wife and the son he had believed to be his.

Jax's first act was to summon Zenas and tell his security chief that he wanted an in-depth private investigation carried out on Kreon Thiarkis and his daughter, Lucy. How the hell had something as basic as Lucy's age been wrong in that file? Her parentage had been incorrectly recorded as well. Lucy *did* have a Greek father. What else could also be wrong? He needed the background and facts he could rely on. He also needed to check out Kreon's ties to his father's first wife, Sofia. And to his father. After all, it was *his* father who had sent that file to him.

Jax began to mull over the other things he had learned. Lucy was still only twenty-one years old? And had been only nineteen when they had first met? Memories swirled in a colourful haze in Jax's head and he marvelled that he had not recognised Lucy's immaturity for what it was. She had been impulsive, outspoken, naïve and unnervingly ignorant about facts he took for granted and a sneaky little unrepentant liar...*obviously.*

And no way was he prepared to marry her! Kreon could not blackmail him into doing what he had never wanted to do, he assured himself stubbornly. On the other hand, Jax also knew he could not stand back and watch his father endure the scandal that would blow up if Kreon went to the press to sell his story. People would enjoy reading about the skeletons hidden in the Antonakos cupboard and his father would lose his dignity. At the age of seventy, Heracles deserved to keep his dignity, Jax decided heavily. He might have been a lousy husband in Kreon's eyes but he had surely not deserved the tragic conclusion to his first marriage. Knowing how badly Heracles had reacted to his own mother's infidelity, Jax could hardly begin to imagine what his father must have felt once he realised that Argo was not his child. Surely Heracles had suffered enough for being a less than stellar husband? How dared Kreon Thiarkis threaten him?

Yet even in the grip of that seething Antonakos rage, Jax could still not stop planning. He knew that it was up to him to control the situation. He reached the stage of listing pros and cons. Were he to marry Lucy, he would get her back into his bed. A sliver of raw anticipation raked through Jax's tense, angry body and he recognised that that was a fringe benefit that he would very much enjoy. At the same time he would also gain a stronger legal right to his daughter and he would not have to fight to gain access to her.

Nevertheless, Jax hated being told what to do and Kreon Thiarkis had just thrown a double whammy at him that came attached to a very high price tag. Primarily he was in a rage because he knew that Kreon had given him a choice but it was the hateful choice of picking between the lesser of two evils: marriage or his aging father's public humiliation. He could tell Kreon to do his worst and then stand by and watch his father get hurt. Unfortunately, family loyalty and a very real affection for his inadequate father warred against that option. But the alternative was to surrender his freedom.

No more hot and cold running women, no more

sexually self-indulgent variety in the bedroom. But then that wasn't quite true, Jax allowed with a sudden strong sense of relief. Even Kreon didn't expect him to stay married to Lucy for ever. Kreon was expecting an eventual divorce, which would still leave Lucy and Bella respectfully acknowledged as members of the Antonakos family and financially secure. *Thee mou*...he could do marriage on a short-term, strictly temporary basis, particularly with Lucy playing the starring role in his bed every night. Furthermore, Bella would have his name and the safeguard of his presence in her daily life. But just how was he expected to cope with a father-in-law he wanted to strike down and kill in cold blood?

As an Antonakos, Jax had little experience of being threatened. He was too rich, too powerful to cross and his father had long enjoyed the same protection. But Kreon was in legal possession of very private and personal information that went right to the heart of Jax's family, the kind of secret nobody wanted exposed and picked over in public. Even worse, one revelation would almost inevitably lead to others. What might be dug up about his own mother? Jax shuddered at the prospect of Mariana's drug-addicted frailties and Tina's death being dragged out into the punishing light of day. At that point it struck him that a wedding ring was a worthwhile sacrifice if it bought peace and left the family's dirty laundry untouched.

Lucy studied the text from Jax with wide incredulous eyes. He had asked her when she finished work.

I'll pick you up when you finish and we'll talk.

Jax? *Talk?* Jax had been known to leave the room or remember a pressing engagement when any form of serious discussion was threatened. Jax didn't believe in talking about stuff. He thought in private and then he acted to fix a problem. He didn't share the reasoning that led to the decision. He believed that talking only heightened the wrong emotions, encouraged divisive stances and made issues seem worse than they were. When she had once tried to talk to him about where their affair was heading he had become angry and he had walked away. Naturally he had, she conceded, because he had known their affair was going nowhere.

But obviously he had to talk to her about Bella, she reasoned ruefully. Even he couldn't make unilateral decisions about the daughter they now had to share. He would want to make arrangements to see Bella again, he would want to ask questions about what the little girl liked and didn't like. That he was prepared to talk was a healthy sign, Lucy told herself heavily, striving to muster some enthusiasm about the idea of sharing her daughter with her father.

Before she even went into work, her own father had lectured her, urging her not to do to Bella what had been done to her. She had grown up without a father because her mother had selfishly chosen not to tell Kreon he had a daughter. Now, quite unnecessarily, Kreon was advising Lucy to take a long-term view and keep her anger and resentment out of the situation.

'I know it's a big ask,' Kreon had conceded, 'but you have to deal with what's happening now and handle it sensibly. Try to concentrate on what's best for Bella.'

Her father's outlook had surprised Lucy because he

seemed to have come to terms with what she had told him about Jax very quickly and had now taken a more detached view of events. Unfortunately everything still felt painfully personal to Lucy. Jax had rejected her but he had *not* rejected their daughter. She knew she shouldn't be thinking that way but she couldn't help it because she was only human.

A car picked her up from the hotel. It wasn't a limo and Jax wasn't in it but she recognised Jax's security guards. She climbed in, smoothed down her denim skirt and worried at her lower lip with the edge of her teeth. She was wondering what Jax wanted while telling herself to keep her temper and her daughter's emotional and physical well-being at the forefront of her mind regardless of what he might say.

Jax had plans as well. He would not confront Lucy about anything until they were safely married. Hopefully by then he would also know how accurate that file he had actually was. But he was also well aware of how deceptive Lucy could be, he reminded himself grimly, thinking of the familiar flash of that red dress below the street lights as she'd walked down that alleyway to have sex with another man. Lucy wasn't the faithful type. Two of his father's three wives had betrayed him with other men and Jax's own mother had never been faithful to anyone. Surrounded from childhood by broken, dishonest relationships, Jax had always tried to avoid emotional involvement and commitment. But when his daughter came into the equation he discovered that he badly wanted to give Bella the storybook family he had never had. Something better, something happier, something lasting…

Lucy walked dry-mouthed and nervous into the

house with the confusing mirrored hall. The elegant drawing room looked more welcoming than it had on her last visit with only a couple of lamps lit to leave the rest of the very large room shrouded in shadow. When Jax stepped out of the shadows, she flinched and stilled on the threshold.

'I ordered supper for you.' Jax indicated the table spread with a selection of snacks.

Jax wore jeans and an open-necked shirt. He shouldn't have taken her breath away in such ordinary garments but he did. The jeans clung to his narrow hips and outlined his long, powerful thighs. The pale shirt accentuated his bronzed skin tone and the blue black of his hair. She sucked in a breath in the tense silence and clashed with shimmering green eyes fringed by black and her heart hammered out a drumbeat inside her.

'Supper,' she repeated, that being the last thing she had expected from him, but she stepped fully into the room to head for the table, grateful to have something other than Jax to focus on.

'Help yourself,' he advised.

Settling down on a sofa, Lucy needed no further encouragement because she was always hungry after work and she was involuntarily impressed that he had remembered that little fact. She filled a plate and poured a cup of tea. 'This is what I call civilised,' she admitted with a wry smile.

'I thought it would be,' Jax said. 'Were you working in that outfit?'

Lucy smoothed a self-conscious hand over her comfy skirt with which she had teamed a black tee shirt. 'Yes…'

Jax gritted his teeth. A tripwire stood in front of

him but he neatly avoided it by refusing to give way to his inner caveman. The short skirt showed off her surprisingly long and very shapely legs and the tee shirt shaped her pert breasts to perfection. Once upon a time he had objected to her wearing the sort of clothing that revealed her body and that had set off heated arguments. Now he was respecting boundaries to preserve the peace. He sank down onto the sofa opposite her while mentally trying to come up with garments that would still be fashionable but which would miraculously shield that glorious body from the visual attention of other men. And he finally registered that there were no such garments on the market. Lucy had always outshone her clothing. From her bright tumbling hair to her luminous skin and radiant blue eyes, Lucy glowed with sheer energy, attracting attention even in a crowded room.

'It's not a short skirt,' Lucy remarked, knowing his flaws.

'No, it's not,' Jax agreed, wishing she hadn't directed his attention to her pale slender thighs and knees because it only made him think about the sheer glory of parting them. Furiously conscious of his growing desire, Jax rocked forward, his lean, strong face taut, green eyes semi screened by his lashes.

'You said you wanted to talk.' Lucy widened her eyes suspiciously. 'Was that a joke?'

'No...' Silence fell while Lucy munched through her third sandwich. 'We have a dilemma and I have come up with a solution,' he spelled out in a roughened undertone as the tip of her tongue chased a crumb from the corner of her mouth.

'Bella isn't a dilemma. She isn't and never will be a

problem,' Lucy assured him quietly. 'I'm not going to be difficult about you seeing her or anything like that.'

Jax breathed in deep, striving to make himself get to the point and bite the bullet. 'If we married, we would be in a position to give Bella far more.'

Lucy put down her sandwich unfinished. *'Married?'* she repeated in consternation. 'But you don't ever want to get married.'

'I didn't plan to have a child either,' Jax reminded her. 'But Bella is here now and that changes the whole picture. I want to give her what I didn't have. A mother, a father and a settled home, all the security that only a traditional family structure can give her.'

Lucy was stunned because she had never dreamt that she would live to hear Jax admit a desire to embrace such conventional ideas. 'Neither of us had that,' she conceded unevenly. 'But life isn't perfect and that's the way it is—'

'But we *can* change that,' Jax sliced in forcefully. 'We don't have to live apart when we could raise Bella together, as a married couple.'

Lucy blinked rapidly, her heart in her mouth, her feet flexing because nervous tension made her want to get up and walk round the room. 'Together?' she repeated in bewilderment.

'We can get married and make a home for our daughter, the kind of home neither of us had the advantage of growing up in,' Jax extended with unearthly calm.

'I don't know much about your background. Well, I know your parents divorced when you were young but—'

Jax stiffened. 'You already know that my mother

was unstable and not a reliable parent. Men came and went in her life. None of them ever stayed. She was too high maintenance. I don't want our daughter to have to adapt to that kind of lifestyle.'

'With respect,' Lucy said uncomfortably, 'I'm not a world-famous, gorgeous actress and I don't think my lifestyle and your mother's would have anything in common.'

Jax released his breath in a small hiss of frustration. 'Do you really believe that your life is going to stay the same now that I know you are raising my daughter?' he pressed in disbelief. 'Do you honestly believe that you can go on working as a waitress and living with your father? Obviously I will take care of all your expenses now—'

'No,' Lucy broke in with a frown. 'I don't want that.'

'But that's what will happen whether you like it or not. Naturally I want my daughter to enjoy the same lifestyle that I enjoy myself and I can't believe that you would deny her what she is entitled to receive. Bella is an Antonakos,' Jax reminded her with pride.

'Yes but...' Lucy's voice ran out of steam as she began to think about everything he had said.

He was asking her to marry him. Jax Antonakos was asking *her* to marry him, offering her the dream conclusion she had once secretly cherished and then buried deep two years earlier. For the space of several frantic minutes Lucy could only stare down into her tea and struggle to come to terms with a proposal she had never expected to receive. A home, two parents and a real family for Bella. That truly was the ultimate ideal for Lucy when it came to her daughter. Her mother had ended up alone raising Lucy and Lucy had ended up alone in the care system because the authorities had failed to trace Kreon. Sometimes she hated herself for making the same mistake with Bella and having to bring her up without a father.

'Are you serious about this?' Lucy asked breathlessly.

'Of course,' Jax asserted levelly.

'But you *never* wanted to get married,' Lucy reminded him helplessly.

'And then Bella came along and turned everything upside down,' Jax confessed with complete honesty. 'This is no longer only about you and me. We have to think about our daughter and about what would make *her* happy.'

'Unhappily married parents wouldn't help,' Lucy pointed out apologetically.

'I see no reason why we shouldn't make a go of it. Even sitting here having a serious conversation I can barely keep my hands off you,' Jax admitted bluntly, his stunning green gaze glittering across her heart-shaped face and watching the flush of awareness slowly build there. 'And if you're honest, it's the same for you.'

Lucy dragged her attention from his sleek, darkly beautiful features with the greatest difficulty. But trying to blank her mind, trying not to look at him was no use when the hunger inside her felt like an insidious virus that refused to die. And she knew what the cure was and that unnerved her. The only cure she knew was the wild, pounding plunge of his body into hers and the explosive release he would give her. And even that wasn't a permanent fix, she thought shamefacedly. She had once craved him as she craved air to breathe. She set her tea down with a jarring crack on the coffee table, her hand trembling.

'Look at me,' Jax urged, breaking the smouldering silence.

And Lucy looked even though she knew she shouldn't, desire clawing at her insides, awakening the yearning buried deep within her body. A ragged breath escaped her, her pulses racing. Her breasts ached but the biggest ache of all was between her legs, at the very heart of her where she was burning with need. That voracious need that hungered for his touch terrified her because it was so ready to rage out of control and sweep all restraint and all common sense before it.

'We're getting married as soon as it can be arranged,' Jax decreed.

Her head flew up. 'You can't just—'

'One of us needs to be decisive. You want to bury your head in the sand and run away from the responsibility.'

'No, I don't.'

'We do it for Bella. Together we make a family,' Jax intoned.

'It's not that simple.'

'Nothing worth having is ever easily acquired,' Jax said drily. 'Everything worthwhile I have ever achieved has come at a cost and there have always been sacrifices involved. Are you willing to make sacrifices for Bella's benefit?'

Lucy leapt upright in frustration. 'Jax! Stop trying to railroad me!'

'In a couple of days the paparazzi will be on to us. I want to pre-empt them with a wedding, a big splashy wedding, which they won't be expecting,' he told her grimly. 'They'll be happy enough to settle for wedding photos.'

'Do you really *want* to do this?' Lucy whispered shakily.

'I want you. I want my daughter. To give her what we both want, to give her what she *deserves,* we have to get married,' Jax countered with measured cool. 'I can handle that. Can you?'

And Lucy thought about that, really seriously thought about that even though her brain did not feel up to that challenge. Even when she had dreamt about marrying Jax two years earlier she had known it was only a dream because Jax had seen too many relationships break down to have any faith in the marriage bond. He had admitted that to her in Spain and afterwards he had seemed unnerved by what he had told her and he had cut their evening short.

'We will fight,' Jax forecast. 'But we're good at making up again.'

Lucy flushed and nodded jerkily and he laughed huskily for they had always ended up in bed after arguments, taking refuge in the sexual unity that bridged their differences.

'And if you don't want to give up work after we're married I'll make a special arrangement for you,' Jax murmured lazily. 'I'll buy a bar and I will be the *only* customer and you can serve me to your heart's content.'

'You say the craziest things,' Lucy muttered, shaking her head while locked to the stunning green eyes gleaming below his black lashes.

'I will say whatever I have to say to get that ring

on your finger,' Jax admitted truthfully. 'The world's your oyster tonight, *koukla mou*.'

But Jax was no perfect pearl for her to acquire, she thought helplessly. Jax was complicated and reserved and unpredictable. Living with Jax would not be easy; it would be a roller coaster of highs and lows. Yet didn't she want to take the chance? It was a chance she had never thought she would have. Yes, Jax had treated her badly in the past but marriage was an equal partnership and this time around she wouldn't have to surrender her independence or her self-respect because money wouldn't be an issue. Giving her daughter the secure and loving childhood she had not had herself would mean so much to her. How could she refuse that offer?

'I'll marry you,' Lucy breathed tautly. 'But you'd better not make me regret it.'

Thinking of the secrets he had withheld and the complete honesty that he would eventually have to practise, Jax breathed in deep. He had given way to blackmail to protect his family but in marrying, he acknowledged grimly, he would be protecting his new family from potential harm as well.

'I should be honest,' Lucy murmured, her blue eyes awash with regret and apology. 'I don't trust you.'

Jax, who had learned never to trust anyone, particularly one's nearest and dearest, almost laughed out loud. Lucy would flourish like a tropical flower in the Antonakos family.

CHAPTER SIX

EVEN A FEW days before the wedding Lucy still couldn't quite accept that she was getting married. She was very tense and stressed. Jax had insisted on picking up the bill for the hundreds of guests invited and her father had been dismayed to discover that he was only allowed to cover his daughter's more personal expenses. In the same way Jax had organised the church and the venue for the reception.

And he had done all of that from a safe distance, leaving Lucy to handle her father's hurt pride and angry complaints. Jax, after all, was the man who had never planned to marry and since the moment Lucy had agreed to marry him Jax had come no closer to the centre of bridal activity than a phone call because he had hired a wedding planner to take care of everything. Lucy had had the freedom to make her own choices but had relied heavily on the planner's advice because she knew nothing about high-society weddings. Her brain was still stuffed, however, with the turmoil of selecting flowers, colour schemes and table arrangements from frighteningly long lists of options and having to discuss every possibility.

Iola had gone shopping with Lucy for a dress and

Jax had been allowed no input there. Lucy had gone for lace and a fancy pleated train that would be removable if she was dancing and she had picked the sweetest little outfit for Bella.

It was ironic that Jax had pretty much vanished as soon as she'd accepted his proposal and that had really annoyed Lucy. He had said that he had too much work to get through and he had only visited the house once when she had insisted he come and meet her father and her stepmother. That had been a very awkward hour of stilted conversation, she recalled ruefully. Jax had been very cool and polite and her father had been stiff and formal. Iola and Lucy's efforts to lighten the atmosphere had made little difference. It had been painfully obvious to Lucy that her father and her bridegroom didn't much like the look of each other.

And then there was the troubling question of her future father-in-law, Heracles Antonakos.

Lucy had assumed that Jax's father would want to meet her in advance but apparently not, and Jax did not seem to know whether or not his father would attend their wedding, an admission that had made her wince. Obviously, Heracles Antonakos was not impressed by his son's decision to marry a waitress and he wanted nothing to do with the event. But Jax refused to be drawn on the sensitive subject and had urged her to be patient.

'It's a delivery…for you,' Iola called up the stairs to Lucy.

Lucy clattered downstairs and signed for the package she was given, turning it over and back before walking into the kitchen to open it. She extracted a letter and a small jewellery box and frowned.

'Is it a wedding present?' Iola asked.

'No...it's from some woman called Polly, who *says* she's one of my sisters,' Lucy whispered in deep shock, reading the closely typed lines to learn that her mother had only passed away a few years before at a hospice and commenting on the fact to Iola.

'I always assumed that Mum had died when I was a child...possibly during the three years I was adopted because of course I wouldn't have been told about it then,' Lucy confided. 'But according to my sisters they too only found out about her death afterwards because she didn't want to see any of us while she was so ill. But she left us all rings given to her by our fathers...and it was only then that my sisters found out that I existed.'

'Strange,' Iola commented. 'But if she was very ill, possibly she wasn't thinking very clearly. Is there a ring in that box?'

Lucy opened the box and extracted a small ruby ring with a smile. 'It's very pretty. I'll wear it when I get married. It's wonderful to have something that my mother actually wore,' she murmured with a sad look in her eyes.

'Read the rest of the letter,' her stepmother urged. 'Tell me about your sisters.'

Unfortunately Polly didn't offer much information beyond the fact that she was married and had children just like Lucy's other sister, Ellie, who was a doctor. What she did say was that she and Ellie very much wanted to meet Lucy and get to know her.

'She couldn't have chosen a worse time to contact me,' Lucy mumbled, settling down to read the letter again. 'She hasn't given me an address or anything but she has given me a phone number, which I could use to talk to her.'

'You could invite your sisters to your wedding,' Iola suggested.

Lucy grimaced. 'No. I don't know them and I don't think Polly knows I'm a mother as well either. It would all be too awkward for a first meeting and in any case they would need more warning than a few days to attend. I'll call her as soon as we get back from our honeymoon. But my goodness, this is exciting,' she muttered abstractedly. 'I wonder what Polly and Ellie are like. Do I look like them? Do you think they have the same father?'

Kreon walked in and Lucy handed him the letter straight away to read. He stared down at the ring on the table and then he lifted it. 'I gave this to Annabel as an engagement ring. It's not a real ruby, you know, but it looks well. It was all I could afford at the time—'

Lucy laughed and removed it from his hand. 'I will still wear it with pride, Dad.'

'You have your mother's bright and beautiful smile,' Kreon told her fondly. 'But you have a kindness as well, which she never had.'

'Maybe I inherited that from you,' Lucy replied, watching her daughter hug her grandfather's knees and raise her arms to be lifted with all the confidence of a child who knew she could always expect a welcome.

Lucy couldn't sleep that night. Jax phoned and she told him about Polly's letter. It shook her that her most driving instinct was to share that very private news with Jax even when he wasn't around. But then Jax knew better than most about complex family divisions, she reasoned, shying away from the inner awareness that she trusted Jax more and wanted to share everything with him more than she was willing to admit.

Jax urged her to do nothing until he had checked out her sisters and she got cross with him then and told him to mind his own business. Not that he could do anything else, she conceded, when there wasn't enough personal information in that letter to allow Lucy or indeed Jax to identify either of her sisters or even work out where they lived. Polly had kept the letter short and sweet as a first approach and Lucy's mind buzzed with conjecture about the siblings she had never met.

Some of her excitement gradually subsided, however, when she thought about Ellie being an actual *doctor*. Ellie was obviously very well-educated and clever and possibly Polly was as well. Lucy could well be the odd one out, the lesser sister, the oddball who didn't fit in. That idea troubled Lucy because it seemed to her that that was the story of her entire life: never quite fitting in anywhere. Not with her mother, not in the foster homes, not even in the short-lived adoption she had enjoyed until her adoptive parents died in a car crash and she was sent back into care. And she hadn't fitted in with Jax either, had she? He had dumped her and walked away without a backward glance. Yet now, he was marrying her. How did that make sense?

He was only marrying her for Bella's benefit, she reminded herself, feeling her pride sting and her heart sink at that awareness. Could their desire to do well by their daughter be enough to sustain a marriage? Lucy didn't want make-believe and she didn't believe in perfect. She believed that she had realistic expectations. But she did desperately *want* to have a real marriage and be part of a proper family. It was what she had dreamt of all her life and never managed to achieve. Now that Jax was offering her that opportunity she planned to make the most of it.

The morning of the wedding dawned bright and sunny and, having done her hair and her make-up for herself, Lucy donned her gown. It was a perfect fit, swirling round her in delicate shimmering white lace. As a mother she had felt self-conscious about wearing white but she hadn't felt the need to make a statement either by choosing another colour. In any case she was marrying the man who had become her first lover and the father of her daughter and she wasn't ashamed of either fact.

A heaving bunch of paparazzi waited behind crash barriers outside the vast Metropolitan Cathedral in the city where the Greek Orthodox ceremony was being held. Lucy was unnerved by the questions shouted and the flash of cameras and she gripped her father's arm tightly as they negotiated the shallow steps and moved below the arches into the church.

'Royalty once got married here,' Kreon murmured with satisfaction. 'I never dreamt that one day I would see my own child taking her vows below this roof.'

The comment lightened Lucy's tension as nothing else could have done. 'Glad I've finally done something to make you proud but why are the paparazzi so interested?'

'You are about to become a member of one of the foremost families in Greece. Naturally, the public want to know who has captured the notorious playboy, Jax Antonakos—'

'I wouldn't say captured is the right word,' Lucy muttered uncomfortably as they paused at the end of the aisle and her father shook out her small train for her and offered his arm to her again with a proud smile.

'He's a very fortunate man. I hope he appreciates that. You look really beautiful,' the older man declared with satisfaction.

Tears stung the backs of Lucy's eyes because she was touched by her father's faith in her. She watched Jax turn his handsome dark head and look at her and the ability to breathe died in her throat. The closer she drew to him on their slow walk down the aisle, the more gorgeous he appeared, his dramatic green eyes welded to her approach. Colour warmed her cheeks and tingling heat surged low in her pelvis. She felt as if all her dreams were coming true in that moment and she scolded herself for being too emotional and sentimental. Jax was neither sentimental nor romantic. He didn't love her and she didn't love him, she reminded herself firmly, but they had Bella to bind them and, in time, maybe they would find that more than their daughter kept them together.

Jax studied Lucy with heavily lidded eyes, his attention roaming over every exquisite shapely inch of her petite body. The gown was a triumph, a delicate lace affair of simple design that enhanced her slight stature and gave her elegance. He didn't look to see how his father was reacting. Only minutes earlier he had noticed his father's absorption in Bella where she sat on Iola's knee across the aisle. Heracles longed for grandchildren, and the knowledge that he had a little granddaughter he had yet to meet had at the very last minute made him decide to attend the wedding. True, Jax wasn't expecting his father to be in a party mood because Heracles hated Kreon Thiarkis and hated that his son was marrying Kreon's daughter, but Jax was relieved that Heracles had put family first and shelved his reservations to share their day.

Some of the ceremony went over Lucy's head, for which she blamed Jax, who had said he was too busy to attend a rehearsal at the cathedral when the services of an interpreter had been available. She concentrated on the simple Greek words that she knew and smiled nervously up at Jax when he slid the ring onto her finger. Their eyes met and the burn inside her spread like wild fire. It was utterly inappropriate but she had never wanted so badly to be kissed. Jax angled his arrogant dark head back and gave her a teasing smile of naked challenge and she went for it as she had always gone for it when he egged her on. She stretched up awkwardly in her very high heels, her hands clutching at his arms to steady herself, and *still* she wasn't tall enough.

With a husky sound of sensual amusement, Jax gathered her up and raised her to his level to taste her lush parted lips for himself. And for a split second, Lucy forgot everything. She forgot that she was in public, she forgot the guests shifting in their seats and the imposing robed Archbishop who had conducted the service. The taste of Jax's mouth was like a shaft of sunlight bursting inside her after a long winter. It charged her up, rendered her helpless with longing, and the plunge of his tongue into the moist interior of her mouth only multiplied the explosive effect of that kiss on her body. Her heart hammered, her pulses raced as

Jax slowly slid her down his lean, powerful frame to stand on her own feet again.

She caught a glimpse of Iola's grin and just as suddenly appreciated that she was still in public view. A swoosh of mortified pink lit up her heart-shaped face as Jax closed his hand over hers and walked her back down the aisle.

Jax was amazed that he felt so relaxed. He had expected to loathe every minute of the wedding. Knowing he was protecting his father was one thing, doing what had to be done when it went against his own instincts was another. But that hot little taste of Lucy's passion assuaged those feelings. She wanted him, she wanted him just as much as he wanted her, and for the moment that was as much consolation for his sacrifice of freedom as he needed.

He had struggled against anger, resentment and bitterness throughout the two weeks it had taken to set up the wedding. He had kept his distance from Lucy because he was afraid that she would guess that he was not the enthusiastic bridegroom he was purporting to be. Deception of any kind had always been a challenge for Jax. He was very talented at keeping his feelings to himself but he was very bad at *faking* anything. He had found the drinks engagement with Kreon and Iola extremely uncomfortable and Lucy's demands for his opinion on the colour of the bridal flowers and such nonsense had simply exasperated him. For two solid weeks, Jax had rigorously reminded himself that he was acquiring Lucy and his daughter and protecting his father by getting married. But even that couldn't disperse the sour flavour of having to do what he had always sworn he would not do and take a wife.

Outside the cathedral the paparazzi went into a frenzy of excitement when the bride and groom appeared. Jax's father stalked silently from cathedral to limousine without pause. It was ironic that Heracles was furious with his son for marrying Lucy. Only after Jax had pointed out that he had had a daughter with Lucy had Heracles gone from raging to dark muttering, finally accepting that a waitress, who was also the daughter of an obnoxious criminal, was entering the Antonakos family. And having learned about that criminal record, Jax had not argued in his father-in-law's favour. Agreeing that Kreon was obnoxious had somewhat soothed his father's ire.

Jax had been tempted to bring up the file he had been given on Lucy two years earlier but he had decided to take a rain check on that line of enquiry until after the wedding. Getting information about Kreon Thiarkis had been surprisingly easy but getting information on Lucy was proving deeply problematic. She had lived in so many different places and had even been adopted at one stage when her name had been changed. Indeed the discovery of just how grim Lucy's growing years had been had saddened Jax. Some years after the adoption she had gone back to using the name she had been given at birth. But Lucy's frequent childhood moves read like a depressing indictment of social services care and the investigator striving to trace her movements during her adolescence was currently at an admitted standstill.

Of course, you could simply ask her for the details, Jax reminded himself wryly. Could he trust her answers? Or would she lie to mislead him, hoping to cover up conduct she might now be ashamed of? Jax needed the confidence of knowing that he had the *whole* truth. Naturally he expected her to deny the drugs offences but, so far, no official record of any such offences had been found. Was it possible that the detective agency his father had used had confused Lucy's identity with someone else's? Was it even remotely possible that she was innocent of the charges in that file? But then hadn't he been equally shocked when he'd seen her with that man in the alleyway? Lucy didn't wear her sins or her flaws on her lovely face.

With the ease of long practice Jax buried the memory of Lucy's betrayal deep where he didn't have to think about it. If he thought about it, he mused grimly, it would drive him off the edge, the way it had two years ago when he had tried to find solace in the bottom of a bottle: the aftershocks of giving up Lucy had been little short of terrifying for a male who needed to stay in emotional control. For a short while he had been overpowered by his conflicting feelings, not something he was willing to recall or relive. In fact even remembering that made him flinch.

They arrived at the hotel and settled down with Bella in a private room set aside for their use to drink champagne and await the arrival of their guests. Poised by the window, Jax tensed. 'That's my father's car arriving. Come on. I want to introduce you and Bella.'

By the time Jax and Lucy reached the grand foyer, however, Iola and Kreon were already greeting Heracles. And then there was one of those strange little moments of absolute stillness as Kreon said something and Heracles backed up and then suddenly lurched forward and punched the younger man with angry ferocity. Lucy was aghast when the fight broke out. Her father responded, lurching clumsily after Heracles to return that punch and then receiving yet another for his pains, for Heracles was very fit and fast on his feet for his age. Further violence was only forestalled by the Antonakos bodyguards who stood between the two men to keep them apart. Heracles let out an angry roar of frustration.

'Stay back,' Jax warned Lucy, striding in to intervene and grip his father by both his arms to restrain him, since it was obvious that none of their staff had the nerve to lay actual hands on their irate employer.

All red in the face and still patently desperate for a fight, Heracles roared something angry in Greek. Jax stole a glimpse at the guests piling through the entrance doors and then stopping dead to stare at the spectacle and he suppressed a groan. He said something to his father and shepherded him over to a door of the private room. Pushing open the door, he gestured to Lucy's father to follow him. Looking reluctant but red-faced and more than a little embarrassed, Kreon finally did so. Jax was trying to sort the argument out, Lucy recognised ruefully while wondering what Heracles Antonakos had against her father that had so overpowered his manners.

'Men!' Iola proclaimed dramatically at her elbow, making Lucy emit a startled laugh. 'Thank heaven, Jax got them out of sight.'

'What sparked off that punch?' Lucy demanded in bewilderment.

'Apparently Kreon and Jax's father have some past history. Kreon didn't go into detail but it's obvious that Jax's father hates him and almost didn't come to his son's wedding because he knew Kreon would be here.' Iola rolled her eyes. 'Don't let it spoil your day.'

'I shan't,' Lucy responded, stroking Bella's curls distractedly while thinking that family relations promised to be taxing with their fathers at odds.

With Iola by her side, Lucy welcomed guests and chatted until she saw Heracles and Kreon emerge again together with drinks in their hands and actually speaking to each other. But when Jax strode back to join her, raw tension was still stamped on his lean, darkly handsome features.

'Evidently you're quite successful in the peacemaker stakes,' Lucy remarked as he steered her into the function room to take their seats, mercifully moving her right before she had to greet Kat Valtinos, who looked ravishing in a cutaway emerald dress teamed with feathers in her hair.

'No, they achieved that without any help from me. I only stayed to ensure that hostilities didn't break out again,' Jax admitted. 'You still haven't met my father and I need to explain what happened out there.'

'Don't break the habit of a lifetime and tell me something,' Lucy urged with helpless sarcasm.

'It's not something I want to talk about but I must,' Jax breathed stiffly. 'However, it's old history and nothing to do with us. No doubt you're wondering why my father went for yours…'

'Kreon does seem to be an acquired taste with some people.'

'This is not a teasing matter,' Jax censured.

As she settled down beside him at the top table Lucy was watching Heracles Antonakos make their daughter's acquaintance. Bella was fearless and she stared up at the older man and handed him her stuffed rabbit. Heracles's craggy face broke into a sudden unexpected smile and he sat down with Iola by his side and accepted the rabbit to make it walk across the seat beside him. Bella started to giggle and clutched at the leg of his trousers to stay upright.

'He likes Bella,' Lucy noted with satisfaction, willing to overlook and forgive a great deal if her daughter was accepted and appreciated.

'He loves children.' Jax fell broodingly silent and she glanced curiously at his lean, taut profile, helplessly admiring the classic perfection of it. 'My father discovered after my brother, Argo, died that he could not have been his child. Argo needed a transfusion after the attack and I suspect it was discovered in the minutes before he died that he did not share my father's or my rare blood group.'

Lucy's eyes widened because she was completely disconcerted by that bombshell. 'My goodness, Heracles must have been devastated to find that out—'

'Particularly as he idolised his first wife and despised my mother…and me…for my mother's infidelity. When he found out that he hadn't fathered Argo he immediately suspected your father because of the close friendship Kreon had had with Sofia.'

Lucy winced. 'I honestly don't think it was that sort of friendship.'

'It wasn't. Kreon saw Sofia as a little sister. His mother, your grandmother on Kreon's side, was Sofia's nanny and as children Kreon and Sofia spent a lot of time together,' Jax told her. 'Unfortunately having married Sofia my father distrusted their friendship and became jealous.'

'In other words, your father is an old dinosaur who can't credit that a man and a woman can have a platonic friendship,' Lucy commented, still watching Heracles as he lifted Bella onto his knee with careful hands.

'I wouldn't appreciate my wife being that friendly with another man either,' Jax admitted.

'Sadly I don't currently have any close male friends to torment you with.' Lucy sighed with unhidden regret on that score.

'You're a little witch,' Jax growled, running his forefinger along the lush line of her full lower lip. 'Why does that make me want to kiss you again?'

'You love a challenge?' Lucy whispered unevenly, meeting those stunning green eyes in a head-on clash and feeling more than a little dizzy with excitement, her lips parting.

'But I don't enjoy an audience,' Jax countered, running a finger back and forth across the delicate bones of her wrist below the level of the table.

Lucy was breathing in rapid shallow little gusts, insanely conscious of her body responding to him on every level. She could feel her breasts full and constricted within the bodice of her dress, her distended nipples pushing hard against the scratchy lace of her bra and then there was the tight locked-down tension and heat between her thighs, not to mention the dulled little throb there that made her ache and stiffen her posture.

'It's showtime—but not for what we want,' Jax murmured drily as Iola took a seat beside him and Heracles settled down beside Lucy with Bella still on his knee.

'She's very cute,' Heracles said of her daughter. 'She knows what she wants.'

'Mum… Mum,' Bella framed, lurching straight off Jax's father into her mother's arms and flopping down sleepily.

'She needs a nap,' Lucy sighed.

'Where's the nanny I hired for the day?' Jax asked.

The older woman was already approaching Lucy, ready to take the tired toddler off her hands, but Lucy stood up. 'I'll come upstairs with you and get her settled.'

'Your bride doesn't take hints, does she?' Heracles remarked with some amusement to his son. 'You'll have your hands full with the two of them.'

Jax, who very much wanted to follow his bride upstairs and have her settle *him* down, grimaced. 'I know it.'

'Well, you can't make worse choices than I did. I won't say anything more,' his father declared piously. 'With my track record, I can't afford to preach, can I?'

'No, you can't.'

'Three marriages ending in one death and two divorces and your mother was almost as bad. We didn't set you much of an example, did we?' Heracles sighed heavily. 'By the way, I've set up the island for your honeymoon—'

Thoroughly taken aback, Jax frowned. 'But you live on Tifnos,' Jax objected, because he had been planning to take Lucy cruising round the Mediterranean on the yacht.

'Tifnos is yours now that you're a father. It was built to be a family home and I'm tired of living there alone in that great barn of a house. I've signed it over to you and I'm in the process of buying an estate outside Athens,' the older man told him in a tone of finality. 'It's time for me to step back and make room for the next generation.'

CHAPTER SEVEN

LUCY CAME OUT of the room where she had left the nanny watching over Bella and smiled at the sight of Kreon waiting for her. 'Dad? What are you doing up here?' she asked with a grin. 'Are you trying to escape all the polite chit-chat? Or have you heard a rumour that the food's going to be bad?'

Kreon shifted uneasily on his feet, his face grave and troubled. 'I have done something wrong and it concerns you.'

'What on earth are you talking about?' Lucy laughed as he urged her into an alcove with seats.

'Talking to Heracles made me see stuff...differently.' Her father selected his words with an air of discomfiture as he sat down. 'It made me appreciate that we've all had our tragedies and our triumphs but it's how we deal with them that makes us who we are. I'd like to be proud of who I am but right now I'm *not*.'

Lucy narrowed her eyes in confusion. 'You don't sound like yourself.'

'Jax's father neglected Jax because he despised Jax's mother, whom he divorced. He knows he can never make it up to Jax and he has to live with it every day, knowing that all those years he left his boy to deal alone with a very difficult woman,' Kreon told her.

'But you and I have a different history,' Lucy reasoned, tucking that fresh information about Jax into her memory to take out and ponder at a more suitable time. 'You didn't even know that my mother was pregnant when you left London and she didn't tell you later when she could have done—'

'That's not what I'm talking about,' Kreon told her heavily. 'For many years I hated Heracles Antonakos because he put me down over my friendship with his wife. I'm ashamed to admit that I took my resentment out on his son.'

Lucy's smooth brow had furrowed. 'In what way?'

'When Sofia was dying, she had a letter sent to me in which she confessed her darkest secret. She didn't have the nerve to tell her husband so she told me instead.' Kreon drew a crumpled envelope from his pocket and passed it to her. 'Give it to Jax, let him decide what to do with it now. In it Sofia confesses to having an affair and she admits that Jax's brother wasn't fathered by Heracles. I went to see Jax a couple of weeks ago and I threatened to take that letter to the newspapers.'

'Good grief…why would you threaten to do something so horrible?' Lucy demanded in total disbelief.

'I wanted Jax to marry you and take care of you and Bella. I thought he owed you that security and I *still* believe that he does but coercing him into doing it was wrong and unjust. He was protecting his father from more heartache and I shouldn't have put him in that position. He is not responsible for his father's mistakes.'

Lucy had turned very pale and her stomach was

curdling as if she had eaten something that disagreed with her. She studied her father in slowly dawning horror and comprehension. 'Are you telling me that you blackmailed Jax into proposing to me?'

As Kreon gave a guilty nod of silent confirmation, Lucy felt as though the bottom had just dropped out of her world. She stared at the brand-new wedding ring on her finger and felt sick. Jax hadn't wanted to marry her. No, he had been *forced* to marry her. It was ghastly. She looked at her father in stricken condemnation. 'Were you insane? I mean, what on earth could persuade you that *that* was an acceptable way to behave towards Bella's father?'

'I was angry with him. I wanted to punish Jax for seducing and abandoning you. It's not an excuse but at the time I honestly believed I was doing what was best for you and my granddaughter.'

'Because Jax is rich and powerful,' Lucy slotted in sickly. 'And now you feel bad about it because you've realised that rich and powerful people like Heracles Antonakos make mistakes and suffer just like everyone else.'

Kreon sighed. 'That's probably it in a nutshell. When I listened to Heracles talking I felt my anger draining away. He was a workaholic who neglected all his wives. But he came to the wedding today even though he didn't approve of you because he was making an effort to be supportive of Jax as a father should. That was the *right* kind of effort to make for a child, mine was wrong. What did I do today? I made a sarcastic comment and provoked that punch.'

'I'm really upset,' Lucy admitted, breathing in deep and slow to calm herself down. 'You'd better go back down and join the guests before Iola starts wondering where you are.'

'I'm sorry, Lucy. I've just felt so powerless since you came into my life. You had had such a rough time and I genuinely *did* want to make your life better,' Kreon confessed before he walked away.

And she understood exactly where her father was coming from *but* he had blackmailed Jax. Nausea stirred in Lucy's tummy. Jax, who would hold a grudge beyond the grave. Jax, who idolised the father who had ignored him for so many years, had been vulnerable. A deep sense of anguish flooded Lucy and an even deeper sense of shame. The father she had so easily come to love had let her down badly and shown her his feet of clay. That hurt as well. Was she always going to be a rotten judge of character?

But what did she do now? Well, the middle of a wedding didn't seem the ideal venue in which to open a very difficult conversation with Jax. Oh, by the way, my father mentioned that he blackmailed you… Lucy cringed and winced and hurt all over again. She hurt for her father and for Jax and for Bella, for surely the chances of such a marriage working out looked very poor. But most of all, she was discovering that she hurt for herself. Jax's apparent desire to marry her had filled her with hope and even unleashed a few dreams.

Only now it was obvious that Jax hadn't actually experienced *any* desire to put a ring on her finger. Her father had used the nastiest form of persuasion available to get that wedding ring on her hand. Hadn't it ever occurred to Kreon that it would be his daughter who had to deal with the aftermath of what he had done? Hadn't he appreciated how angry and aggrieved

Jax would feel? Lucy shivered, suddenly feeling very alone and without support. She couldn't depend on her father and now it was equally obvious that she could not depend on her new husband either.

For the first time she badly wanted to speak to the sisters she had never met. It was crazy but she wanted to reach out and see if she could connect with a sister as she so obviously had failed to connect with Jax or her father. Kreon had lied when he said that she could trust him. And Jax hadn't meant all those fine things he had said about how they could be a couple creating a secure family in which to raise a child. He had been forced to talk like that to convince Lucy to agree to marry him and she groaned out loud, remembering how unusually understated Jax had been that evening. She had already put her sister's phone number into her mobile for fear that she might mislay Polly's letter and she dug her phone out of her small ornamental bag.

She got a bad case of cold feet while the phone was ringing and almost stopped the call before it connected. And then it was answered by this sunny, confidence-inducing female voice and Lucy froze.

'It's Lucy…er…your sister…if that's you, Polly,' she gabbled in an uneasy rush.

'Lucy!' Polly proclaimed warmly. 'I'm so very happy to hear from you. Do you have any idea how long Ellie and I have been trying to trace you?'

'Why were you trying?' Lucy asked in genuine puzzlement.

'Because you're our sister and part of our family. Ellie and I always had each other but until recently I know you had no one. Of course, I appreciate that you have your father now—'

'That hasn't worked out so well,' Lucy mumbled in some embarrassment.

'I'm really sorry to hear that. Are you all right, Lucy?' Polly prompted anxiously.

Lucy stared stonily at the wall, hot prickly tears stinging the backs of her aching eyes. 'Well, not so great today…to be brutally honest,' she framed chokily.

'You sound upset,' Polly remarked with care. 'Naturally I don't want to pry but—'

'I'm not upset,' Lucy insisted chokingly. 'It's my wedding day—'

'My wedding day wasn't great either,' Polly told her ruefully. 'I assume the ceremony has already taken place? Do you love the man you married?'

It was a simple question but it froze Lucy from head to toe. She started to shiver, feeling cold and clammy. 'No, we're not in love. We got married because we have a daughter…at least I *thought* that's why we got married but seems I was wrong about that too,' she mumbled shakily.

'I can't believe you're already a mother at only twenty-one,' Polly exclaimed. 'Somehow our detective didn't pick up on that. You sound so unhappy though. Please tell me what's wrong…'

And Lucy compressed her lips, fighting the tears positively attracted by that soft, understanding sibling voice. 'I *can't* tell you—'

'You can tell me anything,' Polly assured her. 'Ellie and I are here and ready and willing to help you if you need us.'

'That's good to know but I still can't tell you,' Lucy repeated doggedly.

'Is your child's father abusive?' Polly demanded worriedly. 'Are you at risk in any way?'

'No…*no*!' Lucy insisted, hastening to shut down that suspicion. 'Look, I've just found out that my father blackmailed my bridegroom into marrying me! That's why I'm upset.'

'Right…' Polly's momentary hesitation spoke volumes and Lucy winced. 'But you're not responsible for what your father does. Lucy, you only have to say the word and, wherever you are and no matter what time of day it is, we'll have you picked up.'

'That's a very generous offer,' Lucy framed, deeply touched.

'Please think about coming to stay with us for a while…you'd be very welcome and it would give you a breathing space in which to decide what you want to do next,' her sister pointed out.

'I'll certainly think about it but I have to go now. I'm sorry. I'll phone you again when I have more time to talk.'

Lucy thrust her phone guiltily back into her bag, wondering what had possessed her to say so much to a woman she had never met. Now Polly probably thought she was more than a little weird. She headed down to the powder room on the ground floor to repair her make-up. Her mascara had run and she asked herself why she had been reduced to tears. The shock of Kreon's confession? The knowledge that Jax had only proposed to protect his cantankerous old father from the humiliation of having it known that his elder son had not been his? Whatever, it was her wedding day and she was on show and she had to get over her emotional reactions and behave normally.

'Where the hell have you been?' Jax demanded as he strode out of the function room to intercept her and closed his hands round her arms to hold her still. 'Is Bella OK?'

'She's fine. I was talking to someone,' Lucy told him, colliding with his stunning black-fringed green eyes and experiencing a jolt not unlike an electric shock.

Jax stared down at her. 'Have you been crying?' he asked, noticing the very faint hint of pink round her eyelids, which he was certain hadn't been visible earlier.

'No, for goodness' sake,' Lucy parried with an uneasy laugh. 'Why would I have been crying?'

Jax had no idea but he could see that Lucy's naturally sunny aura had dimmed. Perhaps Bella was playing up, he reasoned. Weddings were stressful and a strange place and a strange nanny could well have upset his daughter. He dropped a hand to Lucy's spine and guided her back into the function room and towards the top table.

The meal was served. It melted in Lucy's mouth but she might as well have been eating sawdust for all the pleasure it gave her. Her father-in-law asked her some very awkward questions about her past life and she answered as best she could, struggling to breeze lightly past her years in care and becoming much more animated when he asked about Bella.

A professional singer entertained them and then the dancing began. Jax had to almost drag Lucy onto the floor because she couldn't dance very well and was covered in blushes at the thought of having to perform in front of people.

'I just wish this day was over,' she confided, pushing her face against his chest, realising that he was so tall that, from one angle at least, she could literally hide herself.

'You and me both,' Jax admitted, wondering if his father had said something cutting to make her appear so subdued and feeling surprisingly angry at that suspicion.

Of course, the wedding he had been blackmailed into agreeing to could hardly be a source of pleasure for him, Lucy reckoned wretchedly. And what must he think of her father now? He probably knew Kreon had already spent a couple of years of his youth in a cell and now he would believe that Kreon belonged in prison and would think less of her because of it. People did judge you on your background and relatives. Not that he had ever thought that much of her to begin with, Lucy reminded herself unhappily, recalling how she had been cast off like an old shoe in Spain.

'In another few hours we'll be on our way,' Jax remarked, long brown fingers sliding down her back to gather her closer.

Heat curled between her thighs as she felt the evidence of his arousal. Her mouth ran dry. Evidently blackmail didn't douse Jax's libido. He still wanted her. Was that something to celebrate? Or something more to beat herself up about? Was she supposed to settle gratefully for being his sexual outlet? Was that all she was worth? All she deserved? She didn't know any longer. Her brain in turmoil, she forced herself to relax into the hard, muscular warmth of his hold and allowed him to slow-dance her round the floor. Other people were dancing now as well and she no longer felt like the centre of attention.

'Where will we be on our way to?' she asked belatedly.

'That's a surprise,' Jax admitted, still taken aback by what his father had done.

The little island of Tifnos was the Antonakos home but Jax had yet to even spend a night there. As a boy he had been ferried out there but only on day trips to attend several big family social occasions and as an adult he had flown to the island regularly to consult with Heracles about business. But it had never been *his* home because when he had been young he had been lucky if his father even acknowledged his presence among so many other guests. In truth he had always felt like an intruder and an outsider in his father's house and the startling concept of making Tifnos his base raised all sorts of conflicting feelings.

'Oh…' Lucy framed, drinking in the scent of him with flared nostrils. There was definitely something scientific in the effect of pheromones on attraction, she conceded ruefully. She loved Jax's smell; that indefinable combination of designer cologne and husky male had called to her from his first kiss.

Her eyes prickled again and she wrinkled her nose to hold the stupid tears back. Her husband, *blackmailed* into marrying her. Knowing that, she found it a challenge to believe that she could be a true bride and wife. In fact, Kreon's intervention and use of pressure made a nonsense of the entire day. She felt utterly humiliated. She wondered when she would work up the nerve to discuss what Kreon had done with Jax and how he would react when she did. He could well be furious that she had found out. His ferocious pride would rebel against her knowing that he could be forced into doing anything.

She was heading for the bridal suite to get changed for their departure when she saw Kat Valtinos walking towards her and suppressed a sigh because she wasn't in the mood to be patronised or bitched at over the head of Jax.

'Lucy…' Kat murmured with a bright artificial smile. 'Your big day's almost over.'

'Yes. We're leaving soon.' Lucy busied herself fishing out the card to open the door. Kreon and Iola had already taken Bella home for the night and her daughter would be staying with them for the first week Jax and Lucy were away.

'Well, enjoy it while you can,' Kat advised with saccharine sweetness. 'It's not as if your marriage will last long.'

As Lucy thrust the door open she simply ignored the brunette, refusing to be drawn into an exchange with her. Kat had hated her two years ago in Spain for attracting Jax and, from what she had seen of Jax and Kat in the newspapers, Kat must still have cherished hopes of something more coming from their long friendship.

'Jax will take the kid and dump you again,' Kat murmured lethally. 'Don't say you weren't warned.'

Lucy closed the door firmly behind her. Pale and shaky after that nasty little threat of what could be, she concentrated on removing her gown and freshening up. She pulled on a light dress and thrust her sore feet into sandals, touching up her make-up with a light hand. Kat was such a shrew, she reflected ruefully. Jax would *never* try to take Bella from her. Why would he do such a cruel thing? Or even think about separating a mother from her child? It wasn't as though she was an unfit mother. All right, she wasn't perfect. She had been known to snarl a little when Bella tried to get her out of bed at dawn but she *loved* her daughter. Nothing pleased Lucy more than the ability to give Bella all the little things she had never had herself, the small stuff like bedtime stories, favourite foods and lots of hugs.

Her luggage packed and then collected, Lucy went to meet Jax. A limo ferried them to the airport, where they boarded a helicopter.

'Are we going on the yacht?' she asked before the noise of the engine made any conversation impossible.

'No. Tifnos,' Jax told her simply.

And Lucy nodded, secretly intimidated by the prospect. She had read about the fabled private island Heracles had bought as a base in the eighties. Her father-in-law was reputed to live in feudal splendour there in a house that had never been photographed or shown in any publication. But it was supposed to have gardens that could rival the Garden of Eden, a private zoo and literally hundreds of staff.

Lucy felt inadequate. She was far too ordinary for such a backdrop. She had always been ordinary and had once thought that that was what attracted Jax to her. She didn't put on airs, she didn't say things she didn't believe to impress and when she didn't know something she admitted it. Unexpectedly, Jax closed a large hand over hers and then slowly laced his fingers with her own. His thumb massaged her inner wrist soothingly. It was as if she had hoisted a flag telegraphing panic and he had picked up on it. Or as if he was a little apprehensive too…

An idea she swiftly dismissed, for Tifnos was the Antonakos home and he had to be well accustomed to it.

It was fully dark by the time helicopter landed and Jax scooped her out onto the helipad. Momentarily she was thrilled by the dark heavens filled with thousands of the stars that were never visible in the city. Their luggage was piled into a beach buggy and Zenas took the wheel to drive them up a steep hill road hedged in by a forest of pine trees.

And then at the top the Antonakos house stretched like a giant illuminated cruise ship.

'It's big,' she said abruptly.

'Yep, for a man who doesn't like to entertain, Heracles built a very large house,' Jax conceded wryly.

They stepped into a foyer glossy and glittering with pristine marble and chandeliers. It looked exactly like a plush hotel reception without the desk. A double staircase swanned up to the next floor, each tread wide enough to march an army.

'Think movie set,' Jax urged. 'My mother redesigned the entrance, so there are some very theatrical touches.'

A small middle-aged Greek man approached them with a tray of welcoming drinks. Jax passed her a champagne flute but demurred on his account. 'I don't like champagne,' he admitted.

Lucy drank down hers to be polite while she peered into rooms furnished with the kind of opulence that just screamed old money to her. There were statues and collections and cabinets and elaborate artwork everywhere she looked. Suddenly she understood why there were supposedly hundreds of staff. It would take a fair number to look after so many possessions.

Jax set down her glass for her and closed his hand over hers and told the hovering manservant whom he addressed as Theo that they were going to bed.

'Wasn't that a little…offhand?' she pressed self-consciously as they climbed the stairs.

'It's one in the morning and it's our wedding night,' Jax intoned, his hand tightening on hers. 'We can get chatty tomorrow.'

She thought about what she had been avoiding thinking about and colour mantled her cheeks as Jax walked her into a vast room overflowing with urns of white roses and lilies, ornamented with trailing ivy. It was magnificent but not as magnificent as the vast divan bed on the dais scattered with rose petals.

'Heracles wasn't joking when he said he'd set the house up for the bridal couple,' Jax conceded with forbidding cool.

'It's beautiful,' Lucy muttered, because it was and she was grateful that her father-in-law had been prepared to make the effort on their behalf. 'But maybe a little too grand for the likes of me.'

'The "likes of me" now happens to be my wife,' Jax reminded her in reproof. 'And nothing is *too* grand or *too* good for my wife.'

'I'll get used to it…it's just a little overwhelming coming to a house like this,' Lucy confided.

'It's ours now,' Jax revealed, sharing his father's plans with her. 'I think he's hoping we'll go forth and multiply now for him.'

Lucy shrugged a slim shoulder, making no comment on that possibility.

'I think Bella's enough for us at present. I still have to learn how to be a father,' Jax completed, making his opinion clear. 'Do you want a drink or anything to eat? There're snacks waiting on the trolley.'

'No. I only want to get my shoes off,' Lucy admitted, dropping down into a luxurious armchair with a sigh. 'My feet are hurting.'

'Let me…' In the most disconcerting way, Jax crouched down lithely at her feet and unfastened her shoes to slip them off. 'You have such tiny feet. They used to fascinate me.'

Long brown fingers gently stroked the back of a delicate ankle and Lucy snatched in a sudden startled breath because her skin felt super sensitive, as though he had touched her somewhere much more intimate.

'All that got me through the day was the glorious thought of sating myself inside you again, *koukla mou*,' Jax said huskily, rising to lift her bodily out of the chair and settle her down on the huge bed.

Eyes flying wide, cheeks flushing, Lucy stared up at him with bright blue eyes.

'So, why do you look like a cornered rabbit?' Jax asked pleasantly. 'You've been acting strangely all day.'

CHAPTER EIGHT

'I...I FELT OVERWHELMED,' Lucy told him and it was true.

The cathedral wedding, the sleek bejewelled Antonakos relatives and guests and the absence of any actual friends aside of her father's had weighed her down. The constant stares and the low buzz of conjecture hadn't helped either but when someone as rich as Jax married a waitress, who was the mother of his child, people stared and speculated. The wedding had been a strain and her father's confession of wrongdoing had crushed her. It had been the ultimate humiliation to learn that only Kreon's criminal act had made it possible for her to marry Jax.

And yet what could they possibly *do* about it now? Kreon had confessed too late to change anything. If she and Jax were to part this very night, it would cause a major scandal and she knew Jax wouldn't want to invite that media attention, which meant that at the very least they would have to stay married for a few months to make any breakup appear less worthy of comment.

'I can understand that,' Jax conceded, removing his jacket in a lazy fluid movement.

And Lucy watched him with a fast-beating heart,

still wondering what she should do and how she should be behaving. Yet with a good ninety per cent of her being she craved the intimacy that being with Jax would give her. She wanted forgetfulness. She wanted to sink into the comfortable depths of the massive bed and shut the rest of the world out to take refuge in Jax. Even if he wasn't really hers and possibly wouldn't be hers for very long. His dazzling green eyes gleamed in the low-lit room, so bright against his dark bronzed skin, and her mouth ran dry.

Tugging his shirt from his waistband, he came back to the bed and sank down behind her to unzip her dress. She sat there like a little statue, her heart thudding like crazy in her chest as he lifted the garment up over her head, leaving her clad only in the white lace lingerie she had worn with her wedding gown. Sliding upright again, he unbuttoned his shirt, displaying a wide slice of his torso, well-defined muscles coming into view as he shed the shirt.

And she was as entranced by his sheer male beauty as she had once been in Spain, feasting her eyes on him with feminine appreciation. Jax worked out and it showed. He was all lean muscle and controlled power.

'Take the rest off,' he urged. 'I want to look at you.'

Her face burned as she reached behind her back to unclasp her bra. She had never done that before in front of him. Her clothes had once vanished beneath his skilled hands and she hadn't had to think about it or ever feel particularly naked. But there in that silent bedroom she was insanely aware of her body and its deficiencies as she let the bra fall. Most of the pregnancy weight had fallen away but there was no denying that she was curvier at bust and hip and there was an obvious scar low on her belly from the Caesarean she had had to have. Her waist was bigger too, she thought nervously, anxiously cataloguing every flaw. And this was a guy accustomed to the flawless female bodies of underwear models.

Jax studied the pouting swell of her pink-tipped breasts with intense pleasure, arousal flashing through him with storm-force potency. Everything about her daintiness appealed to him because her slender lines became lush in all the right highly feminine places. And he knew exactly what would happen when he touched her. He knew she would respond to him in a way no other woman ever had and that there would be nothing fake or exaggerated about it. Anticipation gave him the ultimate high.

'I'm not perfect,' she warned him tightly as her fingers flirted with the band of her knickers. 'Well, I never was, but—'

A flashing grin flared across Jax's lean, darkly handsome features as he came down on one knee on the bed and yanked her playfully to him by her ankles. 'You're perfect for me…I only want to see you.'

Sharply disconcerted by that teasing assault, Lucy looked up at him with apprehensive eyes of blue. He hooked his hands into her knickers and dragged them off, lowering her back gently against the pillows and then rearranging her to his own satisfaction, her legs parted and her hands by her side.

'I'd love a painting of you looking like this, all spread out and waiting for me, but I couldn't stand the artist seeing you naked,' he admitted thickly, peeling off his trousers and his boxers in an impatient movement.

Lucy lay there feeling like a sacrifice and yet she was quite ridiculously excited by his scrutiny and the thrusting fullness of his arousal. He was so ready for her, was always ready. He made her feel as though her body were flawless and the desire he made no attempt to hide warmed the sore place inside her where her father's betrayal had contrived to undermine her self-esteem.

Jax joined her on the bed and went straight for her mouth with hungry, driving kisses that parted her lips and sent a current of high-voltage expectation flying through her trembling length. Her fingers clutched into his spiky, messy black hair and tears burned behind her lowered eyelids because she wanted him so much that she hurt with the wanting. It felt too intense, too desperate and that wasn't what she wanted to feel. She needed to stay in control, she told herself, remember what was real and what wasn't real. And what they had now *wasn't* real. Why did thinking that drive a knife through her when it was only the truth?

'I can't get enough of you,' Jax growled between the urgent biting kisses that bruised her lips and the devastating plunge of his tongue that made her slight body jackknife in reaction beneath his.

'We've got all night,' she whispered through rosy swollen lips, eyes glazed with passion.

'I've got a hunger that one night won't come anywhere near satisfying,' Jax told her rawly, fisting a hand in her tumbling curls as he snaked a string of kisses down over her collarbone and found a plump, pointed nipple to torment with attention.

'Oh… Jax,' she gasped, a fire trail of tingles lighting up from her breast to her pelvis where a warm damp sensation pulsed.

With difficulty Jax dragged his lips from her writhing body and stared down at her. She was his wife now. Signed, sealed and delivered. In the strangest way, he registered, he *liked* that, liked that ring on her finger that marked her as his and loved the way she was looking up at him as though he had hung the moon.

'You will be very tired tomorrow,' Jax forecast without hesitation. 'I'm planning to take everything you can offer and then some more.'

Without hesitation, Lucy leant up and claimed his sensual, taunting mouth for herself, revelling in the instant rush of hungry need he betrayed. He scored the edge of his teeth across her full lower lip, dallied over the sensitive skin below her ear and then returned to his self-imposed worship of her full breasts. He lashed the hard little tips into swollen, throbbing sensitivity and her hips rose beneath his long, lean physique until he settled a leg between hers, giving her the pressure she craved at the crux of her body.

The demanding ache at the heart of her spread, sending little tingles through every skin cell, building and building her tension. He teased her nipples with his teeth and the heat of a climax simply exploded through Lucy in a glorious rush that made her cry out and jerk under him.

'That's one…' Jax husked with satisfaction.

'You're counting now?' Lucy mumbled distractedly, dragged into brain-dead lethargy by the shimmering backwash of sheer pleasure.

'I always was goal-orientated,' Jax reminded her, working his passage slowly down her quivering length.

Tell him you know about the blackmail, a guilty little inner voice urged her. But that would unleash a very difficult conversation after an extremely long and trying day. In any case Jax was reasonably happy at this precise moment, she decided, and she didn't want to spoil things. Later they would both be more relaxed and less tense. He tugged her thighs apart and buried his mouth there and suddenly her brain didn't have any space left in which to be rational. Suddenly she became a twisting, gasping creature at the mercy of her own sensual responses.

Jax slid a finger through her silky folds. He stroked her, smiling as she moaned and shifted, striving to urge him on, but in bed Jax was always in control, most particularly because Lucy had no control.

'Torture!' she muttered between gritted teeth, a rosy flush and perspiration slicking her skin as she thrashed under his ministrations, gasping as he hit the exact spot where she was most sensitive.

'I love the taste of you,' Jax growled, the vibrations of his dark deep drawl pulsing through her tender flesh.

Involuntarily, her body erupted again, driven to the point of explosive climax by the intensity of her excitement. She screamed his name and jerked and then fell still, wonder creeping over her that anyone could possibly wreak such havoc with her system and give her that much pleasure.

'*Thee mou*, I want you so much,' Jax ground out as he slid over her, his hands strong on her hips to angle her back.

He entered her slowly, urging her tender flesh to open for him and stretch, and the sensation made her dizzy with yearning and wildly impatient for more. He eased back and then pushed in hard and deep and her body convulsed and tightened round him, intense sensation ravishing her. A string of tiny sounds was wrenched from her parted lips as he ground into her and picked up the pace, raw excitement flooding her as she tilted up to meet him, hot, damp and abandoned as the wild roller coaster of sensation raged on and on. He slammed into her with primal force and her body just splintered from the inside out, taking her apart in pieces so that she slumped back on the bed, barely aware of his muffled groan of completion but welcoming the warm, heavy weight of him.

Empty of all conscious thought, Lucy skated her hands over Jax's smooth damp back and then wrapped her arms round him tightly. He was struggling to catch his breath close to her ear and she smiled and twisted her head to kiss him on the cheek.

Jax froze as though she had crossed some invisible boundary line. He refused to do that stuff with her again. Bone and sinew he rejected any show of affection that came from her and he yanked back from her and rolled away. He wasn't buying into that again with her, no way! She had given him that same hugging and petting and apparent warmth in Spain and he knew it was meaningless. He had known that when he saw her in that alleyway having sex with another man. As that cringe-making memory returned, Jax wanted to smash a fist into the wall.

That was better left buried and he knew it, particularly now that they were married. When he thought about it, he felt seething anger and violent. Forgiveness wasn't in his vocabulary and forgetting wasn't in his nature. There wasn't any reason for him to think about that sordid episode, he told himself grimly. All he had to do for his own protection was remember that she was treacherous and watch out when she was around other men.

When Jax jerked away from her and headed for what she assumed was the bathroom, Lucy felt as if he had slapped her in the face. He had recoiled from her as if she were contagious, as if he couldn't *bear* her touch. After such intimacy, that hit hard and hurt, spelling out the message that once he had had sex, he was up and away, any pretence of courtesy or caring set aside and rejected.

She felt hollow and very, very foolish. This was the aggressive male her father had blackmailed into marrying her and this was the payoff, she assumed sickly. Evidently he had taken the only thing he actually wanted from her and now she was like an abandoned toy, a distraction good enough only to be tossed back in the cupboard until the next time he wanted to take her out and play with her.

'You don't like it when I touch you after sex,' she accused baldly.

Jax shot her a winging glance from narrowed green eyes that glittered. 'Because it's fake.'

Lucy sat up. 'It wasn't fake,' she told him but he had already vanished into the bathroom and within seconds she heard the sound of a shower running.

Well, Jax needn't think that was the end of the conversation just because he wanted it that way, Lucy thought angrily. She scrambled out of bed and grabbed up her handbag to extract the letter that Kreon had given her. Whether she liked it or not, it was time to be open and honest. She opened the bedroom door and found their luggage piled outside. She lifted a case and dragged it in, opening it up to remove a light cotton robe. Nothing slinky about her nightwear, she reflected ruefully. Iola had insisted on buying her some stuff and the prospect of Jax gazing in disbelief at her chain-store PJ's had persuaded her. She wrapped herself in the robe, watching out of the corner of her eye as Jax strode naked into what sounded like an en-suite dressing room because she could hear drawers being rammed open and shut and cupboard doors being slammed. My goodness, he was in a bad mood… so much for her assumption that intimacy would bring relaxation and a release of tension!

Jax reappeared, clad in a pair of faded jeans and a black tee shirt that clung to his muscular torso. He headed straight for the trolley and opened it before lifting a plate and piling food on it. 'Would you like anything?' he asked with studious politeness and she wanted to slap him for his tone.

'Not right now, thanks,' she murmured tightly. 'I have something for you… Kreon gave it to me today.'

Jax swung round, fully acknowledging her for the first time, his lean, darkly handsome face guarded until he saw and immediately recognised what was in her hand and he stalked forward to snatch it from her with a profound look of revulsion.

'Were you in it *with* him?' Jax shot at her accusingly, for most ironically that possibility hadn't occurred to him and right there and then he called himself an idiot for not having suspected her active involvement in Kreon's blackmail threat.

Lucy's chest swelled on a stark indrawn breath of shock as she drew herself up to her full unimpressive height. 'Are you certifiably insane?' she demanded in fiery rebuttal of that suspicion. 'Yesterday, *after* the wedding, Kreon told me what he had done to you because he felt guilty. He knew he'd done wrong—'

'Diavolos...' Jax derided. 'Kreon felt guilty? You will never know what a comfort that is to me!'

'He did wrong but he's not a bad man and the mistake you made was in not immediately coming to me about my father's threat and the existence of that letter,' Lucy condemned with conviction. 'I believe I could've stopped it because he would have been too ashamed to continue with it once I knew about what he was doing.'

'And pigs fly and there's two blue moons in the sky,' Jax scorned, shaking his tousled dark head in wonderment, green eyes as cutting as sword blades. 'I'll ask you one more time…were you aware of his intentions?'

'No, I blasted well wasn't!' Lucy shouted back at him, her blue eyes flooded with angry, defensive discomfiture. 'How can you even ask me that? I wasn't expecting you to ask me to marry you, wasn't even thinking along those lines!'

Jax cocked his proud dark head back, black curling lashes semi-screening his stunning eyes. 'It's done now.'

'Yes,' she acknowledged uncomfortably. 'But I had nothing to do with the blackmail or any idea of what was going on behind the scenes—'

'But it all worked in your favour, all the same,' Jax spelt out with contempt. 'You got to marry into the Antonakos family.'

'Well, from where I'm standing now, on my wedding night, marrying into the Antonakos family is not the triumph it's purported to be!' Lucy shot back at him furiously, an angry flush mantling her cheeks. 'In fact it feels like hell, most particularly when I seem to have a husband who can happily have sex with me and then virtually push me away afterwards!'

'I don't cuddle...*ever*,' Jax stressed.

'Bella needs cuddles so you'll have to revise your rule and I need them too,' Lucy flung back at him rawly. 'So, if you want sex, you'll do it.'

An unholy flare of rage lit up Jax's eyes, lightening them to the brilliance of sea glass gleaming in sunshine. 'I've put up with a hell of a lot but I won't stand for *that*!' he raked back at her, every word slicing through the air like a knife. 'I married you. Be grateful for it because you're getting nothing else from me but the name and the money and a father for your child!'

And as Lucy stood there staring at him, involuntarily unnerved by the sheer force of his rage, she stilled a shiver, appalled by that assurance. 'That's not enough for me,' she muttered shakily.

'Tough,' Jax enunciated with clarity. 'That's all you'll be getting now and in the future.'

With that final statement of punitive intent, Jax strode out of the room and just left her there. Lucy ate through a whole plate of profiteroles and drank coffee and then felt sick. Her whole world had fallen into pieces round her feet and, with it, any sense of security. She lurched into the bathroom where she was sick and when she felt strong enough to stand up again she went for a shower. She knew she would never look at a profiterole again. She would never look at Jax the same way again either for she had just seen a side of him that he had never shown her before.

Now she knew what she really *hadn't* wanted to

know. He hadn't wanted to marry her. In fact he had absolutely hated and thoroughly resented having to marry her. He had suppressed that fury successfully throughout the day and she had provoked him into expressing it by asking for something more: a stupid cuddle, of all things. Her eyes stung and she looked heavenwards as she struggled to control her wildly see-sawing emotions. As far as Jax was concerned he had already given her more than enough: his famous name, his great wealth, his readiness to be a father. *Your* child, he had called Bella, not *our* child.

Why would he care that none of that would be sufficient to make her happy? Why would he care that she was hurting so bad that she wanted to scream with the pain of it? He hadn't asked her to care about him and she didn't know when or how she had started caring again. In Spain it had begun with a smile, a shared look of understanding and discussion, a touch of his hand, six weeks of breathless excitement and more happiness than she had ever experienced before she lost it all again.

But, Jax had reappeared in her life and somehow shreds of those old feelings had taken root again deep down inside her where she didn't explore very often. *She* cared. Much more than he deserved. But was that a true or fair view? Kreon had been vicious and Jax had been strong-armed by family affection into making a sacrifice he didn't want to make. Sadly, Jax wasn't any keener on the concept of marriage than he had ever been.

So, what did that leave her to work with? Lucy blinked back tears and went to clean up her face again, dashing on a little make-up in a desperate hope of relocating a hint of a lingering bridal glow. Unhappily she looked tired and heavy-eyed and pale and even bronzer didn't help. In the end she washed it all off again before she went to look for Jax.

It was the early hours of the morning but everywhere was lit up. She didn't even know what she was going to say to him but she knew that she had to deal with the situation and make something out of the mess Kreon had created. After all, they had Bella to consider and while Lucy was prepared to let go of her own dreams she wasn't prepared to give up on her dream of giving her daughter a normal family life.

She peered into empty room after empty room on the ground floor and then she found him, sprawled with a glass in his hand on a huge fancy padded lounger sited on a wide terrace from which he was watching the sun come up in a glorious multicoloured reflective rainbow over the dark sea far below the house. She hesitated beside the patio doors and then noticed that the phone he was studying was displaying a wedding photo of their daughter. And that discovery softened her and empowered her in a way nothing else could have done into moving forward.

'Jax?' she murmured uncertainly.

'We have to make a go of it…or at least *try*…for her,' Jax breathed in a raw undertone without turning his head.

'Yes…' It was exactly what Lucy wanted to hear and yet she still felt as though her heart were breaking inside her because she knew that she wanted so much more from him.

'I'm drunk,' Jax confided gruffly, wishing he weren't, wishing he were better at handling his own emotional turmoil. 'But drowning your sorrows doesn't help. It only darkens everything more.'

In the tense silence, Lucy dropped down onto the smaller lounger beside his. She didn't recline, she sat on the side of it, rigid-backed and still. A photo lay on the table between them and she lifted it. It was a picture of another little girl, a little girl who looked similar enough to Bella to be her sister.

'Who's this?' she asked worriedly, immediately wondering if Jax had another child.

'My little sister, Tina. The reason why I didn't need to wait on DNA test results to know that Bella was mine,' Jax explained reluctantly.

'I didn't know you had a sister.'

'Hardly anyone knows. When she died it was hushed up,' he muttered.

Lucy frowned. 'Your father's child?'

'No. From my mother's second marriage to an actor. He was half her age. It fell apart quickly. By then Mariana was accidentally pregnant and as a devout Catholic there was no question of her not giving birth. Valentina was born the summer I was twelve. Mariana was determined to keep her a secret because she couldn't bear the idea that her adoring fans would pity her for being abandoned a second time with a child. Unfortunately, she could never keep household staff for long. I looked after the baby that summer—'

'At twelve years old?' Lucy gasped although she was trying hard not to react to what he was telling her. 'Where was your mother?'

'Zonked out of her skull on prescription drugs…the way she always was,' Jax confided grudgingly. 'I got attached to Tina. She was a sweet kid. Mariana got another nanny before I went back to boarding school and for a couple of years everything was fine. I saw Tina in the holidays. And then Mariana had a fight with the nanny the day before she held a pool party…and Tina drowned because nobody was looking after her. My mother was a legendary star and the studio ensured that the death and the burial were dealt with very discreetly.'

'I'm so sorry, Jax,' Lucy whispered shakily.

'The worst part of it was that nobody ever mentioned Tina again. It was like she'd *never* existed.'

Lucy slid to her feet and settled on the big lounger by his side, one arm draping over him protectively.

'I don't cuddle,' he told her argumentatively.

'You're not cuddling,' Lucy assured him. 'I'm cuddling you.'

'I really don't need *or* like that sort of stuff,' he growled.

'Of course you don't. You're just tolerating me to be polite.' Lucy sighed, feeling the rigid tension in his muscles ease and snuggling into the powerful heat of his long, lean frame. 'You have such good manners, Jax.'

'I *do*?' Jax said in surprise, flipping over to face her, green eyes clear as emeralds in the dawn light.

'Most of the time,' Lucy murmured with amusement, colliding with those gorgeous eyes of his, eyes full of so much hunger and uncharacteristic uncertainty. 'I *wasn't* part of the blackmail plan.'

'I know…' Jax rubbed his dark stubbled jaw against her shoulder as if in apology. 'But I think I preferred you not knowing about what your father did.'

'I would've preferred that too,' Lucy admitted. 'But it happened and we have to deal with it.'

Assertive hands tugged at the edges of her robe and the sash before sliding beneath the crisp fabric. 'Naked,' Jax savoured. 'I like, *glyka mou*.'

Lucy bridled. 'I wasn't thinking about that when I came looking for you. I couldn't be bothered poking through another case to find clothes...'

'Shush...' Jax murmured, long brown fingers rubbing with devastating expertise over the most sensitive spot on her entire body to set off a devastating tingling awareness before sliding down below. 'I want you.'

'Here?' she gasped in consternation even as her slender thighs parted and her hips shifted in a rhythm as old as time.

'I sent the staff to bed when we arrived. Poor Theo had kept them all up,' Jax told her. 'I don't need attention twenty-four-seven...except from you.'

Lucy's rosy lips parted on a helpless gasp. 'Twenty-four-seven?' she framed with difficulty.

'I'll make it well worth your while,' Jax promised, crushing her ripe mouth urgently under his as he unzipped his jeans and shifted over her with urgent intent. 'Let's take this back into honeymoon territory...'

And Lucy, at that moment malleable as clay in his expert hands with her body rising and burning and already defencelessly eager, had no objection to that plan. They had weathered the first storm, learned that for both of them Bella was their main focus. That had to be enough, she told herself urgently, a strangled sound escaping her convulsing throat as he pinned her under him and plunged into her with raw, hungry energy.

Pushing for more would only strain their relationship, which meant that *she* had to learn to settle for what she could get. And if that meant forgiving his suspicion that she could have been involved in her father's blackmail, she had to do it. It was early days, she reminded herself.

Yet how could he suspect her of such dishonest behaviour? And why did he assume that her affection was faked? Was his past so littered with unscrupulous lovers that trust was impossible for him?

CHAPTER NINE

'YOU WERE TELLING me about your adoptive parents,' Jax reminded her as they walked along the deserted beach three weeks later, walking Bella between them to keep the little girl steady.

'Was I? They were good people. I was nine years old and very fortunate to get a home at that age,' Lucy declared wryly.

'I imagine you were a very pretty little girl. I'm sure that helped.'

Lucy shrugged, thinking back to that brief three-year period when she had been part of a family. 'They were very academic. When they took me on they were warned that I'd fallen behind at school and straight off they decided to hire tutors for me in every subject.'

Jax frowned. 'Impatient, were they?'

'No, they were trying to help but it put me under a lot of pressure. I was trying very hard to be everything they wanted and then I failed an important exam, which meant I couldn't get into the school they had set their hearts on and they were really disappointed. I don't think I was the right child for them,' she admitted ruefully. 'But when they died in the car crash, all that ended and I went back into care because none of their relatives saw me as being part of the family. At the end of the day and whether you agree with it or not, blood counts.'

'Yes, doesn't it?' Jax agreed, thinking of his late brother, Argo, a good-natured, indolent young man, who with hindsight had been remarkably dissimilar to Heracles and Jax in nature.

Bella tugged her hand free of her mother's and pulled at Jax's jeans to be lifted. He hoisted her high and she giggled and rested her curly head down sleepily on his bare shoulder. Their interaction was so relaxed and natural now, Lucy thought with satisfaction, that it was hard to believe they had only met a month ago.

She and Jax hadn't lasted a whole week on the island without Bella. Lucy had never been separated from her daughter before and had decided a week was unnecessarily long when there was a nanny on the household staff, willing and able to give the honeymooners a break from childcare: Heracles had prepared for every eventuality when he entertained. But the rumour of a private zoo had proved to be just that—a rumour.

The gardens, however, were spectacular although Jax and Lucy had spent more time on the beach, crunching through the pale sand to the water's edge where Lucy, who could not swim, liked to paddle. Never having enjoyed many such opportunities, she was not keen on trusting her body to either a swimming pool or the sea, but Jax had insisted that her learning to swim was a safety issue more than anything else. So, Lucy had braved swimming lessons with Jax, which they had both found equally trying,

Jax because he was naturally impatient and Lucy because she was nervous.

Over the past three weeks they had learned so much about each other, she acknowledged cheerfully. Jax was a morning person, Lucy was a night person. They had spent a wonderful ten days cruising round the Mediterranean on his father's yacht, *Sea Queen*, docking at different islands to see the sights, dine out and shop. She loved to dance and they had enjoyed several really late nights out at clubs. He had bought her loads of clothes in hip boutiques on Crete and Mykonos and he had had a jeweller flown out to Tifnos for her to choose what he deemed to be the basics. A gold watch now encircled a wrist and gold hoops ornamented her ears. She had a diamond pendant, bracelet and earrings as well, which he had referred to as a 'belated' wedding gift. And Bella had a nursery overflowing with toys and clothing and picture books to go with the designer furnishings.

In fact, Lucy believed she already had almost everything she had ever wanted or ever dreamt of having. Jax had spoiled them both. He was marvellous with Bella, far more patient with her than he was with anyone else. He was making a huge effort to be a dad and she appreciated that when so many of his friends, smooth sophisticates whom they had met in the clubs where he was well known, had yet to even settle down. For a man who had never wanted to marry, Jax was settling down into family life remarkably well, she reflected gratefully.

Yet she couldn't forget that Jax was the same guy who had dumped her for 'boring' him two years earlier, the same guy who had seemed perfectly content with her one day and who had then cut her out of his life only days later. That past still made her insecure because she had no faith that she could accurately read Jax and estimate his state of mind with regard to her and their marriage. Of course, he seemed to do and say all the right things, but then he had done that before in Spain and look how that had ended!

'I'm hungry…' Jax curved a hand to Lucy's shoulder and steered her up the beach towards the buggy that would waft them up the steep hill. 'And I think our daughter needs a nap…and maybe I need one too, *glyka mou*.'

Lucy coloured. Heat licked at her feminine core as Jax sent her a glittering green glance of sensual enquiry. Dampness gathered between her legs, anticipation rising because that side of their relationship was outrageously healthy. He still wasn't doing the cuddling thing the way she wanted. No, with Jax what might start out as a cuddle invariably turned into sex. He said he couldn't be that close to her and touch her without wanting to get naked and energetic. There was nowhere they hadn't made love. They had indulged on the beach, in the pool, in the pine forest, in the labyrinthine privacy of the lush gardens, but most often in the delicious comfort of their own bed. The simmering flare-ups of passion that wound through their days felt so natural to her. It was as if Jax couldn't get enough of her, a thought she kept tactfully to herself, and that made her feel safer. She couldn't help viewing sex as a barometer to gauge the health of their marriage because Jax certainly wasn't any keener to discuss such things than he had ever been.

'It's those freckles. I can't resist them,' Jax said huskily, skimming the bridge of her nose with a teasing finger.

Lucy laughed because she hated her freckles, seeing them as imperfections, but Jax thought they looked delightfully natural, which of course they were. Did anyone draw in freckles? She thought not and smiled as they piled into the buggy. A pang of sadness infiltrated her mood because the honeymoon as such was almost over. Jax was meeting with Heracles about some big project in Athens the following morning and she was accompanying him because she planned to take Bella to visit her father and Iola. She was hoping that the passage of time since her wedding day and Bella's noisy presence would make the occasion less tense and awkward.

In actuality, Jax wasn't looking forward to the next day either. He intended to confront his father with the file Heracles had had sent to him on Lucy two years before. From what he had so far managed to establish the file was full of inaccuracies and outright lies and he needed to know if those lies had been a deliberate attempt to break up their relationship or the simple product of a lazy investigator and a case of mistaken identity. He could scarcely censure Kreon's ethics if his own father was guilty of the same lack of moral scruple when it came to getting the result he wanted most.

Even so, he still could not have said which answer he wanted to hear from Heracles because if the older man actually *believed* the contents of that file, it outraged Jax in a way he could not rationally explain. Yet he, more than anyone, knew Lucy was far from perfect. His mind skipped superfast over that acknowledgement and tucked the memory of that alleyway encounter back into the box where he kept it locked away. She had made an unforgivable mistake and he *had* to live with that...for Bella's sake, he told himself urgently, *only* for Bella's sake.

Bella's nanny took the little girl off to bed. Lucy went for a shower because she was hot and sandy and she wasn't at all surprised when Jax stepped into the shower with her, all lithe, wet bronzed skin and rippling muscles. She ran her hands up appreciatively over his torso and as the water jets shot at them, sprinkling even their faces with droplets, his mouth came crashing passionately down on hers. He tasted her with raw driving need and as always the strength of his hunger for her disconcerted her. He gathered her slippery body up and pinned her against the cold tiles, lifting her thighs round his waist while rocking and grinding against the tender triangle of flesh at the heart of her.

That fast she wanted him intolerably and with every probing plunge of his tongue she wanted him more. Evocative little noises were wrenched from low in her throat as skilled fingers teased and played to prepare her for his entrance. And then he tilted her back and thrust into her with vigour while she clung to his shoulders, her ankles wrapped round him. He grunted with raw male satisfaction, his hand supporting her hips as he pounded her yielding body with delicious force. Excitement writhed through Lucy in an unstoppable surge and she reached her peak with an involuntary cry, convulsive waves of exquisite pleasure rippling through her lower body as an orgasmic flush spread over her sun-dappled skin.

'I didn't use a condom,' Jax groaned in her ear as

he slowly lowered her back to her own feet. 'Is that likely to be a problem?'

'Hopefully not,' Lucy muttered after doing some quick calculations and without looking directly at him as she stepped out of the shower and grabbed a towel. 'It's the wrong time of the month.'

What had he meant by that question? Was he asking her if she was willing to get pregnant again? Or was he worrying that she *would* conceive? And for that matter, was she willing to take that risk? Lucy thought not. She had not had an easy pregnancy the first time around and was not in a hurry to do it again, particularly when she did not yet feel secure with Jax. Even so, if she did conceive she would still welcome and love her baby.

But then what would it take for her to feel truly secure with Jax? she asked herself. Perhaps she was her own worst enemy and had quite unrealistic expectations of a marriage in which only one of them loved. She might not like the reality but their relationship was bound to be unbalanced with one of them wanting and hoping for more than the other.

'Did you know that the contents of that file were a complete fiction?'

'What do you want me to tell you?' Heracles slapped the file on Lucy back onto his desk and sighed heavily. 'I will not lie. I did what I felt I *had* to do.'

Sharply disconcerted, Jax tensed even more, anger roaring through his tall, powerful frame because he had somehow expected the older man to try and evade his very direct question. 'Why did you think you *had* to do anything? Why did you even think that it was your place to interfere? It wasn't as though I was talking about marrying her—'

'Jax…in the space of two weeks, you flew back to Spain *five* times to see her,' Heracles traded defiantly. 'That was enough for me to view her as a serious contender for something and when I discovered that she was the daughter of Kreon Thiarkis, well, to be really blunt…that was that. Thiarkis is a slippery customer, always has been, always will be and I will not apologise for not wanting a criminal's daughter involved with my family.'

'I know Kreon's history,' Jax interposed harshly. 'I know what he is and I can understand your concern but I was twenty-six years old, *not* a teenager, and you had no right to interfere.'

The older man stood his ground. 'I know I had no right but I didn't care. Years ago I watched Thiarkis charm my deluded first wife into paying for his legal representation in court when he was charged with fraud—'

'Two years ago, Lucy hadn't even *met* her father,' Jax pointed out rawly. 'What I had with her was our business alone, nothing to do with your ongoing distaste for Thiarkis. And far be it from me to say a word in Kreon's defence but for over thirty years he held onto a letter that would have made his fortune had he sold it to the press…'

Jax settled the letter Lucy had given him down on the desk. 'Your first wife confessed her sins on paper during her last days.'

His father turned grey before his eyes and dropped down suddenly into his office chair, studying the letter as if it were a cobra likely to strike out at him. 'Sofia was never discreet,' he muttered heavily. 'Are you telling me I have to thank Thiarkis for his restraint?'

'No,' Jax breathed in a driven undertone, having decided not to reveal the secret of Kreon's blackmail. 'But it's time you came to terms with the fact that he is Lucy's father and stopped visiting your experiences and your resentments on *my* life. I'm not Argo—'

'I know you're not,' Heracles acknowledged grimly. 'Argo always did as he was told and you *won't*, which is why I went behind your back in the first place. I assumed she would be wrong for you.'

'She's not,' Jax bit out curtly. 'But because of that file I treated her badly and now I have to tell her why.'

Heracles compressed his lips in disapproval. '*Do* you? I don't think that's a good idea. A wise man shares nothing with his wife but a bed.'

'Three wives and you *still* don't know better?' Jax derided with seething bite. 'Well, I do know better and I will not tolerate your meddling in my life. If you ever do anything like this again, I'm *out*.'

'You can't mean that,' Heracles breathed in consternation.

'I do. Blood counts but family counts more and you were out of my life for too many years to be considered family in the same way that I consider my wife and my daughter. They come first…*always*.'

Simmering with angry frustration, Jax sat in his limo in the heavy Athens traffic mulling over that confrontation. Heracles had finally apologised and at least his father had at last told him the truth. Jax hated secrets. He had grown up in an atmosphere of secrecy, continually urged never to tell anyone that his mother was 'ill', pregnant or involved with a man. As a boy, he had reacted to those warnings by deciding to never tell anyone at school that the famous Spanish movie star was his mother. It had been a rather pathetic ploy considering that the name Antonakos was too well known and just about everyone who was anyone knew his father had divorced Mariana for having an affair with one of her co-stars. But the practice of keeping his thoughts and feelings and personal details strictly private had been taught to him when he was very young and had become a habit he couldn't shake…until he'd met Lucy and told her things he had never told anyone before.

And if he was honest that experience had totally unnerved him two years earlier. He had seen that he was veering into dangerous territory and had feared getting too involved with a woman again. *Feared?* No, obviously he had been in no hurry to admit that to himself. His mother had been frighteningly volatile, constantly ranging between high and low moods while using drugs as a crutch to get her through the day. Freed by Mariana's death from the powerful conviction that it was *his* responsibility to look after her, Jax had decided that emotion was a weakness and that a sensible man steered clear of it. Most of the time that had worked very well for him.

Until he'd met Lucy…

Until he'd met Bella…

Jax poured himself a stiff drink and drank it down. He *had* to tell Lucy. How could he *not* tell her? He reminded himself that she had married him even after what he had done in Spain. He reminded himself that she seemed happy. He didn't have to love her to make her happy. Hadn't he already proved that? Together they had the fathers from hell. Not her fault, not his fault either. He would give her the facts. She would be angry and hurt but she would forgive him. Jax knew he wasn't the forgiving type but he was convinced from recent experience that Lucy *was*. They had signed up to be a family for Bella's benefit. And that would be Lucy's bottom line because more than anything else, Jax reminded himself doggedly, after a life of turmoil Lucy craved security.

And he offered security, he offered a *lot* of security, he reflected with growing assurance. But it still really bothered him that she wasn't clingier and more open with him. The Lucy he remembered in Spain had been distinctly needy and clingy and, although he ran a mile from that trait in other women, for some reason he had liked that attribute in Lucy as much as he had liked her once flaky tell-all chatter. He had liked it when he was the first person she looked for in a room, when he was the only one she really smiled at or noticed, when she wrapped herself round him all night as though she was afraid he might attempt an escape. He had liked being told that he was loved even if in the end it had all turned out to be a lie.

But she didn't do those things any more even though he wanted her to. She was wary. Of course she was, he conceded, struggling to be fair, so, putting the truth out there was a sensible move, he told himself squarely. He would tell her what had really happened and she would forgive him because that was what Lucy did. And what choice would she have? a more cynical voice enquired. After all, she had betrayed his trust too…

* * *

'He's treating you well?' Kreon prompted while Iola was playing in the garden with Bella.

'Yes,' Lucy told her father flatly. 'But I won't discuss Jax with you.'

'A wife should be loyal to her husband,' Kreon remarked equably. 'I simply wanted you to be happy—'

'I can only be happy with a man who is happy to *be* with me,' Lucy countered drily, resisting the urge to remind him that he hadn't thought of that angle.

But with Jax being the very practical but reserved male that he was, he was more likely to make the best of a bad job than try to wriggle out of the commitment, particularly when his daughter was involved. Lucy showered and changed while telling herself that she had absolutely nothing to complain about. Whatever else, she was married to the love of her life. There was nothing she could do about the fact that she had only gained a wedding ring through her father's dirty tricks. But she knew that somewhere in the back of Jax's astute brain he would probably *always* associate her with her father's treachery and would never quite forgive her for his lack of choice and loss of freedom.

'He gave in to me very easily. That is *not* an Antonakos trait,' Kreon argued.

'Obviously he cares about his father.'

'I believe he cares more about you.'

Unconvinced by that startling claim, Lucy returned to the city villa with nerves run ragged by the strain of pretending for Iola's benefit that everything was fine between her father and her. She had been surprised that Jax hadn't objected to her visiting Kreon and Iola and then relieved because her father was still her father even though he was imperfect. *Imperfect?* Manipulative, sneaky, quick to jump on a golden opportunity even if it entailed blackmail, Lucy's brain added unhappily. But until she had met her father and learned about the existence of her sisters, she had believed that her father was her only living relative and his support and acceptance had meant a great deal to her. That he was capable of going to such lengths to secure a very rich husband for her still devastated her because of course it had to make a difference to her marriage and the light in which Jax saw her.

If Kreon hadn't interfered, who knew what might have happened? All right, they would clearly not have got married, she allowed ruefully, but at least Jax wouldn't have felt forced into doing something he didn't want to do.

Lucy had only just finished drying her hair when Jax strode into the bedroom. He paused for a second, appreciating the sight of her small slender figure in a summery blue dress, tumbling ringlets framing her piquant face. 'You look ridiculously pretty,' he heard himself say stiltedly, and he almost winced at that ill-timed opener because he had come upstairs to give her the investigation file.

Lucy angled her head to one side and gave him a questioning look. 'You never pay me compliments. What's wrong?'

He had called her pretty, not beautiful, and she was more than happy with that, well aware that her looks weren't on the beauty level. In marrying Jax, she had boxed above her weight because *he* was the beautiful one in their relationship, standing there in his exquisitely tailored silver-grey suit, his stunning bone structure accentuated by a shadow of black stubble, gorgeous green eyes glittering like stars in his lean bronzed face.

'Never?' Jax was taken aback by her claim, only belatedly recognising that she was right. He thought such things but he very rarely voiced them out loud. 'I have something for you to read.'

He looked so very serious that Lucy's heart gave a sudden lurch inside her chest. 'OK,' she said apprehensively.

He extended the file. 'My father sent this to me two years ago in Spain. It's why I didn't turn up that last night.'

Lucy grasped the slim file and sank down heavily on the foot of the bed. 'Your father?' she queried with a bemused frown.

'He had discovered who your father was and apparently he was determined to break us up,' Jax explained flatly. 'The file is filled with what I now know to be lies about you.'

Lucy lowered her shaken gaze to the file, thoroughly off balanced by what he was revealing because it was coming at her out of nowhere. Suddenly he was talking about what had happened in Spain and admitting that he hadn't ditched her simply because he had got bored. 'You *now* know...?' she questioned with an uncertain questioning glance.

'I had my own investigation carried out,' he admitted smoothly.

And Lucy was even more shaken at the enormous amount of stuff that Jax had been hiding from her, not to mention the lowering reality of just how much his father had not wanted her in his family. She swallowed hard and, breathing in bracingly, she opened the file and straight away she could not credit what she was reading. It was a seriously exaggerated character assassination in print, from the outrageous allegation that she had convictions for drug dealing and soliciting sex to the fact that her age was quoted as being twenty-five.

'But how could you possibly have believed *any* of this?' she heard herself whisper with incredulous emphasis.

'It was in the early stages of my new relationship with my father and I trusted him. I had no reason to be suspicious of his motives because I had no knowledge of his acquaintance with your father or his dislike of him,' he pointed out flatly.

Lucy shook her head very slowly, an almost dazed light in her luminous blue eyes as she focussed on him. 'You misunderstood my question. I'm not asking why you believed your father but how on earth you could believe that kind of nonsense about *me*? Soliciting *sex*? I was a virgin when we met!' she reminded him with sudden resentful heat. 'And you knew that!'

Jax compressed his lips, wearing the aspect of a male who would have liked to be anywhere but where he was at that moment. He shifted his feet uneasily. 'A woman can fool a man over stuff like that. She can pretend,' he began uncomfortably.

'Then you must have assumed my acting ability rivalled your mother's!' Lucy slotted in a little shakily because anger was rising now to cut through the shock of what she was learning. 'I just don't know what to say about all this...*stuff*!' she selected jaggedly, tossing the file down on the floor in disgust. 'I thought you *knew* me—'

'I thought I knew you too until I read that file,' Jax admitted curtly. 'But I had no good reason then to suspect my father of setting me up.'

'So, you're telling me then that he was responsible for me losing my job?'

'I didn't go into that with him… I was far too angry,' Jax confessed. 'But it's probable that he *was* responsible for that and for the manner in which you were treated as you were put off the yacht. If I had stayed long enough to get into that kind of detail I probably would have *hit* him…'

'Oh…' Lucy was a long way from forgiving him for having had so little faith in her but she was certainly mollified by that little speech.

'You were pregnant,' Jax pointed out, still stuck on that offence with an anger she could see making his lean, darkly handsome features rigid. 'You could have been seriously hurt. He could have killed his own grandchild…we could have lost Bella!'

Lucy warmed up to him a little more in response to that additional really quite emotional exclamation. Jax had only known her for six weeks in Spain. Six weeks and a handful of dates. They had finally become intimate during the final two weeks of that time frame. Why would he have distrusted his father? The father then riding high on the wave of finally deciding to accept and welcome the younger son he had once ignored?

Lucy felt that she had to be fair to Jax. After all, she had not distrusted Kreon when she first came to Greece, had she? It occurred to her that Jax was probably feeling much as she had felt on their wedding day, angry and hurt and defensive while wondering how someone he cared about and respected could have done such a thing to him.

'I think the very least you could have done was speak to me about the file and give me the chance to answer those allegations,' Lucy told him firmly. 'There is no excuse whatsoever for you failing to tell me about that file two years ago.'

And Jax's long, lean, powerful physique went rigid, shoulders squaring, legs straightening. 'Actually there is...'

'No, there's not.' Lucy could understand and forgive a great deal but he could not justify his complete failure to tell her what was going on either in the past or the present. 'You didn't even send me a text in Spain to tell me we were finished, for goodness' sake!' she exclaimed.

'I had my reasons,' Jax breathed in a raw undertone, his eyes gleaming like polished gems.

'Unacceptable reasons.' Lucy refused to give way. She often gave in to Jax because he had a very forceful personality but she knew she couldn't go through life without disagreeing with him occasionally. 'You owed me an explanation of some kind—'

'I owed you *nothing*!' Jax shot at her with sudden derision. 'I did come to see you the night after I received that file.'

Her brow had furrowed because she was beginning to feel a little lost in the dialogue, as though she had misinterpreted some crucial sentence. 'You *didn't* come to see me—'

'And do you know why?' Jax's hands knotted into

fists because he felt like a volcano about to spew lava and somewhere in the back of his mind lurked a tiny voice asking him if he *really* wanted to say what he was about to say. But Jax didn't back down, had never learned *how* to back down. He only knew how to come out of a corner fighting and how to win. He had had a hell of a day and it wasn't getting better the way it was supposed to, it was only getting *worse* and that thought did nothing to cool his temper. He had done nothing wrong with Lucy, he was, in his own opinion, the injured party. He was not a vengeful man but he would not be accused of something he wasn't responsible for.

'If I did, I wouldn't be arguing with you or trying to get you to see my point of view,' Lucy parried.

'I bet you don't even remember that night...'

'I remember it very well,' Lucy admitted, lifting her chin. 'What's this all about, Jax? I'm getting confused—'

His eyes narrowed, his mouth flattening. 'I drove over to the bar and before I could get out of my car, I saw you walking down the alleyway in your red dress—'

'It wasn't me you saw,' Lucy sliced in thinly. When Jax had failed to turn up to see her the night before Lucy had stayed in her attic room after doing her shift, frantically hoping that Jax would magically appear with an explanation. Like a child waiting for Santa Claus she had refused to believe he wouldn't show up eventually and she had been terrified of somehow missing him. She had had that much faith in him, that much *trust*...

'It was you. You were with a man—'

'You're mistaken,' Lucy told him confidently.

'I followed you because I assumed you were heading for the entrance that led up to your room but you weren't,' Jax informed her stonily. 'You stayed outside to have sex with the man you were with against the wall.'

Her lashes fluttered up on disbelieving bright blue eyes and she stared back at him. 'You think that I had sex with some guy in the alley?' she demanded with a revulsion she couldn't hide. 'Are you kidding me?'

Lean, strong face shuttered and forbidding, Jax stood his ground because naturally he hadn't expected her to own up to her behaviour. 'You know I'm not kidding and what I saw that night is why you never heard from me again. There was no point in showing you that file when you were already with another man,' he proclaimed harshly. 'I don't need to apologise or make excuses for not approaching you again.'

'I agree,' Lucy said with wooden diction, shattered inside herself but holding it all together out of pride. 'If I had been with another man that soon, you owed me nothing. Clearly, it suited you very well to assume that night that the girl in the alley was me—'

'And what's that supposed to mean?' Jax shot at her suspiciously.

'Well, you'd seen that file and learned that your precious father did not approve of me. It was really incredibly convenient for you that in spite of everything you knew about me you decided to accept that file and *assume* that I was the sort of young woman who would have sex in an alley.'

Lucy could feel her cheekbones ache with the strain of keeping her face composed but there was a much deeper ache of pain inside her chest. She knew he didn't love her. She knew he had never loved her. That wounding knowledge had chipped away at her upbeat outlook on their marriage and she had fought it off, telling herself to settle sensibly for what she could get. But for the first time ever, Lucy decided that Jax was *bad* for her.

Never mind the Antonakos fame, the money and the gorgeous looks. Two years back, she had told Jax that she loved him and she *had*, but he had given nothing back, not the words nor any other form of commitment. He had held back from her, he had always held back from her and now she finally knew why. But she deserved better. She deserved a man who would, at the very least, refuse to *believe* that she would have sex in public with some chance-met stranger. And Jax hadn't had that faith in her and probably never would have. A horrible sense of emptiness spread inside her. *Her* loving him wasn't enough.

'It *was* you. I recognised the dress,' Jax bit out, exasperated by the stretching silence and the strange way she was staring at him.

'Yes…you may have done but it wasn't me *wearing* the dress,' Lucy countered tightly. 'I loaned it to Tara that night because she had a hot date and I imagine she was fooling around in the alley because she could hardly bring a man back to the room we shared when I was there. Not everyone has a private room or a yacht available for these things…'

Jax froze. 'It *couldn't* have been her! Why would she have been wearing the dress I bought you?'

Lucy sent him a weary glance of exasperation. 'Because we shared our clothes. We didn't have much but what we had, we *shared*. Half the clothes you saw me wear that summer belonged to Tara.'

'It couldn't have been her,' Jax repeated again doggedly, struggling to remember her friend before dimly recalling the much more worldly blonde whom Lucy had worked and lived with.

Lucy shrugged a shoulder in a jerky movement. 'Well, it doesn't much matter after this length of time, does it?' she traded.

'It matters to me. And it *must* matter to you,' Jax told her with assurance.

'No, it doesn't,' Lucy responded heavily.

Jax hovered and clenched his teeth hard. He wanted it dealt with and then never mentioned again. But could it have been Tara in that stupid dress? It had been dark and Tara had had long blonde hair too. Between the street lights and the shadows, it was possible that he had been mistaken. And if he had been mistaken, it would be the very first time in Jax's life that he would ever be *grateful* to have made a mistake. Didn't she appreciate that? Didn't she understand what believing she would behave that way had done to *him*? Refusing to look at him, Lucy was staring at the tiled floor instead as if she were expecting it to start showing a movie and frustration racked Jax's tall powerful frame. *Women!* She had gone into a weird mood now and he would probably get nothing more out of her.

'I have a meeting. I was planning to reschedule it and take us back to Tifnos—'

'No, go to your meeting,' Lucy urged, her throat convulsing, and she still wouldn't let herself look at him because she didn't want what she felt in her heart to show.

'We can fly back in the morning,' Jax commented. 'The timing would probably suit Bella better than a late flight.'

Lucy listened to the door close on his exit and continued to sit there with tears rolling silently down her cheeks. Jax had just shown her how he really thought of her and how he saw her and it was…it *was* ugly, uglier than she could bear or forgive or comprehend. To think that all those weeks on the island he had believed that she had been unfaithful to him and yet he hadn't said a word, hadn't even given her the chance to explain or defend herself. It was so cruel, so unfair but you couldn't change a man, couldn't alter what went on inside his head.

Jax didn't trust her, had never trusted even a word she'd said. He had been her one and only lover and he couldn't even believe that. She had been too young and immature at nineteen to recognise how cynical and distrustful Jax was. She had realised that he was pretty jealous and possessive but her awareness had gone no deeper than that. She thought of him seeing Tara in that grubby alley and believing it was her and a stifled sob of pain and regret and humiliation was wrenched from her. That hurt so much and it seemed with Jax at that moment that he did nothing but hurt and disillusion her. She didn't want to stay married to a man like that, she *couldn't* stay married to a man who thought so little of her…

And when the wave of conflicting emotions began to tear at Lucy more than she could stand she dug out her phone and rang her sister, Polly, desperately needing a shoulder to cry on.

Polly was a terrific listener. Lucy let the whole

sorry story of her relationship with Jax and Kreon spill out and, very satisfyingly, Polly was even more appalled by the alleyway accusation than Lucy had been.

'Come and stay with us, Lucy,' Polly suggested warmly. 'You need a holiday. I know you felt that you were happy with him at first but Jax doesn't seem to appreciate you the way a husband should. It's possible that he resents you for what your father did.'

To Lucy in that instant the prospect of walking away into a different environment shone like a bright welcoming light. 'I don't even know where you live, Polly,' she pointed out unevenly.

'In a country called Dharia. It's one of the Gulf States,' Polly explained.

Lucy was flummoxed by that news. 'I don't know how I'd get there or even how I'd get away from here.'

'Don't you worry about that,' Polly told her assertively. 'I will arrange everything. If you leave tonight, we'll be having breakfast together in the morning and I can get hold of Ellie and she could be here by this weekend. We really do want to meet you and your daughter, Lucy.'

'Leave…*tonight*?' Lucy gasped in astonishment, wondering if it would be wrong of her to take her daughter with her as well and then deciding that, just at that moment, losing both of them was what Jax deserved for his distrust.

'I don't think you should waste any more time on the Antonakos family. They don't love or value you but we *will*.'

And Polly's enthusiasm was the deciding factor for Lucy, who usually took more time to decide anything of a serious nature. But at least she didn't feel like crying any longer, she registered with relief, because crying after Jax had gone over her like a steam roller with his nasty allegations seemed feeble. Jax didn't want her and his father didn't want her in his precious family and her own father had seriously disappointed her. A fresh start and the friendship of her sisters looked a lot more promising than her current situation.

'Tonight will be fine,' she assured Polly. 'I'll start packing. I suppose it will be very hot?'

'Yes, but the pal—er…my place is air-conditioned,' her sister informed her.

CHAPTER TEN

JAX WAS STUNNED. He ran through the empty wardrobes again as if he expected to find Lucy curled up below the empty coat hangers in hiding. He wandered back to the empty nursery, stared into the even emptier cot and then hurriedly strode back downstairs again.

'Take me through it again,' he urged Zenas jerkily, struggling to master the kind of emotions he generally never allowed to see the light of day. Emotions like panic, fear and insecurity that could tear a man to pieces as they had once torn apart the boy he had been. Having frequently lived those emotions in childhood and adolescence, he had sworn never to give them space again. But there they were still inside him, he discovered, just waiting their chance to jump on him and either paralyse him or urge him to make fundamentally stupid decisions…

Zenas breathed in deep, a wary eye on Jax, who was visibly pale and stressed. 'A diplomatic limousine with a foreign flag drew up. An Arab man in a suit and a crowd of heavies got out. The man had diplomatic credentials but he spoke neither Greek nor English and was unwilling to engage with my questions. Your wife opened the door with your daughter in her arms. She had a stack of suitcases waiting in the hall—'

'And you just let her *go*...?' Jax repeated incredulously. 'You let a bunch of foreigners *kidnap*—'

'She wasn't kidnapped. She went of her own free will,' Zenas told him apologetically. 'We followed the car to the airport where the whole party proceeded through VIP diplomatic channels to which we were denied access. From what we can establish a private jet flew Mrs Antonakos and the little girl to Dharia.'

The name of that country rang a bell of familiarity with Jax. His brow furrowed. There had been some connection. *Thee mou*, his one-time business partner, Rio Benedetti, was married to the sister of the Queen of Dharia...who was coincidentally called... Polly, just like Lucy's long-lost sister. No, he shook away the suspicion until he thought about that slick diplomatic kidnapping—he refused to accept that Lucy had willingly left him—and then the suspicion lodged deep.

Lucy was making a statement, he told himself grimly. He should do nothing and wait for her to get in touch. Lucy would not walk out on him, he told himself. She was annoyed with him. There was nothing he could do about that. He was merely paying the price for having finally told her the truth and if she didn't like the truth, what was he supposed to do about it? Satisfied that he had reached a mature and measured decision, Jax poured himself a stiff drink.

Within the hour he was back pacing the empty marital bedroom. He should not have been imagining Lucy there because they had never yet spent a night in his Athens villa. Yet inexplicably memories of Lucy were everywhere around him. He pictured her on the bed, the softness of her pouty lips, the delicate paleness of her skin, the silky fall of her hair running between his fingers. He snatched in a stark breath. There was a tiny spiralling blonde hair on the dressing table and the scent of the perfume he had bought her in Mykonos still lingered on the air. The bedding was still creased from where she had sat while they'd talked that very afternoon.

Talked? Well, she hadn't really talked, he acknowledged tardily, indeed had been remarkably quiet for a chatterbox. With hindsight it became clear to Jax that she had been upset, *seriously* upset. And he hadn't picked up on that. How could he *not* have picked up on that?

Still locked in the mindset he had had for two long years, Jax had continued to feel like the victim of her treachery. But what if there had been no betrayal in the first place? What if that ridiculous story about sharing clothes was genuine? What if he had abandoned her in Spain two years earlier without any excuse for doing so? And what if he had blown up his marriage over a stupid red dress and a mindless need to finally confront Lucy?

Jax paced, feeling in dire need of another drink but knowing he shouldn't have one when his brain was already leapfrogging all over the place. Lucy and Bella were gone and he could live with that, couldn't he? A divorce, shared custody, parental access…?

Suddenly feeling very short of breath, Jax froze. There was a tightness in his chest and a dryness in his throat and his heart was thundering in his ears. No, he couldn't live with that option, he decided with dizzy abruptness.

And as so often before when life challenged Jax, anger came to his rescue. He wasn't letting the queen of some tinpot country steal his wife and child! Lucy had been lured away from him and misled and he was going to get her back pronto where she belonged, which was in Greece with him.

'By the sound of it, Jax really doesn't know how to deal with the emotional stuff,' Ellie remarked with a wry smile on her lips.

'That's an understatement,' Polly inputted with a sniff. 'That alley business…accusing her of *that*—'

Ellie laughed and Lucy looked at her red-headed sister in surprise. 'But don't you see? It was all still as fresh as yesterday for Jax, which tells you that he never got over it. Two years on he's still agonising over that alley…yet he still decides to *stay* married to you, he takes you on a honeymoon, acts happy, treats you decently in every other way. It took the equivalent of torture to get the story about the alley out of him because he's *ashamed* that he still wants you, regardless of what he supposedly thinks you did. No, really, Lucy…you can learn a lot from reading between the lines.'

Lucy smiled at that more optimistic viewpoint even if she didn't quite believe in it. She coiled back into her comfortable corner of the sofa in the beautiful room with its impossibly high domed ceiling and wished that she could see what Ellie appeared to see in Jax's behaviour. Her two sisters were so different. Polly was warm and caring, almost motherly, while Ellie was very clever and sympathetic and their children, *her* nephews and nieces, she noted with pleasure, were simply gorgeous.

Polly's boys, Karim and Hassan and Ellie's daughter, Teresina were playing out in the shaded courtyard on trikes. Ellie was feeding her baby boy, Olly, with a bottle while Polly was nursing her newborn daughter, Haifa. Bella was watching the older children scoot around on their bikes while chasing a ball. Karim got off his bike simply to move Bella back a little with her toys, looking out for the toddler in the most considerate way for a small boy.

Lucy was shaken to admit that she would have been crazily happy in her sister's gorgeous royal palace were it not for Jax's absence. The discovery that her eldest sister was a ruling queen with her husband, Rashad, and that Ellie was the working wife of a fabulously wealthy Italian had certainly helped to take Lucy's mind off her own problems. The three women had sat up into the early hours the first night they were all together, exchanging histories, talking about the three rings they had inherited and catching up on a lifetime of different experiences.

Talking about Jax had come later and had sent Lucy's mood plummeting again because, even though she still felt that walking out on Jax had been the only thing she could do, there was a hollow place inside her where her heart had been ripped out.

In the back of her mind lurked the conviction that Jax had been hurt so much in life just like herself yet they dealt with emotions in very different ways. Jax buried his, hid troubling issues and lived in virtual denial of his feelings. Lucy wore everything on the surface and picked herself up again emotionally no matter how often she was kicked. But she hadn't reacted that way at her last encounter with Jax, she acknowledged.

He had hurt her too much and for the first time ever with Jax she had hidden her feelings as well.

In a sense that had been cruel of her and hitting him over the head with something large and heavy might have been kinder. Feelings had to be shoved in Jax's face like placards for him to read them. He had probably been very shocked by her departure and he was probably furious that she had taken their daughter with her. But he still wouldn't understand *why* she had left, which bothered her. The truth was all that had mattered to Jax and he had finally told it without grasping the damage he was doing. He had expected her to excuse him for past events soured by their fathers' machinations. He had not been capable of realising that she had been devastated because everything he had said had spelled out the message that he had never loved, respected or even understood her. How could she possibly love someone like that?

'He's a man. He might as well be from another planet,' Ellie mocked quietly. 'Rio was exactly the same, hiding things, holding onto the past—'

'Rashad too,' Polly admitted ruefully. 'So, perhaps Jax *could* be rehabilitated…'

Lucy studied her linked hands, unable to imagine Jax budging a stubborn inch from his own convictions.

The door opened, framing Rashad, the King of Dharia. Tall and very handsome, he flashed a smile at his wife. 'Polly…we have a visitor. He thinks we kidnapped his wife. What would you have to say to that?'

'Lucy's my sister and I didn't kidnap her…I offered her sanctuary,' Polly declared loftily.

'Sanctuary?' Rashad echoed, visibly appreciating

that choice of word. 'I don't think I would employ that particular word with Jax, Lucy.'

'Jax is here?' Lucy flew off the sofa as though jet-propelled and then stilled, colour rising in her cheeks below her sisters' interested scrutiny.

'Let the rehabilitation commence,' Ellie remarked softly.

'*Have* I been interfering?' Polly asked worriedly.

'No, I was hugely grateful for the support,' Lucy told her warmly.

Lucy couldn't think straight. It had taken Jax less than forty-eight hours to come out to Dharia and she was sharply disconcerted. In the back of her mind, she had feared that he would let her go and write off their marriage as a mistake. After all, how could he possibly *want* to stay married to a woman whom he had such a low opinion of? But then letting her go could well be what he had arrived to discuss, she reasoned unhappily.

Jax was in no better mood after his long flight to find himself in a room decorated like something out of an Arabian Nights' fantasy, which dovetailed beautifully with the royal palace of Dharia. Rashad, the King, had seemed fairly normal though, acknowledging that he too would have been very 'put out' to find his wife and child had staged a vanishing act.

And then Rashad had murmured, 'But now that you're part of the family I should warn you that when the sisters get together, they plot and plan. You're either with them *or* against them.'

'You're my brother-in-law...well, *half*-brother-in-law,' Jax adjusted, recognising that the three sisters had all had different fathers.

'They don't think of each other as half anything,' Rashad cautioned him.

'Catching up?' another voice interposed, a voice that Jax recognised and he tensed, slowly turning round to arrange his thoughts before meeting the eyes of his former business partner, Rio Benedetti. 'Well, isn't this a small world?' he breathed uncomfortably.

'Relax,' the Italian billionaire urged. 'I ran into Franca last year and she brought me up to speed on past events. No disrespect to Franca intended, but I had the lucky escape and *you* had—?'

Jax winced. 'I owe you a wholehearted apology for what happened but let's not talk about it,' he retorted wryly of that sobering experience.

'Let's not,' Rio agreed, leaning closer. 'A word of advice though,' he added in a rueful undertone. 'The word "alley" will be etched on your gravestone…'

Momentarily, Jax froze as if a gun had been angled at him and faint colour rose over his sculpted cheekbones. 'Is that so?'

'The sisters don't keep secrets,' Rio imparted. 'Nothing is too sacred to be discussed. Cross one and you cross all three and none of them are batting for you.'

That was information that Jax could well have done without. He knew he had messed up but everyone else knowing how badly he had messed up made him feel worse. He had had forty-eight hours in which to think and he had done more thinking within that forty-eight hours than he had done in all his twenty-nine years. And having reached obvious conclusions, had even decided what to say.

But Jax's prepared speech flew right out of his head

when Lucy walked into the suite he was wafted off to. Lucy was wearing a long flowing dress in shades of blue and it fluttered round her as she moved and just seeing her again, just looking at her again, made Jax feel stuff he couldn't suppress any longer.

'I came because…' he began.

Jax looking gorgeous as usual, Lucy was noting, striving to be cool and composed after Ellie had advised her to play hard to get. But she couldn't play hard to get with Jax, which was the crux of her problem where he was concerned: she loved him. She had always loved him and what had been rather insta-love in Spain when she barely knew him had turned into something much deeper and more binding the second time around. Jax might be hopeless at some things, like talking about feelings and paying compliments, but he was very, *very* good at other things.

'Yes…you were saying?' Lucy prompted, striving to take control of their meeting.

Jax raked a deeply frustrated hand through his tousled black hair, green eyes glinting from below black lashes, and her heart jumped. 'I don't know what I was going to say. I had it all planned out but now it's gone. This is all new to me,' he muttered in a sudden surge. 'But the only really important thing I have to say is that I love you and I need you and I want you to come home with me…'

And just like that and with the unexpectedness of an explosion, Jax stole the wind from Lucy's sails. She didn't have time to try and work out how to play hard to get. He took the breath from her lungs and the arguments from her brain because what he had just said was what she felt as if she had been waiting all her life to hear.

'I've never said those words to anyone else,' Jax admitted gruffly as the silence dragged. 'I married you, not because of your father's blackmail, but because somewhere deep down inside me I *wanted* to be married to you. My head was telling me I didn't want to get married but my instincts were pushing me in a very different direction. Is that weird?'

'No...' Lucy almost whispered the word, scared to move, scared to speak lest she interrupt him and stop him speaking.

'My father reminded me that over one two-week period I flew back to Spain five times to see you. My attachment *was* obsessional,' he conceded grudgingly. 'I loved you then but I was afraid to accept that. Possibly when you said it suited me to believe that file and...*the other stuff* there was a shred of truth in that. Love has always been something that hurt and damaged me. I loved my mother, my father, my little sister, my half-brother and years before I met you I fell for a woman, who turned out to be a very troubled alcoholic, whom I had to place in rehab for recovery. I was determined not to get hurt again.'

Lucy nodded like a vigorous little marionette, wanting so badly to reach out to him and hug him and cover him in kisses but knowing it was wiser to let him say what he needed to say to explain the past and the present. 'I can understand that—'

Jax released his breath on a hiss. 'How can you? You keep on caring about people even when they hurt or disappoint you. That's brave—'

'Or plain stupid,' Lucy slotted in wryly. 'That's just

me. I tend to look for saving graces in people and stay optimistic but you're a giant pessimist, who always sees the worst possible conclusions.'

'Pretty much,' Jax conceded.

'And thinks the worst,' Lucy added with spirit, thinking about the alley. 'Even if there's no justification for it.'

Carefully avoiding the word Rio had advised him to avoid, Jax straightened his shoulders. 'The alcoholic that I fell for was repeatedly unfaithful to me. She couldn't help herself—she was a mess until rehab. But like my mother before her she conditioned me to distrust women. I'd seen that file. I saw a woman I thought was you and it seemed to fit, it seemed to be exactly the sort of thing that happened to me—I had got in too deep and you weren't who I thought you were—'

'Like with this alcoholic lady? That would be… er… Franca?' Lucy checked. 'Rio told Ellie about her and Ellie told me.'

Jax took on board the second of Rio's warnings. 'Yes, it was Franca. After her I was very wary and cynical with women. I didn't have faith in my own ability to read a woman, to really *know* her and, life being life,' he groaned, 'that meant I screwed up very badly with you. I ran when I should've stayed. I thought I was protecting myself but you had already burned me.'

'Burned you?'

'I never got over you. I kept on thinking about you at random times and reminding myself how bad you were…you know the—?'

'*Alley* stuff?' Lucy enunciated with precision, bright blue eyes gleaming.

'Yes, that,' Jax muttered, desperately keen to move on. 'Obviously I was wrong and I am very sorry that I believed that was you. I just saw the dress and the blonde hair and—'

Lucy moved closer and closed both arms around him. 'It's all right,' she murmured softly because his voice was ragged and too troubled for her to bear without touching him. 'It's all right. I forgive you. You made a mistake. It's over, done and dusted—'

Jax stared down at her with suspiciously bright green eyes. 'I don't deserve you. You probably don't even believe that I love you and that I loved you right from the start and I don't know how to prove it to you.'

But Lucy didn't need any more proof. Jax had wanted to stay married to her even though he believed she had once been unfaithful to him and that spoke volumes on its own. He had loved her warts and all, carefully schooling himself to overlook what any man would have seen as a monumental flaw and betrayal and predictably keeping his thoughts to himself. And then he had come clean and what he had been keeping secret had shocked and distressed her but at the same time it had set both of them free.

'I love you too,' Lucy whispered, planting a flyaway kiss on his freshly shaven jaw line, which was as high as she could reach even on tiptoes. 'So much that when you're not there it hurts.'

Jax carried her hand to his lips and kissed the back of it in the most un-Jax-like tender manner. 'You didn't even leave me a note. I felt sick. I didn't know what to do. I experienced pure panic—'

'I would've phoned eventually,' she confided. 'I was so upset but you were right to tell me. It all needed to come out for us to deal with it and then put it away again.'

'Your departure in a royal private jet was fairly straightforward when it came to tracking you,' Jax admitted ruefully, and then he gathered her up into his arms with the attitude of a male who couldn't keep his hands off her any longer.

'The bedroom's next door,' Lucy told him helpfully.

'I even told myself I was only marrying you for Bella's benefit,' Jax confessed. 'I lied to myself all the way down the line.'

'I persuaded myself I was only marrying you for our daughter's benefit as well, so you're not the only one.'

'How's Bella reacting to being here?' Jax queried.

'She's got six cousins to watch and loads of toys to steal. She's having a whale of a time.' Lucy laughed, blue eyes sparkling, and Jax looked down at her with his heart in his own eyes and adoration there, a brilliant smile on his lean, darkly handsome features.

'You are a very special woman, Tinker Bell,' Jax declared, settling her down on the bed with that same heartbreaking smile dazzling her. 'And the saddest element of all this is that my father is now going to be battering down our doors for invites.'

Lucy studied him in bewilderment. 'How? *Why?*'

'Heracles is the son of a pig farmer,' Jax told her with a chuckle. 'Yes, he keeps that little fact well under wraps because he is an enormous snob. When he discovers that your sister is a queen, he will be horribly friendly. He's very easily impressed in that line.'

Lucy shifted an unconcerned shoulder. 'I can live with that. It's not as though either of us can change our fathers. They are what they are but neither of them is going to get the chance to spoil our happiness again.'

'*Can* you be happy with me?' Jax pressed with touching anxiety. 'You do know I'll screw up again. I won't mean to but I will because I won't always get it right—'

'Neither will I,' Lucy pointed out equably as she struggled to get him out of his jacket and tie and then, when he got helpful, embarked on his shirt, spreading her fingers lasciviously across his muscular torso. 'Love is all about making allowances and compromises. We'll get there. Nobody has to be perfect.'

'I think you are. You have a heart as big as any country, *khriso mou*,' Jax told her with a blissful sigh as she knelt over him, cheerfully stripping him.

'And so have you,' Lucy countered, much amused. 'The difference between us is that you put your heart in a cage to keep it safe—'

'And you still worked your way through the bars of my cage,' Jax reminded her appreciatively. 'You've got more power than you realise.'

Lucy let a small hand stray and he arched up against her as if she had pressed a switch and she laughed as he sat up, wound both hands punitively into her hair and kissed her into breathless, leaping excitement. There was no more conversation then. They were both much too involved in sharing their bodies as they had shared their love.

'I suppose we should get up for dinner…or whatever they call it here,' Jax mused hours later. 'I'm being a very rude guest.'

'No, I know my sisters and they know me. They'll have tucked Bella into bed and gone on as normal.

There's no pressure, no expectations. Everyone's family here and that's just the way it is. I *love* it, especially because you're here too now,' Lucy confided, tucking a sleepy head into the crux of a strong brown shoulder and dreamily taking in the familiar scent of his skin, soothed by his proximity and the glorious high of knowing herself loved at last.

'I love you,' Jax muttered, easing her closer, marvelling at how easy it had become to say those words that he had refused to think about for so long.

'Love you,' Lucy whispered, dropping off to sleep, because she had lain awake sleepless while they were apart.

And Jax smiled in the darkness, recognising that for the first time in his life he was truly, joyously happy.

'This place looks amazing,' Polly carolled as she stood in the marble hall of the house on Tifnos and admired the fabulous Christmas decorations and the glittering tree. 'It's wonderful that you have a home big enough to take us all too, so we can get together like this to celebrate.'

'You can thank my father-in-law, Heracles, for that. He built *big*.'

'Was that the little man who kept on bowing to me?' Polly whispered uneasily.

'Yes, that was him, very subdued at being in the royal presence,' Lucy remarked, stifling her amusement.

In the three years Lucy had been married to Jax a great deal had changed. Her father-in-law was a frequent visitor, their children providing a major draw. Lucy had warmed up to Heracles considerably once she'd realised that he genuinely adored children and his grandchildren most of all. Yes, she had had another baby, a little boy called Dmitri, who was almost two years old. Their lengthy unplanned holiday in Dharia after their reconciliation had extended the family. She had enjoyed her second pregnancy much more than the first because she had had Jax by her side and Jax had been scientifically fascinated by every change she had gone through on the road to producing his son. He had shared everything with her and supported her right through the nausea in the early stages to every medical appointment and finally the birth.

During those three years only Lucy's son had been born but Polly was expecting again, freely admitting that she wanted a large family. Ellie had declared that two children would do her nicely but one never knew with Ellie, who could be prone to saying one thing and then quietly doing another. As for Lucy and Jax, they were still young and, while being quite happy with the children they had, they thought that some day they might plan a third child. Ellie had already lectured them hilariously about birth control, pointing out that *two* accidental conceptions was inexcusable, and her audience had only laughed.

Kreon and Iola were regular visitors on the island and Kreon and Heracles politely avoided each other at family gatherings. Her father had faced bankruptcy proceedings the year before and Jax had bought a small business for him and placed him in it, pointing out that Kreon needed to be kept occupied and independent. His kindness had almost reduced Lucy to tears and she was relieved that Jax had finally begun to see and understand Kreon's essential good-heartedness.

'He's your father and you love him,' Jax had said to Lucy. 'We have to do our best for him. After all, you put up with my father and forgive his foibles.'

Jax was a wonderful husband in every way, Lucy reflected gratefully, feeling very blessed. After spending so many years of craving the feeling of being special to someone she had finally found a safe harbour.

Leaving Polly to get settled in with her children and explaining that Ellie had gone straight to bed after a hospital late night shift, Lucy went off to put Dmitri down for a nap because he got very cross and whiny when he got too tired and with all the children in the house and the excitement of the Christmas season, he needed more sleep. The little boy snuggled into his cot, clutching his toy elephant. He was as blonde as his mother, which had been a surprise to his parents, but he too had Jax's green eyes and olive complexion.

Lucy looked out of the window and saw the older children down on the beach with Rashad and Rio. She could just make out four-year-old Bella in her yellow dress skipping through the surf with Polly's younger son, Hassan, and Ellie's Teresina. The cousins had all become fast friends and playmates, which made family get-togethers run more smoothly.

Recognising that she finally had the family circle she had dreamt of having all her life, Lucy vented a contented sigh and went to freshen up before dinner. She was in the shower when another body stepped in beside her and she spun round with a delighted smile of welcome.

'Jax…thought you were going to be late tonight!' she gasped.

'No, I looked round my office, thought of you all here enjoying yourselves without me and decided I was needed at home. I saw the children down on the beach as we flew in.'

'Dmitri's having a nap. He was throwing tantrums all over the place,' his mother confided ruefully.

'I swear he's got my mother's temperament,' Jax said worriedly.

'No, don't be silly,' Lucy soothed, aware that he had that little fear that he might somehow pass on some troublesome gene. 'He's a toddler with a short temper and he hasn't learned to control it yet. When he's not tired he's very good-natured. And, hey, did you join me in the shower to talk about the kids or—?'

'Or, *agapi mou*,' Jax chose, plastering her back against the shower wall and tasting her lush mouth with hungry urgency.

Lucy melted every time he called her his love. He was hot and wet and gorgeous and all hers. Excitement rippled through her in seductive sensual waves.

'Birth control,' Jax growled, lifting her out of the shower and throwing a heap of towels down on the tiled floor as he dug into a drawer for the necessary.

Lucy arranged herself on the towels and giggled like a drain. 'Ellie really got to you with that lecture, didn't she?'

'Ellie knows how to make a man feel irresponsible,' Jax responded. 'And I will *never* be irresponsible with you again but don't tell her that.'

'I promise I won't.' Her amusement dying as they joined, Lucy lifted tender fingers to stroke his jaw line. 'I love you, Jax Antonakos…I love you so much.'

He was too otherwise engaged to speak at that moment but his emerald eyes telegraphed love and passion and need and that was more than sufficient for Lucy, who knew a good man when she found one and held fast to him because he gave her so much happiness.

* * * * *

If you enjoyed the final part of Lynne Graham's BRIDES FOR THE TAKING *trilogy, why not explore the first two instalments?*

THE DESERT KING'S BLACKMAILED BRIDE
THE ITALIAN'S ONE-NIGHT BABY

Available now!

'We have a child. A son.'

Their eyes tangled. *A son.* There was no way that Leandro was going to cave in and believe Abby but...*fatherhood.* It was something he had never considered. Never wanted! He'd seen from his own unstable childhood that the production of children was something that could go horribly wrong. He'd not only learned from his own experience but he'd learned from his sister's. He'd never wished to reproduce and take a chance on being a father. It wasn't in his make-up.

What if she was telling the truth? Faced with that possibility, Leandro suddenly knew what it felt like for one's world to fall apart. He'd sought order all his life, to combat the lack of order that had marked his formative years, and there could be nothing more disastrous and explosive when it came to destroying all that hard-fought-for order than the arrival of a child.

But, no, he wasn't going to think like that.

He was a cool, rational man. He forced his thoughts away from possibilities. *Possibilities* counted for nothing.

'Where?'

'I beg your pardon?'

'You tell me that I'm a father. Then let me see my son.'

Cathy Williams can remember reading Mills & Boon books as a teenager, and now that she is writing them she remains an avid fan. For her, there is nothing like creating romantic stories and engaging plots, and each and every book is a new adventure. Cathy lives in London. Her three daughters—Charlotte, Olivia and Emma—have always been, and continue to be, the greatest inspirations in her life.

Books by Cathy Williams

Mills & Boon Modern Romance

Bought to Wear the Billionaire's Ring
Snowbound with His Innocent Temptation
A Virgin for Vasquez
Seduced into Her Boss's Service
The Wedding Night Debt
A Pawn in the Playboy's Game
At Her Boss's Pleasure
The Real Romero
The Uncompromising Italian
The Argentinian's Demand
Secrets of a Ruthless Tycoon
Enthralled by Moretti
His Temporary Mistress

The Italian Titans

Wearing the De Angelis Ring
The Surprise De Angelis Baby

One Night With Consequences

Bound by the Billionaire's Baby

Seven Sexy Sins

To Sin with the Tycoon

Visit the Author Profile page
at millsandboon.co.uk for more titles.

THE SECRET SANCHEZ HEIR

BY
CATHY WILLIAMS

First Published in Great Britain 2017
By Mills & Boon, an imprint of HarperCollins*Publishers*
1 London Bridge Street, London, SE1 9GF

ISBN: 978-0-263-92523-4

Our policy is to use papers that are natural, renewable and recyclable products and made from wood grown in sustainable forests. The logging and manufacturing processes conform to the legal environmental regulations of the country of origin.

Printed and bound in Spain
by CPI, Barcelona

THE SECRET SANCHEZ HEIR

CHAPTER ONE

THROUGH THE WINDOWS of the airy den tucked away in the west wing of his sprawling country mansion, Leandro Sanchez had a bird's eye view of what could only be called the inevitable end of his six-month relationship with Rosalind Duval.

Only fitting, he thought, that a high-maintenance, spoiled diva should exit on a cloud of over-the-top drama.

It was a little after six in the evening and the last of the trucks that only that morning had delivered food, decorations—including a ridiculous ice sculpture for display in his hall—and several dozen staff was now departing. The specially bought Chinese-style lanterns that lined the long, private avenue leading up to his estate twinkled and glittered in the lightly falling snow and illuminated the dark shapes of the vehicles slowly wending their way away from his estate.

Sensual mouth compressed into a thin line of distaste, Leandro replayed in his mind the events of the last three hours. He had returned from his business trip to New York, fresh off the red eye, to pick up a barrage of text messages from Rosalind that he was to come immediately to his country house where he would find a surprise waiting for him.

Leandro loathed surprises. He was especially put out because, during the past week while he had been in New York, he had decided that his relationship with the very eligible Lady Rosalind Duval had reached the end of its course.

On paper, she had ticked all the boxes. She was beautiful, well-bred and independently wealthy. Her parents, whilst not nearly on the same level as him financially, formed the bedrock of that dying breed known as the British aristocracy. As a bonus, she was friendly with his sister Cecilia, who, indeed, had engineered the initial meeting between them.

Leandro was not in the market for love but he had been...*restless* and Rosalind had stepped into that uncustomary void with the promise of something *different*. It was not to be.

Her background had filled her with high expectations that every single one of her demands would be met with complete subservience. As a privileged only child, she was accustomed to getting her own way, and the fact that she was in her early thirties proved no barrier to her stamping her feet and throwing temper tantrums if things didn't go as she decreed. She had always been the centre of attention and had seen no reason why he, Leandro, shouldn't fall in line and continue the tradition.

She'd demanded his constant attention, phoning him sometimes several times a day and, having had full use of his credit card, had seen absolutely nothing wrong with buying whatever she'd happened to fancy on a whim. From jewellery, to clothes, to an outrageously expensive sports car, finally to an *engagement ring* which, he had discovered to his horror, had been the surprise waiting for him when he had returned from New York.

'Special delivery!' She had beamed as hordes of people came and went, fetching, carrying and getting everything in place for the accompanying engagement party which had been arranged for the following day. 'It should arrive at just the right time for us to pop a cork and celebrate before dinner. It's time we made this official, Leandro. Mummy and Daddy are simply *desperate* for a grandchild and I don't see the point of delaying any longer. We're both in our thirties and it's time to take the next step. Darling, I *know* you're a typical man and wouldn't dream of doing anything about it, so I thought I'd do the necessary!'

He watched the tail end of the last van disappear from view then, flexing his lean muscles, he strolled out towards the kitchen, taking in the detritus left behind in the wake of everyone's hasty departure.

In the hall, the ridiculous ice sculpture of a couple entwined was still perfectly intact and would require removal the following day. He would have to enlist a team of cleaners to return his country house to its 'before' state.

Right now, all he wanted was something strong to drink. The wretched engagement ring was on its way. Another hasty departure would have to be effected, although he was debating whether he would keep the ring or not. It had cost a small fortune. Quite a flawless diamond, he had seen from the receipt that had been flung at him by an incandescent Rosalind. Maybe he would gift it to her. She had, after all, been responsible for sourcing the priceless gem even if it *had* been purchased on *his* credit card.

He grimaced and thought that there was a better than even chance that the gesture would not be met with warm approval.

For once, his thoughts assumed an introspective nature. In the kitchen, Julie, his housekeeper, was busy trying to eradicate all evidence of the blighted party preparations. He dismissed her while he poured himself a drink.

'One more delivery due,' he said absently, swirling the amber liquid in the glass and staring down at it for a few seconds before glancing across to the middle-aged woman who had been responsible for looking after his country mansion for the past five years, ever since he had bought it. 'I will need to dispatch this one personally. I'll be in my office. When the courier arrives, let me know, Julie. They shouldn't be on the premises for longer than ten minutes and then you can leave for the evening. You'll need the usual team here in the morning to finish clearing up this…mess.'

It annoyed him that he was still unable to rein in his wandering mind, because he was a man who had little or no time for pointless raking over the past. Yet now, as he strolled back towards his office, closing his curtains against a view of snow that was falling thicker and faster, he couldn't stop himself from thinking.

Thinking about Rosalind and the chain of events that

had brought her into his life and contrived to keep her there, even though, almost from the very start, he had seen the cracks begin to appear.

His sister, Cecilia, had been instrumental in bringing about their meeting and he knew, in a vague way, she'd been instrumental in making him hesitate before doing what had to be done. He sighed, already predicting what his sister's reaction would be when she received the inevitable phone call from Rosalind, who would surely speak to Cecilia before he had had time to fill her in himself.

He swallowed back the remainder of the whisky in his glass, sat down, pushing the chair away from the big, old-fashioned mahogany desk, and thought back… back to events of eighteen months previously and to another woman who had swept into his life for a matter of weeks and wreaked havoc.

Gold-digger…liar…*thief*...

He had had a narrow escape, had walked away from her without looking back, and it infuriated him to know that, however far and fast he walked, she was still there like a thorn in his side, making itself felt at the slightest opportunity. He hadn't been able to escape her and, in ways he couldn't put his finger on but knew existed, she had been responsible for that lethal restlessness that had made him question the direction his life had been taking. Questions which had subsequently lowered his defences when it had come to contemplating something of a more permanent nature with a woman who'd actually appeared to fit the bill.

His jaw clenched and he swung back to his computer, blanking out his memories of the golden-haired, green-eyed witch who had made him take his eye off the ball. There was no point in resurrecting the past. It was over and done with. Once he had sent the courier delivering the ring on his way back down to London, his chapter with Rosalind would be at an end and life, as always, would carry on.

On that note, he did what he did best—buried himself in work—and, within ten minutes, thoughts of the past were where they should be: locked away and incapable of jumping out at him, at least for the moment.

Abigail Christie was running late. The driver, a trusted employee of Vanessa—Abigail's boss, who had saved her, in a manner of speaking, and who owned the exquisite, upmarket jeweller's from which Lady Rosalind Duval had purchased the diamond—had been under strict instructions to *make it to Greyling Manor no later than five, under penalty of death.* Unfortunately, those instructions had allowed no leeway for the twin assault of vile weather and the accompanying stop-start traffic. They had left an overcast London bang on time but had run into problems the second they had hit Oxford and, from there on, it had been a frustrating race against the clock.

Abigail had not been able to contact Lady Rosalind to advise her of the delay because she hadn't been picking up.

The only silver lining was the fact that, although they were now over two hours behind schedule, they had finally left most of the traffic behind and, whilst the country lanes leading to Greyling Manor might be dark, twisty and frankly treacherous given the weather conditions, their destination was at last within touching distance.

She would thrust the ring at Lady Rosalind, get her signature as fast as she could and leave without further ado.

Doubtless, Rosalind Duval would be waiting with bated breath for them to arrive and would be as keen to see the back of them as they would be to see the back of Greyling Manor, which was buried deep in the heart of the Cotswolds.

No sticking around to gather themselves before embarking on the return journey. No polite conversation with the lord of the manor and no having to contend with whatever arrogant, Hooray Henry types had gathered in preparation for tomorrow's Big Reveal and would want to have a preview of the magnificent engagement ring. Not now that they were running so late. And that afforded Abigail a great deal of relief because the prospect of dipping her toes back into the waters of that rarefied world of the super-rich was something that made her feel physically sick.

It had revived all the worst memories she had of just how unscrupulous the people who inhabited that world could be. She had had her disastrous brush with how the other half lived and she was in no hurry for a return visit.

Indeed, she had done her best to get out of delivering this ring, not least because she hadn't handled the sale. She had only seen Rosalind in passing, but the timing had been bad for Vanessa and typical of a young, rich woman who snapped her fingers and expected all her wishes to be met instantly, Rosalind had set a date for the delivery and had refused to budge.

And there were other reasons why Abigail intended to tell Hal, the driver, to keep the engine running while she flew in, did what was necessary and flew back out.

For the fourth time in under an hour, she checked her phone for any communication from her friend Claire, but a reliable network service had died pretty much as soon as they had hit the first winding country lane and it hadn't got any better the deeper into the heart of the Cotswolds they had travelled.

With a sigh of frustration, Abigail leant back and watched the dark scenery drift past her. There was something eerie about the veil of snow falling steadily into the inky-black landscape, settling over the open fields. She was accustomed to light pollution and the constant sounds of a city. Out here, she felt as though she could have been on another planet, and she didn't like that because it made her think of Sam, her ten-month-old son back in London, and the fact that he would be fast asleep by the time she made it back to her house, even if the turnaround here was faster than the speed of light.

And then, hard on the heels of that, she started to think about the weather, started to wonder whether she was imagining it or whether the snow was getting thicker. It was so hard to tell in the darkness. What if these little lanes became impassable? Right now, they seemed fine, but what if she couldn't make it back to

London? She would have to find a bed and breakfast somewhere, and that would entail an overnight stay, and she had never spent a night away from Sam. She couldn't imagine not waking up in the morning to the sound of his gurgling and little complaining cries that went on until she scooped him up for his morning bottle.

Lost in thought, she surfaced when the vehicle slowed, turned through impressive wrought-iron gates and headed up a long, tree-lined drive that was lit by a series of lanterns. It was beautifully romantic and it was only as they approached the Georgian mansion that she felt the first stirrings of unease.

The place looked deserted, aside from a couple of cars in the circular courtyard. Most of the house was in darkness and she made Hal double check to make sure he had got the address right.

'You'd better come in with me,' she said dubiously and Hal, killing the engine, turned round and looked at her, his cheerful face serious.

'If this is an engagement party,' he said in his usual direct fashion, 'then I'll eat my hat.' He waved the woollen hat lying on the seat next to him and grinned. 'I've seen more life in a graveyard.'

'Don't say that. I have a ring to deliver. Vanessa will be distraught if for some reason the sale falls through.'

'It won't, love.' He smiled kindly at her. 'You'll probably find that the action will kick off tomorrow. That's when the party's due to take place, isn't it? The happy couple are probably just relaxing and enjoying some peace before the big day ahead.'

Ten minutes later, Abigail discovered that that couldn't have been further from the truth.

Leandro had thoroughly cleared his head of the catastrophic mess that had awaited him when he had arrived back from New York. That was the joy of work. It put everything into perspective. It was a world in which everything was clear cut and everything had a solution. Now, as Julie popped her head round the door to inform him that the last link in the 'belly up' chain had arrived, bearing the ill-fated ring, Leandro was obliged to face the final annoying hurdle in putting this matter to rest.

He was, fortunately, in a better frame of mind. Rosalind had shouted and screamed, furious that for the first time in her life someone had scuppered her plans. She had threatened social exclusion, at which point Leandro had made the mistake of laughing, and she had been apoplectic when he had suggested that she was far better off without him, because he simply didn't have the reserves of energy or patience to give her the sort of attention she required. Nor, he had added, had he the slightest interest in having children. In fact, he could think of nothing worse. So the pitter-patter of tiny feet would have remained an unfulfilled ambition.

Rosalind had got the worst out of her system and he felt that, when she eventually descended from her rage, she would find blessed relief in gossiping about him behind his back and painting whatever picture it took for her to emerge smelling of roses.

For his part, burying himself in work had put everything in perspective.

He had no idea what had driven him to imagine that anything could be more important. His abiding memory of his parents was of two spoiled and wealthy people caught up in a hedonistic whirl, incapable of growing up and certainly incapable of looking after the child they had accidentally conceived. Even less had they been able to deal with the arrival of Cecilia years later, another accident. The task of taking care of his much younger sister had fallen to him and, from a young age, Leandro had worked out that the tumult of emotion and the chaos it was capable of engendering was not for him. A healthy aversion to chaos, disorder and unpredictability had been ingrained in him from a tender age.

As a teenager, he had lost himself in his studies, only surfacing to make sure his sister was okay. As an adult, work had replaced the studies, and when his parents had died, victims of their wild, irresponsible lifestyle—speedboat racing at night in the Caribbean—work had become even more imperative because he had had to rescue what was left of the family finances. There had been no time to kick back and relax. Work was and always would be the most important driving force of Leandro's life. Rosalind's hysterics had clarified that for him.

He had told Julie to show the courier into the smallest of the sitting rooms, the one which bore the least evidence of the party that wasn't going to be taking place. He now made his way there, mind half on the business proposal he had been reading before he had been interrupted.

* * *

On tenterhooks, because whatever was wrong was *very, very* wrong and the fast exit she had been hoping for now seemed out of the question, Abigail was sitting upright in a chair in the room into which she had been delivered like an unwanted parcel.

Rosalind was, she was given to understand, not there. Hal was to wait in the kitchen where he would be given something to eat and she was to wait for the master of the house in the sitting room where, she hoped, he would take delivery of the ring.

She heard the approach of footsteps on the marble floor and was already rising to her feet, having rehearsed what she needed to say about getting back to London urgently before the weather took a turn for the worse.

Whatever the heck was going on, it wasn't her problem. She had already reached that conclusion. She'd done her job and, if the loved-up couple had had a tiff, then that was nothing to do with her.

She didn't know who or what to expect. Stiff with tension, with the metal box containing the ring clutched to her chest, for a few seconds Abigail almost thought that her nerves had brought on a hallucinatory attack.

Because there was no way that those footsteps she had heard could possibly have heralded the arrival of a six-foot-two specimen of pure, hard-edged masculinity. There was no way that those achingly familiar tawny eyes, fringed by eyelashes she had once teased could have been the envy of any woman, could now be staring at her. *It just wasn't possible.* Leandro Sanchez *could not* be lounging in the doorway of this sitting room, larger than life.

She couldn't tear her eyes away from him. He was her very worst nightmare and her very deepest, darkest, most forbidden fantasy come to life and she blinked, desperately hoping that the vision would disappear. It didn't. He remained just where he was, an alpha male of such sinful beauty that he took her breath away. He had taken her breath away the first time she had seen him a year and a half ago. Over the weeks of their torrid and doomed love affair, that impact had never lessened.

He was the sort of guy women dreamed about. Olive-skinned, tawny-eyed and with an electrifying, ruthless sex appeal. He was long, lean and muscular, and Abigail thought that she could remember each and every muscle and sinew of that fabulous body.

She had never thought that she'd see him again, not after *everything,* and as the full horror of this accidental encounter hit home the room began to swim. She felt nausea rise in a tide up her throat, and she swallowed back the bile, but she couldn't seem to stop herself from swaying. She felt her legs give way and knew that she was going to pass out before she hit the ground.

She came to on one of the low, cream sofas facing the arched window through which she had been absently gazing only seconds before and struggled up to find that Leandro had dragged a chair over by the sofa and was sitting, watching her.

'Drink this.' He pressed a glass with some brandy into her hand and forced her to take a sip. His eyes were cool and guarded, his hand was steady, his voice controlled.

Not a single thing conveyed his utter shock at walking into the room and coming face to face with the only woman who had got under his skin and refused to budge—and, as if that wasn't sufficiently appalling, it galled him to realise that his ability to recall had been spot-on because she was just as exquisite as he remembered.

Her hair was just as colourful and, from what he could tell, just as long, although right now it was pinned back severely in a bun. Her eyes were as green as he remembered, green with gold flecks that were only apparent when you really took time to look, which he had. Her figure was as luscious and as sexy, a figure that could haunt a man's dreams.

Of their own accord, his eyes drifted down, lingering on the full swell of her breasts pushing against the drab white blouse, and the length of her legs primly hidden under a pair of grey trousers. She was dressed in high street fashion. Wherever life had taken her since they had parted company, it certainly hadn't been into the open arms of another billionaire.

'Leandro…this can't be happening…' She would have stood up except her legs had turned to jelly.

'You're in my house, you're sitting on my sofa.' He stood up and strolled towards the fireplace, putting some distance between them, every nerve in his body electrified by the shock of finding her in his house. 'It's happening all right. I take it that you're the courier with the ring?'

'I... Yes...I am.' Abigail's eyes skittered towards him and just as quickly skittered away. She reached for the metal safety-deposit box and held it out to him. Leandro ignored the gesture.

Propelled into nervous speech, Abigail gave him a stilted, jerky explanation for being in his house, all the while feeling like an unwary rabbit that had suddenly strayed into the path of a voracious predator.

'It seems...' Leandro sauntered back towards her, eyes narrowed as he watched her cringe back against the sofa. As she should, he thought, considering the last time they had been in one another's company she had been revealed for the liar and thief that she was. '...that your boss got the wrong end of the stick.'

'I beg your pardon?'

'That ring was purchased without my consent. Unfortunately, Rosalind misinterpreted the depth of our relationship.'

'But we were told that there was to be an engagement party...'

Leandro shrugged and continued looking at her as he sat back down on the chair that he had pulled over, which was far too close for comfort, as far as Abigail was concerned. 'Crossed wires all round,' he informed her coolly.

'So is Rosalind...? Has Rosalind...?' Abigail struggled to make sense of the situation while her thoughts kept whirling round in utter confusion and her body burned and tingled as though she'd been plugged in to a live socket.

'I never had plans to marry her.' Leandro brushed

aside the question with just a hint of impatience. Now that she was sitting here in his living room, larger than life and just as sexy, all those memories he had carefully locked away were coming out to play. He remembered the way she had felt, the noises she'd made when he'd touched her, the way their bodies had fit together like one. He'd bumped into ex-girlfriends before and had felt nothing for them but a sense of relief that they were no longer around. He certainly had never looked at them and *wanted* them.

But then no other relationship had ended the way theirs had…

Jittery and feeling caged in, Abigail sprang to her feet and began pacing the room nervously, hands clasped behind her back, barely able to think straight. 'So this trip has been a complete waste of time. What am I supposed to do now? With the ring?' *Focus on why you're here,* she told herself feverishly, *and forget about everything else.*

'Now that you've made the effort to bring it here, you'd better let me have a look—see where my hard-earned money has gone.' He nodded to the box and Abigail dutifully extracted the ring with shaking fingers and watched as he carefully held it up to the light and inspected it.

'It's not my problem if you've broken off your engagement with Lady Rosalind,' she said jerkily.

'I haven't *broken* anything off. There was never an engagement to break off. She bought this off her own bat because she wanted to pin me down. The strategy didn't work. I'd already decided to finish with her before I knew anything about this ridiculous scheme and that's exactly what I did when I returned here after my trip abroad.'

Abigail shivered because this was just the sort of ruthless side to him she had finally glimpsed when their relationship had crashed and burned.

She thought of Sam and was overcome with sudden sickening fear and apprehension. 'The ring was sold in good faith,' she told him flatly, taking a deep breath and exhaling slowly because it steadied her shattered nerves. 'I just need you to sign for the delivery and then I can be out of here.'

'Really?' Leandro relaxed, crossing his legs and leaning back in his chair. 'Why the rush?'

'Why do you think, Leandro?' Abigail asked in a high-pitched voice. 'The last time we met you were walking out of your apartment, leaving me with your sister, believing every word she had said about me being a liar, a thief and a gold-digger. So, believe it or not, the less time I spend in your company, the better. If I'd known that you were the man Lady Rosalind was about to marry, there's no way I would have come all the way here to deliver a ring. But I didn't, and now the ring is in your possession, and all I need is your signature before I leave.'

'I'm not going to go down the road of reminiscing over your lies and half-truths,' Leandro told her calmly. 'As for the ring…I may or may not decide to keep it.'

'You have to!' Abigail gasped. 'Vanessa has just taken over her father's business and this sale is a real coup for her. There was stiff competition from other buyers to get hold of this particular diamond!'

'Not my problem, although it beggars belief that you managed to con your way into a job handling priceless jewellery, now that we're on the subject. Does your employer know that you're prone to being light-fingered?'

'I don't have to stay and listen to this!'

'Oh, but you do. Or have you forgotten that you need my signature?' He snapped shut the box with a definitive click. 'I think I'll keep it,' he decided briskly, 'as an investment. It'll make me money. Now, sit.'

'I have to go.'

Leandro looked at her narrowly as she glanced down at her watch with just the slightest hint of panic, as she licked her lips and fidgeted.

'It took much longer to get here than I anticipated,' Abigail said into the growing silence. 'We should have arrived ages ago, at least two hours ago, but the weather… I'd planned on being back in London by eight-thirty. I really have to get back…'

'Why?' he asked smoothly. 'Glass slipper going to get lost? Carriage about to turn into a pumpkin? There's no wedding ring on your finger, so I take it that there's no Mr Right keeping the fires burning on the home front. Or is there?' He found that he didn't care for the thought of a man in Abigail's life and that streak of inappropriate possessiveness shocked him.

But then, why beat about the bush? She'd lodged in his head like a burr and the plain truth was that he still wanted her. It made no sense, because she represented everything he found distasteful, but for reasons he couldn't begin to understand she still turned him on. Something about the way she was put together. He'd been out with some of the most beautiful women in the world and none of them could get to him the way this one could.

It was as infuriating as it was undeniable.

She was still in his system, a slither of unfinished business, and there was only one way he could think of to get her out of his system once and for all.

He lowered his eyes and felt the kick of satisfaction at a decision taken. It would be an insult to fate, which had decided to throw them together, were he not to take advantage of the situation.

'It's none of your business whether there's someone in my life or not, Leandro!' Agitated, she sprang to her feet, challenging him to stop her. 'Now, if you'll excuse me, Hal is waiting in the kitchen. I'll go fetch him and we can head off. It took us hours to get here, and it'll probably take us hours to get back, and I…'

'And you…what?'

'Nothing,' she muttered. 'I just need to go now.'

'By all means, although…' he nodded towards the window '…you might want to reconsider that decision. If you look outside, you'll find that the weather conditions that delayed your trip here are now considerably worse. Leave here and you're liable to end up in a ditch by the side of the road somewhere. That's the thing with these country lanes—they're very picturesque in summer but positively lethal in winter when the weather decides to take a turn for the worse.'

Abigail paled and followed the direction of his gaze,

then she anxiously went to the window and peered outside. The flakes were raining down fast and thick. Already, the extensive grounds of the country estate were carpeted in white. It was beautiful. It was also, she noted with sickening dismay, virtually impassable.

'I can't stay here. I have to get back!'

'Feel free. But perhaps that should be a joint decision taken with your driver.'

'You don't understand! *I have to get back to London tonight.*'

'You're not going anywhere,' Leandro told her. 'This snow is going to get worse before it gets better. You might be willing to put your life at risk in your desperate need to return to the city, but you have your driver to consider. Frankly, what you choose to do with your life is entirely your concern, but I won't be responsible for any accident that might befall your driver. I will ensure that he is fed and settled into one of the guest suites for the night. By tomorrow, you will doubtless find that the driving conditions are improved.'

Abigail was close to tears but there was nothing she could do. 'I can't get a signal on my phone,' she told him, defeated. 'I need to make a call.'

Leandro didn't say anything but he was thinking fast. A man? Not a husband, but a lover? Who else? And would that stop him? He wanted her, but was that want reciprocated?

He had one night, he thought with satisfaction, and one night should be more than enough to put this urge to bed once and for all. He would find out soon enough.

CHAPTER TWO

ABIGAIL HAD EXPECTED similar alarm from Hal about being trapped at Greyling Manor for the night—he was a family man with three young children—but he seemed pleased as punch not to be returning to London.

'Treacherous roads,' he said comfortably as he settled in front of the array of wildly extravagant food which had been laid on for them by Leandro's housekeeper. 'Wouldn't want to risk driving on them, and besides, I haven't been out of London in months.'

While he had tucked into the surplus party grub, with Julie nodding approvingly at his hearty appetite, Abigail toyed worriedly with her food. She had, at least, managed to get through to her friend Claire who was looking after Sam for the evening, and she had cheerfully agreed to stay until she returned.

'I'll be back no later than tomorrow lunchtime,' Abigail had said *sotto voce*, for she had been directed to the landline and was petrified that Leandro might be lurking behind a door and overhearing her conversation. 'I don't care *what* the weather decides to do. There's no way I can stay here.'

'I know you miss Sam,' her friend had said soothingly, 'but it's better for you to wait and travel back when it's safe rather than risk life and limb. I promise to take very good care of the little guy!'

Abigail knew that her friend would. She had met Claire at the handful of antenatal classes they had attended together, and they had hit it off immediately. Both young, both single and both pregnant. Although, in Claire's case, she had had a job at the local nursery. Thanks to Claire, Abigail had managed to get Sam registered and, much as she had hated leaving him there when he had only been four months old, she'd had to in order to work to keep the roof over both their heads. Knowing that Claire was there, looking after him every bit as thoroughly as she looked after her own son, had helped a lot. Just as Vanessa had given her a job when she had needed it most, so too had Claire chipped in and helped her with Sam when she'd needed it.

Claire had no idea where Abigail was and neither did she know why she so desperately needed to leave.

So far, she had inspected the weather a dozen times in the space of the past two hours.

There was some let up but not much. She had barely been able to touch a morsel of food and was only thankful that Leandro had disappeared into the bowels of the house. There was a slim chance that she wouldn't see him again but she knew that that would make little difference to the onslaught of memories, heartache and misgivings that had risen to the surface, like debris washed ashore.

Of course you could never forget the past, but now

the scab that had been formed had been picked apart to expose the barely healed wound underneath.

As Hal was shepherded up to his quarters, as happy as a privileged guest in a five-star hotel, Abigail remained in the kitchen with her cup of coffee, remembering the past she had tried to put behind her.

She could recall the very second she had looked up and seen Leandro standing in front of her, so unbelievably gorgeous that her mouth had run dry and every single thought had fled her head. In that split second, she had forgotten all about the job she had just failed to secure, the uncertain future staring her in the face, the last laugh her philandering, lecherous ex-boss had had at her expense by insinuating in his reference that she had been sacked for theft. She had turned down the pass he had made, had allowed her disgust to show and had paid the price.

She had been at rock bottom. Every single effort she had ever made to elevate herself and get away from a background that had been a slideshow of foster homes and indifferent adults had been for nothing.

Then she had felt a shadow, looked up and there he'd been, all big, brooding and heart-stoppingly gorgeous, and for the first time in her life Abigail had discovered the meaning of sexual chemistry.

She'd spent so many years playing down her looks, telling herself that she would never, *ever* allow anyone into her life because they wanted to have sex with her, and fending off unwanted advances from the age of thirteen, that she'd been quite unprepared to discover that sexual attraction had no time at all for pep talks and earnest lectures.

Indeed, sexual attraction hadn't given a damn about her resolve never to leap into bed with a man who wanted her for her body and not much else. Her mother had been that woman before an overdose had ended her life. Abigail had known that she would never end up selling herself short like her mother had. Unfortunately, the power of that same sexual attraction she had had under tight control had refused to obey her ground rules. It had raced out of the box in which it had been contained with the gusto of a racehorse sprinting from the starting box.

Leandro hadn't even beaten around the bush. He'd just said, conversationally, that it was nearly lunchtime and he knew a nice little Italian just round the corner. He had not bothered to wrap up what he'd wanted in fancy packaging. She'd bowled him over, he had said over lunch, looking at her with those fabulous, long-lashed eyes, the very casualness of his voice at odds with what he was saying. He didn't do commitment, he'd made it clear, but he wanted her and he was going to New York. He'd glanced at his watch with a nonchalance she'd found unutterably *cool* and had told her he wanted to take her with him, but that she'd have to decide on the spot, because his private jet was due to leave in three hours.

His eyes had roved over her with open desire but everything about him had told her that, if she chose to walk away, he wouldn't try to stop her.

He'd been *everything* she hadn't been looking for and

she'd dumped every single principle she'd ever had and gone with him. She'd let him sweep her into his world of chauffeur-driven cars, five-star hotels and every whim granted at the snap of a finger. He'd worked during the day and had insisted that she buy herself a new wardrobe, and whatever else she fancied in whatever store she chose, because money was no object.

But she *had* objected, only to learn that, what Leandro didn't want to hear, he simply chose to ignore, and he hadn't wanted to hear her objections.

'I have never,' he had told her, undressing her very, very slowly, 'allowed any woman of mine to pay for anything. Not going to change the habit now.'

No-strings-attached sex was what he'd offered and it was what she'd taken, greedy for him in a way that had shocked her beyond words. They'd lived for the moment and, whilst she had not lied to him about her past, neither had she told him about it. Somewhere along the line, she'd felt that it would turn him off and quite quickly she'd known that she hadn't wanted to turn him off.

When one week had turned into two and then three, and when, on the spur of the moment, he had decided to take a break with her in the wilds of Canada, she'd begun to hope that what had started out as just sex might end up as more.

But then everything had gone wrong, and it had all happened so fast. One minute she had been dreaming impossible dreams, and the next minute his sister had entered the frame and within three days all her fledgling dreams had lain in ruins around her and she'd been turfed out of his Manhattan apartment without a backward glance.

He'd made no bones about spelling out the sort of unscrupulous guy he was when it came to women and, instead of listening, she had chosen to ignore the writing on the wall because she had been first bowled over by him and then head over heels in love with him.

Abigail stared off now into the distance. She hadn't drawn the curtains in the kitchen and she could see that, whilst the snow wasn't getting any heavier, it was still falling, a flurry of white, shining and beautiful where the lights around the house illuminated the drift.

'So…' a familiar voice drawled from behind her.

Startled, Abigail saw Leandro's reflection in the glass of the French doors through which she had been staring. He'd changed into a pair of black jeans and a long-sleeved black jumper, the sleeves of which had been pushed up to the elbows, and he was barefoot. It might be freezing outside, but this rolling country manor was heated to perfection. Her heart jumped and her mouth went dry as she turned slowly towards him.

'I see you decided to stay rather than brave the snow in an attempt to get out of here. Wise decision.'

'I thought you'd gone to bed.' Abigail said jerkily—the first thing that came to her head.

'You mean you'd *hoped* I'd gone to bed. Why's that?' Leandro strolled towards a platter of cold meats, made himself a clumsy sandwich and poured himself a glass of red wine, offering her one as well, an offer she refused.

She gazed at him helplessly as he sat at the kitchen

table. She'd remembered the way his physical presence could affect her. She'd forgotten *how much*.

'It's awkward being here,' she stammered, finally dropping into the chair opposite him and watching as he ate, his eyes flicking towards her every so often.

Leandro didn't say anything. He thought that awkward didn't begin to cover it, but the hand of fate worked in mysterious ways, and he wasn't feeling uncomfortable with the situation at all.

Indeed, things were remarkably clear cut. Far clearer cut than they had been when they had been seeing one another a year and a half ago.

Then he had found himself, for the first time in his life, in a situation in which normal play had been suspended. The rules he had always applied to his life had taken a back seat and, even before his sister Cecilia had had her say, he had known that the relationship was entering unexplored territory. When he had first laid eyes on Abigail, he had known that he wanted her. Desire had hit him hard and fast and, never one to ignore the demands of his libido, he had done what he had always done, without beating round the bush or going down any nonsensical courtship route. He'd found her attractive and he'd wanted to bed her. A simple equation.

He hadn't reckoned on her being a virgin and he wondered whether that had marked the beginning of all those subtle changes that had pulled him in and frankly terrified him at the same time.

She'd been cagey about her past and he hadn't pressed her for detail, instinctively wanting to hang on to whatever safe ground he could. He hadn't wanted her to start the whole confiding game, which always inevitably led to the sort of cloying situation that he found a huge turn-off. He'd sought to keep her at a distance because he could feel the compulsive drag of being pulled in and, subconsciously, that had seemed the safest way of fighting it.

He'd told himself that he wasn't curious but, even while he'd been trying to hold her at arm's length, he'd wanted to know *everything* about her, had wanted that act of possession.

Perhaps his sister had heard something in the way he had talked about Abigail down the phone. Why else would she have dug up all that dirt on her? He had known that Cecilia was possessive and he had always indulged that and understood the reason for it. He had been her anchor from the day she'd been born, but even so he had seen red when she had descended on his Manhattan apartment, clutching evidence of Abigail's past, challenging him to continue seeing a woman who, if not an outright liar, had concealed the truth—and why else unless she was a gold-digger, playing the long game? He had walked away from the relationship without a backward glance. Problem was that his body hadn't quite managed to forget her.

Which was why the woman had stayed in his head. Which was why, looking at her now, he could feel the slow burn of desire inside him.

She was unfinished business and he still wanted her. The blondes and eventually Rosalind had been sticking plaster over an open cut and now the sticking plaster had been ripped off. There was only one way the cut was going to be healed and that was to sleep for one last time with the woman who had delivered the damage.

Things were different now. He knew Abigail for who she was. Once upon a time, he had almost believed her to be the person she'd been pretending to be, but that was then. Now, he was in no danger of being sucked into anything.

'It's only awkward,' Leandro drawled, 'if you insist on dragging the past in. Personally, I'm the sort of guy who is happy to let bygones be bygones.' He shrugged. 'I'm not interested in talking about why you did what you did.'

'I didn't *do* anything,' Abigail muttered in a driven undertone. 'Okay, so I didn't tell you about my background because I didn't want to put you off. Why is that so hard for you to understand? I'm human. You were everything I wasn't and I couldn't believe that you'd even looked in my direction. I didn't want to spoil the moment and then…things started getting serious and I just never seemed to know when to sit you down and explain that you might have got the wrong idea of who I was…'

Leandro flushed darkly. 'Things *got serious* for *you*,' he corrected coolly.

Abigail nodded. 'I won't sit here and pretend that they didn't,' she told him. 'I felt things for you and, the more I felt for you, the harder it seemed to start telling you about myself and my foster homes and what it was like growing up in them.'

Her voice had sunk to a whisper and Leandro grimly fought off any inclination to feel sympathy for her. She deserved none, and too right he would have seen things slightly differently had he known just how desperate for money she had been. The only thing she hadn't lied about had been her lack of sexual experience, and he'd wondered afterwards whether she'd been saving herself for the right billionaire to come along and elevate her to the status she felt she deserved. She'd certainly taken to the high life like a duck to water.

'And what a stroke of bad luck,' Leandro murmured smoothly, 'to have ended up trying to get a job in one of the hotels I owned. The second Cecilia knew where we'd met, it would have been easy for her to work her way backwards and to have discovered the job you failed to secure because of the reference given by your ex-boss.'

'He lied.' Abigail had been so desperate to make him understand all those long months ago when his sister had confronted him in his apartment, but now she just felt tired of finding herself repeating the same old stuff all over again. It wasn't as though he was going to listen now any more than he had then. In fact, if anything, she repulsed him more now than she would have then because, back then, they at least had been lovers and that would have counted for *something,* surely?

'Of course,' Leandro said soothingly. 'Although I wouldn't get too moral, if I were you, considering you weren't far behind in the lying stakes...'

Abigail looked away.

'And then there was a certain incident I unearthed about a spate of shoplifting for which you received a warning in the heady days of your misspent youth...'

Abigail's eyes flew to his and she blanched, because this was news to her. 'What? You had me checked out *after* we broke up?'

'Call it curiosity.' Because a part of him had wanted to believe her. He couldn't credit himself for being the fool he'd been, but then he'd never felt for any other woman what he'd ended up feeling for her. The memory of that vulnerability made his teeth clench together in frustration and anger.

'I remember that incident,' Abigail said softly. Her eyes clouded over. 'I was only twelve at the time and I was so desperate to fit in. I'd just been transferred to another foster home and...' she sighed '...I just knew that the girls there weren't going to accept me.'

Because of how she looked. It had *always* been about how she looked. Her face had attracted too much attention and, in her circumstances, attracting too much attention had never been a good thing.

'A group of us had gone into the shopping centre for the morning. I'd tagged along, happy as anything that I'd been invited to be part of the crowd. When we got there, I only realised that the reason I'd been asked along had been so that they could make fun of me. They dared me to steal some cheap costume jewellery from one of the shops. They didn't think I would, which was probably why I did.'

She glanced up at him ruefully. 'I made a hopeless shoplifter. I couldn't have been more obvious. Of course, I was caught as soon as I walked out, and hauled down to the police station and treated like a common criminal. It wasn't even as though it made a spot of difference, because when I was returned to the home I *still* ended up standing out and being ostracised. But I learned my lesson, so that's just one reason why I would *never* have stolen anything again.'

Leandro found that he didn't like thinking of her as a kid in a police station, probably confused and scared. In fact, he found himself wishing that he could find whatever policeman had taken her in and beat the living daylights out of him, which was such a crazy reaction that he almost wanted to laugh.

It struck him, in a moment of blinding clarity, that the two of them might have come from wildly different backgrounds but that they had more in common than either of them might think.

Frowning at the sudden bout of introspection, Leandro relaxed back in the chair, topped up his wine glass and looked at her with brooding intensity. 'Like I said, there's nothing to be gained from trips down memory lane. Tell me what you've been up to since we parted company.'

Abigail stilled. She licked her lips nervously and made a big effort not to look away, because that would have been a sure sign of a guilty conscience, and she *didn't* have a guilty conscience.

'I...I managed to find the job I now have.'

She cleared her throat and looked at him as evenly as she could.

'When I got back to London I was out of work, as you know, and I'd gone to a café to try and work out what to do next. I didn't know who would employ me after that reference from my ex-boss. Who was going to believe me? Anyway, while I was having a cup of coffee Vanessa came in, and there were no free tables so she asked if she could sit at mine and, well, the rest is history, so to speak.'

She looked at him wryly and then said with some satisfaction, 'I told her all about my past and the stupid lies that had been told about me and she believed me. She gave me a job on a trial basis and it worked out brilliantly, as it happens. I seem to have a knack for selling stuff, including high-end jewellery. None of which,' she couldn't help adding, 'I have ever been tempted to stick in my handbag and take home with me.'

'And men?' Leandro decided that it was time to push on from a topic on which he had no intention of dwelling on for too long. What was done was done.

Abigail flushed a delicate pink.

'I think it's time for me to head upstairs now. I'm tired. I want to get a good night's rest because I intend to leave first thing in the morning, and if the weather is still poor then Hal and I will just have to chance it.'

She stood up and neatened her outfit, which felt inappropriate, because she was no longer here on business. Her coat was upstairs in the bedroom suite which had been allocated to her, a sumptuous space that felt nearly as big as a football field. As were her handbag and the company laptop which she had brought with her. She had no idea what Leandro had done with the ring. Maybe he would hang onto it for his future wife.

'Have there been other men?'

Abigail's breathing hitched. He stood up and closed the distance between them. She stuck her hands behind her back because she wanted to reach out and flatten them against his broad chest and feel the hardness of muscle and sinew underneath the black jumper. She wanted to fly back in time but that was impossible.

She thought of Sam, innocently lying in his cot back in London, and the series of decisions she had made when she had discovered that she was pregnant. Fear threatened to swamp her, fear and guilt. because, although she had been torn apart at the time, wondering whether she had made the right choice to keep the pregnancy a secret from Leandro, it had been relatively easy to live with her decision because it meant she could relegate their relationship to the past. In her head, she had kept open the option to get in touch with him at some point in the future, but she had lived for the present and so that point in the future had been nothing more than theoretical.

But the future had crashed into the present, challenging that decision she had taken and filling her with dread at just how close she was now to a conflagration that could get out of control.

She wouldn't allow that to happen. Maybe she would now rethink the choices she had made but she would do that coolly and calmly. That settled her and she relaxed a little. She thought about his question. A man in her life? She wanted to burst out laughing because, between work and motherhood, she barely had time to breathe, never mind deal with the complications of a relationship. Not that she had been tempted anyway.

'No, Leandro,' she said coolly. 'I didn't rush back to London and immediately get involved with your replacement. I've been busy trying to get my career going.'

'And no time left to jump back into the dating scene?' Leandro murmured.

'Unlike you.' Abigail couldn't resist the dig. Not only had *he* jumped right back into the dating scene but he had become so involved with a woman that she had actually been led to believe that marriage was on the cards. She turned away, angry with herself for feeling hurt and jealous.

'But it didn't work,' Leandro said softly. He reached out and circled her wrist with his hand. He stroked her skin with his thumb and Abigail wanted to moan and drag her hand away but she didn't do either. Instead, she froze.

'Want to know something?' he asked as his thumb continued to do its damage. 'I understood why when I saw you today, Abby.'

'I don't know what you're talking about,' she croaked, and he smiled crookedly at her.

'Yes, you do,' he corrected gently. 'I can feel the way you're trembling right now. You're still in my system. It doesn't make any sense, because you're the last woman I should still be interested in taking to bed, but against all odds you are. Do you think it's because what we had ended under such…bizarre circumstances?'

He sounded genuinely curious and his voice was calm, neutral and conversational. In fact, she had to sift through what he had just said and replay it in her head just to establish that she hadn't misheard it.

That he still wanted to take her to bed!

She tugged her hand and he tightened his grip on it and focused on her, his fabulous eyes lazy with intent. 'Now you're going to tell me that you have no idea what I'm talking about, aren't you? Maybe you'll express horror that I could even suggest such a thing. Am I on the right track?'

Spot on, Abigail thought. She licked her lips and tried to still her racing pulse. He was still the sexiest man she had ever laid eyes on in her life, but she was not attracted to him. *Because you couldn't possibly be attracted to a man who had insulted, offended and disbelieved you.* That just didn't make sense.

But her skin was prickling and dampness had pooled between her legs. Fascinated and mesmerised, she stared at him, sucked in by the low, honeyed seductiveness of his voice.

Leandro could feel the racing of her pulse under his thumb. Her skin was so soft and his recall of her so clear. Just touching her like this made him remember how it had felt to touch her all over, to hear the little cries and whimpers she'd made as she climbed towards an orgasm, the way she'd moved and wriggled under him. He was so turned on he had to adjust his stance to try and subdue the discomfort of his arousal.

His eyes drifted downwards to her parted lips.

Abigail knew that he was going to kiss her before his mouth covered hers and her body strained towards his, as natural an instinct as a flower leaning towards a source of light. His lips, when they touched hers, detonated a series of little thrilling explosions inside her. She wanted him. She'd never stopped wanting him. She hated him and was terrified of being here, in his company, carrying a secret she knew could be as devastating as dynamite, yet she couldn't get enough of his kiss.

With a helpless little groan, her fingers curled into his jumper and she angrily pulled him towards her even as he propelled her towards the wall without breaking physical contact.

His hands were hot and hungry on her, reaching to tug the prissy white shirt free from her trousers, then pushing underneath the shirt to cup her breasts and massage them until her nipples were pushing against the lace in a desperate bid to be caressed.

Leandro was shocked at how fabulously familiar her body was and even more shocked at how novel he still found the experience. Familiarity, in this instance, was showing no signs of breeding contempt.

He wanted, he *needed* more than just some schoolboy groping through a bra, and he discovered that his hands were shaking as he undid the tiny pearl buttons of her blouse. Given the option, he would have ripped the thing open, so desperate was he to suckle what his hands were touching, but taking his time at least had the advantage of imposing some control on his runaway libido.

Buttons finally undone, he delicately peeled aside her blouse and lifted her bra, pushing it up so that her generous breasts were on show.

'You're so beautiful,' he said in a ragged undertone. He held her breasts in his big hands and rubbed his thumbs over her nipples, watching as they promptly stood to attention, the pink tips hardening and peaking under the caress. He looked at her. 'I want you so much it hurts,' he confessed, and Abigail shuddered because this couldn't be more wrong and yet it felt so right. 'Tell me right now that you don't want me back…'

CHAPTER THREE

'WANT YOU BACK? *Want you back?*' Abigail fought the heat suffusing her body and pushed him away but her hands were shaking as she busied herself trying to re-arrange her clothing.

In response, Leandro planted both hands on either side of her, caging her in, and he looked at her without batting an eyelid. 'Shameful admission, I know,' he murmured. 'But the truth, nevertheless. I know you're not acquainted with the fine art of truth telling, but personally I find it rarely pays to ignore it. And the truth is that we're still where we were a year and a half ago—burning up for one another.'

This time Abigail *did* laugh. 'How can you call me a liar in one breath and then tell me that I'm still stupid enough to fancy you in the other?' Backed against the wall, and trapped by the sheer steel wall of his body inches away from her, she folded her arms defiantly and stared at him.

'Because lust has nothing to do with whether you like someone or not.'

'Maybe not for you!'

'Shall we put that to the test? Oh, we already did. You failed.'

Abigail could feel the little nerve jumping in her neck. She should really *hate* all this cave man, macho stuff but the truth was that Leandro did it all so well. He'd always had that intensely masculine air of cool self-assurance and a careless assumption that the world would jump when he told it to. She'd found it novel, strange and a massive turn on all at the same time and she hadn't even been able to work out why. She just had.

Now, he was exercising that self-assurance again and she could feel herself getting addled.

'Leandro, this is crazy,' she muttered. 'If it hadn't been for your ex-fiancée, I wouldn't even be here. We wouldn't have met again.'

'I wish you'd stop calling her my ex-fiancée,' Leandro said irritably. 'That was all wishful thinking on her part.'

'You were very well suited.'

'Really? I had no idea you knew her.'

'Oh, stop being so sarcastic, Leandro. You know what I mean.'

Leandro flushed darkly. In the space of only a handful of weeks, she had become the only woman who had never shied away from saying exactly what she thought. She hadn't been impressed into obedience and he had liked that. 'We're moving off topic here,' he drawled. 'We were talking about this thing that's still here between us. You were busy trying to pretend that there was nothing and I was on the brink of proving to you that there is.'

'I didn't say that there was...that there was *nothing*,' Abigail denied in a harried undertone. 'But whatever there is, it's inappropriate.'

'I don't care about what happened in the past,' Leandro lied smoothly. He cared all right but, in the end, this was an even better situation in a way. Shorn of emotion, this became a sating of their physical appetites and the most natural thing in the world. It was unthinkable that she would dig her heels in and deny what was obvious and, if she did, then he had every intention of using every bit of ammunition to hand to batter down her defences.

She was probably right. If she hadn't shown up on his doorstep, their paths would never have crossed again.

But she *had* shown up and he had seen in a blinding flash that she was still in his system and would always be in his system unless he did something about it.

'But I do,' Abigail said stubbornly. 'I didn't have the greatest of backgrounds, and I was a coward for not admitting that to you from the beginning, but I didn't deserve...' She looked away, bright red, teetering between calling him out for the blind loyalty to his sister which had made him judge her without giving her a fair hearing, and just running as fast as she could away from him and the crazy feelings he had stirred up in her. 'It doesn't matter,' she muttered, staring down at her feet. Her heart was beating like a drum inside her chest and her fingers were digging into her forearms as she continued to focus on the ground while his dark gold eyes raked over her.

'Look at me, Abigail.' He stood back and tilted her

chin with one finger so that their eyes met. 'I wouldn't be standing here if I didn't think that there was something *inevitable* about this accidental meeting.' Eyes still on her, he carefully traced her collarbone, and she was helpless to do anything about it. 'What happened to end things happened, and the truth is that they would have ended at some point anyway.' Something stirred uneasily inside him and he frowned briefly. 'If it's any consolation,' he confessed gruffly, 'it did make me realise how possessive my sister had become over the years without my realising.'

'Really?' Abigail's eyes widened because this was some admission, coming from a guy who would sooner have all his teeth yanked out with pliers than admit to any form of weakness, and admitting that he had allowed his sister to take control—and had misjudged the situation—was a form of weakness.

Not that it made a blind bit of difference because, as he said, things would have ended anyway. She had fallen in love with a man for whom things were always going to end. She was always going to reach a sell-by date.

'Family dynamics.' He shrugged as he realised how easy it still would be to be lulled into thinking that she was someone she wasn't. 'Will you let me see you?'

'I beg your pardon?' Now that she wasn't caged in, Abigail knew that she could terminate this conversation and briskly walk towards the door, head for her bedroom, lock herself in and make sure that she left the following day without laying eyes on him. Instead, she heard herself saying, 'I don't know what you mean.'

'Take off your shirt. I loathe that shirt anyway. Very prim and proper and we both know that you can be the opposite of prim and proper.'

'Leandro…'

'I've always loved it when you said my name like that—in that breathy, husky voice of yours.' His words were like a physical caress, pulling memories from where they had been hidden and wreaking havoc with her prized common sense.

'There's nothing wrong with my shirt.'

'There's everything wrong with it. All those infernal buttons. Very starched and white.'

'It's my work outfit.'

'I hate it and I'd really like you to take it off.'

'I can't believe you're saying that, Leandro.' But she wondered why she was surprised when he had always been the king of the outrageous demand.

His voice was as smooth as caramel and he made everything sound so easy. Two people, no strings attached, no thorny past to contend with, thrown together *for a purpose.* He almost made it sound as though it would be an insult to fate were they not to take the opportunity to jump right back into bed with one another simply because they happened to be unexpectedly sharing the same space.

Her mouth was still tingling from his hungry kiss, and her whole body was on fire, and the worst of it was that he knew it. He knew it because he *knew her.* She might have kept stuff from him—not through design but by default, almost—but really she had opened up to him in ways she'd never dreamed she would.

He had known what she thought about everything under the sun, and he'd certainly known how she'd felt when he touched her, when he'd whispered into her ear. That was why he knew exactly what was going on inside her and was certainly part of the reason why her feet seemed to be nailed to the floor and her wilful body was determined not to listen to calm reason and get the heck out of the kitchen and away from him.

'Or…'

His voice lingered seductively on that one syllable, stretching it out till her nerves were on the point of shredding.

'I could always do the taking off for you… Will you let me?'

Rendered speechless, Abigail just stared and he grinned and tilted his handsome head to one side. 'You're not saying anything. Either you've decided to consent through silence or else I take your breath away. Maybe both.'

'You are *so* full of yourself, Leandro Sanchez.'

'I know,' he said ruefully, 'and, believe me, it's something I'm trying to cure.'

'How can you flirt with me when you don't even like me?'

'I don't know,' Leandro replied with a lot more honesty than he'd intended. 'Let's stop talking.' He began to undo the buttons she had fastidiously done up only moments before and she felt her knees buckling as she let him.

His hands were very gentle on her, barely brushing her skin as he eased the shirt off and then unhooked the bra from the back and removed it. He'd moved closer to her and the only indication that he was turned on was his unsteady breathing and the hot, drowsy look in his eyes.

Abigail knew that if she touched him through his jeans she would feel the rock-hard length of his arousal, and just thinking that chipped away even more at her non-existent defences. Hard on the heels of that thought came another memory, the memory of how he filled her up, the surge of sensation as he thrust inside her, moving and building a rhythm that had never failed to take her over the top.

Pressed against the kitchen door, she arched back and her eyelids fluttered as he lowered himself down in front of her. It had been so long and, yes, she had missed this so much. It was a bitter pill to swallow because it defied all logic, but he was right. She could still want him, *want this,* even though their relationship had collapsed, even though there was no affection left between them, but instead the biggest secret of all that had the power to blow his world apart.

That secret should have stopped her but by the time his mouth was sucking on her nipple she was already too far gone into a world of heightened sensation where nothing mattered but what he was doing to her.

She plunged her hands into his hair and then half-groaned and sagged back as his questing mouth travelled lower, tracing her stomach then pausing as he reached her no-nonsense grey trousers, which doubtless he also loathed.

All those muddled thoughts were zooming around

in her head as he began to unzip them, tugging them gently down until they pooled at her feet.

Her fingers were still entwined in his dark, springy hair, her eyes were shut and she could barely breathe as he pressed his face against her underwear, breathing her in.

He'd introduced her body to the art of making love and she could remember the way she had jerked back when he had first gone down there. She hadn't been able to imagine such an intimacy, but she had quickly become a fan, and her body now quivered in anticipation of his mouth and tongue delving into her. She was so turned on.

He nuzzled for a while, breathing her in, then delicately he pulled down her panties and she shimmied obligingly out of them. Her body was incredibly familiar even though Leandro dimly registered that she was slightly more rounded than he remembered. If possible, that made her even sexier. Her hips were fuller and her belly was still flat but slightly softer.

Same musky scent, though, that had always been able to work on him like a drug.

He placed his hands on her inner thighs and gently eased them apart and then he flicked his tongue into her, finding the tight, throbbing bud and tickling it until she was melting.

He wanted to pleasure her so badly it hurt. He craved the feeling of her coming against his mouth and he continued to lick and suck while her stifled whimpers turned into low, barely audible groans, and then she was coming, her spine arching, her whole body stiffening and flailing as she couldn't hold on any longer.

Abigail practically collapsed against him. Her climax was so explosive that it blew her legs from under her. Hot, naked and shaking, she clung to him and Lord knew what would have happened next in that scenario if the shrill sound of the landline hadn't interrupted what had been, as she came to realise faster than a bolt of lightning, a moment of complete and utter madness.

Leandro swore under his breath and stalked across to snatch the receiver of the kitchen phone up, at which point he had a brusque and intensely irritated conversation with someone who seemed to be calling from a catering company.

By the time he turned round, Abigail had managed to shove her hot, disobedient body back into its suit of armour, even though she knew that she looked a mess—hair all over the place, lips swollen from where she'd been thoroughly kissed and her whole body still flushed in the aftermath of her orgasm.

Just thinking about what she'd done made her feel sick.

'I am *not*,' Leandro grated, 'seeing this!'

Abigail flinched. 'This should never have happened!' She knew just how that sounded, and she hated herself for the picture she was painting of a woman who was happy to lead a man on and then slam the doors firmly shut in his face once she'd got what she wanted. But she wasn't going to fall into his arms again. *She couldn't.* Now that sanity had been restored, there was so much at risk here that her blood ran cold just thinking about it.

She literally burned with mortification.

'Care to explain why?'

Abigail hugged herself. 'I know what you're probably thinking.'

'You have no idea what I'm thinking!'

He was now standing directly in front of her, towering and darkly, scarily angry. However much she quailed inside, and however ashamed she was at her appalling lapse of judgement, Abigail knew that she just couldn't afford to be steamrollered by Leandro. She stood her ground with shaky legs and met his glare head-on.

'It was a mistake,' she offered with choked sincerity.

'Why?'

'Because…' She opted for part of the truth 'I can't help being turned on by you. Maybe it's because you were my first…' She went bright red but ploughed on. 'Or maybe you're right and it's because things ended… well…maybe there's some unfinished business there. I… You touched me and I…I remembered, Leandro…'

Leandro flushed darkly, swung away and hooked his thumbs into the pockets of his jeans for a few silent seconds. He didn't care to be reminded of the power of those memories because, whilst he could acknowledge that to himself, he had no intention of sharing any such admission with Abigail. To do so would have signalled a fundamental weakness he wasn't about to expose. He disliked the notion of anything or anyone having power over him and memories fitted neatly into that category.

'But it would be wrong for us to go there,' she volunteered tentatively. Part of her thought that it was rich suddenly to come out with all of this when she had only just descended from a climax that had blown her apart.

She glanced down quickly to see that the bulge was still there, pushing against his jeans, and she licked her lips and hurriedly raised her eyes to catch him looking at her. 'And I'm sorry if I gave you the wrong impression.'

Leandro didn't miss a thing. If the damned phone hadn't interrupted them, he would have taken her up to his room and he would have lost himself in her. As it stood now…

He was in line for a very long, very cold shower… and afterwards?

He wanted her and he knew why she had backed away with a sudden attack of conscience. She was dwelling on what had happened between them and allowing it to get between them.

He raked his fingers through his hair and sighed. 'Why were you afraid to tell me the truth about yourself all those months ago? You can hardly blame me for reaching the conclusions I reached and acting the way I did. Concealment always carries the stench of something underhand.'

Startled, Abigail stared at him. This was the first time he had come close to giving her a chance to explain. In the aftermath of their break-up he had been happy to walk away without giving her any opportunity to defend herself.

'I told you,' she said, clearing her throat. 'I was overawed by you. I'd never met anyone like you in my life before. Also,' she added with complete honesty, 'around you I didn't feel like myself.' She grimaced, relaxing a little, because he wasn't attacking her for stringing him on when he could have been and she would have understood. She managed to get her legs to do something constructive and shuffled to one of the kitchen chairs, promptly sinking into it with relief.

'I was somebody different—somebody *normal*—and I liked how that felt. I'd spent my life being cautious around men but you swept into my life and all of that changed in a heartbeat. It was like being on a roller-coaster ride.' He strolled towards the table to join her and she raised her huge, clear, green eyes to him. 'And once I was on that ride, there was no room to raise uncomfortable topics about my past. Besides, I didn't think it would last as long as it did.'

Long enough for her to fall head over heels in love with him.

'And when it carried on…the right time just never seemed to be there.' She stood up and smoothed down her trousers, uncertain, because he had gone from rampant lover to inscrutable spectator. 'I should head up to bed now.' A glance through the window told her that the snow was still falling but lightly. She hoped for the best. She couldn't possibly stay another day in his house.

Their eyes met and for a few seconds she thought about what she had done and the secret she had kept to herself for all the right reasons. She ran through some of those reasons in her head right now. They had parted on the worst possible terms. He had never cared about her. For him, she had only ever been a short-term fling and he had never encouraged her to think otherwise. When she'd found out that she was pregnant, she had been determined to hold onto her baby, because no one had ever held on to *her.* By then, Leandro had been out of the picture.

She had imagined contacting him to give him the glad tidings, then she had gone further and wondered whether he might feel inclined to take the baby from her because, at the end of the day, he would be its father. If he'd chosen to do that, she wouldn't have stood a chance and, after the way they had broken up, he might very well have seen it as an opportunity to get some revenge for, as far as he was concerned, having been lied to.

Abigail had known that she would never risk losing her baby and, after several weeks with Leandro, she had seen for herself that he led the sort of high-octane, high-pressured lifestyle that was not compatible with living with a young child.

Fear created by dark thoughts about worst-case scenarios, heartbreak at being dumped by the guy she had fallen in love with because she wasn't good enough and hormones coursing through her system had propelled her into a decision she now realised had been a life-changing one.

Yet it had been a curiously easy decision to make in the aftermath of their relationship.

She had even told herself that it was responsible not to foist an unwanted child on a guy who had not planned for a pregnancy. Why should an inveterate bachelor be made to pay such a high price for a simple mistake?

But now, things didn't seem quite so clear cut. She expected him to try and stop her but Leandro remained where he was, watching as she headed for the door, and she turned round when her hand was on the doorknob to inform him that she would be leaving first thing, whatever the weather.

'And no need for you to see us off,' she decided to tell him, to which he raised his eyebrows and kept looking at her until the colour crawled into her cheeks. 'We'll let ourselves out,' she finished lamely. Face flaming, Abigail dashed out of the kitchen, headed straight to the bedroom she had been allocated and only allowed herself to relax when that bedroom door was well and truly locked behind her.

She woke to the sound of knocking on her bedroom door, and when she sat up she realised with some dismay that it was after eight-thirty. She had planned to be up and out before seven. So much for that.

There was no service on her phone. It seemed that service was only available here and there in the house and her bedroom was not in that category. Still, she had texted the situation to Claire from downstairs the evening before, and could only hope that everything was all right. She was dying to get back to London.

The knocking continued. Abigail didn't have time to think about her state of undress. She'd had to sleep without anything on, because the alternative had been her work clothes, so she wrapped a bath towel round her and opened the bedroom door a crack to see Leandro outside, bright-eyed, bushy-tailed and looking unfairly drop-dead gorgeous in a pair of low-slung jeans and a thick cream jumper. She was conscious that the towel tightly wrapped round her barely skimmed her thighs.

He pushed the door open further with one foot and then folded his arms. 'I hate to wake Sleeping Beauty,' he said, eyeing the bank of windows behind her, across which the curtains had been tightly pulled, 'but I'm the bearer of bad tidings, I'm afraid…' Leandro watched with male appreciation at the enchanting picture Abigail made as she bolted towards the windows and yanked back the curtains with one hand while the other kept a tight hold on the towel.

She'd blown him off but there was no way he had any intention of retreating humbly to the sidelines to lick his wounds. That wasn't his style. He'd already determined the reason behind his malaise ever since they had broken up and he intended to do something about that. It would just take slightly longer and require slightly more thought than he had originally imagined.

For instance, he had optimistically harboured the assumption that one wild night in the hay would do the trick. So she'd knocked him back but, even if she hadn't, he could see that one night might not be enough to get her out of his system.

He'd somehow managed to forget the effect she could have on his libido. He was supremely confident about winning her over to his way of thinking because he had proved that she was still as turned on by him as he was by her. He was already gearing up for the thrill of that challenge as he heard her utter a soft exclamation of anguish as she saw that the snow, which should have gone away, hadn't. Out here, in the countryside, there were no gritted roads to give the illusion of things being done to remedy the situation either. The open fields that surrounded his palatial country manor were white and untouched. Not a gritting tractor in sight.

Abigail spun round to find that Leandro had entered the bedroom and was standing right behind her, and she jumped back and looked up at him. Their eyes tangled and for a few seconds she recalled what it had felt like to have him down between her thighs, bringing her to an orgasm that had been as devastating to her peace of mind as a runaway train mounting a crowded pavement. Dampness pooled between her legs, shocking and embarrassing.

'And it's only going to get worse.' He didn't bother to try and soothe her into any positive thoughts on that score. 'Out here, the snow can last for days. That's why I seldom risk coming here in winter. What I'm saying here is that there's no way the car that brought you here can take you back. In fact, if you turn around and angle your body to the left, you can just about make out the shape of it semi-buried under white. Hal's been out to have a go at it and he managed to drive it a few metres before giving up. I doubt he could even get the thing out of my drive, and it's miles from here before you're lucky enough to hit any kind of road that might have been salted.'

'No, don't say that,' was all Abigail could find to respond, aghast at this development. 'You don't understand, Leandro. I *have* to get back to London.'

'I've talked to your driver and he's more than happy to wait it out here, which will in all likelihood be for another night. I shall ensure that he is fed and watered. Between us, I get the impression that the man sees this as a weekend break from a household of tetchy kids.'

'I don't *care* about whether Hal is willing to stay another night here!'

'Well, you should,' Leandro pointed out, 'considering he's your means of transport out. Unless you're insured on the car? But either way it's moot. The country roads will be impassable, anyway.'

Abigail wanted to sob. 'This is *all your fault*,' she accused in a wobbly voice and Leandro shot her a perplexed look that further inflamed her because it reeked of insincerity.

'Explain,' he said drily. 'You must think I have superhuman powers if I can conjure up a fall of snow simply to scupper your plans for leaving. But, before you pull another "damsel in distress" fainting act, you'll be reassured to know that I have a similar problem. I, too, need to get down to London. Bear in mind that this weekend here was sprung on me as an unfortunate surprise. I hadn't planned on opening up the house until early spring.'

Abigail glumly wondered what that had to do with anything. So both of them would be stuck here. Little did he know that, whatever important deal he had to close, it was as nothing compared to the responsibilities she urgently had to return to.

'So what?' she said shortly.

'So you should go and change,' Leandro murmured.

Which was a sharp reminder to Abigail that she was still clutching a towel with absolutely nothing on underneath while he stood there, smirking.

She saw red and swallowed hard because this was not how she had envisaged her ring-bearing trip to the

Cotswolds ending. Everything had gone wrong. The weather had been hideous. There had been no loving fiancée for the ring she had carefully transported. She had crashed into her past when she had least expected it. She had become a stupid victim of all those physical responses she knew she should have put behind her and, to top it off, meeting Leandro again out of the blue had forced her to confront all the decisions she had made in good faith.

And, as if all that wasn't bad enough, she was now going to be stuck here with him because fate couldn't do the decent thing and clear a path for her to return to London where she would have the peace and space to think things through.

'I will need to make some calls,' she muttered, and wanted to smack him very hard when he grinned at her.

'You're getting worked up over nothing,' he said in a placating voice that made her teeth snap together. 'Hal is going to be staying on another night because he will have to drive the car back down to London. Fortunately for you, there is alternative transport.'

'What do you mean?' Abigail frowned because, aside from skiing their way cross-country, she couldn't think of any other means of manoeuvring in the snowy conditions. And that wouldn't work because she had never been near a pair of skis in her entire life.

'I've had my guy fly my helicopter up this morning. I have a landing pad and, as long as the snow isn't too deep, it is always possible for me to get out if I need to.'

'You had your *guy* fly *your helicopter* up?'

'It's a luxury, I know,' Leandro imparted smugly.

'So…we're going to take a helicopter down to London?'

'Hence it's imperative that you slip out of your towel and get back into your working clothes.' He strolled towards the window and peered out before turning his attention back to her. 'The snow's fine but it's piling up fast. Leave it too long, and we really will be stranded here with Hal and an all-you-can-eat buffet of unused party food.'

Leandro truly felt that sometimes things happened for a reason and this snow was a perfect opportunity to deliver her back to London, minus her driver, and directly to her house, to discover exactly where that might be.

He felt extremely satisfied at being in control of the situation. He was particularly pleased because, the last time round, control had not been at his disposal and that had been a big mistake.

'Meet me in the hall in half an hour.' He headed for the door without looking back over his shoulder but in his mind's eye he could see her with that scanty towel trying hard to cover her up, and then he pictured her without it at all.

Naked and sexy and the stuff of all his fevered imaginings.

She'd had a night to think about…things. A night to realise that it would be futile to try and ignore the fire still burning between them. Her blushing and coy backing away had told its own story. She was as jumpy as a cat on a hot tin roof around him and he was convinced that, once she was in her own comfort zone, having been solicitously dropped off by him, she would relax and be open to exploring the chemistry between them.

Abigail watched Leandro shut the door behind him without a second glance back at her. Helicopter? That would make nothing of the trip and she would be back in her house within a couple of hours, if as long as that.

He would go his own way and she would really have to think about what happened next now that he had resurfaced in her life.

CHAPTER FOUR

ABIGAIL MANAGED TO find service on her mobile in the hall and she made a harried call to Claire while Leandro was outside, doing whatever had to be done to direct his pilot. She would be back within a couple of hours—so please could Claire hang on a little bit longer?

Hal was in the kitchen being fed. He couldn't have been happier at being left in the snowy Cotswolds, in a sprawling country mansion, with limitless supplies of wonderful food and drink. He would drive the car back down to London just as soon as the snow cleared.

By the time Leandro re-entered the house, she was a little more reassured that all was right on the home front and that there had been no problems with Sam. It was the first time she had ever left him overnight and she had been worried sick.

She was fidgeting to leave and Leandro looked at her curiously.

'How many more times are you going to look at your watch?' he drawled, cupping her elbow in his hand and propelling her towards the front door. He had already given his instructions to clean the house and then close it up until he could arrange to pay a return visit.

'I'm anxious, that's all. I've never been in a helicopter before.' Outside the snow continued to fall, the flakes small and sharp, the wind biting and instantly putting red into her cheeks. She hadn't banked on such severe weather and her trouser suit, even with her coat, felt like inadequate protection.

'Looking at your watch a hundred times isn't going to make you less anxious. Don't worry, you will be delivered to London safe and sound and in once piece.'

Ushered into the helicopter, a monstrous black beast that looked as though it could survive Arctic conditions, Abigail had some time to think as the machine roared into life, head-butting the lashing wind, and rising up and up.

'I'm sure I will be,' she said eventually, over the roar of the helicopter as it swung and made its way south. She risked a look at him and shivered because he was just so *dominant,* so incredibly overwhelming. He induced raw, forbidden excitement and dreadful, paralysing apprehension in equal measure. Since she had never thought to lay eyes on him again, the apprehension was winning hands down just now as the helicopter buzzed its rapid path away from the snow towards cold, leaden skies that became clearer the further south they travelled.

She had begun unhappily questioning the road she had taken and the choices she had made and now, as London drew closer and closer, she felt faint with the sickening suspicion that she might have made the wrong decision.

Abigail didn't want to think this way. She fought

to recover some of the conviction she had felt all those months ago when she had decided not to contact Leandro.

She forced herself to remember that she had never known her parents. She had no idea who her father was because he wasn't even registered on her birth certificate. Her mother was now only a vague memory because Abigail had been taken into care when she had been just seven years old. She had known little but the indifference of strangers who had been paid to make sure that she was fed, watered and educated in a manner of speaking.

The system in which she had grown up had made her fiercely protective of her baby even before he had been born.

That was why she had chosen to keep the pregnancy a secret, she reminded herself. She hadn't dared risk Leandro, rich, powerful and filled with hatred after the break-up of their relationship, trying to lay claim to his child. Of course, he might have chosen to walk away completely, given the option, or offer some financial support and nothing more, but that had been a risk she had been unwilling to take.

Who knew what the future held? she had asked herself. Maybe in time, when her baby was old enough to start asking questions, then she would reconsider the decision she had made, but by then she would be on her feet financially, would hopefully own her own house, and would certainly have many years of successful motherhood behind her to ensure that no one could take her child away from her.

In that manner, she had been able to shove any guilty conscience out of sight, and out of sight had been out of mind.

Her guilty conscience was certainly making up for lost time as she lapsed into silence during the short helicopter flight down to the outskirts of London.

The snow which had been falling steadily in the Cotswolds was not in evidence when they landed. It was cold and windy but, instead of snow, they exited the helicopter into freezing rain and Abigail wrapped her coat tightly around her and stood for a few seconds, getting her bearings.

'My car.' Hand propelling her gently behind her back, she found herself tripping along beside Leandro towards a gleaming black vehicle, at the side of which a smartly dressed middle-aged man was standing with the passenger door open.

With a stomach-churning feeling of someone on a rollercoaster ride, Abigail was deposited in the back seat of the car with Leandro next to her before she had time to consider what would happen next.

'Right.' Leandro slid shut a partition screen so that they were enclosed in complete privacy. 'Address?'

'Address?' She stared at him in alarmed silence as he waited patiently.

'Where do you live, Abigail?' He clicked his tongue impatiently as she continued to stare at him, cheeks a dull red, her mouth parted, her eyes wide. 'I need to tell my driver where to take you.'

Abigail closed her eyes briefly and rested her head against the leather seat. All the chickens had come home to roost now. She had closed the door on all those '*what if?*' questions which foolishly she had been sure would never see the light of day.

What if Leandro discovered that he had a son?

What if she had chosen to tell him the moment she had discovered that she was pregnant?

What if he threatened to fight her for custody?

'You don't have to drop me to my house, Leandro,' she said with a touch of desperation. 'You can drop me to the shop. Vanessa will be keen to hear how the whole thing went. I tried emailing her yesterday but I don't think it was sent.'

'You're still in the same clothes from yesterday.'

'That doesn't matter. They're clean! And…and…'

'Just tell me where you live. I'm sure your boss can wait another hour for the urgent debrief.' He clearly wasn't going to take no for an answer.

Defeated, Abigail just looked at Leandro's bronzed, handsome face. She'd really and truly thought that she had put him behind her. She'd made a big mistake and fallen for someone utterly out of her league, and she had only discovered *just* how unreachable he was when he had believed his sister and the lies her ex-boss had told and refused even to allow her to give her side of the story.

She had fallen for a guy who had chosen to ignore everything they had shared because all he'd seen was a lying gold-digger who had used him. It hadn't mattered that they had done more than have sex. It hadn't mattered a jot that they had laughed, talked and done all the things that couples falling in love with one another do. Except, she had misread the signals. While *she* had been falling in love, *he* had just been having a bit of fun. All Leandro had shared with her was his body.

She'd been bitterly hurt and heartbroken when they had split up, but she'd had a lifetime of having to pull herself up and get on with things, and she had done it again. Her eyes had been opened and she had put him behind her as a mistake she had made.

One sidelong glance to her right was enough to confirm that she hadn't even come close to putting Leandro behind her. Her biggest mistake right now would be to let him see how vulnerable she still was as far as he was concerned.

She drew in a deep breath and said steadily, 'I think we need to talk before you drop me off at my house. Would you have some time? We could go to…a café close to where I live…'

Leandro leaned against the door and looked at her. Talking could only mean one thing and he controlled a kick of satisfaction at knowing what it meant. She'd had time to think about what he had said and the offer he'd put on the table was one that she was going to accept. Lust was a powerful thing and of course, he thought with cool rationality, there would also be the lure of money because she knew from experience that he was a generous man.

He smiled. 'I could spare the time,' he murmured. 'And we could always go to your place instead, or even mine. I have a place in Belgravia. Why don't I tell my driver to take us there and when we're finished…

talking…he can drop you back to your flat? How does that sound?'

Abigail couldn't think of anything worse. As soon as she could, she would have to phone Claire and tell her to hang on for just a teeny bit longer, but there was no way she was going to his place in Belgravia, or anywhere else aside from a busy café, surrounded by people, where she would be able to say what she had to say and the fallout would be diluted. She knew very well why he'd want nothing more than for her to go to his house.

Not going to happen in a million years.

'No,' she said simply.

Leandro shrugged. He realised that he didn't care how much money he had to part with. He'd never wanted anyone the way he wanted her, and the fact that her CV as a woman who had lied to him and cosied up to him under false pretences left a lot to be desired didn't seem to have diminished her appeal.

He was willing to throw the rule book out of the window just to get her out of his system once and for all. At least this time round he was in full possession of the facts and would be able to control the situation.

Abigail gave him the address of a café she had occasionally visited in the past and he dutifully relayed the information to his driver. Then—not because she was interested, but to break a silence that was beginning to make her skin prickle—she said, 'Your country house is magnificent, Leandro. How often do you get up there to stay?'

'A couple of times a year.' She had tied her hair back

once again but in his mind's eye he was seeing it in all its glory, hanging low down her back, vibrant and colourful. A few stray strands hung down on either side of her face and he wanted to tuck them neatly behind her ears and then pull her towards him so that he could feel the cool softness of her mouth on his.

'What a shame that you have so many houses in different parts of the world and you seldom get to enjoy them.'

'Perhaps, for me, it's the ownership that counts and that none of my properties will ever lose me money. I keep a sharp eye on them all and, over the years, they have done sterling work when it comes to increasing in value.'

'There's so much more to life than money.'

Leandro laughed shortly. 'Is this where we start going over old ground so that you can try and convince me that you're as pure as driven snow, despite the fact that you made no effort to tell me the truth about your background or about why, indeed, you were sitting in my hotel foyer in the first place?'

'No. I don't want to go over old ground any more than you do. I was just making small talk.'

'Feel free to skip the small talk.'

'If you dislike me so much, why do you still want to...sleep with me? How can you sleep with someone you dislike?'

'Do you have to ask that?' Leandro questioned roughly. 'Aren't we in the same boat? Driven by the same urges that haven't gone away? Or are you telling me that you have feelings for me? Because, if that's the case, then I should be clear right now and tell you that, sex or no sex, this is about wiping the slate clean and nothing more.'

Abigail resisted the urge to tell him that he was crazy if he thought that she wanted to talk to him because she had come round to his way of thinking, but then that would lead to all sorts of questions, and eventually to the conversation she knew would have to take place, but not in the back seat of his chauffeur-driven car.

'I don't have feelings for you, Leandro.' She stuck her chin out at a defiant angle. 'How could I?'

'Well, at least we're agreed on that score. I expect this conversation you want to have is to do with the terms and conditions of any liaison we enter into?'

'Yes, but not in the way you imagine,' Abigail told him truthfully.

Leandro shot her a half-smile. 'I'm a big boy, Abigail, and too experienced to be surprised by anything. Terms and conditions are a good thing in this situation.'

'Are they?' She was pretty sure that, firstly, he *wasn't* too experienced to be surprised by anything and, secondly, the terms and conditions she had in mind would take him so far out of his comfort zone that describing them as *a good thing* would be the last thing he'd do when she was done talking.

Done telling him what she'd never envisaged telling him. She should be scared stiff, but she felt very, very calm as the car continued to eat up the miles to the café. Sam was nearly one. She'd had months of motherhood and she felt much stronger than she had during those tumultuous months of pregnancy. Then afterwards, when she had held her new-born baby in her arms, she'd been torn between marvelling at the miracle of life looking at her with unfocused big, black eyes, and sickly wondering how on earth she was ever going to cope.

'Of course they are,' Leandro murmured, tilting her chin so that she was looking at him and actually *seeing* him instead of staring off into the distance, almost as if he no longer existed. 'I like terms and conditions. They're practical. They help keep things on an essential business level.'

Abigail's breathing quickened. His touch electrified her and that wasn't going to do. She wrested herself away but the blood had rushed into her face. 'If you'll give me a minute, I have to make a call before we get there.'

'We'll be there in under twenty minutes. What's the big rush?'

'I have a friend staying with me and I need to get in touch with her.'

'Friend? What friend?' His eyes narrowed and he shifted impatiently.

'My friend Claire is at home.' Abigail was already dialling. She'd planned to wait for a snatched moment when Leandro was otherwise occupied to make this call, but what did it matter now? Still, she kept the conversation brief, merely informing her friend that she would be home soon and thanking her for helping out.

'Helping out with what?' Leandro stared at her, frowning. Curiosity about her wasn't part of the deal and yet he was curious. Hushed conversations, he reasoned, had that effect on a person.

Abigail chose to ignore that because he would find out soon enough. 'I won't be able to hang around for long,' she said instead.

Leandro scowled at the brush-off but he decided to let it go. 'Nor will I,' he informed her. 'This whole sorry mess has screwed up my schedule. It might be Sunday but I've had to cancel several conference calls.'

Abigail felt a pang of sympathy for the woman who had now been reduced to the creator of a *sorry mess* that had put his work schedule out of sync.

She glanced through the window to find that they were already in North London, and it wasn't long before the car was pulling to a stop in front of the café, disgorging them both into damp cold and the onset of a fine, grey drizzle.

Her stomach clenched into knots as they found a table. She'd thought that it might have been busy but in fact the little chi-chi café, usually packed with yummy mummies or nannies with their little charges, was relatively empty.

'So…' Leandro wondered if she could look any more nervous. Should he help her out with the 'terms and conditions' chit-chat? Maybe ease the path by talking about his generosity as a lover? Clear the way for her to ask him what she wanted? Maybe not. 'Let's cut to the chase. Tell me what you wanted to talk to me about.'

They'd ordered coffees and these had now been brought to them, along with a selection of pastries, which she looked at without touching. He had no such qualms, breaking a croissant and looking at her steadily as he ate.

'Do you remember the time we went to that lake?'

Leandro paused mid-bite and gently replaced the croissant on his plate. He sat back, his big body loosely relaxed and yet tellingly still. He had no idea where this was going and that, in itself, wasn't working for him. He also didn't like the way she was fidgeting, playing with the rim of her cup and studiously avoiding his eyes.

'I remember,' he said abruptly. 'Five days in a little cabin by a lake just outside Toronto. Why do you ask? Trip down memory lane? I thought we'd agreed that there was no profit in going there.'

Abigail looked at him without any outward sign of the nervousness tearing her up inside. His lean, handsome face was closed and she knew that he would be annoyed because this was not what he had been expecting to hear. 'Something happened there, Leandro,' she said quietly. 'Do you remember?'

Leandro shook his head and raked his fingers impatiently through his hair. 'Are you going to carry on speaking in riddles, Abigail? Because I haven't come here to play guessing games with you.'

'We made love by the lake. Do you remember?' Her voice had grown wistful without her realising it. 'It was really warm and we'd been lying out on the jetty with a picnic lunch and a bottle of wine and we...we made love right there, out in the open.'

Leandro remembered it all. In fact, it had been the

first time he had really felt as though he'd been on holiday, and he'd never felt so relaxed in his life before. Unfortunately, there was always a serpent lurking in paradise, and he wasn't going to be sucked into dwelling on a memory that didn't deserve an airing considering the revelations that had come later.

'We didn't use any contraception.'

Five little words dropped into the silence like unexploded bombs, except that it took a few seconds for them to sink in. She was looking at him carefully but his mind had gone blank and he felt like his thoughts were wrapped in fuzzy cotton wool.

'What are you saying?' he asked eventually.

'You know what I'm saying, Leandro.' Abigail's voice was gentle. 'I know you're probably going to be enraged, and maybe you'll think that I should have told you then, but I'm telling you now. We had unprotected sex and I got pregnant.'

'You're lying.'

'That's why I was so desperate to get back down to London. Claire, the friend I just spoke to, had agreed to look after Sam because I had to deliver the ring, but I never expected to get stuck up there.'

'If this is some sort of gimmick to get me to part with money, then you're overplaying your hand.'

They hadn't used any contraception. He'd been so turned on that he'd taken a risk. For the first time in his life, he had taken a risk.

'He's ten months old.'

'I refuse to believe a word of this.' But the burnished

bronze of his golden skin was ashen. He *didn't* believe what she was saying, but he was still doing the maths.

She sighed. 'I would have told you right at the beginning, Leandro, but I was scared. We'd broken up under some pretty horrible conditions, and I was scared because I thought you might try and take Sam away from me.'

Leandro reached for his coffee cup and was surprised that his hand was unsteady.

'You need time to process all of this. I can see that.' Abigail stood up and began backing away from the table. 'If you let me have your mobile number, then I will give you a call in a couple of weeks' time, once you've…um…come to terms with…everything. And I just want you to know that I'm not expecting anything from you.'

The sight of her scuttling towards the exit galvanised Leandro faster than a rocket blazing into outer orbit. He slammed some money on the table and was by her side before she had time to do a runner.

Two weeks? Then she'd be in touch?

She'd just dropped a hand grenade into his lap and she really and truly thought that she could disappear and then resurface after he'd dealt with the fall out?

Had the woman lost her mind?

'Where the hell do you think you're going?' His hand circled her arm and he yanked her to a stop, ignoring her wriggling attempt to break free. 'Don't think that you can spring this on me and then vanish!'

'You need time to process…'

'Spare me your pop psychology! You tell me that you have a child…'

'*We* have a child. A son.'

Their eyes tangled. *A son.* There was no way that Leandro was going to cave in and believe her but…fatherhood. It was something he had never considered. Never wanted! He'd seen from his own unstable childhood that the production of children was something that could go horribly wrong. He'd not only learned from his own experience but he'd learned from his sister's. He'd never wished to reproduce and take a chance on being a father. It wasn't in his make-up.

What if she was telling the truth? Faced with that possibility, Leandro suddenly knew what it felt like for one's world to fall apart. He'd sought order all his life, to combat the lack of order that had marked his formative years, and there could be nothing more disastrous and explosive when it came to destroying all that hard-fought-for order than the arrival of a child.

But, no, he wasn't going to think like that.

He was a cool, rational man. He forced his thoughts away from *possibilities. Possibilities* counted for nothing.

'Where?'

'I beg your pardon?'

'You tell me that I'm a father. Then let me see my son.'

'Leandro…'

'This isn't going to play out the way you had in mind, Abigail. You don't get to spring something like this on me and then walk into the blue yonder. So you tell me that I have a son? Fine. Let's go and have a little meet and greet, shall we?'

He was clinging to this whole nonsense being a lie, but why would she lie about this? As fast as he tried to reason away the horror of what had been placed at his door, the counter-arguments piled up.

'I don't think—'

'No!' His voice cracked like a whip and she flinched and looked around her, but the street was quite empty of people. 'This situation is no longer within your control! You opened a door and now you can reap the consequences.'

Abigail stared at him, her eyes huge with dismay.

'Where do you live? And no beating about the bush, Abby. We go there and we go there *right now*, whether you like it or not.'

His car had been waiting on the other side of the road and Leandro hustled her towards it.

If his driver was in any way curious about the little sketch unfolding, he revealed nothing as he drove the ten minutes it took to get her to her house, a tiny rented place in a row of similar terraced houses.

Of course Claire would be agog. She had no idea that Sam's father was back on the scene because Abigail hadn't told her. But everything was happening so swiftly that this wasn't the time to launch into explanations.

But, as she hugged her friend and gently told her that *of course* everything was fine, she could practically inhale the scent of Claire's curiosity.

'Sam's asleep,' was the first thing she told Leandro, spinning round to look at him as soon as the front door was shut.

The house felt ridiculously tiny and his large, looming, threatening presence ate up the oxygen, making her light-headed with foreboding.

'I want to see him.'

'Do you still think I'm lying?'

'So, you have a son.' Leandro looked at her with flinty eyes. 'Who's to say that I am the father?'

'I would never lie to you about something like that.' She looked away because she didn't want to get into a squabble about the past and the lies he felt he had been told. Also, it hurt. It shouldn't, because he thought nothing of her now, but it still did. She blinked away an urge to cry. 'Follow me.' She spun round and he followed her as she made her way up the stairs to the little landing and to her bedroom, where Sam's cot was pushed up against the wall. It wasn't an ideal set up, but rents were high in London, and it was the best she could afford.

She always kept the side light by her bed switched on. It was dim and it ensured that she didn't risk waking him up when she retired to bed for the night. The light was on now because the curtains had been drawn to block out the watery early-afternoon light.

It cast a mellow glow through the bedroom, which was as neat as a pin and done up in calm, neutral colours.

She stood back and Leandro walked towards the cot. He looked down.

He was so tall, so stunningly gorgeous, and she felt

the sharp, piercing stab of real guilt that she had kept his son from him. Seeing him there, looking down into Samuel's cot, deprived her of all excuse for what she had done. A father looking down at his baby son. Sam was sleeping on his back, his short, chubby legs bent like a frog's at the knees, his arms raised on either side of his head.

Even in the dull, grey light the mop of dark hair and the faint olive of his skin was dramatic proof of paternity.

Staring into the cot, Leandro had no idea how much time passed by because it seemed to stand still. He'd looked out for his sister but he couldn't remember the time when she'd been as small as this.

Something filled him and he didn't know what it was. A vague, aching discomfort that was a nasty hollow in the pit of his stomach. The little boy had very dark hair like him, and he was olive-skinned, also like him. Clinging to the notion that he wasn't a father felt like a fantasy.

But he knew that he had to cling to it for a while longer. He would take nothing for granted. That just wasn't his nature and so he would not take this for granted even though somewhere deep inside he knew that the child was his.

And Abigail had kept him from him, would have *carried on* keeping him from him, had fate not forced their paths to cross.

Leandro had never thought about having children but now he was filled with the slow, steady pulse of rage that he'd been kept in the dark about the biggest thing that was possible to happen in anyone's life.

He turned away from the cot and looked at her, his face all angles and shadows. Then he moved towards her.

'Time…to talk.'

CHAPTER FIVE

'I'LL WANT A DNA TEST,' was the first thing Leandro said the second they were in her kitchen. He hadn't paid a scrap of attention to his surroundings, but now he did, and he didn't like what he saw. A small, shabby house hardly big enough to swing a cat in. Fresh paint and cheerful posters couldn't quite conceal the fact that the place was probably held together by masking tape and glue, and the rage that had swept through him earlier on, after he had looked down at the dark-haired baby in the cot, swept through him once again—a red tide that made him clench his jaw in an effort to exert some control.

There was still room for doubt.

Abigail was hardly noted for her fervent adherence to the truth. She'd spent weeks papering over her background and the small matter of the theft hanging over her head. She'd effectively lied to him, and right now he chose to disregard all the reasons she had come up with for her evasions. Right now he could only think that, if that baby upstairs was his, then life as he knew it was about to be turned on its head.

Abigail paled. 'You mean you don't believe me,' she said flatly.

'You come with a reputation. Taking you at your word would be a ludicrous act of charity on my part.' He pulled a chair and sat down, pushing it back so that he could extend his long legs. He felt like a giant in a playhouse.

The thought of any baby of his being raised in this sort of environment set his teeth on edge, and just like that he was shocked that his thoughts were already travelling down that road, already accepting possibilities.

One step at a time, he reminded himself grimly.

He would deal with the situation only when full paternity was revealed.

But the maths made sense…then there was that physical resemblance…and did he truly, in his heart, believe that she was the sort of woman who somehow would have thrown herself into bed with another man the second they'd parted company?

Leandro had a moment of complete terror, because suddenly he could see the ordered and well-oiled life he had built for himself falling apart at the seams.

'You're Sam's father, Leandro.' Abigail tilted her chin at a mutinous angle and held her ground but her world was shifting on its axis and she had no idea where it was going to end up. Right now, that look on his face was sending shivers of apprehension up and down her spine.

He'd wanted her for five minutes, wanted to have her back in his bed to *scratch an itch* until the itch went away. There had been no lingering affection behind that. Indeed, he had made sure to tell her that, so what on earth would he be thinking now?

Surely he must realise that a DNA test wasn't necessary? But then, Leandro's opinion of her was so low that he might actually believe that she would have disembarked at Heathrow airport over a year ago, broken-hearted, and headed for the nearest bar so that she could pick up a random stranger and drag him off to bed somewhere.

He loathed her, so where did that leave them? She should have been regretting bitterly the impulse to confess, but she wasn't. Seeing him standing over the cot and looking down into it had made her realise that she couldn't keep Sam from him. She had made her decision to say nothing for reasons that had been right for her at the time but, whatever the consequences now, it was right that he knew.

Which didn't help when it came to trying to figure out what happened next.

'I'm not asking for anything from you,' she said quietly. 'You didn't ask for this situation and you don't have to think that your life is going to be messed up because of it.' She'd sat opposite him and she was very much aware of how tiny the kitchen was because he took up so much space in it. In fact, she was very much aware, ever since he had entered the house, of how confined her surroundings were. Her heart began a slow, scared drum roll inside her chest.

If *she* could see the limitations of where she lived, and she'd grown accustomed to it over the months, then what must *he* be seeing?

This was a man with a helicopter and flash properties worth millions scattered across the globe. He snapped his fingers and everyone around him jumped to attention. A house wouldn't be a house for him unless every bedroom came with an *en suite* bathroom and a separate dressing room.

He was going to get a stupid DNA test, which would come back positive, and what then? Would he want to rescue his son from these surroundings? He couldn't. The sensible side of her saw that, because mothers had rights too, but he could provide so much as Sam's father and he could fight her with all the time and money at his disposal if he felt so inclined.

It suddenly seemed imperative that she persuade him that having his life remain as it was was what he wanted and needed.

'It was an honest mistake.' She smiled reassuringly at him. She felt about as sincere as the wicked witch smiling at Hansel and Gretel while she tried to lure them into the gingerbread house. 'You didn't ask for a child, Leandro, and I know what your lifestyle's like. Your feet hardly ever touch the ground! You said yourself that you rarely get to visit your beautiful country house. I'll bet you're hardly ever in England at all!'

She cleared her throat and wished that he would say something. Agree with her, preferably. Or at least give some indication that he was hearing what she was saying. He was looking at her with brooding intensity and it was doing nothing at all for her equilibrium. Or for the sensible, rational part of her that *knew* he couldn't sweep in and carry Sam off with him just because he was rich.

'What I'm saying,' she finished with a lot more bracing confidence than she was feeling, 'Is that I wouldn't want you to stop living the life you're living because of this. I'm perfectly capable of bringing Sam up on my own.'

'I will make arrangements for a paternity test.'

'Is that all you can say, Leandro?'

'What would you like me to say?' His voice was deathly quiet. 'That if you're right, and he's my son, that I'll oblige you by disappearing because it was all an *honest mistake*?' He stood up and looked down at her. 'I have no intention of taking your word for anything,' he said calmly. 'I'm a very rich man and whether I believe what you're telling me or not makes no difference. I am an easy target for gold-diggers.'

'I'm not a gold-digger, Leandro, and you should know that.'

Leandro's heart clenched at the genuine hurt in her face but he wasn't going to retract a word of what he'd said. He'd been invigorated by the thought of pursuing her to take her to his bed so that he could finish something that had been started, something that needed a proper conclusion so that he could get on with his life, but now things had changed. Very, very dramatically.

'What will the procedure be?' she asked, defeated. 'Will Sam have to go to a hospital for the test?'

'It will be handled discreetly. You will hear from me tomorrow about arrangements for the test and once the results are known…' He looked at her narrowly and thought about the small, softly breathing shape in the cot. Something threatened to engulf him, a depth charge as powerful as an earthquake. 'We will take it from there.'

'Leandro…' She stepped towards him then hesitated and remained where she was, hovering and uncertain.

'I'll be in touch.'

He didn't get in touch, but by lunchtime the following day she was contacted by a consultant employed by him to perform the test, and by six that evening the technician had come and gone and she had received a call from Leandro informing her that he, too, had been tested in accordance with the paternity-test requirements.

If Abigail had been hoping for some kind of clue as to what he was thinking underneath the clipped voice and the curt words, then she'd been barking up the wrong tree. The conversation, the first she'd had with him since he'd left her house, lasted ten seconds.

But the DNA test results would take at least a week, when you factored in overworked and underpaid health service workers who couldn't jump to attention and put their particular kit to the top of the queue. A week of breathing space. It would give her time to plan ahead for all possible eventualities.

She hadn't been expecting to see Leandro three days after he had left her house, and she certainly hadn't been expecting him to show up at the shop in all his dark, avenging glory.

About to leave for the day, Abigail looked up and

there he was, standing in the doorway, a tall, commanding presence that made her breath hitch in her throat and set up a nervous drum beat in her chest.

Everyone in the shop instantly stopped what they'd been doing. Two customers fell silent and stared. Brian, who worked alongside her, gaped. A woman, who looked no older than twenty-one and was dripping in jewellery, started breathing far more quickly than could be deemed healthy. Leandro ignored them all. He strolled towards her, face cool, expression unreadable.

Like a rabbit caught in the headlights, Abigail was finding it a challenge to move a muscle. In fact, she was finding it a challenge to breathe as he continued to close the distance between them.

'The results are back.'

She blinked and unfroze. 'I…I thought you said that you were going to call me.'

'I thought that breaking the news face to face would be a far better idea. We need to talk, Abigail, and unless you want us to have this conversation here then you're going to make your excuses and leave.'

'But I'm not due to finish for another two hours!'

'I don't care if you've just stepped through the door to start your day.' He looked around him, caught Brian's eye and turned back to her. 'That the guy in charge?'

'Give me five minutes… And, please, could you wait outside?'

'I'm very comfortable here.'

Abigail glared but had a hurried, low-key conversation with Brian and within minutes they were outside, back in the freezing February cold.

'My car is over there.' Leandro nodded towards the black chauffeur-driven car. 'Here's what we're going to do. We're going to go to my apartment—which is twenty minutes away—we are going to have a civilised conversation, and then we are going to go and get my son from whatever day-care place you've stuck him in.'

'You can't order me around.' But Abigail heard the weakness in her voice that signalled capitulation.

'You should be glad I've decided to go down the civilised route, Abigail. Because, right now, the last thing I feel is *civilised*.'

'Look...' She turned to him as the car into which she had been channelled like a kidnap victim pulled away, 'I can understand that you might be a little...annoyed...'

'A *little annoyed*?' Leandro looked at her with scathing disbelief. She was wearing practically the same drab outfit she'd been wearing when she had crash-landed back into his life days before. Her hair was tightly pulled back and her face was bare of all but minimal make-up. She looked like a mid-level career woman. Neither in her demeanour nor in her svelte shape did she betray any signs of being a mother. There was no way he could ever have guessed that she was, and again it hit him like a sledgehammer that she had kept his son from him.

She'd given him a way out with her speech about not wanting anything from him and, although he had never contemplated fatherhood, that 'way out' had struck him as offensive and insulting. His reaction had surprised him in its ferocity, as had the surge of primitive emotion that had gripped him when he had slit open that hand-delivered report to discover what he had known all along: the chances of him being Sam's father were ninety-nine per cent.

'What gave you the right to withhold my son from me?' Leandro gritted. 'Did you think that because we had broken up I was no longer due the decency of being told that I had fathered a child?'

Abigail flushed. For a man who was so good at keeping his emotions in check, those few words were incendiary.

They fired her up into a burning anger that matched his. What gave him the right to lay into her? They hadn't just *broken up*. He had rid himself of her the way someone would rid themselves of vermin. He had dispatched her as a criminal and a liar and now had the barefaced nerve to accuse her of lacking the *decency* to tell him that she had been pregnant!

'Start as you mean to go on' was the saying that sprang to mind, and Abigail suspected that, if she started by lying down and becoming a doormat he felt free to walk all over, then that would be her role forever, whatever joint way forward they finally found.

'I wasn't exactly filled with confidence that, if I threw myself at your feet and told you that I was pregnant, you wouldn't do your best to hurt me for all that stuff you'd been told by your sister!'

'The truth, you mean?'

'There you go! It was over three months after we broke up before I even found out that I was pregnant. I was so anxious about my future, so desperate to get a job, so worried about where I would end up living because all my savings were running out, that I didn't even notice that my periods had stopped! And, yes, I suppose I *could* have come running to you for help, but guess what? When you're accused of being a liar and a thief and a gold-digger, the last thing that occurs to you in a moment of blind panic is to turn to your accuser for help.'

'I wasn't just a random ex-boyfriend.' Leandro wasn't going to let her get away with that, 'I was the man who'd fathered the child you were carrying.'

He sighed with frustrated impatience and bit down hard on the bitter recriminations that begged to find a way out. They would be at his apartment in under five minutes. He'd drawn the partition and his driver couldn't hear a word they were saying but he still felt that he needed her somewhere entirely private in which to have this life-changing conversation. The back of a car just wasn't working for him.

'I told you,' Abigail reminded him in a driven voice, 'I was scared. Scared that you would try and take him away from me—that I would never be able to fight you, because you're rich and powerful, and at the time I was jobless and virtually unemployable, thanks to that scumbag of an ex-boss who'd lied about me.'

'What makes you think that I won't try and do that now?' Leandro asked.

Abigail froze and looked at him with horror. 'You wouldn't dare!'

'It's always a mistake to lay down a challenge to a man like me.' Leandro let the silence stretch between them, interminably long. Why not let her imagination go wild? It was the very least she deserved, as far as he was concerned.

'We're here. We can continue this conversation inside.'

Abigail, who could hardly think for the blind panic racing through her, and the worst-case scenarios filling her head, glanced distractedly at the elegant white building in front of which the car was slowing. Precise, black wrought-iron railings enhanced the windows, which were perfectly spaced and perfectly rectangular—like a child's drawing of what the outside of a house should look like, with all the dimensions of ruler-like precision. They entered a large hallway, tiled in original Victorian tiles, and were whooshed up in silence in the lift to his apartment, which she found extended over two floors and was as big as a house.

It was all white, aside from the dramatic, abstract works of art on the walls. The floor was blonde wood. There were no curtains at all, just shutters. The staircase that wound up to a galleried landing was the least child-friendly item of house décor she had ever seen in her entire life. Metal and with a token safety railing that would encourage any adventurous toddler to fall under. She was horrified.

Leandro was watching her carefully, and he frowned, because his apartment never failed to impress. He'd employed the best interior designer in London who had sourced materials from across Europe to create the perfect place. No expense had been spared and that was obvious, from the rich grey granite in the open-plan kitchen, to the pale wood on the floor which had been specially flown in from The Netherlands at great cost. Half of the paintings were by iconic and recognisable artists, the other half were investment pieces by up-and-coming artists, and their value increased weekly. The furniture was all bespoke.

'What's wrong?' he asked irritably and Abigail swivelled round to look at him, her hands belligerently folded.

'I hate this apartment,' she said bluntly, spreading one arm wide in a gesture of dismissal that got on his nerves.

'Don't be crazy. Of course you don't. No one hates this apartment.'

'It's…it's…soulless…cold. A *mausoleum* would have more atmosphere!'

Leandro glowered and remembered that she had never been shy about speaking her mind. In fact, she'd been the only woman in living memory ever to have disagreed with him about anything and he'd enjoyed it. She'd always been magnificent when she was arguing. She looked bloody magnificent now. He stared at her in brooding silence, noting the hectic flush in her cheeks, the pinkness of her full mouth and the fiery glitter in her bright green eyes.

Faster than a speeding bullet, his body responded to her with shocking enthusiasm. He hardened and his desire increased. Disgusted with himself, Leandro turned away and headed for one of the cream sofas artfully arranged around the only rug in the apartment, a grey hand-woven affair with a bold white, abstract pattern.

'Speaking of residences,' he told her coldly, 'let's

move away from the shocking condition of mine and let's talk about yours. When you were thinking about yourself and making your far-reaching decision to exclude me from my son's life, did you ever stop to think that he might have benefited from the financial support I would have been able to give? That, instead of condemning him to a house the size of a matchbox, his life may very well have been improved by being somewhere bigger? Understood, at the age of ten months it's not that urgent, but what when he begins to crawl? To walk around? Were you so busy being selfish that you managed to happily justify denying him all the advantages my money could have brought to the situation?'

Abigail flushed, dismayed at being labelled selfish, yet seeing it from his point of view and not at all liking the picture he was painting of her.

'And what about,' Leandro continued mercilessly, 'when my son got old enough to start wondering where his father was?'

'Stop referring to Sam as *your* son. He's *our* son.' Warmth spread through her because, unwittingly, she had joined them up, voiced what she had denied for the past year and a half: that she wasn't the only parent involved in this equation. She'd pretended that she was, but that was no longer the case, and she thought uneasily that perhaps it shouldn't have been the case at all. Not that she was going to start apologising for anything.

Leandro didn't miss that slip of the tongue and was quietly pleased because it showed that she was no longer fighting him. It didn't make it any easier to stomach what she had done but, in truth, he could almost see her point of view. He *had* walked away without giving her the chance to defend herself. He had taken his sister at her word and had refused to see that the woman he'd been sleeping with, the woman he'd felt he'd known, might have had her reasons for not being quite as open with him as she could have been. He'd reached conclusions and he had thrown those conclusions at her and, yes, they'd pretty much added up to her being a thief, a liar and, by extension, a gold-digger.

Well, if time had proved one thing, it was this. She was no gold-digger or else she would have landed on his doorstep within seconds of finding out that she was pregnant. She wouldn't have avoided him, she would actively have sought him out, because—he had to face it—she would have been holding the ultimate trump card.

She was telling the truth when she said that she'd been scared and he knew why—because he was ruthless. She'd been terrified of him trying to take her child away from her, and she'd had good cause to be apprehensive because of the way they'd broken up. And not just that, he was forced to concede with searing honesty—he had always made it clear to her that he wasn't interested in commitment, even though he had come uncomfortably close to revising that decision during the time he'd been with her. He grudgingly admitted to himself for the first time that this was possibly why he had rushed to believe Cecilia, but had rushed to break off the relationship with Abigail, a relationship that had come way too close to challenging his long-held beliefs.

He thought of her alone—scared, broke and dealing with a momentous situation on her own.

Had there even been anyone by her side when she'd delivered Sam? Or had she got herself off to hospital on her own?

'I *did* think about what might happen when Sam was old enough to start being curious,' Abigail muttered uncomfortably.

'And what conclusions had you come to?' Disconcerted by the introspective route his thoughts had taken him, Leandro's tone was sharper and cooler than he'd intended. 'Had you decided that you'd write off my existence on a permanent basis to make life easier for you? "Lost at sea" or something like that?'

'No!' Abigail was horrified that he could come to such a conclusion. Was he being serious? 'I would never, ever have done anything like that!' She found that she couldn't bear the thought of anything happening to him. Indeed, she felt physically ill at the thought.

His tone softened at the distraught expression on her face. From old, he knew that her fire was counterbalanced by a real capacity for empathy.

How was it that he hadn't seen that at the time, when he had walked out on her without a backward glance?

'You need to think past yourself,' he urged, leaning forward, forearms resting on his thighs, all his leashed power at bay but ferocious intent still stamped on his lean, beautiful face. 'Think about what Sam will think if years down the road he believes that you deprived him of a lifestyle that could have been within his reach.'

'What are you talking about?' Abigail frowned in confusion at this new angle he'd decided to explore.

'Don't you think that if you wait until he's a teenager, demanding to know who I am, that one look at the privileges that have passed him by might lead to a certain amount of resentment?'

'I would never raise any child of mine to be materialistic,' Abigail countered gamely, while her mind took hold of this whole new disturbing slant and began to chew it over.

'That's as may be,' Leandro continued remorselessly, 'but, human nature being what it is, unless you manage to raise a saint he will look at what could have been his and sooner or later blame you for denying him the opportunities that could have been at his disposal.' He allowed a few seconds of silence so that she could mull over this scenario in her head.

He knew that he was battering her from all sides, and he quelled his guilt, because guilt was the last thing he should be feeling. The truth was that he meant to see this through to its inevitable conclusion and he was determined to get the result he wanted whether she liked it or not. She was just going to have to see past herself and absorb the bigger picture, so painting all the potential minefields that awaited her should she not come round to his point of view was necessary. Simple as that, because all was fair in love and war.

'Unless,' Leandro mused thoughtfully, 'you plan on scaling the dizzy heights of financial success.'

'I hate you.' She glared at him and he raised his eyebrows in response.

'You hate what I'm telling you, but you have to hear it, because we're in a situation that requires a solution—and before we can reach that solution it's important for you to stand back and look at everything from all possible angles.'

'How can you be so…so…*unemotional* at a time like this?'

'Aren't you pleased that I am? What's the alternative? That I sit here sobbing and wringing my hands in despair?'

His wry humour leapt out at her, almost but not quite making her want to smile. Why couldn't he just be a complete bastard instead of reminding her that there was so much more to him? Right now, the last thing she wanted was to see the complex guy she had fallen in love with, the guy who could be as clever as the devil and as funny as any stand-up comedian. She didn't want three-dimensional.

Agitated, she sprang to her feet and began pacing. She glanced at everything around her, at the opulence dripping from every surface.

'My house may be tiny but this apartment is ridiculous when you think about putting a child in it!' she burst out accusingly, moving to stand directly in front of him with her hands on her hips, then immediately wishing that she hadn't because the powerful effect of his personality made her giddy.

'I appreciate your honesty,' he said gravely and she glared at him.

'No, you don't,' she snapped. 'I don't suppose you've ever welcomed anyone being *honest* with you.'

'Wrong. You were honest with me about some things when we were together. I distinctly remember you telling me that I lived in an ivory tower, and then taking it upon yourself to introduce me to the fun of fast-food dining. You called me a show-off who liked to flash my money around and laughed because I was outraged.'

A wave of colour flooded her cheeks and she stared at him, taken back in time for a few seconds, amazed that he remembered that incident—when he'd obviously never really been attached to her the way she'd been attached to him because it hadn't taken him two minutes to find her replacement.

Flustered, she bought herself some time by continuing to glare at him. 'Everything in here is white.' She looked pointedly at the off-white sofa on which he was sprawled. 'A toddler would wreak havoc with all your furniture, and that excuse of a handrail…' she glanced behind her to the culprit before returning her triumphant gaze to his admittedly unfazed face '…well, that's an accident waiting to happen.'

'So you've decided that eliminating me from the picture isn't going to do. Good. We're on the same page with that.'

Abigail sat back down. She guessed that this was where the conversation would really begin, the starting point for making arrangements for visiting or whatever. She was staring at a future in which he would be part of her life for evermore, two people on parallel tracks joined together by the child they'd produced. Rattled, she gulped and stared at him.

'I guess we can sort out visiting rights,' she conceded

faintly. 'Would you want me to sign something? And, if you want to contribute financially, then that would be fine.' She drew in a deep breath as she remembered that vague threat he had issued earlier. 'But there's no way I would ever let you try and take Sam away from me.' Abigail found her courage and met his eyes without blinking.

'I wouldn't dream of it,' Leandro assured her.

'You said…'

'I advised you to contemplate the option.' He looked at her thoughtfully. 'Here's the thing…' he murmured in a soft, low voice that made her shiver and did weird but idiotically predictable things to her nervous system. 'You're right about my apartment.' He sat back and gestured to the expanse of pristine white surrounding them without taking his eyes from her face. 'Not user-friendly when it comes to children, and you can work on changing that.'

'I beg your pardon?'

'Think of it as a blank canvas, and do whatever you want to bring it up to scratch.'

'I'm not following you…'

'And then, when you've got it exactly as you want it,' he continued into the bewildered silence, 'we can set about hunting for somewhere outside London—but not as distant as my Cotswolds place. In fact, I have had several people champing at the bit to get their hands on Greyling. I might just give one of them what they want and then we can search for somewhere more commutable. What are your thoughts on Berkshire?'

'I'm not following you, Leandro!'

'Of course you are,' Leandro said silkily. 'We have a child, and I'm not going to get embroiled in visiting rights and custody battles. I never thought about fatherhood but, now that it's appeared from a great height, I intend to deal with it in the most logical manner possible. A child deserves both parents and the stability of a unified background.'

He sighed heavily and sifted his fingers through his hair. 'My parents were married,' he informed her quietly, 'but that's where the unity stopped—and you should know exactly what I'm talking about. We have a child between us, whether it was planned or not, and I intend to make sure that our child is brought up with both of us present, in a stable atmosphere. Nothing less is going to do.'

'So you're saying…'

'Marriage, Abigail. Like it or not, there's no other way.'

CHAPTER SIX

'No other way?' Abigail parroted, shock writ large all over her face. She had gone through a million and one scenarios of what could happen ever since she had told Leandro about Sam, but a marriage proposal hadn't featured in any of those scenarios.

'Correct. As I've made clear, I'm not going to subject our son to a back-and-forth situation between us.'

'Leandro, we can't *get married*.' Her voice had gone up a couple of octaves and was bordering on hysterical. She swallowed and breathed deeply, in and out, slowly and evenly, counting to ten, because approaching this situation with ranting was going to settle her firmly on the back foot before their negotiations had even begun. 'In an ideal world, a child is a cherished addition to the family unit and is blessed with two loving parents, but it's not an ideal world. Telling me that that's what we would be providing for Sam if we got married is just… just a *fantasy*.'

Leandro flushed darkly. He had offered to make the greatest sacrifice he knew for the sake of their child and he was incensed that she could throw his proposal back in his face without bothering to think things through. Buried beneath his anger was also a certain amount of pique. Countless women would have bitten his hand off for the proposal she was self-righteously tossing aside.

'Since when is it a fantasy to want the best for a child?'

'It's not,' Abigail told him in a long-suffering voice that really got on his nerves. 'Marriage is just not necessary in this day and age.' She jumped up and once again began pacing through the gloriously all-white room. Just looking around her was enough to show her how great the differences were between them. They were chalk and cheese, and it was no wonder his sister had been appalled when she had found out about their relationship. When he had turned his back on her, she had been left in his flash penthouse apartment in New York to pack her things and clear off, and she had had the pleasure of listening to his sister rant about her unsuitability for her brother.

'Leandro needs someone of his own class,' Cecilia had stormed, while Abigail had packed her bag in frozen silence, too distressed with Leandro's disappearance really to pay much attention to what Cecilia had been telling her. 'You're no good for him. He can't get involved with a thief, and it's just a good thing that I had the wit to get involved and rake up that stuff about you or else heaven only knows what might have happened!'

Nothing would have happened, as it turned out. The fact that Leandro had found it so easy to walk away had said it all. Now, here he was proposing marriage, but she was still the same person who was unsuitable for him, the same person he had found it easy to walk away from.

'I'm willing to let you see Sam whenever you want to,' she told him. 'And I get it that you can give him opportunities that I would never be able to in a million years, so of course if you want to contribute financially then I have no problem with that. But it would be a complete disaster for us to get involved in any other way. I mean, the world is full of kids who grow up perfectly happily when their parents are divorced or separated.'

'I don't care about those cheerful kids you tell me thrive when their parents are separated,' Leandro said calmly.

'Why won't you *listen* to me?' Abigail burst out. 'We don't come from the same world,' she enunciated in a low, urgent voice. 'It would never work. Your sister was right about that. I'm from a different class and never the twain shall meet. At least, not unless you want to become infected by me. So, marriage? It wouldn't last five seconds, and a break-up would be worse for a child than two adults who can communicate in a friendly fashion but aren't saddled with one another.'

'Rewind.' Leandro was frowning. 'What are you talking about?'

'It would end in tears, Leandro. You can't stick two people together who don't like one another and hope it works out for the sake of a child, especially when that child is the result of an accident.'

'What did Cecilia say to you?'

'What?' Perplexed, Abigail stared at him. It was always dangerous doing that because she found that, once she started looking, she couldn't stop and it was no different now, even though they were in the middle of a heated argument. Or, at least, she was. Leandro was so assured, so controlled, so stupidly beautiful. It was no wonder she had fallen head over heels in love with him and it was no wonder that even now, when the love bit had crashed and burned, her body still responded to that dark, powerful magnetism in ways that left her feeling addled and all at sea.

'I admit that there was no need for Cecilia to ride in to my rescue.' Leandro grimaced because his habit of indulging his sister had never left him, even though now he could see that she was wilful, where once that could have been interpreted as restless and youthfully energetic. 'But she did it with the best of intentions.'

Abigail couldn't help herself. She rolled her eyes, gritted her teeth and clenched one fist because for a guy who was so clued in he could be shockingly *stupid.*

Momentarily distracted, Leandro frowned. 'She's protective of me.' He gritted his teeth. 'It comes with the territory. I effectively looked after her because our parents were too busy pretending that they didn't have to grow up.'

'Cecilia isn't protective,' Abigail said in a rush. 'She's possessive and it's not healthy. Okay..' she was constrained to be fair '...she might be protective, and she might have been anxious that you'd get wrapped up with someone who might have been after your money, but that's not the only reason she was determined to break us up. Cecilia didn't think that I was good enough for you and she made that perfectly clear once you were out of earshot. "A common little tramp who should go back to the dustbin she crawled out of" was how she put it!' She sighed and sat down, spreading her fingers flat on her lap and staring down at them. She felt mean talking about his sister when she wasn't there to defend herself but why shouldn't Leandro know what she thought? Their class differences were just another thing to take into account, whether he liked it or not.

'Cecilia and I are not as close as we once were,' Leandro murmured reflectively. Had he been too generous in forgiving a side to his sister that it had been easier to ignore than acknowledge? He thought back to Cecilia's enthusiasm when he had taken the bait and started going out with Rosalind, the perfect mate on paper with the right pedigree and all the right credentials.

'I apologise for having said anything, Leandro,' Abigail told him stiltedly, 'but Cecilia had a point. We don't come from the same background.'

'We're getting off topic here.' He would think about his sister later. He'd taken his eye off the ball with her, and maybe it was time to correct that oversight, but right now there were more important things to focus on.

'We're not. I'm just trying to make you see why this marriage proposal of yours doesn't make sense.'

He looked at her, his brilliant eyes veiled. 'I am not prepared for you to have another man in your life,' he said bluntly, 'who will inevitably have influence over my son.'

Abigail laughed because it seemed ludicrous for him to be thinking about another man in her life. She hadn't so much as glanced at anyone since Leandro and she drew a blank when she thought about moving on and doing normal stuff like going on dates and getting to know other men.

Who could possibly ever compare to him? Reluctantly, she looked at him and did a quick mental comparison between Leandro and every other single man she had ever spoken to, communicated with or even set eyes on in her entire life.

Leandro won hands down, and it wasn't just because of the way he looked. He was larger than life in his dynamism, his vitality, his overpowering sexual magnetism. She had sensed that the very second he had approached her in that hotel foyer and she had allowed herself to go with the flow. Only afterwards had she worked out that a man like Leandro could have any woman and that the relationship that had become more and more significant for her had, for him, remained firmly on the same footing on which it had begun.

'How do you feel about another *woman* in *my* life?' he asked shrewdly, and Abigail snapped out of the wistful reverie that had swept over her. She blinked, focused and thought about what he had said.

Wasn't it far more likely that he would be snapped up? Women with a child in tow were never seen as sex sirens and, on a practical level, Abigail knew that she would struggle to find the time to go out and paint the town red anyway. She would carry on with her job, because she would want to maintain her independence, and between her job and looking after Sam—even if there *was* an injection of cash that made things easier—her life would be as hectic as it always was.

But a man with an infant in tow, a *sexy, eligible billionaire bachelor with an infant in tow,* would be even more of a catch because there was nothing sexier than a guy pushing a pram. Leandro wouldn't even have to try. He would be targeted and there would be another Rosalind out there who would snap him up sooner rather than later. Chances were that, with a child to consider, he would be far more amenable to the concept of getting married. Subconsciously, he would be seeking out a mate with whom he would be able to share parental duties.

How would she feel about that?

She broke out in tingly perspiration. Of course this was what sharing a child was all about, she told herself stoutly. Blended families. It happened every day of the week!

Unfortunately, thinking about a blended family with Leandro in the starring role, and some gorgeous, upper-class blonde as his co-star, made her feel sick.

She started when he suddenly stood up and looked at his watch. 'What time do you collect Sam?'

Dazed, Abigail looked at him and blinked like an owl. 'Not for another couple of hours,' she admitted.

'You put him in childcare every day, nine to six?'

She bristled and followed him to the kitchen, where he began rummaging in a cupboard, fetching the ingredients for coffee. 'Vanessa is very generous with my hours,' she told him. 'I get in at nine-thirty and work until four and I have Fridays off. I usually catch up with whatever admin is outstanding then. She understands the pressures on working mothers. Not many employers do.'

Abigail's mind was still furiously playing with the image of a Leandro all settled down with a woman, a woman actually destined to wear the engagement ring he had kept for investment purposes. Wasn't it fair to say that she would resent some other woman holding Sam? Cooing at him? Pushing him on a swing in the park?

Would she be laughing up at Leandro, holding his hand and planning the perfect little family holiday with Sam...?

'I don't approve of my son being stuck in a nursery for hours on end.' Leandro delivered this on a note of finality. 'Do you? Honestly?'

Abigail hesitated and then blurted out defensively, 'What choice did I have? I had to get out there and earn a living to keep the roof over our heads.'

'And yet you never thought to seek me out and ask for help.'

'No. Not once,' she said honestly.

'You must have been lonely,' Leandro suddenly commented, surprising himself and her with the incisive remark, and Abigail blushed and hesitated. Without her noticing, he'd brought her coffee, and oddly he'd remembered how she took it—strong with very little milk.

'I got through it,' she said, tilting her chin at a bullish angle and leading him to think of her as a kid out there looking after herself, doing whatever it took to put one foot in front of the other. Which made him think of the shoplifting charge against her, and he had a sudden wave of sympathy for her youthful desire to fit in.

'So you did.' He looked at her reflectively until she went bright red and began to toy with the handle of the mug. 'I'm making this sound like a business deal,' he drawled, and Abigail flicked a glance at his lean, thoughtful, outrageously handsome face.

'Isn't it?' she questioned. 'You've found out that you have a child and…and…I'm *sorry* that I didn't tell you at the time. Perhaps I should have but, at the time, keeping it to myself felt like the right thing to do.' Abigail sighed and absently curled one long, escaped strand of hair round her finger, then undid the little bun and smoothed her hand through its long mass, before propping her chin in the palm of her hand and staring at him. 'And now you're approaching the *problem*—and, yes, that's what you called it, Leandro—with the most logical solution you can think of that fits in with your desire to be a full-time father, now that you've been put in the position of having to do something.'

'All true.'

'Most men would understand where I'm coming from. They would see that it's totally impractical to think about marrying someone you're not in love with for the sake of a child.'

'Also true.'

'But you have to be different, don't you, Leandro?' she said with a mixture of helplessness and frustration. She stood up and walked across to the deep, gleaming stainless steel sink, and stared through the window for a few seconds at a view that couldn't have been more different from the view she had from her kitchen sink, then she turned around, leaned against the counter and stared at him. 'So tell me how this isn't a business deal, and tell me how approaching marriage like a business transaction can *ever* be a good thing.'

'Well,' he said pensively, 'in point of fact, I happen to think that a marriage undertaken as a business proposition stands a far better chance of staying the course. Look at the other options when emotions are involved—either there's the soul-destroying disillusionment once the gold veneer wears off and the rust starts creeping through or, even worse, there's the never-ending high passion that leaves no room for anything else and ends up destroying everything around it.'

'You're so cynical.'

'I'm being realistic, Abby.' Leandro looked at her steadily. 'Set alongside those, a business transaction becomes a gold-plated, blue-chip option. But…' He stood up and strolled towards her and she felt the hairs on the back of her neck stand on end as he drew closer. 'Like I said, this isn't just a business transaction, is it?' He stopped in front of her and leaned forward, caging her in by placing his hands flat on the counter on either side of her.

'Of course it is,' she spluttered.

'Business transactions don't take into account the sort of chemistry we have,' Leandro told her flatly. 'Business transactions are cold, calculated and devoid of the sexual charge that makes it hard for us to keep our hands off one another. In one way, it would make sense for us not to complicate a situation by giving in to what we both want. And of course, if you dig your heels in, then we won't complicate things. We will accept that other people will enter our lives.'

He shrugged. He was playing a wild card, but she could be as stubborn as a mule, and he couldn't appear to force her hand. Under the casual tone of voice and the nonchalant, cool indifference, he found that he was wondering tensely how this would play out. 'I am a highly sexual man,' he admitted. 'I would be unable to remain celibate for any length of time.'

'That's so tacky, Leandro.' But thinking about that made her feel sick.

'I prefer to call it *honest.*' The silence pooled between them and then he leant towards her and feathered his lips over hers. 'And if I'm to be honest again,' he murmured, his voice a caress that made her shiver and that squashed the voice of reason telling her to push him away politely but firmly because this just *wasn't going to do.* 'I would rather be a highly sexual man with you.'

'Leandro…'

'I want you, Abby, and I don't just want you for my wife because you are the mother of my child. I want you for my lover because no other woman has ever turned me on the way you do.'

He kissed her again and this time the kiss was deeper and hungrier. His tongue lashed hers and she moaned softly into his mouth. He took her hand and guided it to the bulge between his legs and he pressed her hand firmly on it. The sensation was exquisite. He was past caring whether he might scare her off. He could feel her *want* radiating from her in waves and it matched his.

Not giving her time to start formulating a bunch of reasons for them to stop, Leandro tugged the prissy white blouse free from her trousers and began unbuttoning it, giving up at some point and tugging it off her, to hell with popping buttons. Pretty soon, she'd have enough money to buy as many prissy white blouses as her heart desired. His big hand curved round her breast possessively and he massaged it through the lacy bra, finding the stiffened bud of her nipple and rolling his thumb over it until her breathing thickened and she was squirming against him.

Wrong, wrong, wrong, her head was yelling, but the truth was that she couldn't get enough of him. She'd *never* been able to get enough of him. She shimmied closer, her hand still feeling his hardness, her whole body keening towards him and resenting the barrier of their clothes.

Still kissing her, Leandro pulled back slightly so that he could get rid of his shirt, then he brushed her hand away, and undid the trousers.

'I'm in heaven,' he breathed hoarsely as her hands curved beneath the opened shirt. He freed her breasts, then unhooked the bra. Without giving her time to think, he swept her off her feet and carried her out of the kitchen and up the flight of stairs to his bedroom. Her feeble protest was met with a plundering kiss that drove all thoughts of resistance straight out of her head.

Her whole body was flushed and trembling as she watched him move quickly towards the shutters, closing them so that the watery afternoon light suddenly became muted. By the time he hit the bed, where he had deposited her, he was unclothed.

Beautiful. He was as beautiful as a statue of a Greek god, all muscle and sinew and a six-pack stomach that was as flat as a washboard. He moved to stand by the bed and she sat up, half-closed her eyes and took him into her mouth.

Leandro breathed in sharply and plunged his fingers into her hair. She knew just how to please him, moving fast then more slowly, her hand gripping him and turning him on in all kinds of places. He only eased her off when he knew that he would climax in her mouth if she carried on, and he wasn't going to do that.

He was going to take her slowly and thoroughly. She wasn't just his lover, she was the mother of his child, and he felt a kick of pride and ferocious possessiveness that he'd never have thought possible.

He undressed her. It was familiar and exciting, rediscovering the body that had always had the ability to drive him out of his mind. When she was naked, he straddled her and looked down at her exquisitely delicate face and her full, beautiful breasts tipped with circular discs that he wanted to lathe with his tongue.

'You drive me wild.' He groaned, and she smiled drowsily at him.

'Less talking.' She reached out and traced the tip of his manhood with her finger, keeping her eyes on his face and loving the reaction that tiny gesture evoked.

Leandro growled a response. 'I was going to take my time…'

'Who said I wanted you to do that?' She wriggled under him and opened her legs, which was his cue to nudge against her. She was so ready for him and he eased his finger into her until she was bucking against his hand. He had to hold himself to contain a driving urge to ejaculate. He couldn't wait. She didn't want him to wait.

He levered himself over her, propped up on both hands and drove into her. She had a body that had always seemed fashioned especially to fit him, sheathing him tightly and taking him to soaring heights of pleasure with the speed of a rocket launching off.

Abigail cried out. Her short, square nails dug into the small of his back and she raised her legs and wrapped them round him as he drove deep and hard into her.

She arched back as she came in an explosion of a thousand fireworks that splintered through her. Her cries were loud and guttural and barely recognisable. With Leandro, she'd learned to lose all her inhibitions. She crested, dimly aware that he, too, was surging towards an orgasm. Wave upon wave of indescribable pleasure rolled over her, an unstoppable tide of sensation that brought tears of real joy to her eyes.

Coming down filled her with such utter contentment that it was hard to remember the gravity of what they had been discussing and the repercussions of decisions that would have to be made. In a gesture born of habit, she sighed and hugged him.

She liked snuggling. Leandro recalled that, just as he recalled that he had enjoyed that too, even though it was something that should have gone against the grain, because he had always been accustomed to vacating the bed pretty much the instant he'd finished having sex with a woman.

Post-coital chit chat had never been his thing, far less cuddles.

On the verge of dozing off, Abigail's eyes flew open and she pulled back and stared at him with horror.

'We didn't use contraception!' She gasped. When he failed to respond with an equal show of horror, she repeated, just in case he'd developed temporary loss of hearing, 'Did you hear what I just said, Leandro? We didn't use any contraception and I'm not on the pill or anything!'

'Marry me, Abigail.' He pulled her back towards him, inserted his thigh between her legs and moved it slowly against her, rousing her all over again.

'Leandro…'

'Can you deny after what we've just done that there isn't a powerful bond between us?'

'Sex isn't a powerful bond,' Abigail denied with a frightening lack of conviction. 'And is that why you wanted to make love to me? So that you could prove a point? That would be a really hateful thing to do.'

'That's not why I wanted to make love to you,' Leandro said with complete sincerity. 'I wanted to make love to you because I can't resist you.'

'Lust disappears,' she was constrained to point out.

'Most things do but who says that it disappears any faster than all that heady emotion people call *love*? You might be pregnant by me right now.'

'That would be appalling,' Abigail wailed, but he was still doing that thing with his thigh, and she was finding it hard to keep track of why she should be horrified.

She *should* be horrified, shouldn't she? He didn't love her and he never would, and lust *did* fade, and when it did it left nothing behind, nothing concrete that could ever shore up the walls of a relationship. Without love, those fortifications would crumble the minute the sex went off the boil.

But he was still moving his thigh between her legs and she could feel herself climbing again towards a climax. She gyrated against him and orgasmed, shuddering, moaning and clutching his broad shoulders, not caring that he was looking at her flushed face and open mouth, hearing the sounds of her physical satisfaction. In fact, she rather enjoyed the sensation of being observed. It was wanton and really, really sexy.

A thought flew through her head, like quicksilver. *If he didn't mind the thought of getting her pregnant, what did that say?*

It told her one thing and it was that he wanted their relationship to work. He didn't want to marry her with divorce as an option to be kept within sight. If that had been the case, he would never, ever have risked her getting pregnant with a second child.

Could what they had really work? she wondered. In a rush, she saw all the upsides to a situation she had previously discarded as being ridiculous.

Sam would have both parents there for him and that could only be a good thing. When it came to parenthood, you had to put all your selfish traits to one side and do what was best for your child, and she was unwillingly aware that being in a couple with Leandro would be best for their son.

Then there was the little matter of the separate lives he had talked about. If they were together, she wouldn't have to worry about him heading straight into the arms of some woman who wanted to prove that she could be suitable stepmother material. She wouldn't have to face a future riven with jealousy she was forced to conceal.

Because she *would* be jealous. She couldn't bear the thought of him sleeping with anyone else.

Because she was still in love with him.

The realisation didn't jump out at her like a jack-in-the-box, a shocking revelation. It crept out as something she had known all along, deep down. Lust didn't last, but if they both worked truly hard at making things work between them then who was to say that he wouldn't, one day, come to love her the way she loved him? He knew everything there was to know about her now. He knew who she was and where she had come from.

The future suddenly glimmered in front of her, full of possibilities.

'You're not saying anything.' Leandro had a surprising urge for Abigail to put him out of his misery. 'Tell me what you're thinking.'

'I bet that's something you've never asked any woman to do before,' she teased, and he relaxed. It was crazy but he felt quite heady with relief because she wasn't fighting him. He intended to capitalise on that if it killed him.

'Well…?' he pressed impatiently, and Abigail sighed, smiled and looked at the familiar lines of his beautiful face.

'You're right,' she said softly. 'Sam deserves the chance of both parents being there for him. But…' She hesitated and then ploughed on. 'I won't marry you. Let's live together, Leandro. Let's see if we can work together as parents…'

It wasn't what he wanted but he figured that it was a great deal better than nothing. 'If that's how you want to play it,' he conceded gracefully, already making plans to improve on that concession with the greatest possible speed, 'then very well. We'll see if it works between us. For our son's sake.'

CHAPTER SEVEN

ABIGAIL STOOD LOOKING at the little cottage. It was in a beautiful location, forty-five minutes out of London and accessed via picturesque little lanes.

She still had to pinch herself that Leandro was the same man who had pronounced only several weeks ago that the only thing he wanted from her was sex, because as far as he was concerned she was no more than unfinished business waiting for a line to be drawn under it.

When she had decided to tell him about Sam, she hadn't known what to expect. He didn't love her. In fact, he felt the opposite. Nor had marriage ever been on his agenda before. Not even Rosalind, with her impeccable connections and shared social circle, had been able to persuade him otherwise.

Yet, after the initial shock, he had rallied his forces and handled the explosion thrown at him with admirable aplomb. His proposal of marriage had been from a keen sense of duty, which was something she figured out, because the minute he had been given an out he had been happy to accept the far less committed alternative.

Since they had reached the decision to live together

nearly two months ago, Leandro had been a model of attentiveness. Anything, it would seem, to further his desire to be a good father. Abigail wasn't entirely surprised, because Leandro always had been a man who threw himself one hundred per cent into everything he did, which was one of the reasons why he had become so successful at such a young age.

Faced with the shock of ready-made fatherhood, he had not run from commitment, but instead had dealt with the situation head on.

It would have been so tempting to think that he had feelings for her and not just for Sam, but she wasn't stupid. He would have married her because, traditionalist to the core, he had seen nothing wrong in making the ultimate sacrifice for the sake of his son. Over the past few weeks, she had come more and more to understand why. Occasionally, when his guard was down, he would let fall little snippets of information about his own childhood and she now had a little more idea of the boy who had become the man.

However, happily released from the duty of putting a wedding ring on her finger, Leandro was doing the next best thing, which was proving to her that he could be the best father possible.

The only fly in the ointment was the fact that she thought that she knew why—once he had proved himself sufficiently, he would walk away from her, safe in the knowledge that she would never try to break the bond he had been at pains to create with Sam. She still felt sick when she thought about him walking away straight into the arms of another woman, but the marriage offer was no longer on the table, and she had had good reasons for turning it down.

Yet everything was so perfect. She just wanted to believe the impossible and she was constantly having to wage war against being lulled into thinking that all the grand gestures meant more than they actually did. But surely, she caught herself thinking more and more as time went on, things were changing between them? To all intents and purposes, they were a couple, and if Leandro didn't have the same feelings for her as she had for him then who was to say that that wouldn't change given time? Hope, she knew, could be as much an enemy as a friend, and she *really* tried to avoid it like the plague, but it still crept in, filling her head with fantasies and presenting a future that was rosy and bright.

This idyllic cottage was definitely high on the 'rosy and bright' spectrum.

'When you said you had a surprise for me, I hadn't expected anything like this,' she murmured, walking towards the chocolate-box white picket fence and then just standing there, lost in pleasant day dreams about how perfect life could be here. She wished they had brought Sam, but at five in the evening it was perilously close to his dinner and bath time, and the nanny Leandro had engaged several weeks previously had persuaded her to leave him back at the apartment. Abigail had been easily swayed, for she knew just how demanding her son could get when he began getting tired and hungry.

'Like it?' Leandro moved smoothly to stand next to her. He couldn't have arranged this on a more pleasant afternoon. Spring was in the air and, although the sun was low, the charm of the place with its climbing roses and neat path to the front door was inescapable.

He had taken great pains to lay it on thick with the estate agent, and it was just the sort of place he was looking for. He could have summed it up thus: *the sort of place I would never normally have glanced at in a million years.*

But, despite her background and the toughness that had seen Abigail through hard times, including the pregnancy she had borne on her own, she was a romantic at heart and that was something he had recognised when they had been seeing each other the first time round. She didn't like his white, modern, minimalist apartment because what she *did* really like was exactly what she was gaping at right now, round-eyed and thrilled to death.

'I absolutely love it.' She turned to him and smiled and, looking down at her, Leandro wanted to do what he *always* seemed to want to do whenever he was anywhere near her—whisk her away like a cave man and have his wicked way with her. She could still get his libido going in five seconds flat and that showed no signs of abating, which was something of a minor miracle, given his predilection towards a fast turnover when it came to the opposite sex.

'But…' she frowned and looked at him seriously '…we agreed that every decision we took would be one we both wanted, Leandro. Is this sort of place really your kind of thing? It's nothing like your apartment.'

'Should we look inside before we start having this conversation? The place is vacant and the estate agent said we could take our time and then drop the keys back with them through the letter box.'

Abigail looked at the mesmerising beauty of his tanned face and couldn't help falling a little faster into the seductive hope that all of this thoughtfulness might add up to more than just the considerate behaviour of a decent guy who wanted to build a solid friendship with her before he disappeared out of her life.

'Okay.' She grinned happily as he unhooked the gate and ushered her up to the front door. 'I just never thought that this was your kind of thing…'

'Things are slightly different when there's a child to consider,' Leandro pointed out and Abigail stifled a sigh because, of course, all of this was being done for Sam.

After his first uncertain steps in the bonding department, Leandro had become increasingly confident with his son. From picking him up and holding him, arms outstretched, with the puzzled expression of someone not too sure about the wriggling bundle in his arms, Leandro was now confident enough to bathe his son, and didn't seem to mind grubby fingers on his expensive clothes. He showed limitless patience now that Sam was starting to walk and, if there was one fault, it was that he had a tendency to overindulge his son with presents that were far too grown-up for a one-year-old.

'Greyling would have been far too big,' Leandro pointed out with irrefutable logic, 'and my apartment is, as you've said, far too…*white.* This seemed a good compromise.' He pushed open the door and in they stepped.

Leandro had visited the place with the estate agent

only a couple of days previously. He knew what to expect. Now, he watched as Abigail turned a slow circle in the small hall with its attractive flagstone tiled floor.

'Wow.'

On closer inspection, Leandro could spot a couple of cracked tiles by the wall, but he went along with her enthusiasm as they explored the cottage which was deceptively big and quirkily laid out.

She gushed over everything, from the coving and dado rails, to the range in the kitchen and all the open fireplaces in the rooms. She waxed lyrical about the utility room and the larder. Abigail confessed that never in a million years had she ever thought that she might end up living in a fairy-tale cottage such as this.

They ended up in the garden, which was a riot of flowerbeds and fruit trees.

'Commuting is going to be difficult for you,' Leandro remarked as they sat side by side on a wooden bench placed strategically under one of the apple trees. It was cool but clear and the silence of the countryside felt like an antidote to the chaos and noise of London life.

'I hadn't thought of that,' Abigail responded in some dismay. She had continued with her job, albeit working shorter hours, because she hadn't wanted to lose the small amount of financial independence it afforded her. Deep down she wanted to leave, to spend far more of her time with Sam, but she couldn't bring herself to be so completely dependent on Leandro.

What about when this happy charade ended and Leandro returned to his normal life? Of course, he would ensure that there was a hefty financial settlement involved, but how would she feel about accepting his money and becoming, effectively, a kept woman?

The downside of rejecting his marriage proposal was like the steady drip of acid wearing away all her good intentions, yet what was the point of marriage if it was undertaken for the wrong reasons? The more she was with Leandro, the more she wanted love from him and not duty.

'It wouldn't make sense for you to leave here at a ridiculous hour in the morning to get into London and do a job that you are not required to do in the first place.'

'You don't understand…'

'You're right. I don't understand. You should be overjoyed that there is no financial imperative for you to go out to work.'

Abigail tensed. 'I can't be dependent on you, Leandro. You're being generous because of Sam but, face it, if I hadn't accidentally fallen pregnant then we wouldn't be here now.' She hated the way she hoped that he would refute that, although she couldn't imagine what he could say to do so.

'There's no point dealing in "what if?"s,' Leandro said with deflating logic. 'The fact is that we're at this point now and you have a choice to make. Either you relinquish the job in London and move in here, or we stay at the apartment and you continue working. What's it to be? If you decide that this is the sort of place that would suit you, then say the word and I can have this deal wrapped up by the end of the month.' Leandro turned to her and watched her averted profile like a hawk.

The longer he was with her, the more convinced he

was that 'gold-digger' she certainly was not. But he hadn't understood her determination to carry on working, even though the hours had been shortened. Whilst she accepted a modest allowance from him for Sam—far, far less than he would be happy giving her—she still persisted in using her own money to buy anything for herself. He had only just managed to persuade her to stop buying food supplies with what she earned. On the few occasions when he had presented her with items of jewellery, little gifts she could wear out when he took her somewhere flash for dinner, she had accepted, but politely, wearing them once for his benefit then stashing them away in her bedroom drawer.

She got that close but was determined to get no closer and he couldn't blame her. She couldn't forgive him for having walked away from her the first time. She never harked back to it, but why else would she have turned down his marriage proposal? There was still a part of her that distrusted him. Leandro was certain of it.

'I suppose I could work from here…' Abigail flicked a sideways glance at him. He was just so…perfect. If they moved here, would she be letting herself sink ever deeper into a situation from which it would be more and more painful to extract herself? Would this cottage existence with the man of her dreams, the man who didn't love her, just feed the illusion that what they had might end up being the real thing?

Another, darker thought hit her.

Was this his way of removing her from London so that he could gradually resume the life he had put on hold? Was this step one in distancing her from him?

'I expect you'll find it pretty tough to commute from here yourself,' she said lightly, making sure not to look at him, because she didn't want to see her worst suspicions confirmed.

'What are you talking about?'

'Well, it's not exactly next to a railway line, is it?' She forced herself to laugh carelessly. 'If *I* can't commute easily to Central London, then *you* won't be able to either, will you? I mean, you'll have the same problems as I have.'

'I own the company,' Leandro pointed out gently. 'I can work whatever hours I want, and I have a driver to accommodate the travel situation. There isn't the same necessity to get in and leave by certain times. I also don't go to work just to prove a point.'

'I'm not doing that!' Abigail flushed angrily and glared at him.

'Aren't you?' he said wryly and she had the grace to remain silent.

'Anyway, it doesn't matter. I just want you to know that.'

'Sorry, but you've lost me. What doesn't matter?'

'If you need to stay in London overnight.'

'If I need to stay in London *overnight*?'

'Yes. *If* we *both* decide that this is the best place for Sam to grow up, then I don't want you to feel that you have to come home every single evening out of a sense of obligation.'

'It's no obligation when it comes to seeing my son,' Leandro grated, enraged at the not-very-subtle dismissal in her voice.

'I just thought I'd mention it,' Abigail pointed out. 'It's going to be inconvenient for you to be travelling back and forth each day, every day.'

'Why don't you let me decide for myself what I find inconvenient and what I don't?'

She shrugged. 'Sure. Maybe I'll go and have another quick look around before we go.' She sprang to her feet, angry with him for no reason whatsoever.

When he talked about *obligation* it only reinforced her suspicions that the glue that was temporarily binding them together wasn't going to last longer than the blink of an eye. But, whilst being out here would give him ample opportunity gradually to break free, didn't it work both ways? She would gradually get accustomed to having him around less and less. She would be able to distance herself and pull back.

She lost herself in reviewing the cottage all over again and finished up back in the kitchen, and was looking around, when Leandro surprised her from the doorway.

'It'll need work.'

Abigail turned around and looked at him across the width of the kitchen. Due to the lack of furniture, their voices echoed. She hugged herself and raised her eyebrows in a question.

'The cottage,' Leandro said patiently, moving towards her. 'There will be work to be done on it.'

'It's perfect the way it is!' Abigail said immediately, wanting an argument.

'I'm taking it that you have decided that you're happy with the place?'

'I can see myself living here with Sam,' she conceded. 'But I don't want you getting some interior designer in who will get rid of all the traditional features and turn it into a replica of your apartment.'

'Why would I do that?' He strolled towards her and curled his fingers into her silky hair. 'Are you trying to have an argument with me?'

'Of course not. Why would I do that?'

'You *chose* not to change anything in the apartment.'

'I didn't feel comfortable doing that.'

'Your choice. You can do what you like with this place and, for your information, it will be entirely in your name so you don't have to feel that I own the roof over your head.'

'You don't have to do that.' Abigail wondered whether that was another sign of him distancing himself from her.

'I want you to feel secure,' Leandro said gently. 'And I know you're proud, so I don't want you to feel as though you're indebted to me. You're the mother of my child and I intend to look after you.'

He tilted her chin and feathered a kiss on her mouth, at which point her defence system was well and truly knocked for six. Of their own accord, her arms lifted, curved around his neck and pulled him towards her.

Sex. It always came back to this. Aside from his sense of duty, it was the thing that powered their relationship but, oh, how it left her feeling vulnerable. Yet, she couldn't help but take what was on offer, torn between making the most of what she had while she had it and trying to resist so that she could start building her defences for when they parted company.

And there were times, such as now, when he was just so *nice* that she didn't have it in her to resist him.

He could be so tough, so ridiculously forceful, yet at other times so unbearably tender that it took her breath away and left her feeling as helpless as a kitten.

She kissed him back, holding his face in her hands, and whispered guiltily, 'We *can't.*'

'But I'm hungry for you, Abigail. Ravenous.'

'Is sex the only thing you think about?' she half-joked.

'Is it my fault that you continue to do crazy things to my libido?' He drew back and smoothed her hair with slightly less steady hands than he would have liked.

She was wearing a pair of jeans and a long-sleeved red tee shirt under a trench coat and she looked amazing. Fresh, wholesome, shockingly pretty and absolutely lacking in artifice.

'I admit it wouldn't be right to make love here,' he conceded with obvious reluctance. 'What sex on the ground gains in reckless impulse, it loses in sheer discomfort.' He grabbed her hand and headed out of the cottage, carefully locking the door behind them and putting paid to any impulse she might have had to do another quick turn round the place.

He reversed at a pace back into the road. 'But I can't wait until we get back to London.'

'Don't be outrageous, Leandro.'

'You make me outrageous.' He shot her a look that was bone-meltingly sincere, and Abigail shivered and wondered whether he knew just how achingly addictive he could be without even realising it.

Soon he was gunning along the lanes, dusk falling steadily around them. With no traffic to speak of, they would have been back in London in less than two hours, so she was surprised when he swung the snazzy silver sports car into the courtyard of a country pub that was as picture-postcard perfect as the cottage had been.

'I said I couldn't wait,' he growled.

Not even stopping to enjoy a glass of wine, they headed for the room he had rented for the sake of an hour and made love, wild, passionate love, that left her weak and clinging to him and crazily, stupidly happy.

'That was such a decadent use of money,' she giggled as they headed back down to London. 'And what must that poor hotel manager be thinking?'

'That he got a good deal,' Leandro remarked wryly. 'He rented us his most expensive suite and we were there for under an hour. He's laughing all the way to the bank. Tomorrow I'm going to seal the deal with the house.' He reached out and covered her hand with his. 'Will you leave the job, Abby?'

Was that why he had made that very unusual detour? she wondered with unexpected cynicism. He knew that she was putty in his hands when they made love. But, no, she couldn't credit him with that amount of deviousness, even though he *was* a man who was accustomed to getting what he wanted at whatever the cost.

'I guess I will,' she said at last, knowing that she truly did want to spend her time with Sam, even if it meant giving Leandro his way. 'But I shall miss working there. Vanessa has been very good to me and I owe her a huge debt of gratitude.'

'So do I,' Leandro said gravely and she looked at him in surprise.

'What do you mean?'

'I mean,' he glanced at her briefly, 'It's bad enough thinking of you broke and down on your luck while you were pregnant, but it's worse when I think of what might have happened if you hadn't had that lifeline extended to you.'

Sam was asleep by the time they returned to Leandro's apartment at a little after seven-thirty. The nanny—a lovely young woman who absolutely adored the baby—spent a few minutes telling them what escapades he had got up to in their absence, and as soon as she had gone they both went into the room which had been turned into his nursery and gazed down at their son.

Typically, no expense had been spared in the decoration of the room. The walls were a pale blue with a hand-painted scene from a popular children's movie on one of the walls. In the corner of the room, a tepee had been erected with a sheepskin rug in which he could cocoon himself. Next to the tepee was a giant stuffed toy—a surprise present from Leandro, bought a couple of weeks previously.

Leandro gazed down at Sam and Abigail gazed furtively at Leandro. The only light in the room came from a tiny night light. Her heart clenched, for this was what it looked like to see him shorn of his toughness. His face was softened in the mellow glow. He had never looked at her like that, with open tenderness, and once upon a time she might have thought that he was incapable of that depth of emotion. He wasn't. She squeezed his arm and he glanced across at her.

She padded down to the kitchen, where food had been prepared for them by the housekeeper who came in daily to make sure that the apartment always resembled something you would see in a fancy interior-design magazine.

For some reason, the thought of leaving London made her feel all shaken up. She had burrowed into a comfort zone here, in this apartment, with one foot still connected to her old life working at the jewellery store and another placed squarely here, surrounded by this unbelievable luxury.

But now everything was changing and that unsettled her. The future seemed shakier than ever and she realised that, without even being aware of it, she had rooted herself into the pretence of thinking that what they had was a real relationship instead of a stitched-together one for the sake of their child. She had subconsciously latched on to the changes she had seen in Leandro—his attentiveness, his consideration, his real efforts at being a dad—and had translated them into something they weren't.

Not once had he ever expressed any feelings towards her. He knew how to make her feel sexy, and he was eloquent on the subject of her physical attributes and what effect they had on him, but that was where it all ended.

Now, she would be moving out of London, giving

up her job, and whatever Leandro said now about being able to handle the commute she knew that it wouldn't be long before he settled into a pattern of overnighting at the apartment when he had to work late. And how long before he was tempted to relax in his apartment with a woman to massage away the stress of the day?

Of course, he would still see Sam, but it wouldn't be long before he would suggest having Sam on his own, and by then Sam would be old enough to stay overnight with him.

Abigail knew that she should be taking one day at a time instead of projecting down the road but, as she began dealing with the food that had been prepared, she could feel a thousand possible scenarios zipping in and out of her mind like angry, buzzing wasps.

She surfaced to find Leandro lounging in the doorway, arms folded, his amazing eyes fastened to her face.

'Spit it out,' he said without preamble. 'What's going on?'

'Nothing!'

'Then why are you looking as though you've suddenly realised that the sky might start falling down?'

He strolled towards her but before she could scrabble to provide a reason for her sudden, unexpected shift of mood his mobile phone buzzed in his pocket and he held up one hand to silence her.

Standing only inches away from him, Abigail heard a woman's voice and all the fears which had been playing out in her head congealed into the certainty that this was why Leandro was suddenly so keen to shift her out of London to the house of her dreams.

Not only was he talking to a woman, but he had lowered his voice and was leaving the kitchen.

He was on the phone to a woman and he didn't want her to overhear the conversation.

Gripped with a sickening sense of apprehension, she remained glued to the spot until he reappeared in under five minutes, shoving the phone back into his pocket as he strode back into the kitchen. He should have been looking as guilty as the worst of sinners but there wasn't a trace of guilt etched on those devastating features.

Abigail kicked herself for even thinking that she should expect him to feel guilty because he had been talking to a woman on the phone, having an intimate conversation he hadn't wanted her to overhear. But *still...*

'Who was that?' she was horrified to hear herself ask, in an accusatory voice, and Leandro stilled and looked at her with veiled eyes.

Every instinct in him rallied and railed against the querulous note in her voice. 'No one that should concern you,' he offered coolly.

Trembling, because as fast as that he had become a stranger just because she had asked him something he hadn't wanted to hear, Abigail dug her heels in and stood her ground.

'You were talking to a woman,' she flung at him.

'I do not want to get into this, Abigail.'

'But you were, weren't you?'

'Would you say that that's a crime?' Leandro asked tautly. Unaccustomed to having to justify his behaviour, he had reverted to type. Did he want to argue with her? No. 'You need to calm down and not over-excite yourself about it.'

'Who was she?' Abigail demanded. 'No!' She held up an imperious hand, shaking like an engine at full throttle. 'Don't bother telling me. You don't have to. You can do exactly as you please. I don't care!'

'Don't you?' he asked with considerable intent, eyes narrowed on her flushed face.

'Of course I don't!' She spun away to gather herself, took a few deep breaths and then looked at him with a lot more control than she felt. 'I apologise for having questioned you,' she offered. 'We don't owe one another anything and I realise that.'

'Even though we're lovers?' Leandro questioned and she waved that aside.

'We both know that that doesn't mean anything.' She cleared her throat. 'You can do as you please.'

'So you wouldn't mind if that woman on the phone was someone I intended to sleep with?'

Pain slithered through her as sharp as broken glass. 'Of course, I would expect you to break off our relationship before you start hopping into bed with someone else.'

'I don't believe I'm hearing this,' Leandro muttered darkly.

Abigail ignored him. In fact, she barely heard what he'd said. She was far too taken up with the images racing through her head, like a cinematic reel on fast-forward.

'How long will it take before I can move into the cottage with Sam?' she asked, already settling on that as the only way to break the catastrophic effect he had on her. If he wanted to carry on with some other woman, then she wasn't going to be around to witness it in the shape of late arrivals back and unavoidable meetings.

It was astounding that he could seem so preoccupied with her, so crazily *in lust* with her, and still make time to start playing the field. Just thinking about it ripped her to shreds and she could feel tears beginning to glaze the back of her eyes.

'Well?' she demanded forcefully and his lips thinned.

'I will sort out the finances tomorrow and I can have the whole place brought up to scratch in record time. You can be in within the fortnight.'

CHAPTER EIGHT

LEANDRO STARED OUT of his office window, brow pleated in a frown of dissatisfaction.

He couldn't concentrate and he loathed that. He had cancelled three meetings in the past ten days and had rescheduled his trip to New York for the following month. Right at this moment, his secretary was under strict instructions to hold all outside calls, even though the documents he should be getting through while all those calls were being conveniently held were still sitting in front of him on his computer, waiting to be checked.

Scowling, he vaulted upright and strolled towards the window to gaze down at an unseasonably fine spring afternoon.

Everything was coming along a pace. The cottage had been bought and without a chain, or the thorny problem most people faced of having to get a mortgage, he had been able to rush things along and work had already started on some essential renovations.

He had discussed those renovations with Abigail in the atmosphere of cool politeness that had characterised the time they now spent together.

She'd made a fuss over that phone call and had assumed the worst of him and when he had, quite rightly, put his foot down at launching into a grovelling explanation of a simple phone call, she had resorted to the oldest female trick in the book. The cold shoulder.

And no sex.

God only knew exactly what was going through her head but it didn't take the IQ of a genius to figure out that whatever outlandish scenario she was conjuring up probably involved him in a compromising position with a woman.

Frustrated beyond measure, he cursed softly under his breath.

This entire episode could have been avoided, he knew, if he had simply told her that he had been speaking to his sister, but the conversation with Cecilia had been an unusually abrupt and inconclusive one and he had been in no mood to deal with Abigail's crazy suspicions.

Why should he?

He'd never had much time for people who made demands of him. What man did? A demanding woman always turned possessive at some point and there was no way he would ever contemplate having any such relationship.

It infuriated him that, after all those very reasonable pep talks he had given himself in the past week and a half, he was still out of sorts. He hated the saccharine smile she produced every time he walked through the front door and, for the past few days, she had somehow managed either to ensure that the nanny had dinner with them or had invited Vanessa or one of the other employees of the shop over so that any time spent alone together had been frankly reduced to zilch.

And then there was the lack of sex.

Leandro couldn't work out how it was that he missed her warm, willing and incredibly sexy body so much.

Sex was a bodily function, wasn't it? A very pleasant bodily function but nothing upon which the entire world could stop turning on its axis if it wasn't around.

And yet…

He glanced at his watch, noting the slow passage of time and cursing the tendency to introspection that seemed suddenly and inexplicably to have taken up residence in him.

It took a lot of focus and concentration actually to get down to reviewing the complicated legalese that had to be picked over for the deal he was in the process of closing and, the next time he looked at his watch, it was after seven.

For the first time since she had re-entered his life as the mother of his child, Abigail was going out for the evening. She had handed in her notice and Vanessa was throwing her a little party at a club not a million miles away. Not only were the employees of the company invited, along with a few of Abigail's friends she had made during the time she had been working in London, but some of their more regular clients who had dealt with her over the years were also going to be there.

This information had not been volunteered by Abigail, but by Vanessa, when she had come over two evenings previously for dinner. Leandro had surreptitiously scrutinised Abigail's face for a show of excitement but he hadn't been able to glean a thing from her lack of expression.

But he had had to face the stark truth, which was that they were no longer sleeping together and, effectively, she was a single woman who could do as she liked.

Which, of course, would be nothing, because if there was one thing he had worked out it was that she wasn't the sort to jump into bed with a man just because the opportunity happened to present itself.

He almost laughed at the thought of her going to some office party and throwing herself around.

Yes, they would be going to a club, and indeed he knew the club they would be going to and had once been a regular there back in the day. And yes, sure, there would be music and dancing, although he personally had never been one of those gyrating on a dance floor, but doubtless she would miss Sam and would make her excuses to leave as early as possible.

He'd bet on it.

Abigail looked at her reflection in the mirror of the spare room she now occupied. The wardrobe spanned one entire wall and was completely mirrored. There was no escaping the reflection staring back at her. It felt odd to be dressed up when she had spent so many months in an array of unexciting work garb or old stay-at-home clothes that were suitable for holding a baby.

Since Leandro had re-entered her life, her wardrobe had undergone a radical transformation because he had insisted that she buy herself stuff she could go out in.

He had even bought a couple of dresses for her himself, which had seemed extraordinary at the time, but she had quietly put those to the back of the wardrobe because she was assailed by a weird feeling of guilt whenever she thought about wearing them.

She'd extracted one of those dresses now and she had to admit that it fit like a dream.

It was figure-hugging, short and, despite the very modest neckline and three-quarter-length sleeves, still managed to look incredibly sexy.

Maybe because it was fire-engine red. For better or for worse, one look at her and people would stop dead in their tracks, and that was exactly what she wanted them to do because her confidence levels were at an all-time low.

Things between Leandro and herself had changed so quickly from wonderful to nightmarish.

One phone call.

Why couldn't he have told her what it had been about? How hard would it have been for him just to have said that he had been on the phone to a work colleague? Very hard, she reckoned, if that phone call had been from a prospective lover, and surely it had been or he would have explained the situation?

He was seeing someone else. Or, at the very least, he was contemplating it.

Abigail couldn't bear the thought of it. When she had heard a woman's voice down the end of the line, the jealousy that had gripped her had been as powerful as a vice squeezing her heart. Since then she had feverishly found herself imagining *what* woman. Blonde?

Brunette? Tall? Short? Past flame? Potential flame? She'd been driven crazy with her imagining.

And, when she hadn't been busy *imagining,* she had been sensible enough to work out that their trial period—which she could now see she had optimistically undertaken in the wild hope that he would find himself loving her, and proposing to her all over again for the right reasons—was at an end.

She had taken herself off to the spare room on the night of the phone call. Leandro hadn't objected. He had watched her move her stuff out and close the door on sex and he hadn't tried to win her back. Considering the sex had been so powerful, that pretty much said it all as far as she was concerned.

Her heart was breaking, but she was keeping it together, trying to make sure that she behaved like an adult for Sam's sake. She wasn't going to run away or take out her sadness and hurt by being mean to Leandro. Once upon a time, she'd let her emotions determine her behaviour and had deprived him of the first ten months of his son's life and, looking back, she could see that although she had done that without malevolence she'd been misguided.

So she was polite to him. They made conversation. She kept her distance and communicated the way she would have communicated with a perfect stranger, even though every time she looked at his lean, achingly beautiful face her heart squeezed tighter and the hollow in the pit of her stomach hurt more.

She would have to move on with her life, whilst recognising that he would still be a part of it whether she liked it or not. She would still have to see him. When she moved out to the cottage, he would probably show up one day with the very woman he had been talking to on the phone in that guilty, hushed voice. And she would have to face her replacement with equanimity and get on with it.

'Getting on with it' meant having a life of her own. She'd decided that step one to achieving that would be to go out to the party Vanessa had arranged and have fun.

Hence the dress. And the make-up, which was deceptively light but definitely effective. And the hair, which she'd had styled at the hairdressers. Trimmed and straightened, it hung down to her waist in a colourful golden curtain.

She had already settled Sam and, sticking her feet into some very high sandals, she had a few quick words with the nanny and then hurried out to get into the taxi which she had ordered earlier. She could easily have taken Leandro's driver, but not relying on such luxuries seemed a vital step in reasserting the independence which she had gradually forfeited during the time she had spent succumbing to Leandro's charms and nurturing hopeless fantasies about happy-ever-afters.

The club was in the centre of London and by the time Abigail got there, having texted Vanessa to warn her that she would be arriving—so that she didn't turn up at the place and find herself on her own, having to order a drink at a bar and hope she didn't look as if she had been stood up by a hot date—it was already heaving.

Taking a deep breath, she headed in, very much

aware of heads swinging in her direction, and decided that she was going to have fun if it killed her.

Leandro wasn't quite sure how, at a little after nine-thirty, he found himself outside the club where Abigail's leaving party was taking place. It seemed that one minute he'd been engrossed in the finer points of due diligence, and the next he'd been in the back of his car on his way to Valentino's.

Outside, there was a polite gathering of well-heeled, well-dressed thirty-somethings, mostly smoking and holding flutes of champagne. The men had dispensed with their obligatory jackets but the women were still decked out in their finery, even if they were beginning to look a little less groomed than they had probably looked two hours previously.

The doormen looked bored. Valentino's was an exclusive members-only club and the opportunities for getting rid of riff raff would be remote.

Leandro wasn't sure where his membership card was, but in any event it didn't matter because he was known here. He also carried that air of unassailable power and opulence that encouraged people to bow, scrape and open doors before they even realised what doors they were opening.

It had been well over a year since he had been there, but he was familiar with the layout. Like other private clubs, this was a dark, intimate place, with a very cleverly thought out décor that encouraged intimacy, relaxation and therefore a great deal of expensive drinking and eating. The bar snacks were unusually good and the food, which was served in separate rooms, had won Michelin stars. To one side, the actual bar was a curving oak semi-circle that brought to mind old-fashioned movies involving the mafia. The dance floor was a raised podium with low lighting and sufficient space to house a live band, which was often the case, although not tonight. Sofas and comfortable chairs were interspersed between low wooden tables.

As always, the place was heaving. Jean Claude, a Frenchman of impeccable good manners and frightening efficiency, ran the show with a hand of steel. Drinks were never spilled, bar snacks were always delivered with aplomb, food was never served cold.

Leandro had been prepared to cut short the preliminaries and flatly ask him where Abigail's party could be found, but he didn't have to because, eyes narrowed, he saw for himself where his quarry was.

He clenched his jaw and remained standing where he was, towards the back of the dark room, a towering, vaguely menacing presence that was attracting all sorts of sidelong looks from the people edging past him.

No wonder Abigail hadn't waxed lyrical about the leaving party, he thought through gritted teeth. She had managed very successfully to keep her excitement under wraps.

She'd barely had time for him for the past couple of weeks. Indeed, they had moved seamlessly from passionate lovers to nodding acquaintances—but what a fool he would have been to have thought that she might have been missing...well, missing *him*.

It appeared not.

It seemed that she had been ticking off the days until she could let her hair down and revert to the single life she had clearly never intended to leave behind.

So much for that sweet, sexy smile and those big doe eyes when she had told him that she wouldn't marry him, but would live with him and see how things went. She'd failed to mention that the slightest hiccup and she'd be off in a puff of smoke.

Every muscle tensed, he watched through narrowed eyes as she danced with some guy who looked as though he would have jumped all over her given half a chance. Her eyes were half-closed and her movements were as rhythmic as a professional dancer's. Around her, everyone else faded in comparison. It was as if she exuded an unbearably bright glow which was, quite literally, unmatchable.

The over-eager man curved his hand around her waist to gather her closer and Leandro didn't wait to see how she would react.

Galvanised into furious action, he strode through the crowds, the tables and the waitresses holding huge, circular trays above their heads. By the time he hit the dance floor, fury was coursing through every vein in his body. He made no effort to think straight or to analyse why he was behaving the way he was.

'Mind if I cut in?' He barely glanced at the younger man who stepped back with an expression of alarm. Every scrap of his attention was reserved for the woman who had now snapped to attention and was frowning at him in a way that suggested perhaps one glass of champagne too many.

'How much have you had to drink?' he demanded.

Abigail blinked and laboriously tried to work out an answer to that, while trying to process the unexpected appearance of Leandro in the middle of the dance floor. He'd appeared out of nowhere—and he wasn't dancing.

The music had changed from upbeat to a ballad and she tugged the lapels of his white shirt and shimmied closer to him. 'Can I interest you in a dance?'

Aware that the eyes of the world were beadily swivelling in their direction, Leandro curved his big body against hers, shifting and settling her against him so that he could murmur into her ear, 'I'm dancing. Now, how much have you had to drink? No, scratch that. Who the hell was that guy you were dancing with? If I hadn't arrived in time, you would have had to peel him off you…or was that what you wanted? Have I interrupted a romance in the making?'

He tightened his grip on her and pulled her a little closer. Her breasts were pushing against him. When he thought of that guy and pictured him getting into a clinch like this with her, Leandro saw red, and he had to bite down the urge to find the man and thrash the living daylights out of him.

It would never happen, of course. Leandro abhorred that sort of extreme reaction. And yet…*his fingers itched...*

'I haven't had *much* to drink.' Abigail knew that her inhibitions were lowered. She had come to have a good time and had knocked back three glasses of champagne in quick succession in her quest not to be a party pooper.

The champagne had gone to her head, and had done wonderful things to loosen her up and relieve her of some of the terrible stress and sadness that had been plaguing her every day since she and Leandro had begun pulling away from one another.

Right now, it was also allowing her really to enjoy the firmness of his body against hers and the husky, urgent whisper in her ear and that tone of...*possessiveness* was frankly thrilling.

She cosied up to him and he didn't pull away.

'Shane,' she murmured, curving her hands behind his neck and linking her fingers together.

'Shane?' The woman was sex on legs and Leandro's blood ran more hot the closer she pressed herself against him. He fought to remember that this was the same demanding woman who had laid into him simply because he had failed to answer a question which should never have been asked in the first place. He didn't do nagging, even though she was in a different category from anyone else who'd ever tried. However, his body was not making the necessary connections, and he knew if he wasn't careful soon he'd be as hard as steel and painfully in need of relief.

'Don Andrew's son.' Abigail was proud of her ability to think clearly even though she knew that the drink had gone to her head. 'Don Andrew,' she enunciated with precision and clarity, 'is a regular customer of ours. Shane is his son by his first marriage. He came in with his girlfriend a couple of months ago to buy a diamond bracelet for her.'

'And where's the lucky girl now?' Leandro bit out.

'Hiding behind a pillar? Waiting for him to get back to her just as soon as he's done making a pass at you?'

Abigail pulled back and stared at him in apparent fascination. 'Are you *jealous*?'

Leandro flushed darkly. 'I don't do jealousy,' he denied, voice cool and clipped. 'Never have, never will. You've had too much to drink. I'm taking you home.'

'But I've only just got here,' Abigail trilled. 'And we've barely danced together at all.' She pouted up at him, all lush pink lips and bedroom eyes, and Leandro swore softly and fluently under his breath.

'Don't do that,' he said roughly. They'd managed to find their way to the side of the dance floor where the light was even dimmer and the music was low enough that they could hear themselves talk.

'Do what?' She fluttered her lashes with a shameful lack of reserve and giggled.

'Ask for something you might not be intending to ask for,' Leandro growled. Never had self-restraint felt so hard, and his desire was so painful he could barely move properly.

'Maybe I am intending to ask for what you don't think I should be *intending* to ask for…or something like that…' She pulled him down towards her because she just had to, and her body went up in flames as his cool lips met hers, then lingered and then devoured, tongues meshing, her little moans shattering proof of how much she'd missed touching him.

Leandro was the first to pull back and he was shaking as he raked his fingers through his hair. 'I don't believe in these public displays of affection.' He looked at her long and hard, and wanted her with every bone and muscle and tendon in his big body. 'Besides, you're not in control. Where's your boss? I'm taking you to her, and you're going to make your excuses and then we're going home. And don't even think of telling me that you're *not ready to go yet.*'

Leandro didn't give Abigail time to mull anything over. They were out of the club in under ten minutes and in his car, heading back to the apartment. She was pressed against him, her body soft and pliable like a rag doll, and it took the will power of a saint to keep his hands to himself.

He would settle her into the spare room and in the morning she would wake up with a thumping headache and there would be no question of him having taken advantage of her.

That plan worked pretty much until he'd shut his bedroom door. He'd settled her into her room, having made sure to check on Sam. He'd even made sure she'd wriggled out of the cling-film dress which, if he had his way, no other man would get to see her in again. He'd politely turned his back, in true *ex*-lover style, while she'd got into whatever sleeping clothes she'd found in one of the drawers after she'd banged about searching. Then he'd reminded her that there were paracetamol in the cabinet in her *en suite* bathroom, and told her to take two, because she wouldn't like how she'd feel when she woke up in the middle of the night.

Then he'd gritted his teeth in pure frustration and taken to his bedroom and then…

And then his door had opened and she'd been there.

As quiet as a wraith and as beautiful as the most tempting of sirens.

And, as she'd climbed onto the bed with him, Leandro reckoned that he was, after all, just flesh and blood.

Now, as she lay staring intently at him in the silvery light filtering through the shutters, he sighed and shook his head.

'I want this,' Abigail said, as sober as a judge. She could scarcely credit that she had walked into his bedroom, which was next to hers, as naked as the day she'd been born, not caring about the consequences. She wanted him and she was sick to death of telling herself that wanting him was no way to move on with her life. Being a martyr hurt like hell, especially when they were both living under the same roof. For one night, she didn't want to be a martyr. Having lost him, she had woken up to how much she had lost, and it hurt more than she could ever have thought.

'I'm not going to take advantage of you.'

'No, you're not,' Abigail agreed. '*I'm* going to take advantage of *you*.'

He laughed in exasperation as Abigail unbuttoned his trousers and pulled them off before working on his shirt. He was the very picture of a man who was exercising as much self-restraint as he possibly could and she loved him—yes, loved him—for that.

Loved him even though he didn't love her and even though he probably had some stupid woman in the background ready to take her place. Abigail loved him so much that she wanted to take what was here right now and think about the consequences later. After all, she'd have a lifetime to pay her dues, wouldn't she?

She pushed him onto his back and climbed onto him, moving slowly and sinuously against his bare chest while she eased the shirt over his shoulders, only pausing and shifting so that he could rid himself of it. Leandro seemed to give in to his desire and put up no resistance.

'Don't let me get in the way of you taking advantage of me,' he said huskily with a smile that turned her on even more, from the soles of her feet to the top of her head. He hooked his thumb provocatively under the waistband of his boxers and tugged it suggestively, just enough to show her how aroused he was, then smiling the smile of the victor when her eyelids fluttered and she moaned softly.

'Have your wicked way with me, my darling, because I've missed you.'

Don't say stuff like that, she wanted to yell, because lines like that were what had got her where she was now, had made her think that there was more to what they had than there actually was.

When he said that he *missed* her, what he really meant was that he'd *missed the sex.*

Which meant that there wasn't another woman. Not yet. Because he wouldn't be here if there was. She just knew that.

Right now, she just wanted to hold him tight. She planted her hands on either side of him and leant over, lowering her breasts for him to take into his mouth, a nipple at a time. Head flung back, she groaned without restraint as he laved one hardened nipple with his tongue, while holding her other breast and massaging it. He moved between the two and took his time.

Then he cupped her behind and Abigail daringly edged up, straddling him and inching her way towards his mouth in small, sinuous stages until she positioned herself just where his tongue could flick devastatingly against her. He tickled her with the tip of his tongue and she released a long, shuddering moan. Her breathing was shallow and fast and, as he continued to taste her between her legs, she moved against his mouth. She felt little shivers of excitement racing like quicksilver through her veins, signalling an orgasm if she didn't stop to gather herself, but for a little while longer she enjoyed what his mouth was doing.

He was big and hard for her when it was her turn to taste him. Leandro angled her body, sliding her over him, and they tasted one another.

He couldn't get enough of her. He'd gone mad when he'd seen her dancing on that dance floor, seen the way other men had been eyeing her, and the way that guy had been circling her, waiting to make his move.

Was it simply possessiveness?

Something weird and disconcerting kicked inside him and he buried the odd sensation in the only way he knew how.

With sex.

He took over and Abigail loved it. He was so powerful and yet tender between the sheets. Her body was thrumming when, after an eternity, he thrust into her with long, deep strokes that drove her wild. Fingers biting into his waist, she moved against him, finding the rhythm that was theirs and moving to its beat, their bodies as one as sensation built and built between them.

She climaxed on a wave of shuddering ecstasy that went on and on and on, taking her to ever higher peaks which were made all the more amazing because she knew that he was coming as well, his body arching and stiffening under the impact of his own orgasm.

In sex, they truly became one person.

As they descended back down to Planet Earth, Abigail marvelled that she could have translated that complete physical union as a uniting of the mind, soul and spirit as well.

And what, she wondered in sudden raw confusion, was she going to do now?

He was back in bed with her and she didn't want to let him go, but thinking like that made her feel like a coward after the stand she had taken. How could she love someone who was so indifferent to her that he'd point-blank refused to answer a simple question? When he knew that the answer would have meant so much to her? They might not be married, but they'd been lovers and parents to a child. How did secrecy fit into that scenario?

Bitter tears tried to push their way through as stark regret began to invade her. Yet when Leandro scooped her against him she was happy to let him. She flattened her hands against his chest and breathed him in deeply, then sighed.

'Okay,' Leandro told her roughly. 'You win.'

Abigail drew back and squirmed into a position that allowed her look at him. 'What have I won?'

'You asked me who I was talking to on the phone.'

'You don't have to tell me anything you don't want to,' she lied with a dull flush. 'And it's not some kind of game, Leandro. We were supposed to be…*trying*…and it…it *hurt* thinking that you were talking to a woman on the phone. And it *hurt* to realise that you couldn't even respect what we had enough to tell me who it was. I know I have no rights over you but you wanted to know who that guy was…the one I was dancing with…and I told you. You'd rather walk away than tell me and, for me, that could only mean you were talking to someone you plan on sleeping with.'

Leandro groaned, lay flat on his back and stared up at the ceiling because everything she said made sense. He'd been an idiot and he couldn't blame her for laying into him. He'd let his pride rule him. 'I'm not accustomed to…answering to other people,' he admitted gruffly. 'But I should have just told you and I…I apologise.'

Abigail closed her eyes for a few seconds, astounded that she had won this concession, and astounded that he had apologised to her. True, it wasn't a flowers-and-chocolates kind of apology, but she knew instinctively how much it took for someone like Leandro to say sorry, someone who didn't, as he had said, *answer to other people.*

'So, who was it?' she asked coolly, pressing him for an answer.

'My sister. I was talking to Cecilia.'

CHAPTER NINE

ABIGAIL STIFFENED AND drew away from him. Aside from that one conversation two months ago, Cecilia had not been mentioned. Where was she? She could have set up residence on Mars, for all Abigail knew. Leandro never mentioned her, and Abigail knew better than to initiate any conversation about her, because she was all too aware of the unshakeable bond between them. At least, out of their sight, she could do no more damage—although why on earth hadn't Leandro said at the time who he had been talking to? Unless the conversation had been an awkward one. And it didn't take a genius to figure out what that *awkward* subject might have been.

'How is she?' Abigail asked, trying to sound concerned, and Leandro looked at her wryly.

'I'm sensing real interest there,' he remarked, but his face was serious and thoughtful and she couldn't help but feel a wave of unease. He would always at least partly believe the picture Cecilia painted of herself and presented to him. Lately, it might have taken a dent, and perhaps he wasn't quite as forgiving in his responses as once he might have been, but essentially

Cecilia could do no wrong. She was his kid sister, he had always taken care of her, and caretaking was a habit that could never be broken.

'She hasn't been around.' Abigail lay flat on her back, pulled the duvet up to cover her nakedness and stared at the ceiling, although in her mind's eye she could see his face, shuttered and inward thinking.

'That's because she's been on the other side of the world opening up my boutique hotel in Fiji. It's been non-stop for her. She's barely had time to surface. She's also got involved with one of the project managers working with her, so she hasn't had any interest in flying back to the UK when she can holiday on a South Pacific island if she needs a break.'

'Why didn't you tell me that she was the woman you were talking to on the phone?' Abigail demanded, turning to look at his profile.

'Like I said,' Leandro returned without missing a beat, 'I'm not accustomed to having questions asked about who I'm talking to, or where I'm going or with whom.'

Abigail inhaled deeply. 'I know we're not married,' she began, 'and that in fact you'd probably feel the same way even if we *were* married, but as far as I'm concerned that's not an acceptable attitude to take.'

'Come again?' Leandro turned to her, astounded that she would flatly choose to start an argument when he had earlier offered her an apology for not having told her what she had wanted to know, and when he had volunteered the information in a move that, for him, was a massive concession.

Abigail wasn't going to back down on this but the brooding disapproval in those eyes was wreaking havoc with her levels of courage. 'I mean you need to make a choice, and then we can take things from there.'

'I'm not following you,' he replied, but all his senses were on red alert. He shifted so that he was on his side and they were looking at one another, eye to eye. It hadn't escaped him that she had tugged the covers up to cover herself, and from that he gathered that this was a serious conversation, a conversation in which accidental nudity had no part. 'What choice am I supposed to be making?'

'We're living together,' Abigail began with a great deal more assuredness than she was feeling. Indeed, she was floundering so much inside that she marvelled that her voice hadn't dried up completely. 'You may think that I overreacted to your silence, but I've had real doubts as to whether it's a good idea to let something develop between us.' She sighed and looked at his shuttered, unrevealing face. At least he hadn't turned away. At least he was listening. As far as she was concerned that was a case of so far, so good.

'Did you honestly think that I was on the phone to another woman? Planning a *rendezvous* with her—whilst sleeping with you? On the one hand, I'm flattered that you think my energy levels are through the roof, but on the other hand I'm insulted that you would even think that I might be capable of what you have accused me of.'

'I haven't accused you of anything but there's no room for those sorts of silences between us. If you really feel that there's no need for you to ever explain your actions, or tell me where you've been if I ask, then say so right now and I will pack my bags and leave this apartment in the morning. I'll move into the cottage with Sam, and I will never, ever try and limit your contact with him, but there will never be anything more between us. You'll be free to do whatever you like, without anyone questioning you. In essence, you would be free to remain a bachelor and behave like one—but if we're to be together then, as far as I'm concerned, you might not be married but you're no longer a bachelor.'

Just like that, Leandro knew that the rules of the game had changed and, whilst instinct was telling him to make a stand—a *justified* stand, because the only rules he had ever played to had been his own—there was a third party involved.

Was he prepared to risk his relationship with his son? Because, say what she might at this point in time, if he chose to turn his back on her now, when she had effectively told him that she was prepared to give it another go, his rejection would fester inside her, and everyone knew that old saying about a woman scorned.

And the world was full of men ready and willing to try it on with her, even if she came with a child. She had the sort of looks that guaranteed that she wouldn't be left on the shelf for longer than five seconds. Everything in him demanded Abigail remain *his*.

'If you insist on terms and conditions,' Leandro drawled, 'then I have a couple of my own.'

'You still haven't answered what I asked.'

'I will do my utmost…' he flushed darkly and she

met his accompanying glare with serenity '…to keep you in the loop and, if you're curious about any of my activities—which I assure you will be above board, whatever you might think—then I will satisfy your curiosity with the appropriate explanations.'

'Okay.' She paused and registered the heady relief flooding her because the past days had been hellish and she knew, seeing him tonight, that she just wanted him back whether it made sense or not. 'What are your terms and conditions?'

'You don't turn your back on me and play the *no sex* card every time you want to make a point. I understand that you were hurt, but don't think you can try to turn me into a person I will never be and then, if you think your efforts are failing, decide to withdraw sex.'

A person who will never be in love with me, Abigail thought bravely, *because if you were in love with me, compromising would come as second nature. It wouldn't feel like a great, big sacrifice.*

It proved just how committed he was to being a good father for Sam but it still hurt her.

'You stop acting as though it's torture to take and spend the money I've been putting into your account.'

'I do spend it. Some of it.'

'You buy things for Sam and food for the house. Occasionally you might treat yourself to something cheap and cheerful. I find that insulting.'

'How?' Abigail gasped. 'How can it be insulting if I don't use your money?'

'Take what is given in the right spirit, in the spirit in which it has been given,' Leandro told her bluntly. 'I see you stubbornly refusing what I can give you and it makes me think that it's your way of telling me that your pride is greater than your desire to adapt. I have a certain lifestyle and it makes sense for you to adapt to it.'

'I suppose you have a point.'

'I know I do. Furthermore, we set a time limit to this exercise in self-discovery.'

'What do you mean?'

'Here's what I mean.' Leandro didn't beat about the bush. 'I proposed to you because it was the preferred solution. Our son would benefit from having us both there, at hand, rather than being bounced around between us. You turned me down, and I appreciate that the end result was for you to establish whether we could be a functioning proposition, but there has to be a time limit to this probationary period after which we sit down and decide whether we tie the knot and make this permanent, or else walk away, knowing that we gave it our best shot.'

Never had she seen more clearly how little love featured in his life plan that was all set to include her. Effectively he was telling her that theirs was an arrangement with benefits, and if, at the end of the day, the arrangement wasn't working, they'd wash their hands of it and move on.

'How do you set a time limit on something like that?' she asked jerkily and Leandro shrugged.

'Good question. It's impossible because there can never been any guarantee that we have reached a point of knowing, for sure, that we are compatible on a long-term basis, which is why I propose we give it three months, at the end of which we decide.'

'Good idea,' she agreed painfully. 'Three months and then, if things haven't worked out, we can go our separate ways and get on with our lives.' She paused and digested this, knowing that it was the best solution and would stop her from drifting hopelessly on uncertain waters, becoming more and more incapable of taking a stand, hanging on to see whether he would one day tell her that he loved her.

Moving out to the cottage felt like a final cutting of ties with life in London. The frantic noise and constant buzz that had been the backdrop of her life for so long gave way to the sounds of nature. Their possessions had been taken the day before by a professional removal company, including furniture from both the apartment and Greyling.

'Cherry pick whatever you want.' Leandro had shrugged. 'And bear in mind that everything will probably be replaced at some point because I can't imagine you'll want to furnish the place in things you haven't personally chosen.'

Abigail could have told him that being fussy was not a trait she was acquainted with. But she didn't make a song and dance about being parsimonious and being the sort of girl who didn't need to throw money around. She had taken on board what he had said to her and had realised that her continual refusal to accept his lavish generosity was indeed something he found both bewildering and vaguely offensive.

For the first time, she shopped for herself and really enjoyed it.

On her way to the four-wheel drive in which she and Sam but not Leandro would be travelling to the cottage, she paused to look at herself in the mirror.

She'd found her own style. She wasn't interested in flashy designer labels and, left to her own devices, with Leandro's explicit instructions ringing in her ears, she had gravitated towards the clothes she had more or less always worn but this time well cut, well tailored and just that bit smarter. Today, she was in a pair of perfectly fitting designer jeans with designer rips at the knees and a polo shirt with a very small, very discreet logo over the breast pocket. Blue jeans and a white top, accompanied by a pair of flat, tan-and-white leather pumps. She looked *stylish.*

From behind, she registered Leandro strolling towards her, Sam in his arms.

She knew that, to any outsider, they looked as if they could have stepped straight out of the pages of a magazine. She turned and smiled. 'I'm surprised he's not demanding to get down.' Abigail reached out for her son who lunged for her and then, predictably, squirmed until they settled him on the ground. These days he crawled and cruised everywhere with the sort of reckless enthusiasm that kept them both on their toes, sweeping aside breakables and covering sharp corners.

It never failed to amaze her just how naturally those simple things came to Leandro. He had embraced fatherhood. No one could accuse him of not putting his all into it. And by night he embraced the physical closeness that always left her wanting more of him. He was the very essence of what any woman would consider herself lucky to have ended up with. He was as amusing, intelligent and wildly, crazily sexy as he always had been, but scratch the surface and she knew that she wouldn't find the love she desperately wanted.

Never, not once, not even in the heat of passion, had he uttered any unguarded words that could have led her to think that he had the sort of feelings for her that she had for him.

'Want' was a staple in his vocabulary but 'love and need' were ostensibly missing and, with each passing day, she wondered what would happen to them when their three months were up.

He never discussed it and neither did she. She was plagued by the suspicion that she was on trial, and cautious about how she responded, because she knew that what he wanted was a functioning business arrangement and not the sort of complicated emotional involvement that love brought with it.

Deep down she knew that if, at the end of the three-month period, he repeated that offer of marriage then she would accept. They got along, they were bonded in their love for Sam and the sex was mind-blowing. Many marriages worked quite happily on less.

Was she selling herself short? She didn't think so because, whilst she had never envisaged being married to a guy who wasn't madly in love with her, she also couldn't imagine anyone else completing her the way he did.

She wondered whether he would get bored of her and feel tempted to stray but uneasily that was a bridge she was prepared to cross when she came to it.

'Penny for them.' Leandro scooped up his son, leant to brush a kiss on the side of her neck and then held Sam up high until he squealed with laughter, before handing him over to Abigail.

'Just thinking about the move,' she said brightly.

'Sorry I won't be able to come with you now,' Leandro told her. 'but I'll be there later.' He grinned. 'You'll probably get a lot more done without me around,' he told her. 'I would probably get under your feet. Or perhaps just under you.'

Abigail blushed bright red, reminded of just how much he thought about sex, practically to the exclusion of everything else aside from Sam and his work.

Determined not to dwell on what was missing in her life, but to focus on what she had, Abigail spent the drive to the cottage making lots of mental lists of what she would do and how she would apportion her time.

She had been out several times to see it, had supervised the arrangement of the various bits of furniture which had arrived over a period of three days, yet an hour later, when the four-wheel drive drew up in front of the cottage, she was charmed all over again.

The cottage had been upgraded to a very high standard, having been repainted, with new units put into the kitchen and landscaping done in the back garden, as well as hand-made, built-in furniture having been installed in the bedrooms. She and Sam explored the place. She had given the nanny a few days off so that she could accustom herself to the cottage, just Sam, Leandro and her, and as Leandro's driver disappeared back to London Abigail felt the stirring of excitement at this new step in her life.

She allowed Sam to run around the sitting room, where there were no hard edges or glass, then she played with him in the garden and, by the time his afternoon nap time came at one-thirty, he was exhausted.

The kettle was boiling for a cup of tea when the doorbell went and her heart leapt at the prospect of Leandro being here much earlier than anticipated.

She dashed to the door, pulled it open and then fell back in surprise to see Cecilia standing on her doorstep, as stunningly gorgeous as she had been the last time they had seen one another. Both Leandro and his sister shared the same colouring, both olive-skinned with black hair and perfectly chiselled features. Where Leandro's beauty was hard-edged and aggressively masculine, his sister's was aristocratic and intensely feminine. She was the puma to Leandro's tiger. Abigail associated pumas with cunning and danger, which was why she remained blocking the doorway.

'Aren't you going to invite me in?' Cecilia peered past her and took a step forward. 'Great place. I nabbed a peek at the particulars in Leandro's apartment when I arrived a couple of hours ago but it's even better in the flesh. I can see that you've really landed on your feet, Abigail. Must be nice for you, all things considered.'

'Why are you here?' Leandro hadn't mentioned, not even in passing, that his sister was due back in the country today. Had that been a deliberate oversight on his part? Or had Cecilia descended on him without warning?

'To catch up. Why else? I *have* driven all the way from London. The *least* you could do is invite me in for a glass of something.'

'I thought you were in Fiji.'

'Two weeks off. Thought I'd come and see my darling brother. In fact, I just left him with a few things to think about.'

Abigail stilled and she stood aside and quietly invited Cecilia in, guiding her immediately to the kitchen, while the other woman made a big show of looking around her and exclaiming with delight at everything she saw, from the pictures on the walls to the bottle-green range in the kitchen.

'Hats off to you. You've done well. Bet you never thought you'd end up in a fancy cottage with a wad of cash to spend on yourself! Clever of you to get pregnant,' she mused, glancing at her exquisitely manicured nails and buffing them with her thumb before fixing huge, almond-shaped eyes on her.

Abigail didn't say anything, instead turning away and taking her time to make a pot of tea. Her heart was hammering and she knew, with a sickening feeling, that this conversation was going somewhere and the destination wasn't going to be very nice.

But, now that the other woman was in the cottage, she had little option but to travel down the circuitous route of icy small talk laced with sugar-coated insults. She bit her tongue. There was no way that she was going to open up a can of worms by getting into an argument with Leandro's sister.

'He tells me that marriage is on the table,' Cecilia

said abruptly. They were sitting at opposite ends of the cleverly weathered wooden table, which had had pride of place in the kitchen at Greyling, and Abigail nodded and met the other woman's eyes squarely.

'We feel that Sam would benefit from having both of us around.'

'Stop talking about yourself and my brother as though you're a *couple,*' Cecilia hissed. 'You're *not* a couple. You weren't then and you aren't now.' Her eyes welled up. 'I knew you were trouble the minute you met Leandro the first time round. He barely had time to talk to me when you appeared on the scene!'

Concerned, Abigail flew to her feet and rummaged in her handbag which she had slung on the kitchen counter, extracting a wad of tissues and shoving them over to Cecilia.

'I should have known that something was up when he sent me halfway across the world to oversee that hotel in Fiji.' Her voice wobbled but the glare was intact. 'It was impossible to talk to him, what with the time difference and the problems with the Internet! But I found out everything today when I confronted him. You are *not* going to marry my brother. You are *not* going to take him away from me.'

'I—I'm not planning on taking him away from you,' Abigail stammered.

'He doesn't want to marry you!' Cecilia's voice had risen and Abigail worriedly glanced at the kitchen door, which was open. The last thing she needed was a shouting Cecilia and a screaming toddler. 'You're all wrong for Leandro and the last thing he wants is to *marry* you.'

'Did he tell you that?'

'Of course he did!' Cecilia shouted. 'We discuss *everything*! He told me that you're forcing him to marry you because of the kid. He told me that you're not really his type. He doesn't *care* about you. He doesn't *love* you!'

Abigail looked down. Cecilia had a vested interest in saying all those things, in causing as much chaos as she could. But was she lying? She was only confirming what Abigail already knew.

She expected another shrieking tirade from the other woman, and was rising to her feet to forestall that by leading her firmly out of the cottage, when Leandro's voice from the doorway of the kitchen stopped her in her tracks.

She hadn't heard him enter the house. Of course, why would she? He had a key and she had been entirely focused on Cecilia. She wouldn't have noticed two yetis if they had walked past the kitchen door holding hands.

'Cecilia.' Leandro's deep voice was cool, as was the gaze arrowing towards his sister as she spun round, reddening before rushing to his side. But before she could hug him he held out his arms to stop her. 'What are you doing here?'

'I—I came to say hi to my nephew,' she stammered, 'but *she* wouldn't let me.'

Abigail opened her mouth to protest and then was overcome by a feeling of deep hopelessness. Why would Leandro believe her? He didn't love her. It was going to be just as it had been nearly two years ago when he had listened to Cecilia and refused to give Abigail a fair hearing. He had been judge, jury and executioner to their relationship and why would it be any different now?

Perhaps he had already been persuaded that without love he was better off without her, whatever he said about wanting to stay with her because of Sam. Perhaps he might have drifted into a relationship with her, but he was no doubt open to being persuaded by Cecilia. Abigail could easily envisage a situation where she managed to convince him that there was someone better for him out there, someone who shared the same background, someone he could love rather than like, and with whom the ties would not be centred around obligation and duties to an infant he had never asked for.

Her imagination was running riot but through all that she couldn't help but notice that he wasn't chastising his sister. Indeed, he was drawing her to one side, although his eyes were firmly focused on Abigail.

'I'll make sure Cecilia gets back to London,' he said without any inflection in his voice at all that could have given her a clue as to what he was thinking.

Which made her fear that he was already thinking the worst of her. He had descended out of the blue to be told that she was the cruel woman withholding a nephew from his aunt. Cecilia could work a sob story like an Oscar-winning actress.

And yet, in receipt of a sly look from the other woman as she was gently led out of the kitchen, Abigail couldn't help a pang of sympathy for her. That plaintive voice had been real. Cecilia was hurt because she had felt ignored by the big brother who had always had time for her. The hint of tears had not been phoney.

Not that any of that changed anything. The three months might barely have started, but if Leandro could not give her the benefit of the doubt now, and remain behind to hear from her exactly what had transpired between herself and his sister, then he would never be prepared to give her the benefit of the doubt over anything.

In short, nothing had fundamentally changed between them since he had turned his back on her all that time ago, except that he was now a father. His attitude towards her remained the same.

He would hand-deliver Cecilia back to London, all those protective instincts that had been fostered since youth would kick into gear and he would indulge his sister and whatever lies she chose to tell him.

Lord knew, he would probably head straight back up to the cottage to fling another one of his *terms and conditions* in her face, specifically one banning her from upsetting his sister.

Suddenly weary beyond belief, Abigail went out into the garden and headed straight for the lovely gazebo that had been erected under one of the fruit trees. Sam's window was flung open and she knew that she would be able to hear him should he wake up and start crying, although his afternoon naps were long, and she knew that he wouldn't be up for at least another hour.

Precious time during which she would try and get her thoughts in order, try and reach a conclusion to the ebb and flow of life as she had recently been living it.

Her thoughts became muddled as she closed her eyes.

It was a fine day, the breeze just the right side of warm. Nature had its own sounds and with her eyes closed she could really appreciate all of them. The sound of the leaves in the trees rustling, the birds chirping and, in the distance, the roll of traffic because although the cottage was in the middle of nowhere this was something of an illusion, because the road to London was not terribly far away.

Drifting into a light doze, she had a dream of Leandro walking away from her and, with every panicked step she took closer to him, the faster he moved away, glancing back towards her and walking on even though he could see that she was upset.

She started violently when his deep, familiar voice said, way too close and way too vibrant to belong to a dream, 'Falling asleep in the sun is never a good idea.'

Abigail's eyes flew open and she gaped. 'I thought you were dropping your sister back down to London!'

'She came in a car,' Leandro said drily, 'and there's no reason why she can't return in it—although my driver brought me here, so I've had him deliver her back down and leave my car here.' He stood where he was, hands in his pockets, his dark, beautiful face revealing precious little.

He looked away briefly, and when he raked his fingers through his hair she finally identified that unrevealing expression on his face for what it was. Discomfort. Since she had never seen him out of his depth, that was a piercing cause for concern, and suddenly all the doubts and insecurities she had nurtured under the surface rose to the top, clamouring to be heard.

Heart in her mouth, she cleared her throat and said quietly, 'I think we should have a chat. I'm not sure what your sister told you, Leandro, but she did tell me what you said to her about… Well, put it this way, about your heart not being in making this relationship work, and it's no big deal.'

'It's not?'

'It's nothing that I didn't know, and I want you to know that I really appreciate the effort you've made in trying to stay together for Sam's sake. It was never going to happen, of course,' she said ruefully, lowering her eyes. 'You can't fit a square peg into a round hole, which is what we have been trying to do. I'm sure you'll agree with me.'

She looked at him and flushed because he was staring at her with such a curious look of hesitancy that she didn't know whether to carry on in the same vein, shift course or bolt for the back door.

She did none of those things. Instead, she plastered a smile on her face and prompted, 'Well? Say something, Leandro. Because Sam is going to be up soon and if we have to have this talk then this is the best time to have it…'

CHAPTER TEN

'I HAD NO idea that Cecilia was going to show up at my apartment today. At least, not without warning.'

'But you spoke to her on the phone.' Abigail restively stood up and began heading into the cottage, because outside was for relaxing and she wasn't feeling relaxed. She was aware of Leandro following her. It made the hairs on the back of her neck stand on end. 'She must have told you,' she carried on, swinging round to look at him, hand on one hip. 'I mean, she made it clear that you tell each other *everything.*' This last was slung at him in an accusatory voice and Leandro glanced away, jaw tensing.

When had all his control started seeping away? Control was the one thing he had always aimed for. Control in his professional life and control in his private life. When had that all disappeared? Could he have stopped it somewhere along the way or was it just a process that had begun when Abigail had first entered his life, a process that had simply been temporarily halted when she had left, only to continue the moment she'd returned?

He certainly didn't feel in control now. He felt…like

any red-blooded man would feel if he had one foot dangling off the edge of a precipice.

She sat down at the table but was staring off into the distance.

'She has always been dependent on me,' Leandro explained heavily. 'Our parents had little time for us and Cecilia relied heavily on me for pretty much everything. Of course, as time went on, I assumed she was becoming more independent, and certainly on the surface she had a good life. She never wanted for anything and she had a lot of friends. She still came to me for advice. She still confided in me. I found it amusing, and I suppose it was a comfort zone that worked. She did her degree, immediately started working for my organisation in the hospitality field and she was, and is, excellent at it.'

He sighed and linked his fingers together. 'I never really noticed how possessive she was of my relationships, because I took everything at face value, and they were never meaningful. When you came along...'

'When I came along,' Abigail filled in for his benefit, 'she couldn't wait to blow it out of the water because she wasn't in control of it.'

Leandro's mouth quirked. 'She couldn't wait to blow it out of the water because she sensed that it could become serious,' he corrected quietly. 'She sensed something I myself wasn't even really aware of. I wanted you the minute I laid eyes on you, Abigail.'

'So you told me,' she responded with an edge of bitterness in her voice. 'I've always known that. You want me and you find me attractive. You'd be surprised how insulting that can feel after a while. It was heady when we first met. I'd never met anyone like you in my entire life. How would I? You moved in the sort of circles I would never have been allowed to enter. I've said this before but I'll say it again—that was why I kept quiet about my background. I wanted to enjoy you without all those judgements being formed about me because of where I'd come from. Cecilia must have thought that she'd struck gold when she dug and found out all that stuff about me.'

'I should have listened to my conscience,' Leandro admitted, 'instead of accepting the evidence against you and jumping to the wrong conclusions.'

'What are you saying?' Abigail looked at him defiantly because she refused to get her hopes up. She'd had them dashed too many times.

'I was wrapped up with you, Abigail. I don't know how it happened, because I always thought I was well protected against emotional involvement, but you managed to work a way through to me… Maybe that was why I was so quick to pigeonhole you as a gold-digger. You'd lied, and it was easy and lazy to believe the worst of you, because if I didn't I would have had to admit to having feelings for you that went way beyond wanting to have sex with you.'

Abigail's heart leapt. 'I didn't tell you I was pregnant because I knew what you thought of me…'

'I understand. When I saw you again, I realised that I still wanted you,' he confessed. 'I'd just broken up with someone who, on paper, should have been the perfect match. Cecilia introduced us.' He grimaced. 'I suppose at that point I should have read the writing on the wall and realised how important it was to my sister that she should never feel threatened by any woman I chose to date.'

Abigail allowed herself a glimmer of a smile, because if there was one type of reading Leandro didn't do it was reading writing on the wall. She could understand that because, if you never dug deep, you never found yourself out of your depth.

He stood up and paced the kitchen, vaguely taking in the small steps she had already made towards turning it into a home. There were two framed pictures of Sam on the wall by the table and some herbs in pots on the window ledge. She'd done the same when she'd been living with him. She had somehow transformed his apartment in incremental ways, from a cold space to something homely, and she'd done it without him even really noticing.

'I heard what she said to you,' he stated flatly. 'It was impossible not to overhear because she wasn't making the slightest effort to keep the noise levels down.'

Abigail tensed and stared at her linked fingers on the kitchen table.

'I had no conversation with her along the lines she intimated. I should be furious that she should take it upon herself to come here and purport to be my mouthpiece, but I'm not.'

'Because she paved the way for you to…tell me what's been obvious all along?'

'Something like that.' He reached out and held her fluttering fingers still until she was forced to look at him. 'This is hard for me to say,' he told her in a low, driven voice. 'I've never believed in love. I have always associated it with something destructive. I thought I was immune to its effects but I was wrong.'

'What do you mean?'

'I mean I was half way to falling in love with you the first time round, and this time round I've managed to complete the job. I'm head over heels in love with you, Abigail, and I think I've known that deep down for some time now.'

'You're in love with me?' she whispered, eyes as round as saucers.

'I buried it under the excuse of rising to the occasion and doing the right thing, but when I proposed I should have asked myself how it was that I wasn't appalled at the change it would bring to my cherished lifestyle. I was blind and I drove you away.'

'You drove me away because I wanted so much more than you were offering. I wanted the whole package. I wanted you to love me the way I loved you.'

She smiled at him and he returned her smile, relief mingled with satisfaction.

'I never allowed myself to feel confident around you,' she confessed. 'I was too aware that we came from opposite sides of the tracks. I was scared when you got that call from Cecilia,' she carried on, 'because I could project and see the damage she had done being done again. When you left with her again earlier on today, I was convinced that the next time I saw you it would be to learn that you'd decided to take the road away from me, the road I'd paved for you to take. I had a lot of principles about marrying for the right reasons. I mean, I wanted my future to be completely different to my past. I wanted the whole package deal—romance and love with all the trimmings. Except I fell in love with you and there weren't any trimmings. I felt I couldn't walk into a union with someone for the wrong reasons and, somewhere along the line, I decided that perhaps you would start to feel the same things I felt.'

'Will you marry me, my darling?'

Abigail nodded, stood up and moved to sit on Leandro's lap. She curved her hands around his neck and drew him to her. 'Of course I will. Believe it or not,' she conceded sheepishly, 'I was desperate for you to pop the question again because marrying you—even if you couldn't love me—felt a whole lot better than the alternative, which was not having you in my life.' After a pause, she said, 'What about your sister?'

'She won't be back to air her views,' Leandro said shortly. 'I will, naturally, continue to see her when she happens to be in the country—but she overstepped the boundaries and that's unacceptable.' He sighed deeply. 'Protecting my sister has become a habit over the years and it's blinded me to some of her failings. She will continue to run my hotel in Fiji but she won't be bothering you in the future. Now, let's stop talking about Cecilia and let's start talking about...*us*.'

EPILOGUE

ABIGAIL GAZED AT her reflection in the mirror with a smile of satisfaction because this was exactly how she had wanted to look. Not flashy, no overkill, but not so understated that she could have been going to a cocktail party.

This was the perfect wedding dress. It was straight and simple, with exquisite silvery beading against the cream background. The neckline was modestly scooped while the back dipped a little lower. It was the last time she would be able to fit into something as tight as this—she was ten weeks pregnant and she could already spot the incipient signs of an expanding tummy.

Tonight, she would tell Leandro, and she couldn't wait to see his face when she broke the news. He had missed out on her being pregnant with Sam and she knew that he would be the most attentive husband, lover and father-to-be with the baby she had found out she was carrying only a few days ago.

That would be surprise number one.

Surprise number two would be his sister. Cecilia had been firmly put in her place and given her marching orders, to hold the fort on the other side of the world and never again to interfere in his life. Abigail knew Leandro and, whilst he was the fairest man she could ever have hoped to meet, he was not a guy who believed in beating about the bush.

When he had informed her that he had told his sister to cease and desist, Abigail had very quickly imagined a terse and unapologetic two-sentence conversation. Whatever Cecilia had done, it was fair to say that she had done so against a backdrop of issues that had made her overly dependent and fragile and therefore vulnerable to the thought of her brother no longer having time for her.

A week ago, Abigail had spoken to her on the phone. The conversation had been awkward, halting and, at least to start with, defensive on the part of Cecilia, but Abigail had persevered and two days previously, unbeknown to Leandro, Cecilia had arrived in London. They had met and Abigail had taken Sam along with her.

'You're his aunt,' she had said gently, 'and it's important that you get to know him. Every child needs a fun aunt. I've seen the movies.'

Cecilia had offered a grudging smile, but after five minutes she was no longer holding Sam with outstretched arms as though he were a parcel that might contain hazardous bio-waste material.

Abigail wouldn't go so far as to say that they had bonded at first sight, but Rome wasn't built in a day.

And, just at the moment, everything was looking pretty wonderful. Leandro had no idea that his sister would be attending the wedding. Abigail drily thought that, for a man who notoriously hated surprises, he was in for a fun-filled day and evening.

From behind, she saw Vanessa enter the room with a smile and low wolf whistle.

She grinned. 'I think that the groom is going to be a very happy man when he sees his radiant bride.'

Abigail turned around, mirroring her friend's smile with one of her own,

'Let's go,' she said, smoothing down the fabulous dress and allowing Vanessa to put some finishing touches to the beads in her hair. The stylists and the beauticians had gone and this was going to be her last few moments as a single girl. She knew that there was no one she would rather walk down the aisle to than Leandro. 'The rest of my life is waiting.'

* * * * *

'You're offering to *buy* my baby? Are you out of your mind?'

'I'm giving you the opportunity to make a fresh start.'

'Without my *baby*?'

'A baby will tie you down. I can give this child everything it needs,' Ariston said, deliberately allowing his gaze to drift around the dingy little room. 'You cannot.'

'Oh, but that's where you're wrong, Ariston,' Keeley said, her hands clenching. 'You might have all the houses and yachts and servants in the world, but you have a great big hole where your heart should be—and therefore you're incapable of giving this child the thing it needs more than anything else!'

'Which is?'

'Love!'

Ariston felt his body stiffen. He loved his brother and once he'd loved his mother, but he was aware of his limitations. No, he didn't do the big showy emotion he suspected she was talking about and why should he, when he knew the brutal heartache it could cause? Yet something told him that trying to defend his own position was pointless. She would fight for this child, he realised. She would fight with all the strength she possessed, and that was going to complicate things. Did she imagine he was going to accept what she'd just told him and play no part in it? Politely dole out payments and have sporadic weekend meetings with his own flesh and blood? Or worse, no meetings at all. He met the green blaze of her eyes.

'So you won't give this baby up and neither will I,' he said softly. 'Which means that the only solution is for me to marry you.'

He saw the shock and horror on her face.

'But I don't want to marry you! It wouldn't work, Ariston—on so many levels. You must realise that. Me, as the wife of an autocratic control freak who doesn't even like me? I don't think so.'

'It wasn't a question,' he said silkily. 'It was a statement. It's not a case of *if* you will marry me, Keeley—just when.'

'You're mad,' she breathed.

He shook his head. 'Just determined to get what is rightfully mine. So why not consider what I've said, and sleep on it and I'll return tomorrow at noon for your answer—when you've calmed down. But I'm warning you now, Keeley—that if you are wilful enough to try to refuse me, or if you make some foolish attempt to run away and escape…' he paused and looked straight into her eyes '…I will find you and drag you through every court in the land to get what is rightfully mine.'